VOLUME
III
KINGSLAND

The Heir

DEBORAH HILL

To Cathy

Deborah Hill

NORTH ROAD
PUBLISHING

Copyright © 2014 by Deborah Hill

ISBN: 978-0-9844414-7-1 (softcover)
ISBN: 978-0-9844414-8-8 (epub)
ISBN: 978-0-9844414-9-5 (kindle).

All rights reserved
Published in the United States by
North Road Publishing Corporation

www.northroadpublishing.com

Cover photo credits: Cnicbc © iStockphoto (Tall Ship Confrontation II), 101imges © Shutterstock (man's face), EHStock © iStockphoto (man's shirt), Bereta © iStockphoto (woman's face), Anouchka © iStockphoto (woman's shoulder). Image manipulation by RD Studio.

The Fell Types (body text and ornaments) are
digitally reproduced by Igino Marini. www.iginomarini.com.
Book design by DesignForBooks.com

For Doug

Author's Note

The Heir is set on Cape Cod, in a fictional town called Waterford. Its roots are known to readers of earlier volumes in the Kingsland Series; however, these roots are not a necessary introduction to the novel. Knowing the fictional families whose lives are followed in *This is the House* and *The House of Kingsley Merrick* is not a requirement, either. Both reflect the customs, dreams and values of their times; *The Heir* is an independent twentieth century reflection of contemporary customs and dreams and, for many, a search for a new Promised Land.

The confrontation which is the background of this story has been seen in many sections of our country; I have located it on Cape Cod because that is where I witnessed it. The destruction of this tiny part of America did not happen exactly as I describe it, for this is a work of fiction. But I have not invented its occurrence, nor the way of life that did exist on Cape Cod, a way of life deeply entrenched in the heritage of our nation. I have tried to preserve it in a web of words in order to make its values more tangible. It is my hope that these values might be encouraged to flourish in the places where they yet exist, and that they might be regained in places where they have been destroyed.

For without them the Promised Land, wherever it lies, is lost.

D.H.

Contents

1. Emily ~ 1
2. The Child ~ 89
3. The Allies ~ 113
4. Waterford ~ 141
5. The Bastard ~ 163
6. The Annhilation of Charles Sinclaire ~ 193
7. The Nomads ~ 209
8. The Heir ~ 253
9. Jenny ~ 271
10. The Runaway ~ 289
11. Diana ~ 305
12. Kingsland ~ 333
13. The Legacy ~ 257
Epilogue ~ 365
Merrick Geneology ~ 378

CHAPTER

Emily

1928

Shortly before the American Civil War, an immense silver trophy was captured by the New York Yacht Club. It was awarded by England's Royal Yacht Squadron when the schooner America beat the Royal's ship in a race around the Britain's Isle of Wight. Queen Victoria, watching from the finish line, is said to have asked who was second. "Madam, there is no second," was the reply.

Fifteen years later, after the Civil War, only the America's cup remained to celebrate the glory of sail. The merchant fleet, formerly crowned by clipper ships, now was powered by steam-driven paddle-wheelers.

Boston, a pleasant, tree-shaded town, had been submerged by the tidal wave of Irish immigration. As Europe's troubles mounted, other immigrants arrived—Italians, Polish, and East European, to work on the docks, man the machines, and proliferate. Merchant monarchs grew ever more powerful, exploiting the overflowing labor market. Riots bloomed, were quelled, bloomed again, but as the century turned, these difficulties were gradually brought under control by the federal government. In the south, the white supremacist kept the African population under a control of its own.

Immersed in these challenges, the nation paid scant attention when an obscure archduke from a far-away country was assassinated in 1914.

In Waterford, on Cape Cod Bay, the once-admired mariner was compelled to earn a living elsewhere than on the sea. Unless he had saved enough, he settled for employment in banking or insurance and moved away to one city or another. Those more fortunate opened their houses to boarders or ran small businesses from their parlors. A gilded society of summer wealthy provided income for the town's tradesmen; the tranquil village ran its own affairs and looked after its own people.

Over it all rose the house of Kingsley Merrick, three stories high with a portico and a four story tower, square in the middle of Waterford where no one could miss it. To the west of it was the first Merrick house, a Georgian Colonial. To the east, the First Parish Church of Waterford, Unitarian. Within, the woman who directed the summer society, made provision for its entertainment, established the rules for its decorum, and maintained careful control over those who were included and those who were not.

She was Elizabeth Edgarton, a granddaughter of Kingsley Merrick. There was one other grandchild, whom the summer society never heard of, nor from, until well into the 20's.

She was Alice Bradley.

✦∽ I ∼✦

THE MORNING SUN danced in Kingsland's dining room chandelier, sprinkling the walls with small rainbows. Emily Merrick dreamed among them, drifting slowly along until Mother said her name, sharply, as though she'd spoken before, probably just a few moments ago.

"Sorry," Emily said, without meaning it. "What did you say, Mother?"

"I asked if Charles was taking you to the party tonight."

"No, I thought I'd walk over. Then, if it's boring, I can come home whenever I want to." Thus eliminating an opportunity for Charles Sinclaire to kiss her goodnight, as he so loved to do.

"Walk!" exclaimed Cousin Elizabeth from the head of the table. "Where is this party going to be?"

"At the old house," Mother told her. It lay on the edge of what had once been Kingsland's property, sold recently by Elizabeth to summer people from New Jersey. "The Marshalls are having a get-together tonight for the young people, to introduce their children to everyone."

"Still," pronounced Cousin Elizabeth, "It seems quite improper for a young lady to walk alone anywhere after dark."

How tedious she was! Emily was tired of battling her way through Cousin Elizabeth's old fashioned thinking. She was a Victorian, a vestigial remnant. Girls today no longer wore long dresses or hobble skirts. Girls smoked cigarettes and drank alcohol when they could get it, danced the Charleston and kissed boys they hardly knew. Girls were in control of their own lives!

When they could get away with it.

"It'll be light on the way over," Emily pointed out, as patiently as she could.

"Surely the whole thing should be decided by your mother," Elizabeth sniffed. "I don't know what young people are thinking of these days," she went on. "When I was a girl, children were seen and not heard. They did not tell their parents what they were going to do. Their parents told them."

"How tedious for you," Emily smiled sweetly. "Did you do as *your* mama told you?"

Mother flicked a warning glance in her direction. Liberated or not, as girls seemed to be, impertinence was not an option. Besides which, Emily was now entering the mine field of family dysfunction—deliberately, from the look of it.

"Suppose we check the back path, Emily and I," Mother said quickly. "If it's well enough marked, and I'm confident Emily won't get lost, I'll consider it. If not, the issue will be resolved all by itself. Please excuse us, Elizabeth."

"Certainly." The witch rang the little bell by her plate and stalked off to the library. A maid came to clear the table, and meekly, Emily followed her mother into the back yard, to the path just past the well that entered the tangled underbrush there. It was wide and well maintained. Even by night, once the eye became accustomed to the darkness, it would be easy to follow. They meandered along it toward the old house, to check its accessibility at the other end. This proved to be satisfactory, too, as they both had known from the start.

"I'll be safe enough back here," Emily said. "Why is she so stuffy, Mother? She must know how well the path is taken care of."

"Some people resist change." Mother shrugged. "They insist on trying to keep old standards alive. Cousin Elizabeth's are a little outdated, I'll admit, but she is still owed respect. I'd like to speak to you about the remark you made in the dining room," she continued.

"Sorry about that," Emily said insincerely.

"It was cruel, and you know it." Mother's face was set in grim lines, her tone censorious.

Well, yes, perhaps it was cruel, asking if Elizabeth always did what her mother asked. Everyone knew that she had been so estranged from her parent that she had not even attended Augusta Merrick Edgarton Bradley's funeral ten years ago. All because she disliked the man her mother had married after her own father, Harold Edgarton, died. As a result, her own sister—well, half-sister—Augusta and John Bradley's daughter, was not received here in Waterford, among the nicer sort. This was the worst act of enmity a woman like Cousin Elizabeth could fathom.

"Do you want me to apologize to her?"

"Definitely not. Less said, better mended. But I wish you'd show a little consideration, Dear."

Emily sighed. "I'll try."

"Trying's not enough. Grounding is still an option, if you remember."

Yes, she remembered! Liberated or not, Mother and Daddy held the whip hand, and would not hesitate to use it if they must, in order to protect Her Highness who was their ticket to Kingsland in the lovely Cape Cod summertime.

"I promise I'll be more polite. But is it all right if I walk to the party tonight? Will you tell Cousin Elizabeth you approve?"

"Yes," Mother agreed, and then smiled. "But don't let Charles Sinclaire's mother know I agreed to it!"

Emily peeked through the barely opened pantry door, watching the entry hall where the hostess welcomed the guests too loudly. It had been only by the stroke of wildest luck that she'd been in the kitchen and could hear Mrs. Marshall, whose voice was shrill and carried easily. "Why hello! I'm so glad to see you again, Miss Bradley."

Had she heard correctly? Was the pariah of Waterford's elite actually here? Hastening to the pantry, which adjoined the entry hall, Emily peeked and ascertained that indeed, the blacklisted Alice Bradley was right there shaking hands with Mrs. Marshall, wearing a very up-to-date dress that shimmered, belted at the hip and stopping short enough to reveal that she, too, rolled her stockings.

"And I'm glad to see you, too. May I introduce my cousin, Tim? I thought you wouldn't mind if I brought him along." Beside her was a young man tall and nicely built, with dark curly hair and eyes the color of the summer sky. He was the bees knees!

Emily knew she must—must—meet him! But unless and until she gritted her teeth and girded her loins (if it could be said that ladies had loins to gird) and went out there to greet Alice, there'd be no way to get introduced. And greeting Alice Bradley was somewhat daunting, considering how the Merricks had treated her.

The flagging victrola was wound up again; the door on the kitchen side of the pantry was flung open. "I've been looking everywhere for you!" exclaimed her best friend, Pris Warden.

"Quiet!" she hissed.

Approaching, Pris peeked over Emily's shoulder to see what was so interesting in the front hall. "Oh, so that's it. Alice Bradley."

"Maybe you'd like a megaphone," Emily suggested. "So everyone will know."

"Sorry," Pris said. "It's just that I'm so surprised. Looks like she's making quite a hit." All of the gang had been invited this evening. No doubt they wished they hadn't come; the Marshalls apparently upheld Prohibition, and the party was dry. But everyone was stuck now, and so had gathered around Alice Bradley whom they had never met. Being new, she must have something interesting to offer....

"This party's so dull, anything different would make a hit," Emily snorted.

"Well, Alice Bradley's different, all right," Pris agreed.

"Really, have you ever met people so déclassé as Annabelle and James Marshall?" Emily asked breezily, as though the Marshall children were as interesting as Alice Bradley. Déclassé was a word often used at Bryn Mawr, and fitted the Marshalls, young and old, right down to the ground.

"Well, now that we know what they're like, we needn't bother to come back," Pris said.

"Most likely their mother is hoping for an invitation to your house."

"My mother says the Marshalls are tacky." Pris tossed her head so that her bobbed hair would sway in front of her face. "She says she wouldn't invite them to our house under any circumstance."

Mrs. Warden had done little entertaining for the last five years, due to her preference for sherry instead of orange juice for breakfast, martinis in lieu of lunch, and bourbon for supper. The chances of her receiving anyone, let alone a stranger in town, were negligible. Still, the point was well made. The Marshalls would find Waterford could not be manipulated by the presence of new wealth.

"How long do you plan to hide here in the pantry?" Pris wondered.

"I don't know what to do about Alice," Emily confessed.

"What would you like to do?"

"Ignore her, but then there'd be no way to meet that yummy boy."

"The one standing beside her? He is cute. And you're right. If you want to talk to him, you'll have to talk to her, too. Good luck to you,

Emmie!" Everyone knew the Merricks and the Bradleys were not on cordial terms. Pris had only sympathy for her friend, who was being squashed between the millstones of family dispute.

"And then, there's Charles," Emily said in further despair. He was a fact of her life that she couldn't do much about, like chicken pox and measles, because his widowed mother was such a dear friend of the Merrick family. By using the back path and walking over to the party, she'd been able to avoid him, but sooner or later he'd find her and make a nuisance of himself.

"I'll try to divert him," Pris plotted. "Let's go out through the kitchen and around to the front. We can come in again, and you can swoop down on the handsome guy while I introduce myself to Alice. I'll be your buffer. Come on, Emily. You can do it!"

The party having started early—another Marshall faux pas—there was still light enough to find their way around to the front of the house. What would Elizabeth Edgarton say when she learned that Alice was back in town, Emily wondered as she followed Pris to the front door. And that, at this very moment, she was hob-nobbing with the gang.

Mrs. Marshall gave a squeal as Emily and Pris bore down on the group crowding the entry. "Haven't I seen you girls somewhere before?" Her raucous peel of laughter shook the chandelier. "I have! You've arrived already! You sweet things, you probably remember my son James, and my daughter Annabelle?"

The two young Marshalls, no doubt embarrassed by their mother, smiled weakly.

"I think we've met before," Pris giggled, and turned to Alice Bradley. "How do you do? I'm Pris Warden."

"Oh! Where are my manners?" Mrs. Marshall gushed. "I should have introduced you myself."

"No matter," Alice reassured her as she shook hands with Pris. Emily remembered she was supposed to introduce her own self to the handsome New Man. Although the gang was hovering closely, she managed to twirl around, a pirouette that placed her face to face with him.

"How do you do! I'm Emily Merrick."

"I know," he smiled. A wonderful smile, warm and somehow intimate. Momentarily she lost her place, as though she'd been reading a script and dropped the pages. In disarray, she was off stride as Alice, turning from Pris, smiled and said softly, "Hello, Cousin. How nice to be able to talk to you, at last."

"We're roommates at Bryn Mawr," Pris interjected, doing her best to run interference. "Emily and me."

"Cousins," cooed Mrs. Marshall.

"I've been out of town for quite a long time." Alice, undeterred, explained to the hostess. "Emily and I haven't seen one another for a while. And the family?" she asked. "How is everybody?"

"Oh, um, everyone's fine."

"If you think they'd be interested, you might mention that I've come back to Waterford. And that I intend to stay."

By now, Emily was ready. Tossing her head much as Pris had done, she said, "Everyone will be so super-glad to hear that."

"I'll just bet they will." If they had drawn swords and crossed them, the battle could not have been more clearly joined.

Mrs. Marshall, refusing to be excluded for long, edged her way in. "What will you do here, Miss Bradley? I mean, in so small a town?"

"My father is getting along in years," Alice told her. "So I thought I'd take care of him in his old age. And teach at the district school in West Waterford."

"Teaching," extolled Mrs. Marshall. "How lovely!"

"Very nice," the young Marshalls nodded, as if their opinion mattered.

"There you are, Emily!" Charles Sinclaire broke through the crowd. "I wondered where you'd got too. We've rolled up the rug. Want to dance?"

"No, thanks." Charles was definitely not an acceptable alternative even to this minefield.

"Come on," he cajoled.

"Gee, Chuckles, I was hoping you'd ask me," Pris pouted.

"Later perhaps," he said, as though relegating her to his line of admirers. "Just now it's Emily I want. Come on, Em!" He took her arm and pulled.

"Miss Merrick has said she doesn't care to dance." The New Man spoke firmly. He was twice the size of Charles, who shrank back.

"Well, I certainly didn't intend to be rude," Charles apologized. "Excuse me, Emily. Let's not dance."

"Perhaps, Miss Merrick, you'd enjoy getting a little fresh air," said the New Man.

"Oh, thank you. That would be very nice!" She smiled shakily. Without so much as excusing himself or her to Mrs. Marshall or to Alice or to anyone else, he whisked her out of the old house and onto the Low Road.

"You've really saved my skin," she said, regaining her shredded poise. "Charles can be very insistent. But I'm afraid I didn't get your name."

"I'm Alice's cousin, Tim Bradley."

From the frying pan, into the fire. Two Bradleys at the same time!

"Everyone's a cousin to someone, here in Waterford," Emily gabbled blithely, trying to absorb this new information. "But I don't think I ever knew about you."

"Well, since I'm a Bradley, that's not surprising," he grinned.

"You mean because of the trouble between my family and yours?"

"Yes, that's just what I mean."

"We're not really as bad as it sounds. At least, my parents and I aren't. It's Miss Edgarton who's to blame for it."

"I understand," he assured her. They'd reached Main Street by now.

"How did Alice get herself invited to the Marshall's party?"

"When she came back to town, she learned that they'd bought the old Merrick place," he explained, "so she made sure she accidentally ran into Mrs. Marshall and got an invitation to the party."

"Why did she want one?"

"So she'd be in a position to strike."

To strike! Bad enough Alice was in town, apparently to stay, but to have a plan that involved striking?

They were passing Kingsland now, nearly indistinguishable so far from the road, its lights low. But its occupants were awake, she was sure, Mother knitting, Cousin Elizabeth reading. They'd wait up for her, most likely. At least, Mother would.

"Explain yourself, sir!" she exclaimed, forcing brightness and gaiety into her voice. "What kind of strike?"

Brightness and gaiety were a required part of any girl's repertoire. Along with dressing according to the style of the day and being pretty. Emily Merrick was pretty, her smile cheerful and also sultry, if necessary; her figure, flattened according to the standards of the day, was pleasantly rounded when not bound.

They had reached the Rockford road. "I'll explain Alice's strategy while we walk down to the beach. If you'd like to go down, that is," Tim Bradley offered.

"Sure."

He held out his arm to steady her on the uneven road. It was muscular. A refreshing change from the pudgy softness of Charles Sinclaire!

"You mentioned Alice is getting in a position . . ."

"To strike. Yes."

"Dare I ask who?"

"Why, her sister, of course. Elizabeth Edgarton."

"Half-sister."

"Half-sister," he agreed.

"Dare I ask how?"

"Well, she'll start with introducing herself to the summer crowd. She'll get them to like her, and want to be around her."

"Why, for pity's sake?" Sand began filling her shoes, and the smell of low tide was pervasive. "I think we've arrived. I've got to get barefooted. If you'd turn your back?"

"Oh! Sure!" Dutifully he turned.

Whatever was he talking about, she wondered, removing her shoes and stockings and shoving them beneath some nearby sweet peas. They approached the flats and began to walk along the edge.

"Why is my gang so important to Alice?" she asked, getting the flow of information back on track. Information, from the sound of it, she would eventually need.

"She plans to lure your friends to her side, win their loyalty, and then pry them loose from their parents' acceptance of Miss Elizabeth's standards. When the older generation is underground, poof! The exclusive society will be gone. Forever, Alice says."

Into Emily's mind crept the image of a monkey, throwing a wrench into the middle of everyone's life. "She has a pretty high opinion of herself, if she thinks she can manipulate us so easily."

"She has a huge advantage. She's nearly ten years older than your friends, and has had time to move along on her own path. Younger people tend to admire someone who has done that. Especially a girl."

Being assigned to a group of juvenile admirers was unpleasant. This must change. "Have you moved along your own path yet?"

"I'm about to. I've just graduated from Amherst, and in the fall I'll start learning how to run my father's business."

Hah! He was only two years older than she was! He was on her side of the age divide in respect to Alice. "What's your Dad's business?"

"Manufacturing shoes," Tim answered. "Not very exciting. Let's change the subject. I have a very risqué suggestion to make. I'm carrying a little something in my hip pocket. Since we're missing the party, I think it would be nice to have a little celebration of our own. If you agree." He slipped a flask out of his pocket, offered it.

"What's inside?"

"Gin."

"Nice gin? Or bathtub booze?"

"My father has a Philadelphia supplier," he replied with dignity.

Gamely she took the flask, gasping as the swallow burned all the way down.

Tim Bradley took a long pull. "Warms you right to your toes, doesn't it! Let's sit down somewhere and do the juice justice."

"Sure," she agreed, taking his marvelous arm again. They found a dune from which to look out over the flats, glimmering here and shadowed there, under the newly risen stars.

Settling himself into the sand, propped up by an elbow, he asked, "How do you like Bryn Mawr?"

"It's OK," she said, taking another swallow and handing the flask back. "But I'm trying to persuade Daddy to let me leave and take a job in Boston."

"Sounds adventurous. Like something Alice would do."

"She's not the only girl to go out on her own," Emily declared with spirit, diverting him. "I want to get an apartment with my roommate, Pris Warden, who's a bit on the wild side—but so much fun!" Reaching for the flask, she took another swallow. "And you? Are you spending the summer here?"

"Yes. I'm repainting the old Bradley house on Main Street."

"Why haven't I seen you around town before this?"

"Actually, I haven't been here much since Alice's mother died. Right about then I got sent to prep school, then Amherst. And now, here I am, helping Alice hog-tie the younger set."

"Hog-tie?"

"Yes, indeed."

Her laughter rang raucously, even to her own ears. She must tone it down, lest she sound like Mrs. Marshall, trying too hard to please. "Hog-tying is an art, you know," she said, working at being sophisticated. "From the perspective of the pig, at least."

"True. And I have yet to find out how much Alice knows about doing it. But I told her I'd take her where she wants to go this summer, and to keep out of the way until she wants to go home."

"Oh, yes, I see," Emily nodded, though she didn't. "And tonight? She doesn't need you?"

"Nope. She can walk back to her own house from the Marshalls.

So she suggested that I find someone fun and not worry about her. And that's what I've done."

He reached over and slowly pushed her prone alongside himself. "So I suggest we have fun. You and me. If you want."

Oh, yes! She wanted! "What kind of fun did you have in mind?" she murmured.

Languidly he leaned over, came close, closer, closest until their lips were touching tentatively, in a get-acquainted sort of way and she was aware of her heart beat, aware of his arms gathering her up as the kiss deepened and became urgent. Something within her stirred, something that had never moved before.

It took all her resolve to break away and resume the conversation, sitting up. "Is there any more gin?"

"Sure is," he answered good-naturedly, accepting the limit she had imposed and handing over the flask.

"I know you're tired of talking about it, but how did Alice come to be so mean? Wanting to break up something that means so much to so many people?"

"To a very few people," he corrected. "I think the idea's been growing on her, over the years. Ever since her mother died, and Miss Edgarton didn't come to the funeral. Did you know about that?" He lay back on the sand, arms behind his head, regarding the arrival of new stars.

"Yes." Emily nodded. When she stopped, the world continued to bob up and down for a second or two. Perhaps she'd better not have more gin....

"After her mother died, she went to the Rhode Island School of Design on a scholarship. And then she got a job at Gilchrist's in Boston, setting up fashion shows and organizing all kinds of things. She's very good at it."

"Sounds like Alice is good at whatever she's doing."

"She is. She's an amazing person."

Attuned to him by now, sensitized by the gin, Emily heard it in his voice. "You're in love with her!"

Tim was silent for a while, working on the flask until there was one swallow left. He offered it to her, and finished it off himself when she held up her hand in refusal. "Alice is opposed to con-n . . ." He struggled with his gin-thickened tongue. "Con-sang-guin-u-ity. So it dozen madder if I'm in love with her or not. She'd never marry me."

"Consanguinity never bothered the rest of the Merricks," Emily observed. "After all, the great Kingsley Merrick married his cousin, the great Julia Merrick, Waterford's gilded society maven."

"Besides being con-sanguine, Alice thinks I'm a phil-philistine because I'm going to run Dad's factory."

"What would she prefer?"

"Someone who does something less m-material." Pocketing his flask, he rose a bit unsteadily to his feet, held out his hand to assist her. "Philistine. Doesn't sound flattering, does it?"

Emily found herself becoming indignant on his behalf. "Just because you're going to work for a living?"

They staggered back toward the road. "No. It's something to do with—with . . ." He gestured widely at the stars. "It's sorta deep. Since I'm a ph-philistine, I can hardly be expected to understand, can I?"

His feelings had been hurt, Emily saw, and she was sorry. "I don't think you're a philistine. I think you're nice." Turning, she searched among the sweet peas for her shoes and stockings, tucked them under her arm.

"Gee," he said, taking her free hand as they started back up the road. "Do you? Think I'm nice?"

"Yes, I do," she said stoutly. "And if you let Alice push you around, and bully you, you're crazy. Running a factory and making money doesn't make you a philistine. Or your father, either."

"It doesn't?"

"No."

"What does, then?"

"Depends on what's important to you. It's a state of mind, is all. Do you think money's more important than anything else?"

"Certainly not."

"And your father? Does he think money is the best measure of success?"

"I don't th-think so." Tim considered it. "And even if he does, he's still a good father."

"I'm sure he is," she said softly. "And I'm sure he deserves your loyalty, even if Alice disdains him and his achievement."

Tim stopped walking and turned to her. "Thank you, Emily," he said softly, and reached out, touched her hair. "That's damn sweet of you."

"I didn't say it to be sweet," she breathed. "I said it because it's true."

"Still, you wanted me to feel better. And I appreciate it."

"Well, you're welcome," she whispered as he drew her close again. Standing up was quite different from lying beside him, because he was quite a lot taller than she was, and in the kissing, he completely engulfed her and her shoes and stockings.

But it could not go on forever! "I'm afraid I have to go home," she murmured into his perfectly shaped ear.

"I was afraid of that, too."

Gosh, she just had to see him again. Did he want to see her? Should she try to find out?

Of course she should, she advised herself. If she waited modestly, she'd lose the opportunity. "The Hallets are having a party next Friday," she offered. "They live in Yarmouth. The Waterford gang is going. It's an open invitation; friends of friends are always welcome."

Would he grab the chance?

"How about Alice?" he asked, crushing her. "Would she be welcome too?"

"It's an open invitation, like I said," Emily rallied.

"What time does it start?"

"Eight or nine o'clock, I suppose. Parties usually do."

"I take it that I would be your guest?"

"One or both of you, however it works out. Alice can bring her hog-tying equipment."

He laughed loudly, the pleasant sound of it echoing in the night as they strolled onto Main Street and into the driveway of Kingsland.

"Perhaps this'll do," she said, stopping on the far side of a tree in the front yard where he would not be seen by any chaperone who might yet be awake. "Thanks again for getting me out of that awful party at the Marshalls'."

"You're welcome." He kissed her again, very lightly this time, and watched in a protective sort of way as she climbed the front porch stairs and let herself in.

The house was quiet. In the library, Mother was alone, dozing beneath the portrait of Kingsley Merrick, Waterford's Great White Father.

Emily put her shoes on, balled up her stockings and tucked them into her girdle. "I'm home," she whispered, nudging Mother's shoulder.

"Oh! There you are! Now I can go to bed!" Mother whispered too, so that Cousin Elizabeth wouldn't be disturbed. "How was the party?"

Considering what she had learned this night, keeping Tim and Alice a secret was probably a good idea. "Dull," she whispered. "The Marshalls are a lost cause."

"Did you use the back path?"

Oh dear. A bald-faced lie was required. Something Emily disliked, though she had done it often enough, when necessary.

"Um, yes. And I could see just fine."

"Good." Mother nodded and turned off the lamp. Together they carefully climbed the stairs, making no noise at all, and kissing one another goodnight, went into their separate rooms.

Now she could think about Him. Now she could make plans, beginning with the Hallet party next weekend. Everyone would be going, and her parents were never worried if the gang was together—though they should be, she thought. The gang could get a little wild, all things considered. But if the kids were all together, everyone's parents figured they'd look after each other.

There'd be a party at the Wardens' house the week after that, already planned by Pris and herself. It would include a snipe hunt designed to amuse those-in-the-know at the expense of Charles Sinclaire, Waterford's goat. Charles had never gone to summer camp, the origin of snipe hunts, thus would be easily victimized. With him out of the way for a while, the opportunity to pair up with Tim Bradley might just naturally, in the course of things, happen. Perhaps they could arrange some time in close proximity, too.

Her toes curled up at the very thought!

※∞ 2 ∞※

The Hallet's party was delightfully noisy. Pris fox-trotted by with Jacky Pollard, the two of them, despite the heat in the room, glued flat together. Jacky's hand, which had been pressed to the curve of Priscilla's back, crept downward, cupping her bottom, and it was a full five beats before Pris, reaching behind, put his hand back where it belonged.

In a dark corner Becky Levering was necking with an unknown Yarmouth boy; Evvie Thayer lurched by with a cigarette hanging from her lips. Bobby Blake peered around the pillar on which Emily was leaning, blew a smoke ring and asked her to dance, went away unoffended when she waved a refusal. Neddy Winslow leaned against the pillar for a while, too, trying to chat, saw that she did not care to spend her time shouting over the noise, and considerately left, too.

In the living room the rugs had been rolled up, the furniture pushed into the corner, all lights but one extinguished. Soon that one, too, would go, and then there'd be no way to see if Tim came in. Staying in one place was Emily's strategy of the moment, so he could find her if he ever did arrive. Her confidence waned as more time went by. He must come!

The music, warbling, slowed. The lone light went out with a crash, and the party roared to a higher pitch than ever. The girls squealed and the boys laughed and in her ear Tim Bradley's voice said, "Alone in the dark with Emily. Again."

"Oh!" she exclaimed. Her gladness broke loose and flew free. "Hello!" she yelled. "I'd about given up on you!"

"Oh? Sorry I'm late."

"What?"

"Sorry I'm late," he shouted. "I lost an hour trying to persuade Alice to come. Then I jumped into my car and got here as fast as I could, hoping to find you."

Her joy knew no bounds. Even without Alice, he had come here. Looking for her! Clasping her glass firmly to control the shaking of her hands, she leaned languidly against her pillar as though she were entirely at her ease, as though she had not spent most of her waking moments since last Friday thinking about him.

"Have you got a drink?" she asked loudly.

A different lamp was turned on, and in its light Tim held up his glass by way of answer.

A new record was found, the victrola wound up. The din of the party continued anew, loud as it wanted to be because Mr. and Mrs. Hallet were wisely elsewhere.

"Dance?" Tim gestured to the livingroom as the Charleston crashed through the racket and the whole room was instantly in motion.

"You bet!" Throwing her drink into a nearby potted plant, she jounced her way onto the floor and turned to face him. He danced well, light on his feet and able to do the Charleston even while hanging on to his highball.

"What have you been doing this week?" she called.

"What?"

"What have you been doing to keep busy?" she yelled.

"Scraping paint."

"What?"

"Scraping paint." He made a scraping gesture which appeared to be part of his dance routine. She scraped back, and by mutual consent they danced without trying to converse until the record was done. While a new one was being found, he drew her outside, onto a side terrace.

"Whew! Hot! Now we can talk. What have you been doing this week?" he asked, hardly out of breath at all.

The summer night was suffocating and would remain so until the land breeze shifted; at least once during the summer Cape Cod was embraced by these doldrums. "Tennis," she panted.

"In this heat?"

"Early morning," she told him. "I spend the night at Pris Warden's house, and we play as soon as we wake up. Well, we don't really play. We just lob the ball back and forth, and by the time we're out of steam, breakfast is ready. Then I go home and play dutiful daughter."

"Ah! And do you think that just now we could play 'sit down'?"

"There are walls right here," she pointed out. "Let's find a place." A lot of couples were perched on them, while some stood around and others wandered on the lawn or hovered on the edges of the yard, ready to slip into the surrounding woods for some serious petting.

Charles was nowhere to be seen, probably hiding behind the draperies in the house with Ginny Porter, a girl who would put up with him, even pretend to be amused by his obnoxious humor and pretentious British accent, when he remembered to use it. The field was clear at the moment, thank goodness.

Tim settled himself on the stone wall, expectantly looking up at her, one long leg swinging time to an unheard, unhurried beat within.

"Why didn't Alice want to come?" she asked.

Waving meaninglessly, signifying his inability to understand his cousin, he said, "She's concerned with overexposure. She thinks she did pretty well at the Marshall's last weekend, and the Hallet revels include Yarmouth people who don't interest her. Miss Warden asked her to a party next weekend, so she's decided to save her ammunition until then."

Frowning, Emily sat beside him. "She's going to Pris's party?" Somewhere, like distant thunder, malaise rumbled.

"Yes, indeed. She's been led to believe there's going to be a snipe hunt." His smile was mischievous, friendly, but Emily's dismay increased as she thought about the implications of Pris's invitation.

Why had her friend said nothing about it? "Did that Sinclaire fellow bring you here tonight?" Tim asked.

"He drove a lot of us," Emily said, bringing her thoughts to the present moment. "It's not like a private date or anything like that."

"Then I don't suppose he'd mind if you and I played 'sit-in-my-car'?"

In his car!

"We could stay here and just talk," he added, "but we might get interrupted by Sinclaire if we do."

"A distinct possibility, yes."

"So how about this." He held up his glass. "I'm running on empty. How about I get us both a refill and we take it to my car? Since I was the last one in, it's a pretty good distance from the house. Plenty of privacy."

Charles was still nowhere in view. "Perfect," she smiled. "I'll meet you on the front porch. That way I won't have to go through the house and risk running into him. Check on the time while you're at it. I should be back here by 11:30."

That definitely put a limit on their time together, as was the expectation. The girl generally set the boundaries.... A chill chased itself up one arm and down the other. Wandering to the front of the house, she waited until Tim appeared with the promised two drinks. Putting one in her hand, he took her elbow and they strolled down the driveway.

"I wanted to tell you," he said, "that I used your argument against Alice, and it stopped her cold."

"What argument?"

"About a person's state of mind defining what he is. I'm very grateful to you for giving me that little tool. There's no disputing it, and Alice doesn't try to talk me out of working in my father's factory anymore. Makes things more restful, since I aim to work there whether I want to or not, and own and operate it one day, whether I want to or not."

"Gee, Tim, that sounds grim."

"It isn't, really. I think a lot of my father. I certainly don't plan to make a shambles of his plans, just to gratify my cousin. As for myself—well, I'm sure I'll enjoy it, once I get into the swing of it."

"Good luck!"

His car was a long way from the Hallett's house, just as he had promised. Their privacy was complete, and for an hour, they took advantage of it.

At 11:30 he returned her to the back yard, leaving her in the shadow of an overhanging tree. "Very nice," he murmured. "See you next week at the Wardens."

He melted into the night just as Charles shouted from the terrace, "Emily, dahling! Where've you been, Schweetheart? Everyone wantsh to go parking." Staggering down the steps to the tree, he slipped an arm around her waist, kissed her cheek sloppily. She wiggled away.

"Cut it out, Charles. I'm not going parking."

"She saysh she won't go!" Charles called.

"Come on, Emily! Be a sport!" Pris yelled, clinging to the draperies at the terrace door. They gave way and she fell into a velvet heap.

Jacky Pollard hurried to fish her out. "I hope you didn't ruin the curtains!" he scolded. "The Hallets might not let us back."

"Thanks for your sym-sympath-y," Pris hiccupped.

Charles dragged an unresisting Emily over to the velvet pile upon which Pris now reclined. "She saysh she won't go parking," he repeated gloomily.

"Oh, Em." Pris sighed. But even drunk, she understood. "Better luck next time, Ch-Charles. Here, let me kiss you and make it well." Reaching up for his hand, she pulled him down onto the draperies, kissing him more ardently in jest than Emily had ever done in earnest.

"It looks like we'll just have to go home," Jacky observed. "Come on, Pris. Break it up. Unless you let him go, he'll never be able to drive us."

"He's not going to drive us," Emily dictated. "I am."

"What?" cried Charles from his velvet nest.

"You're drunk," she said flatly. "I can handle the car better than you can."

"I am not drunk," he insisted. "My Gawd, Em, do you think I'd risk precious cargo by driving when drunk?"

Arguing with him was not an option. "I'll walk, then." As if to prove it, she stalked away, her own sobriety returning fast.

"I'll drive, if you think I'm a better bet," Jacky offered, following. "I'm not drunk, either."

Sitting in the backseat with Charles, having to fend off his mauling and manhandling, wasn't an option either. "I'll drive, or else I'll walk," she repeated.

"Your Mater and Pater will think itsh very strange," said Charles, trailing after Jacky, dragging Pris along. "My Mater will think itsh strange, too. Maybe we ought to put the top up, Schweetheart. Then no one'll know itsh you who's driving."

Drunk or sober, Charles would not be capable of putting the top up. It had been down all summer, just for that reason. "Everyone will be asleep, Charles dear, so no one find out. Get into the car, dammit."

"Oh, Emily girl, you have got clash," he sighed, happy to let her boss him around since it implied a relationship of sorts. "Dahling, where the hell were you all evening?"

He was her passport, after all, and must be placated. She could go anywhere if she were with him. It did not occur to her parents that Charles might take their daughter to an undesirable place, like a speakeasy or a wild party. His mother had raised him right, they were sure.

"I was down at the beach, looking for a snipe."

"Did you find one?"

"No."

"Have you ever even seen one?"

"No, but Pris's brother has."

Becky Levering had been sick all over the fender of the Sinclaire Ford and was draped now over its hood with Bobby Blake patting her back.

"If you think I'm going to ride with her, you're out of your mind," Pris objected. "She'll throw up all over me. She'll ruin my dress."

"You can sit on my lap, honey," Jacky said. "We'll put Bobby in the middle, between us and her, and she can upchuck on him."

"Thanks," said Bob.

"I'm dying," Becky gasped. "And all you can think about is who gets thrown up on."

"Everyone aboard, please," Emily called. Grumbling, groaning, giggling, the two couples squeezed into the back and Charles pushed on the door until it clicked shut; he let himself in the front and sheepishly dropped the key into her palm. Pris and Jacky, she saw in the mirror, fell instantly into an embrace from which they would probably not surface until the Warden driveway had been reached. Becky was already asleep on Bob's shoulder. The engine caught—the recently invented self-starter was a godsend!—and Charles passed out, not waking up even when Becky and Bob got out at the Leverings. He was still asleep when the car rolled up to the Warden's front door.

"Well done," Pris sighed, adjusting the narrow straps of her dress and rearranging her rhinestone headband. "Wake up, Charles. We're nearly home."

"Oh, do leave him alone," Emily begged. Once she got him to his own house, she could just leave him to sleep it off in his own driveway.

"Nonsense. You shouldn't be driving around in the dead of night alone. Wake up, Sinclaire," Pris called into his ear. "Wake the hell up."

"I'm awake," Charles mumbled crossly.

The pair stood at the edge of the driveway, waving farewell while they waited for Jacky's erection to subside. Emily pointed the car toward the Sinclaire garage, only a few miles away.

"You can walk me back to Kingsland from your house," she instructed Charles. "If anyone asks why, just tell them we wanted to, because it's such a fine night."

"It is rather nice, just now." Charles was recovering and his words were clearer. "Hot nights are especially delicious, don't you think, Emily dahling?" He loved to drawl, an affectation he believed made him sound like one of the Newport elite. "I'd be glad to walk. Especially with you."

"Hummm," she hummed ambiguously.

"Did you enjoy the evening at the Hallets'?"

"Nifty. It was nifty."

"Where were you, during which time you were enjoying the evening?"

"Like I told you, looking for snipes."

"For the longest time, dahling, I couldn't find you," he complained.

"Tell me you didn't take advantage of it by necking with Ginny Porter."

"I didn't!"

"You did."

"Well, I may have. But that's not the point, dahling. I'm supposed to take care of you. That's what your parents expect, and that's what my Mater expects, too. How can I do that if I don't know where you are?"

"You knew I was there somewhere."

"But with who? Whom?" No doubt helped along by either anxiety or anger, he was sobering up fast.

Hauling at the wheel, she aimed the car up his parents' driveway, past the side door of the house, stopping in front of the garage. Before Charles could pin her behind the wheel, she slipped out and started for home. Quickly he caught up with her, wrapping an arm around her waist as they walked toward the tree-darkened driveway of Kingsland. The porch lamp was on, winking through the maples.

"Great place, your house," Charles said as they climbed the front steps. "I like it much better than ours." Kingsland was a mansion, and suited Charles' pretentions well. Turning her toward the light, he examined her closely, put a finger on her chin. "Is that whisker-burn I see on your face?"

Backing away and out of his grasp, she retorted, "What if it is?"

"I thought you were looking for snipes."

"Yes, at the beach."

"Obviously, not by yourself. Who were you necking with?" he demanded.

"I don't have to tell you, Charles. We are not engaged. We aren't going together, even, and there's no reason for me not to enjoy myself the way I want to when the gang goes out as a group. Just as you did with Ginny."

Crushed, he stood slumped and sad looking.

"I've told you I'd like to be your friend," she added, "and I really don't see why you won't let it go at that."

"I can't," he said abjectly. "I'm so crazy over you, Emily. I'll be leaving for my new job in Boston the week after next. Will you write me when I'm gone?"

"Of course," she soothed, wishing he were in Boston this moment.

"Well, that's some consolation!" Then he kissed her, roughly and hard, because he was under the impression that irresistible passion was muscular. Finally he was done.

"Good night, Charles." Did she say it without conveying hatred? She turned off the lantern, letting herself into the house without looking to see if he was clear of the porch steps. Leaning back against the closed door, she worked on ordering her thoughts.

Alice would be at Pris's party. Pris, her friend, had invited the very person Emily Merrick was never even supposed to mention at Kingsland! She must have done it at the Marshall's party—but she had not said so all this week, when they'd been together. Alice, of course, had probably started her hogtying at the Marshalls, and somehow Pris must have fallen under her influence. There was no other way to explain her friend's secrecy.

It would have been easy to mull that over and over and over, but there was no point in it. The deed was done, and she could hardly complain about it, even though she believed Pris had betrayed her. No. Better to think about Tim, instead. Mother was doubless in the library, napping. Emily would wake her up, and the two of them would creep quietly upstairs, and then, in bed, waiting for sleep, she'd relive her hour in his car, and the passion he'd stirred up, and the possibility of more. "See you at the Wardens," he'd said.

Oh, yes, she'd think about him.

3

Deep in the house, dancing was in progress, the music competing with the chatter and laugher on the Warden's back terrace. It was there Emily found a portion of the gang gathered around a seaweed-draped crate. The girls were pretty in their pastel dresses with hip-encasing waistlines, their hair short in back, longer in front, easily tossed one side or the other as they smoked and laughed and flirted. The boys wore summer whites, hair in high-crested pompadours or plastered down with a part in the middle, tan because they were the collegiate sons of the wealthy who could swim at high tide and play tennis at low.

Among them Mary Ann Hall passed trays of canapés, collected empty glasses to take back to the kitchen.

"You'll be happy to know that Tommy has had a stroke of extraordinary luck," Pris said. Emily observed that the Warden heir, like a king on his throne, sat proudly on a white-painted iron chair, accepting the accolades of his peers and sampling the contents of the case of bootleg gin he'd found on the flats. A rumrunner, with a federal revenue cutter in hot pursuit, had been forced to jettison his cargo with the hope of finding it later, when the feds and the tide were gone. A futile hope. If a beachcomer like Tom Warden didn't get it, a thirsty Waterford local would.

"A whole case, Tom?" Emily asked. "None broken?"

"Nary a one," Tom said proudly, if thickly.

The music began to wind down, and someone unseen revived the flagging victrola; the crashing of a glass and a Rebel yell indicated that sobriety was not entirely the order of the evening. More dancers came out onto the terrace to assist in the sampling of the gin.

It occurred to Emily that Pris's mother was not present, that her father was still in Boston, along with everyone else's father, that none of the men would arrive in Waterford until the midnight train. Without the dampening presence of adults, it promised to be quite a party, the best ever.

"I take a sh-shovel every time I go out on the flats," Tommy was explaining, "so I can dig into sushpicious humpsh."

"Suspicious humps!" Emily scoffed, working her way around Tommy's wrought iron throne, as far from Charles as she could get without making it obvious.

"You never know what the tide will do," the monarch of the moment pontificated. "Cover shomething over with shand one day, uncover it the next. I dig up everything, just in case. Usually it's only horseshoe crabsh, though."

"You beast," cried Becky Levering, having left the victrola in favor of the gin. "Probably they're only harmlessly taking a nap out there and you have to go and dig them up."

"Nap, nothing!" Tommy pronounced. "They're for-fornicating."

"Fornicating!" the gang murmured reverently.

"In the name of decency," Tom went on, "I believe the crabsh ought to go shomewhere else to fornicate, shomewhere I can't shee them. They'll end up cor-corrupting my morals. The rumrunnersh are bad enough."

"Where's the ice?" Charles asked.

"Pantry," Pris informed him.

"Is there any tonic or orange juice to mix in with it?" Emily querried. Drinking that stuff undiluted was unacceptable. She needed to be on her toes, because Alice and Tim weren't here yet. Surely they'd arrive at any moment, and when they did, she wanted to be sober.

"Kitchen table," Pris instructed.

"Charles? Would you get me some?"

"I'd be delighted, dahling."

Free of him for the time being, Emily made her way onto the Wardens' side porch, sat at a wrought iron table, on an uncomfortable iron chair, listening to the babble of her friends. It was on this very porch, earlier in the week, that she'd finally confronted Pris.

"Yes, I asked her at the Marshall's party," Pris said. "The gang seemed to really enjoy her, and a couple of kids asked me if she was coming..."

"And you figured you could invite whoever you want."

"Well, it's my house, isn't it?"

Indeed, it was.

"She's the cat's meow, kid. You'll get used to her, I'm sure."

"Oh, I can get used to her," Emily shrugged, covering her anxiety. "But I'm not so sure about my family."

"What do you think they'd do about it?"

"It could mean I won't be allowed to go to parties anymore."

"Oh, really!" Pris laughed. "Surely it's not that bad."

"It might be," Emily sighed.

Now she could hear a crescendo of voices on the terrace, welcoming someone newly arrived. Maybe the Bradley cousins. Peeking around the corner, she could see Alice. But no Tim. Her heart sank.

"How did you ever get stuck out here without a drink?" It was Him! "Pris said I'd find you here. I brought you a little something to refresh yourself."

In his hands were beverages for each of them, with ice clinking in the glasses. Setting them on the table, he pulled out a chair for himself and gestured at the other.

Happily, she returned to her seat. From the porch the immaculate expanse of Warden lawn spread out and out, a soft evening green, and a bird dipped and soared over it. The bay was azure, a hue that only happened in the summertime. At the water's edge Charles, apparently having forgotten about the ice he'd promised, was wading with rolled up trousers, hand in hand with Ginny Porter.

Thank God.

She sipped, gasped. "Is there anything but gin in this?"

"Ice," he grinned.

Caution would be required. Putting the glass down, she said, "Tell me about all the progress you've made this week with the ancestral Bradley house."

"Paint and putty. Putty and paint," he answered, leaning back cautiously in the little chair that was not large enough for someone his size.

"But you're making progress?"

"Oh, yes. Besides that, I'm learning a lot. Whenever I'm not sure what to do next, I ask my uncle John—Alice's father. He can tell me whatever I need to know."

"Are you staying there? At Alice's house?"

"Nope. I hang out at the old place."

"All by yourself?"

"Yup."

"Isn't it spooky?"

"Awful," he said. "Drives me to drink." His glass was half-empty, while she had hardly been able to make any inroads on hers. "Something wrong with the gin and tonic I fixed you?"

"Well, it's a little gin-ny."

"It's supposed to be. It'll make this wonderful party into an even happier occasion." His tone was sardonic.

"You wish you hadn't come, don't you?"

"Somewhat."

"Maybe you're not in the mood for a party?"

"Maybe I'm not," he admitted. "Everyone here is going to get smashed. I'm not sure I want to watch."

"You won't need to. You'll be pretty well oiled yourself in about half an hour, if you keep on making your drinks this strong."

"Oh, I wouldn't make them this strong all night," he explained reasonably. "That'd be silly. I thought I'd just make them that strong until Alice leaves. She has a date with a fellow from Boston, who is driving down especially to see her. He'll be coming along almost any time now."

His smile was crooked.

"Then you won't be taking her home?"

"No, sir-ree. I'm not her date, only her chauffeur. And tonight I'm her one-way chauffeur. She made that clear. I was rather hoping I could adopt you as my date, Emily, once I got here."

"That's a pleasant prospect, I must say," she purred.

"But I haven't quite figured out how to get you home," he went on, watching her closely, "considering that the Bradleys are persons *non grata* at your house."

Now was her chance, and she took it. "Look, Tim, I'm really sorry about this situation. I can't figure out what to do about it, but I think you and I could at least get creative. Like leaving your car at the beach and walking me to my house. I can let myself in through the back door."

"And that Sinclaire fellow won't say anything? Complain about being discarded?"

"Only to me. I'm pretty sure he won't say anything to my parents, because I might get back by telling his mother he's not a teetotaler, like she thinks he is."

"I feel better already. Let's leave now, before the mood is spoiled."

"Alice will wonder where you disappeared to."

"She told me to get lost. I'd like to get lost with you. Come on!"

His car—how conveniently!—was again the last one in the driveway.

They climbed in as dusk slid into the velvet arms of night on Cape Cod Bay, drove into town, past the church and past Kingsland and the library and the town house, on down to a beach far west of the old packet landing. Pulling into a clump of bushes, Tim parked and in the silence, the sounds of life on the waterfront whispered. Anchored were several sailboats, and pulled up on the beach were several dories.

"I didn't think anyone ever anchored a boat anywhere else than the packet landing," she observed. "I've never even been here before."

"Only a few people use it," Tim said in the darkness. "Uncle John is one of them. His boat is the second on the left."

The small craft bobbed freely. The tide was either high or still incoming.

Tim fetched a flask from the glove compartment. "I'm very glad you came with me," he said, and she could guess at his smile in the dark. "Will you have a drink? Good for motion sickness."

"We aren't moving."

"Soon we will be. We're going to Provincetown."

"We are?"

"If we leave right away, I'm sure we can get over and back tonight. The tide looks about right."

The tide was never right. It always seemed possible to get to Provincetown and back in one tide cycle, but very few people had ever done it successfully.

"Sounds like fun," she said, reckless in her need for him. "Let's go. I'll have a drink later."

"Your dress might get ruined, scrubbing around in a boat," he warned.

"I'll risk it."

"I have a blanket in the trunk. You can sit on it once we're under way."

"I knew you'd take care of everything, Tim."

"You had better take your shoes and stockings off, though," he said. Climbing out, he went to the back of the car, took a blanket out of the trunk and a bottle of gin while Emily whisked behind a rock and divested herself of shoes, stockings and, at the last moment, girdle. She was wearing almost nothing as a result—just panties and a constricting bra to keep her figure flat, but it would be unbearable to be trussed up. She'd done plenty of sailing; she knew. The girdle must go.

They did not speak as he dragged one of the dories into the water, helped her in and rowed to the second boat on the left that swayed, side to side, looking larger than it was. The night breeze was steady and gentle, and there was a swell that spoke of a distant storm long gone, with only waves to tell of it. The dampness took the edge off the warmth, and Emily shivered as she hopped onto the bow and into the little cockpit. The floor of the craft was dry.

Tim handed over the blanket and the bottle. Securing the dory, he raised the anchor, and together they hoisted the sail and headed out.

"You're a pretty good sailor, for a girl," Tim remarked.

"I'm a pretty good sailor, period," she answered pertly. She'd spent summer in Waterford all her life, after all. "My Daddy taught me."

After a time, Tim loosened the lines and released the tiller. The sail swung out over the water and hung there quietly. From nowhere a glass appeared and gin was heard to splash in it. "Let's just drift for a while," he said. "Come over here." His voice sent chills from one end of her spine to the other. Obligingly she crawled to his side, and when he reached for her, the wonder of this secret night grew greater, his arms around her warding off the chill. They snuggled closely and intermittently shared the contents of the bottle. She did not resist as he spread the blanket, lay down on it and pulled her to his side. His lips were warm on her throat, her ear, on her mouth, exploring in a manner she had never experienced before, to which she could not help responding as though she'd done it all her life. His hand stealthily found her bosom.

She drew back, as much as she was able in the confines of the cockpit. Never had she let a boy touch her without first establishing limits.

His hand moved up, touched the vein in her throat. "Are you frightened, Em?" he asked softly. "Your heartbeat's fast as a bird's." Her breath seemed caught there, beneath his fingers.

"No, I'm not," she managed to say.

"Good," he whispered, the hand on her throat dropping to her breast again. "I wouldn't want to scare you."

"Well," she murmured, putting a restraining hand on his, "it's just that I don't believe in p-petting on the first d-date."

"It isn't the first," he protested. "But I certainly will respect your wishes." His hand withdrew. It had been warm, his touch thoughtful, and she wanted more—but surely could not ask for it; she would appear to be loose, wanton, amoral. Looking up at the night sky, trying to think of what to say, she watched the mast, like a pointing finger, wag from a star in the east to a star in the west and then back. Her stomach lurched uneasily as, fascinated, she watched the mast again describe its arc. The little boat was lifted, let down, lifted again and again her stomach lurched.

"Oh-oh," she groaned and quickly sat up, looking for the horizon, which often quelled sea-sickness if you were quick enough about it. But the horizon wasn't there in the darkness, and internal upheaval crowded out everything else.

"Can we make it back?" she asked feebly. "Is there enough breeze?"

"Back? Do you want to?" he asked, concerned. "Are you OK?" He sat up.

"No," she confessed. She tried to keep her voice happy and lilting, and not heavy like the pit of her stomach. "I don't want to go back. But I have to. I'm going to be sick if I don't get to land in a hurry."

"Ahah! You looked at the sky while you were lying down."

"Afraid so," she apologized. "I forgot not to."

"We'll be steadier when we're moving." He hauled on the lines that controlled the sail, and took the tiller. If he was disappointed, he didn't show it.

Straightening out her dress, she dragged the blanket up and over her shoulders, knowing she had ruined her chances but too nauseated, now, to care.

Tim stirred the water with backward and forward sweeps of the tiller, coaxing the sail into the proper spot to take advantage of what little breeze was stirring and use it to its best advantage.

"You're a good sailor, too," she remarked, hoping to divert herself from her increasing misery. "I wouldn't have thought you'd do it so well, since you haven't been on the Cape very often."

"We used to visit Alice and her folks a lot, before her mother died. I seemed to get the hang of it fast. My uncle says I'm a born sailor," he said proudly. "We Bradleys come from a long line of mariners. How are you feeling now?"

There was nothing like seasickness for misery, she was discovering. It permeated her whole body, occupying all her thought, commanding the center of all her emotions. But it was growing no worse, now that she was sitting upright and now that the little craft was picking up headway. "I think I'll make it," she said cheerfully as she could. "If we're not out here too long."

"Eastham's not too far."

"Eastham!"

"That's the quickest route to shore. Otherwise I'll have to tack toward Waterford, and it would take quite a while to get there. The tide would be low and we'd be stranded on the outer bar," he said amiably. "We could walk in from there, but frankly I'd rather not. It's a terrifically long way."

"I guess I'm more confused than I thought," she said. "I could have sworn the tide was rising when we were at the Wardens'."

"It turned."

It turned and he knew it, and probably he thought she had known it too. Probably he figured she knew exactly what she was doing, coming out here with him, and it seemed quite probable that he knew, himself, exactly what he wanted. That was one of the problems dating older men, she'd been told. They were experienced....

Indecisively she waited while they moved along. Unless she said something, they would continue straight to Eastham. They would not get home before her 1:00 curfew. She'd be out all night, with a forbidden Bradley. The repercussions at Kingsland were beyond imagining, but she was too sick to care.

Then the bottom of the boat scraped, bumped, scraped again. Tim pulled up the centerboard and jumped out, towing the small craft in as far as the falling tide would permit. He dropped the anchor in the sand and pushed it down firmly with his foot.

"We're here," he announced cheerfully. "You'll feel better soon. When the boat is floating again, we'll leave. There's a box under the bow—can you reach it?"

On hands and knees she crawled there, and slid it out. As if it weighed nothing at all, he leaned over and picked it up. "I'll take it. Too heavy for a delicate flower like you."

"A sick flower," she reminded him.

"Yes, poor thing! Do you think you can manage the blanket?"

"Probably." Gathering it up, she slid over the side. The wet sand was unpleasant beneath her bare feet, oozing coldness up between her toes. Meekly she followed him to the beach and to a hollow where dunes would protect them from the night breeze and nearby boulders radiated heat like an oven, creating a small, warm amphitheater. The inner churning increased, but it was not caused by seasickness. There was dread, and excitement, and curiosity, drawing her to him like a magnet.

In the box was a flask, two small tin cups, some sandwiches, and a great heap of sugar cookies. "I made them," he said proudly. "And the sandwiches, too."

Even in her befuddled state, Emily understood that he had planned to bring her here all along. Plucked like an apple, she had fallen into his hands, ripe for whatever he wanted to do. Giddy, (the effects of gin did not wear off as easily as other liquor) and hopelessly enamored, she wanted only to please him so he would love her.

"What a nice spot," she said, because it seemed as though she must say something. Her scalp tingled with her tension and all she could hear was the racing of her heart.

"I thought you'd like it. Let's have a sandwich. I think you'll feel better if you eat something. Or have a cookie. Or both."

"It's worth a try." She spread out the blanket while he opened a sandwich, unwrapped some cookies, poured small cups of gin, and set them on top of the box. "I think I'll try a cookie first," she ventured. "See how it settles."

The cookie went down fine. She took a bite of sandwich—cheese—and that went down fine, too.

"How did you know about such a place? How did you find it in the dark?"

"A friend told me about it, quite a few years ago. A local kid who was interested in bringing girls here. You find it at night by keeping the Provincetown light on your left."

Another cookie. A sip of gin. The beach tipped a little, up, then back. "Very nice picnic."

They ate and drank for a while, and then it was time. She knew it, without understanding how. They lay down together and he put his hand on her bosom and kissed her mouth, very gently.

Again she stopped his hand.

"I think you're afraid," he murmured in her ear, his body's heat pouring onto her.

"A little." Afraid or not, her own heat was increasing, her body swelling with need and pure wanting. She did not stop him from reaching under her dress. There was a tugging and then the releasing of her bra, and with a touch very gentle, well calculated to arouse her, he stroked her unbound flesh.

"It's too late, you know," he said softly, his hand more urgent, as though he had sensed her increasing arousal and moved to meet it.

"To late for what?"

"Too late to stop. It's been too late ever since you got into that boat."

She tried to protest, but could find no words.

"Don't fight me," he whispered. "Say you want me. Say you want me, Emily, because I want you—so much." He eased her dress up and slipped it over her head. Along with the bra, he tossed it away. His shirt followed. He leaned to kiss her bared breasts, and then held her to his naked chest and kissed her slowly, with leisure, as if they had all the time in the world—which they did—and then somehow he divested himself of his trousers and underwear and reached into the warm and wet territory between her legs.

She forgot about resisting and let him lead her. "Tim, oh Tim," she murmured as he straddled her, his elbows planted in the sand above her shoulders so she could not move away. Overwhelmed by her clamoring, devouring need, she found herself holding onto him, her fingernails digging into his back, her mouth searching, reaching for his, and then there was stabbing, pushing pain.

She was unprepared for it. "Stop! Oh Tim, stop!" And he did stop, drawing a sharp breath. They waited. "Try to relax," he whispered. "We'll lie here like this for a while. Just quietly. Try to let yourself feel the nice part, not the hurt part. I'm sorry it hurts! I'm sorry!" His lips traveled over her forehead and temples, ears and throat as he waited, and she waited, and sure enough, the pain subsided a bit and she became aware of a throbbing, warm vitality that seemed amazingly to increase and become irresistible and she was compelled to rise toward it, to reach for it, to meet it despite the pain.

"Tim!" she whispered. A white heat burned and built higher from the depths of herself, from a place she had only wondered about before, now unlocked because of loving this warm and passionate man, who even now created an agony of pleasure that soon became lost in the pain of penetration.

She could not help crying out again, but he did not stop this time. He drove deeper, faster and then cried out, too, calling something she could not name. Gradually his weight settled upon her and he was still; then he rolled away, onto his back, and gathered her up so that her head was on his shoulder, his arms tight around her. Eastham's rapidly draining flats breathed and sighed and the night air caressed them and somewhere in the beach grass a night bird chuckled.

Oh, Tim. Oh, Tim Bradley. Do you love me, she wondered.

The prow of the cat-boat once more scraped bottom. Tim buried the anchor in anticipation of higher water, and they bound the sail to the boom. Farther toward the shore the other boats lay on their sides like beached whales, waiting for water enough to float. When the tide had risen a little, later in the morning, he'd haul the small craft closer to the beach. Meanwhile, there was now.

Emily looked over the expanse of the bay, at the pinking of things and the brightening blue of the sky and the shining water creeping toward the shore, speechless at the miracle of the morning, flooded with the peace of it and the joy of loving Tim Bradley.

"It's often this way early in the day," he said, looking fondly down at her at as they walked. "Sometime, perhaps, will you meet me here at dawn?"

"Sometime, and gladly." Her heart soared, swooped, danced—and yet, beneath, lay melancholy, poignant longing for something she could not name. She had held nothing back from him, and now she was sore and exhausted. An unacknowledged part of herself, somewhere very deep, was bereft at parting from him, and she winked back tears.

"What'll happen now?" he asked. "About your parents?"

"I hate to think," she said wearily.

"You'll be in for an awful lot of trouble. Staying out all night."

"I'm afraid so."

"With me."

"That too."

"I can't leave you until we've faced them together, Emily."

Tingling happily in response to the "we", the soaring began again. Yet she could not bring him to her family, because of Cousin Elizabeth, who hated all Bradleys.

"I think I'd better talk to my parents on my own," she said slowly, thoughtfully.

"No man worth his salt would let a girl take the blame for what happened last night. The least I can do is apologize for not getting you home on time."

"That's the most you'd better apologize for," she laughed softly. Then she stopped and he turned to look at her. "I have no regrets, Tim!"

"Neither do I," he said, his tone intimate. "But I am worried for your sake. Just look."

In the distant parking lot there were two cars. One was Tim's, she was quite sure. And certainly the other was not.

"Do you see what I see?" he asked.

"'Fraid so."

"What do you think?"

"I think I'm going to throw up," she quavered. The headache she'd been nursing got suddenly worse.

He put his arm around her shoulder, supporting and affectionate. "I'm glad we left the blankets and booze in the boat. Somehow I think it wouldn't look good if we were caught with them. And it does look as though we are going to get caught."

Love me, Tim, her heart begged. Love me.

"If it's your father, I'm glad," he said stoutly. "At least there'll be no question of your talking to your parents alone."

Elizabeth wouldn't be part of the conversation, either, Emily thought, and took heart as they walked closer and closer to Daddy.

There was still some distance to cover, during which time she must come up with a battle plan. In her fatigued, overloaded brain only one certainty stood out, loudly, clearly: if she had to perjure herself before the whole of Waterford, let alone her own family, she would gladly do it for the chance to lie with Tim Bradley again.

If you're going to fib about it—and you'll have to, she told herself—do it right. Do it mightily. Do it with conviction. She would! Her fatigue fell away and a different Emily took over as she walked with Tim, a self she recognized vaguely as the person she had been as a child, before she grew up and learned to be nice, a person hard and reckless in pursuit of what she wanted, self-serving without a qualm.

"Let me do the talking," she cautioned. "It's really easier that way. I can think better if I don't have to worry about you."

"I won't let you take the blame alone. I'll stand between you and him if he raises a hand to you . . ."

"He never has," she reassured him, thrilled to the core at the image of Tim taking a blow for her sake. Flashing him a grateful smile, she tried to put herself in her father's shoes, looking at the scene as Daddy must be seeing it.

Habitually he took the night train from Boston to Waterford on Friday night; he would have arrived at midnight. Emily's absence, when he first got to Kingsland, would not have been alarming. He wouldn't have thought much about it until the one o'clock curfew had been breached. After that, somehow, he had managed to find out that Emily was not with Charles, but instead had left early with Tim and had deducted that the two of them had gone out sailing, there being little else to do at night. How he managed to zero in on this particular beach, one unknown to Emily herself until now, was a mystery. But he had probably not slept a wink, had suffered in the city heat all week, was probably in a towering rage, implacable. Emily's cards had better be played exactly right, because the chances were good there would be no chance to play them again.

Her walk with Tim was nearly over. It must not be the last. She would take on her only advantage—the assumption of innocence, ingenuous innocence in which her father must be made to believe. And if she succeeded, the day would come when she would never have to let go of Tim's hand as she was letting go now in order to take off his coat which she'd been wearing against the morning chill.

When they were within hailing distance, she said loudly, so Daddy could hear, "Thanks for a lovely sail."

"Um, you're welcome," Tim stumbled, catching on. "I'm so glad you could come."

"Hi, Daddy!" she exclaimed. "Isn't it a beautiful morning?"

Daddy did not move until they were directly in front of him. "What is the explanation for this?" he asked Tim, his voice cold.

"I'm afraid I misjudged the tides, Mr. Merrick," Tim began. "I guess I'm not as familiar with them as I thought."

"So we spent the night floating around," Emily said breezily. "It was fun!"

But Daddy looked only at Tim. "This is inexcusable, young man."

"I'm awfully sorry, Mr. Merrick," Tim said. "It's entirely my fault, and I can't apologize enough."

"No, you can't. We would consider it a favor if you kept away from our daughter in the future." Daddy's face was murderous. "I'm sure your good father would be as upset as I am if he learned about your conduct. Which he will do if I find that you have tried to contact Emily again. Do you understand?"

"Yes, sir."

"Tim is my friend," Emily protested. "You can't decide who my friends are going to be, Daddy."

"Just watch me," her father said. "Good morning, Mr. Bradley."

Tim nodded and turned away. Slinging the coat she'd borrowed over his shoulder, he walked toward the boat and did not look back. She watched his long, loose stride, his broad shoulders, his sleek hips, strong legs. He had only a little dark hair on his body, and his skin was fine and pure....

She willed herself not to cry, because it would put her at a disadvantage. She must be careful not to sulk, which would make Daddy even more angry. Putting her chin up and throwing her shoulders back, she began. "No doubt you're upset, and I'm sorry to have inconvenienced you, Daddy, or worried you and Mother. But I wish you wouldn't take it out on my friends."

Marching past him to the car, she climbed in and stared at the beach, a silent, lifeless place without Tim on it. Daddy slid under the wheel.

"How did this happen?" he asked, watching her closely. His voice was dull and heavy. Whether he wanted to know what had happened on the boat or how it happened that she had gone out in it, was unclear.

She chose the easiest path. "Tim Bradley and I didn't want to stay at Priscilla's party. Her brother had found a case of gin on the flats, and everyone was drinking it and making fools of themselves. So Tim offered to take me sailing. Sailing was certainly nicer than staying there, and where else could we go? I was quite sure it would have been a mistake to bring him back to Kingsland."

"Yes, it certainly would have been. Bad enough that Charles Sinclair showed up at one thirty and announced that you had up and left with the Bradley boy. He said you tricked him, seems to think you had it planned all along."

"Charles would. He's always complaining if I'm friendly with anyone but him."

"He picked you up. He took you to the Wardens'. He was responsible for you. He was supposed to bring you home and you know it. He was very disturbed, and naturally your mother got very upset."

Of course, Mother would.

"So you got away from Charles and went sailing."

"Yes," she said simply. "And if it's an apology you're looking for, I'm glad to apologize for causing you worry and inconvenience. I'll try, somehow, to make it up to Mother and you."

"I would like an explanation of these." He reached into the back, brought out her girdle, wrapped snugly around her stockings and shoes.

"Oh, thanks!" she exclaimed "I was wondering where these had got to." Her father looked a bit disconcerted and she thought that, after all, she was on the right track. Continuing the charade, she said,

"If someone else had found them, I can just imagine what they'd think! Thank goodness it was you!" Carefully she thrust her hand into one of the stockings and inspected it on all sides. "Good as new," she said with satisfaction. "I knew that if I wore them sailing, I'd surely snag them."

"And, of course, no one sails in a girdle," Daddy remarked, his color becoming two shades redder.

"It would certainly be uncomfortable," she agreed. "And at least when you found my things, you must have figured out where I was."

"How could I know they were yours!" he shouted. "I'm hardly familiar with your underpinnings. Bradley probably knows a hell of a lot more about them than I do!"

A diversion was needed. "How did you find this particular beach?" she asked. "I didn't know anything about it."

"I got Tim's uncle, John Bradley, out of bed. He was pretty sure he knew where his nephew would have gone, and we came here to see if his boat was missing."

"I didn't know you were acquainted with Mr. Bradley."

"I am. I've known him for a long time, but that's beside the point. I'd have gotten him out of bed even if I wasn't acquainted. I was worried about you, Emily. What if you were hurt? What if someone had abducted you?"

Finally she did feel ashamed, and had no more to say.

"Tim Bradley's been around long enough to know you can't make Provincetown on one tide," Daddy grunted, turning the key. The car was a new model and had an electric starter, like Charles'. Daddy backed around, heading up the rutted road. "Everyone knows it can't be done."

"I think he really believed he could do it."

"But you knew." Daddy concentrated on steering so he wouldn't have to look at her. Probably he was fighting it out with himself, wanting to probe more deeply and not daring to, for fear what he might find. Pulling into the circular driveway of Kingsland, he drove around to the kitchen door.

"Needless to say, it would be best if you don't argue with your mother, Emily."

Nodding, she followed him into the house. Mother was waiting at the kitchen table, her eyes heavy, with dark pouches beneath them. There were lines etched into her face that Emily had never noticed before, and she felt a pang of true remorse—a pang she quelled instantly.

"Where have you been?" Mother's face was distorted, her voice rasping.

"I went sailing. The tide was wrong, and we couldn't get back. I suppose everything would have been fine if I'd been with Charles," Emily began.

"That's enough," Daddy said, quelling the incipient rebellion. "Just don't you get fresh. I gather they merely waited until there was enough water to get near the beach, darling," he said to Mother. He did not mention the girdle and stockings.

The night's exhilaration had faded, and Emily found herself in the middle of a yawn. As if it were a signal, her parents instantly attacked.

"We were careful not to wake Elizabeth up; she's still sleeping," Mother said. "She must never—ever—know who you were with, Emily."

"I've already told the Bradley boy to keep away from her, dearest," Daddy said comfortingly. "The real issue is Emily's disobedience. She's been out all night, with a young man of whom we disapprove. It must not be repeated." He looked meaningfully at the culprit, and she understood that he would not bring her undergarments into the discussion if she did not force him to, if she didn't give him any trouble about Tim. Still, she couldn't just take it lying down, could she?

"Staying at Pris's would have been far worse than leaving," she ventured. "You wouldn't believe . . ."

"Perhaps you ought not to see so much of Priscilla," her mother observed, and the discussion careened off like a herd of stampeding buffalo. "I've been wondering how well she's supervised. What's your thought about that, Daniel?"

"I don't know," Daddy said. "It's her brother that got ahold of the gin, after all. But clearly no adults were present. I'll admit to wondering if Emily wouldn't be more interested in completing her course of study at Bryn Mawr if Priscilla weren't egging her on about a job and an apartment in Boston."

Ah. Now he was using her indiscretion as a tool to give up her independence. Was there no end to this? "Pris and I have both been reconsidering it, as a matter of fact," she lied placatingly, and was rewarded by the little leap of hope in her mother's eye. "And as far as a night sail is concerned," she pressed on, "I thought it was positively inspirational."

Daddy tried not to smile.

"It isn't funny, Dan," Mother snapped. "We need to set limits for Emily, and do it now, before Elizabeth comes downstairs."

"Yes, of course." He thought about it for all of four seconds. "From now on I'll expect you to stay in the house, Em, unless accompanied by your mother or Cousin Elizabeth."

"Daddy!" she protested, appalled. "For how long?"

Daddy appeared to be unbearably satisfied with this sweeping control of her life. "Until August, I should think."

August! It was a month away!

"If Emily is grounded for more than a week or two, our friends will wonder why," Mother ventured. "We'll have to tell them something."

"Just tell them I have a communicable disease," Emily sulked. "That'll take care of it."

Daddy threw her a dirty look.

"If she had merely stayed out too late, being grounded for a month seems a little extreme," Mother went on.

"Yes," he sighed. "But she was with someone at the party we don't know. And Charles, who was responsible for her, became distraught when he couldn't find her. So we have two offenses to consider. That Emily stayed out past curfew, and that she appears to have hidden from Charles. On purpose," Daddy caught her eye again. Don't you balk, he seemed to be saying. "So let's use two weeks for breaking curfew, and one for giving Charles such a hard time. Three weeks in all."

"Can her friends come here?" Mother asked.

"One at a time," Daddy decided. "And it goes without saying, Emily, that you may not see the Bradley boy again. Ever."

She would see him. She would!

"Charles is coming to call on her after lunch. He said he would, last night," Mother reminded him.

"That's fine, if Charles comes here," Daddy announced. "She's still in the house. Or on one of the porches."

"Or under one, where he can't find me," Emily scowled.

"It's time you went to bed," Mother said. "Do it now, this instant. Use the back stairs, in case Elizabeth is coming down as you're going up."

They waved her away, and continued to talk. The quiet rumble of their voices faded as she crept up the stairs and into her room. There was, as yet, no sign of Cousin Elizabeth.

In the unfamiliar light of the early morning, she lay in her bed, her groin throbbing and abraised, wondering what Daddy would do with her girdle, wondering what had happened at the party. When would there be another one? It was important to find out, for it was at these gatherings that she and Tim could meet—and she would meet him! She would! She must! The cry volleyed back and forth in her brain as her exhaustion numbed her and she fell away from the morning now in progress.

"I don't think it was very nice of you, just going off and leaving me like that." Charles' face was grim, taut with anger.

"I'd say it was you who left me." The afternoon air fanned past the west porch, overlooking the tree once used by the gang as home base. The lawn, sweltering in the sun, seemed to grow crisper and crisper as they sat there, rocking in the swing.

Her head ached. Her skin was sticky and itched, and her eyes were gritty from too little sleep.

What was Tim doing now, she wondered. Was he thinking of her, as she was of him?

"You could have at least told me you were leaving," Charles growled.

"For all I knew, you were going to spend the evening in the bulrushes with Ginny Porter," she lashed out. "The last I saw of you, it looked like you were going snipe hunting."

It was cruel and she knew it, but he was a convenient target of her own anger. Due to him, Daddy had gotten to the beach before she and Tim could get away without a confrontation.

"So you knew about the snipe hunt. Why didn't you put me in the know? It was really mean of the gang. Do you know what I'd do if I had a chance?" he said fiercely. "To get back at them, get even? I'd tie them up and leave them in that damned marsh, all of them. I'd strip them naked and let them get eaten alive by bugs, and I'd listen to them moan and I'd watch and I'd laugh." His smile was unpleasant. "They used to do that, you know, to Negro slaves. Tie them naked to a tree, leave them to the swarms of mosquitos hovering around the swamps until they went mad and died." He glanced at her, saw her stare. Shakily he laughed, covering his malice. "They did. They really did. I read it somewhere. Well, next time, I'll know better when Pris proposes a snipe hunt!"

Disturbed by the cruelty she'd glimpsed, Emily patted his hand to distract him. "I don't blame you for being mad. But you're a jolly good fellow, and everyone must have thought you'd be a good sport about it." They were words calculated to placate, and they were successful. He relaxed, and his scowl disappeared. "Besides," she chided, "you can't tell me Ginny Porter didn't creep into the swamp with you."

Did Tim Bradley think of her every waking moment? Did he dream of her when he got to bed today—if indeed he got to bed at all?

"Who told you?" Charles asked.

"I saw her heading in that direction," Emily lied. "I know she's crazy for you. Everyone knows it."

"Yes," he sighed. "I suppose she is." The swing had coasted to a stop. "Are you going to tell me who you disappeared with?" His tone was sharp again.

"No. But, since I wasn't there, are you going to tell me how the party went after the snipe hunt."

After she left and went sailing with Tim Bradley and made love with him on the Eastham beach . . . An insatiable longing swept by, wrenching her.

"You don't know!" Charles crowed. "Of course you don't. You haven't heard!"

"No, I haven't." How long would he play this scenario out, she wondered wearily, tantalizing and teasing.

"Priscilla's Pater came home before midnight!"

"Mr. Warden!"

"He motored down with someone from his company."

The catastrophic impact of Mr. Warden returning early was unimaginable. "What was going on when he arrived?"

"Pris and Jacky and another couple were skinny-dipping in a tide pool. Thomas and a girl from Yarmouth were fornicating on the grass. Everyone else had passed out and were scattered about the house, on whatever bed or couch they could find."

"Fornicating on the grass," she groaned.

"Truly," Charles remarked wryly. "It was an interesting scene, I can tell you. There the Warden Pater was, ranting and raving, and Pris was trying to tell him that repressions are bad for you—that Dr. Freud himself said so, and Jacky was hopping around trying to get his trousers back on—and that was when I realized you weren't there." He cast her a reproachful glance.

"I'll forgive you for not noticing before then, Charles, if you tell me what Mr. Warden did next."

"He loaded his car with anyone he could find, and took them home. Then he came back and ferried another load, and then another. That left just Tommy and Pris and me."

"Why did you stay?"

"I wanted to be able to drive home so the Mater wouldn't know I'd been, ah, under the weather. And I had to tell your parents that you were gone, too, so I chatted a while with Pris and Tom until I sobered up. By then, the Warden Pater had distributed everybody to their respective doorsteps, and he could deal with his offspring. I heard him threaten to send Tom to a military school in Pennsylvania. And he said the Warden Mater must go away, too."

"Mrs. Warden?"

"This morning the grapevine has it that the Warden Mater is now in residence at a drying-out place. Mr. Warden holds her alcoholic propensities responsible for allowing such goings on. Tom has been sent to a relative somewhere. I don't know if the military school thing will really happen or not. But the big news is that Pris's freedom has come to an end. She's getting a duenna."

"A what?"

"A chaperone."

"A chaperone!" she snorted. "Who'd ever be a match for Pris Warden, I'd like to know."

"Why, that new girl. Alice Bradley."

Alice Bradley.

Emily felt something in the region of her heart sinking, down and down. "She's free for the summer, until school starts. And she's older than Pris, quite a lot older, and can probably handle her, judging from what I've seen. She's moved right in, so Pris won't be home alone, what with her mother gone. I'll get more lemonade if you'd like some, Emily. You look like you could use it."

"Thank you," she heard her voice say distantly.

Alice was going to live at the Wardens? Accompany Pris to all the gang's parties, hang around making sure her charge behaved herself? When Mother and Daddy learned that Alice was part of the Warden establishment, they would surely forbid Emily to go there even after her three weeks of penance had expired.

And she would never see Tim Bradley again.

Oh, God, she thought miserably, appalled by the dimensions of her difficulty. Help me. Help me.

A new thought came to her. Perhaps Tim was as desperate as she was. He wanted to see her, too, after all. He'd said so. If she could get a message to him, set up a time to meet secretly, once she was free, she could tell him how impossible her situation was, and between them they might be able to figure how to get around it. There was only one way to do this, of course. She'd have to ask Alice to deliver the message. Unless Tim Bradley found a way to come to her and she would be spared having to beg a favor from the pariah.

4

She had not understood what it would mean, waiting for those three weeks to pass. Had not understood how painful every minute of every hour could be, how long each one was, how interminable. Had not known how much despair one person could contain as the last light of evening lingered, and another day disappeared without Tim in it.

Never had she cared so much before.

Never had she given so much.

And she could do nothing but wait.

As expected, Cousin Elizabeth was enraged to learn of Alice's return to Waterford. She even went to Pris's father, urging him to find another chaperone, a request Mr. Warden regretfully declined. He'd plain forgotten about the animosity between the Merricks and the Bradleys, he confessed. And now having hired the young lady, he could hardly fire her just because someone wanted him to.

Besides, Alice had done wonders for his daughter already, he explained, and further, he knew of no one else who could. Might it not be possible for Miss Elizabeth to live and let live? No? Well, Pris would surely miss Emily.

No one at Kingsland seemed to be concerned about how separation from Pris and the gang might affect Emily herself. Daddy had yet to forgive his daughter's duplicity. Mother was so busy consoling Elizabeth over Alice's appearance on the Waterford scene that she had no time to care, and meanwhile, Emily was dying a thousand times a day.

Three weeks crawled by.

Once she was liberated, she sought him everywhere. Was he hiding behind the shelves at the library, waiting for a chance to see her? Was he lingering at Snow's Store, across the street, watching for her to come there on one errand or another? Or was he at the old Bradley house, painting and repairing things? When she went there, ladders were leaning against walls, paint cans littered the front steps, but Tim was absent.

The summer was half over. She couldn't just lie around dreaming of that wonderful moment when he would pop up from behind a bush somewhere. She must get that message to him, asking him to meet her at dawn on the beach.

Taking her bicycle from the barn, she wheeled it around to the back and along the path to the Rockford Road, peddaled on up to Main Street and east to the Warden's, without anyone even knowing she was gone.

Mary Ann Hall opened the door and smiled in welcome. Her hair was covered by a kerchief, the rest of her by a commodious, well-used apron.

"Hello, Miss Merrick! Pris is on the side porch. Go on through, if you like."

"Thanks."

Propelled by her urgent purpose she forgot to notice that the Hall girl had called Pris by her first name; striding through the shadowed opulence of the Warden mansion, she found her friend reading in the conservatory, seated on a wooden glider that she could set in motion with a little push now and then. Sunlight flooded in, and Pris looked exactly as she should, the daughter of a wealthy banker, whiling time away while others did the work.

"Hello!" Emily called, her voice as merry as she could make it.

"Emily!" Leaping from the swing, Pris closed the book on her finger, marking her place. "How good to see you!" An air kiss was deposited. "Does your father know you're here? Have your parents relented, after all this time?"

"No. I mean, I expect they will, Pris, but just now I had to see you . . ."

"Oh, I know what you mean!" Pris exclaimed. "So often I've felt that I just had to see you, too! Come right here and sit down."

Pris turned to the swing and steadied it, laying the book, the newest one by Sinclaire Lewis, face down on a nearby table.

"Mary Ann? Fetch some lemonade, won't you?" Pris had only raised her voice a little, but the Hall girl answered instantly.

"Right away!" It was obvious that she'd been nearby, hoping to hear what was going on.

"Well!" Pris clasped her hands in a gesture that mirrored her mother. "This is quite a treat! How's everything?" Her brightness was just a bit brittle and, instantly, Emily was on guard.

"I've got a little problem, actually," she said, carefully feeling her way along. "I'd hoped you could help me."

"You know I'd do anything in the world for you, Emily." Pris looked earnestly at her, blinking a few times as though to clear her vision and better see what needed to be done.

Emily made herself smile. "Do you remember when we arranged the snipe hunt a month ago?"

"Yes, I sure do!" Pris discarded her pose of silly sincerity. "And it seems to me, if I remember correctly, that you disappeared with Alice's cousin, and were never seen again."

Emily produced a good imitation of gay laughter. "Oh, yes, that!" Elaborately she looked around. "Does Alice still come here?"

"Oh, yes. Regularly."

"Is she still your duenna?"

"Not exactly. She doesn't come here in that capacity. She comes because she wants to." Pris hurried on. "The Hall girls take turns staying here at night, so I won't get lonely. Alice stops by during the day. She and I have become close." Pris looked modestly down at her folded hands. "She likes me as much as I like her, even though I can't begin to keep up with her. She's willing to befriend me, even so." A very great distance had opened between them now. "I think you'd like her, Emily, if your family would ever give you the chance to know her like I do!" Pris's face lit up eagerly. "Look here! We're going to have a gathering this Saturday, the gang and some of Alice's friends from town. Maybe your parents would let you come. Just tell them Alice isn't my chaperone any more—which happens to be the truth. It suggests she wouldn't be here, doesn't it?"

The most reasonable solution would be to give Pris the message, tell her to pass it along to Alice with the instruction to pass it to Tim. That way, Emily would not be required to lie. But Pris might not be reliable, having apparently been hog-tied by Alice. Emily must deliver the message, herself.

"A gathering," she repeated, as though she were trying to decide if it was worth her time. "That's an odd name for a party."

"It's a work party. Sounds dull, but it's not. It's loads of fun." Apparently life was flowing along in somewhat different channels, without the presence of Emily Merrick.

The rattling of ice against the sides of the crystal pitcher told them that Mary Ann was coming with the lemonade.

"Did you bring enough for yourself?" Pris asked as the girl set the tray on the low table near the swing. "I was just beginning to tell Emily about the gathering on Saturday."

Mary Ann glanced up with a swift flick of the eye in Emily's direction. "And the Fall Fest? Did you tell her about that?"

"I haven't, yet. Here, Mary Ann. Sit right here and tell her yourself while I pour the lemonade."

Mary Ann Hall perched on the edge of a nearby rattan chair. "Everyone's going to exhibit a craft at the Fall Festival," she explained. "We meet Saturdays and work on our projects for the exhibition."

"The Fall Festival? At Kingsland?"

"Yes! Everyone's so excited!"

The Fall Fest had been started by Cousin Elizabeth several years ago. The whole town was invited to view examples of high society's summer fun—collections of rocks or shells, paintings or poetry written in fancy script, needlework or flowers grown in the gardens of the upper crust. It was one of the few occasions when the grounds of Kingsland were open to the town.

"The Festival's always been for the summer folks, to display their projects. Is it open this year for other people's exhibits, too?" Emily knew for a certainty that it wasn't.

"No," Mary Ann giggled and glanced at Pris.

"We're going to crash it!" Pris announced.

"Who?"

"All of us."

"Please, Pris, you explain," Mary Ann begged. "I've really got to finish the kitchen floor."

Emily watched as she disappeared, not quite believing it: Pris had invited the maid to have lemonade with them, invited her to spring the news about the Fall Fest, and had accepted Mary Ann's decision to return to the kitchen before she, Pris, had dismissed her....

"So you're going to crash the Fall Fest," Emily prompted. "Who's idea was that?"

"Why, Alice's!"

"Unbelievable," she murmured as calmly as possible. "If she thinks her sister Elizabeth will welcome her with open arms..."

"No, no, that's not the point at all!" Pris scoffed. "The point is that all the kids in town will be bringing crafts and things and our parents will see there's so much to offer here..."

Emily shook her head. "Maybe you'd better start from the beginning. I'll just sit here and listen."

"Well," Pris began, "Alice had my father's consent to do just about anything she thought would get me out of the rut I was in. She was in charge, and it was amazing, Em, how quickly things started falling into place. I don't know how she did it—well, yes I do. First she introduced me to some new people so that I wouldn't constantly be with the kids who do nothing but party."

"Kids like me?"

Pris went on without acknowledging Emily's remark. "And I began to see that life could be different from the way I'd been living it. Of course, she's a lot older and more mature..."

If she heard another word about Alice Bradley, Emily believed she would scream.

"She's put everything together," Pris was droning on. "She's found the answers to life's questions. They were already there, she said. She makes the gang feel that they have the answers, too, deep inside, and they can discover who they really are if they don't do things that will get in the way."

"And the two of you have dawdled around this past month discussing these things?"

"No," Pris smiled gently, as though Emily were perhaps not bright. "We take walks and play tennis, and she's taught me how to arrange flowers. According to Japanese principles."

"Which are?"

"The earth-man-heaven triad. I'm going to show several arrangements at the fall fest. Becky is quilling some wonderful Christmas stars. Jacky is whittling animals."

"Alice can teach all of these things?"

"No, the town kids do. Steven Stone is helping Jacky. His sister is showing Becky how to quill."

"And the town kids are bringing crafts, too?"

"You bet! Canned carrot and beans. Little people made of straw—that's an Irish tradition, by the way."

"Don't get me wrong, Pris," Emily said. "Those kids are nice and their parents are nice people, too. But they aren't your kind of people, and they never will be. It's a mistake to mix them, thinking there's no difference."

"There isn't any difference when Alice is around," Pris argued. "You'll see that if you come Saturday. All the girls will bring what they're working on, help one another if need be, enjoy one another's company. I hope your parents will let you come."

"They won't. But I believe Charles would help if I asked him. I'll have him take me for a drive, with a detour along the way. My parents never refuse to let me go out with him."

"He'll come all the way down from Boston just to drop you off at a gathering?"

"I expect so, if I promise him the rest of the afternoon and evening. Just the two of us."

"That'll do it," Pris laughed. "Good enough! Be here around two o'clock."

"Okay." In as casual a manner as she could contrive, Emily rose from the swing and waved. "I'll let myself out. Don't bother Mary Ann. She's probably busy studying the rules of etiquette in polite society." It was a nasty crack that she immediately regretted having made, and she cursed herself as she hustled through the dining room and then the living room and the foyer and out to her bike where she'd left it, leaning against a tree.

Behind her back the whole gang had reassembled, and were meeting with the town's young people—a very unusual thing—and not one of them had mentioned it when she'd seen them at the store or after church or at the library. Why did they hide it? Did they think she didn't belong in their ranks any more, just because she'd been in seclusion most of the summer? Or were they excluding her out of deference to Alice?

Well, they couldn't keep her away this Saturday. She'd write a note to Tim and give it to Alice to deliver and that was the most important thing. If it turned out that her old friends no longer accepted her out of their new-found loyalty to Alice, what of it, she asked herself defiantly. If that's the kind of friendship they have to offer, you're better off knowing it now.

But it didn't feel better. It felt worse. Pedaling back to Kingsland, her tears dropped, hot and useless, into the dust.

∞ 5 ∞

"I guess I don't have to tell you that I'm just a bit disappointed," Charles complained. The vein in his left temple was jumping, and

Emily was unpleasantly aware that he had a temper which she had never, ever suspected was there. "Here I come all the way down from Boston, breaking my neck to do it. And jeopardizing my progress at Sommerset and Troy by taking Saturday off. And what happens when I get here? You want me to leave you at the Warden's house and cool my heels for two hours while you weave baskets."

Furiously he turned into the Warden's driveway, so abruptly that she lost her balance and was slammed against the car door. He pulled up to the front of the house with a flourish of dust and flying pebbles, stomped on the brake and stalled the car which bucked in protest, then subsided with a shudder or two.

Never had she seen him like this.

"Charles," she soothed, taking his hand and holding it in both of hers. "It's a little too complicated to explain, but I had to get here this afternoon without my parents knowing about it. So I thought—what a perfect opportunity! A perfect excuse to see Charles again. Surely he'd come down to Waterford, surely he'd help me—and I'd get a chance to spend time with him as well as to go to Pris's craft party."

Desperately wanting to believe her, Charles asked, "Did you really think you needed an excuse, Emily?"

"Of course I did, Silly! I know how busy you are, up there in the city! I know you don't have time for me anymore, Charles, and I understand. Your career is the most important thing in your life just now—as it should be!"

"I always have time for you," he protested.

"Then pick me up at the stroke of four. We can talk to our hearts' content then! You can tell me all about Sommerset and Troy—I'm dying to know what you're up to, Charles!" Kissing his cheek, she quickly let herself out. "I'll see you later."

"All right," he said, mollified though unhappy. "Make sure you'll be ready."

Her arm hurt where she'd knocked it against the car door, but she marched to the Warden's porch and rang the bell without touching or rubbing it, in case he was looking. It was important not to let him know he'd caused her pain, so he wouldn't get out of the car and rush to her side and....

"Emily!" Pris trilled. "It's so nice you could come!"

Such gusto most likely disguised nervousness. Emily gritted her teeth. "Hi, dear." She kissed Pris's cheek. "I'm glad to see you."

Behind Pris hovered Caroline Curtis, trying to look casual. "Hi, Em!"

Instantly she was aware that Alice was standing by the doorway to the dining room, and turned to Caroline, whom she'd known for years, said, "Your dress is marvelous!"

"I made it myself!"

"I didn't know you could sew."

"Oh, Alice showed me how."

"Emily," Pris interrupted, "do you know Ellen Shaunessy?"

The Shaunessy girl's father was the man who delivered parcels and people from the train depot. "Ellen is going to Vassar next year," Pris said. "So we're getting her bridge game in shape."

"If Vassar is anything like Bryn Mawr, she'll need to get it in shape!" Emily laughed, nearly as fraudulently as Pris.

Ellen Shaunessy blushed, tongue-tied in the presence of Emily Merrick, whom she'd seen around town all her life and never once spoken to.

"And this is Amy Stone," Pris announced. "And I guess I don't have to introduce the Hall girls," she gushed.

"No, indeed." She waved to them, sitting on the couch together as though they were Siamese, joined at the hip. "Hi, Evvie," she said to Evangeline Thayer.

"Hi, Em," responded Evvie without enthusiasm, as though she were not truly glad that Emily Merrick had returned to the bosom of their group.

"And you remember Alice, of course," Pris said reverently, leading Emily to the dining room doorway.

"Yes, of course." She used the smile she'd rehearsed for the meeting with the Merrick pariah, a smile that she hoped was disarming and frank, that would cause Alice to believe that Emily Merrick did not share her family's prejudices.

"Well!" Pris exclaimed, her words nearly garbled in her excitement. "The dining room table is all set up. Since you're the one responsible for bringing our latent skills out into the open, Allie, you shall lead the way." Deferentially, she backed up and gestured widely toward the crafts.

Alice glanced at Emily, then smiled and beckoned the group forward as though she were starting a regatta. The girls fanned out, each to her own project, all mixing together, laughing and chatting, while Alice, wandering from one group to another, made a suggestion here, a correction there.

No one paid attention to Emily, standing to one side, watching. In time, Alice fetched up beside her.

"Everyone seems to be doing fine. Let's go out to the conservatory and chat." At last! A chance to ask if Alice would deliver the message. "Pris says that you and she were roommates at Bryn Mawr."

"Yes, we were."

"Pris says she'd like it if you were her roommate again, this fall."

"She would?" Emily asked. "She's going back?"

"Yes."

Pris hadn't said anything about this new turn of events—but, after all, their conversation had been about Alice, not about Bryn Mawr.

"Have you thought about going back, Emily?"

They sat down in the swing. "My parents have, I assure you."

"But not you?"

"Both Pris and I were a bit bored with it all."

"I'm sure that's only because you haven't taken full advantage of everything Bryn Mawr offers. College expands your horizons tremendously. An education gives you wings to soar, a chance to discover who you really are, and what you really want to make of your life."

Waiting, she looked at Emily expectantly, ready to listen, really listen, instead of merely pretending until her chance came to speak again. But Emily had not taken all this trouble to chitchat about her chances of self discovery.

"Your cousin Tim told me you used to work in Boston," she said, working closer to her goal. "Did you soar there?"

"I was a fashion designer. I think anything that taps into the creative..."

"Like Japanese flower arranging?"

"Yes, indeed. Like that."

The ball had been returned, and Emily shot it back. "Tim told me that you were going to hog-tie Waterford. Does that tap into the creative instinct?"

"Hog-tie!" Alice's laughter was spontaneous, even raucous. "Oh, that Tim! He just would say something like that! Wait 'til I get hold of him!"

"And speaking of Tim..." Emily dug into her purse for the note, "I was wondering if you..."

There was an uproar of female voices from the house, and the sudden rumble of a male one, and Emily thought that surely—surely it must be her imagination, because it sounded like...

"That must be my fiancé," Alice said. "I'll have to be on my way. What message, Emily?"

"Your fiancé?" Emily asked faintly. The blood had stopped coursing in her veins, and she suddenly retreated, very distant from the porch and the swing and Alice, sitting beside her.

"Have I come too early?" Tim asked from the doorway. "I thought you told me four..." Then Emily's presence broke through the intensity of his attention to his cousin, and his face deepened to a dark red as Alice went to him, drawing him forward.

"Tim, do you remember my cousin Emily Merrick? You met her at the Marshalls. She's been telling me that you think I'm trying to hog-tie Waterford."

"I'd say you were succeeding, too," he smiled, avoiding Emily's stare.

Onto the porch burst Pris. "Charles is here, Emily. He wants to take you away—now!"

"You bet I do!" Charles followed, taking charge of the moment so effectively it was as though Tim Bradley and Alice did not exist. He put a possessive arm around Emily's waist, inadvertently sheltering her.

"We'll talk about the message later," she said to Alice over his shoulder, refusing to look at Tim in case he was not looking at her. Herself so fragile, like porcelain, ready to shatter.

"Okay, then." Alice nodded and looked up at Tim. "We'll be on our way. Don't clean up the mess, Pris. I'll come over in the morning and the two of us can tackle it."

The young Bradleys left.

Inanely Pris sighed. "Handsome couple, aren't they? They've been in love for years."

"Really?"

Pris looked at her closely and steadily. "They've tried to get involved with other people, but it just never seems to work. They can't get each other out of their respective systems, no matter how many other people they try to love."

Thus did Pris tell her erstwhile friend Emily that Tim Bradley had only sought refuge from the insolvable difficulty of consanguinity when he'd made a play for her; thus did she tell her former friend that the difficulty had been overcome. That Alice came first now, first for everyone. It was not possible to know when Tim's relationship with her had been resolved, or how it had happened or if Tim had only ever played with Emily's feelings in the manner of fickle men everywhere—nor did it matter.

Because Tim was gone.

"Well, it's all been simply charming," she said to Pris, hating her. "But unfortunately, Charles and I must leave now."

"We sure must," Charles agreed, rushing her past the maelstrom in the dining room and to the front door. In the driveway Tim was closing the passenger door of his car. Charles had parked behind him, and they must pass by as Tim came around and slid into the driver's seat. He nodded to her in belated acknowledgment as he pulled his door shut. Somehow she must make it to the Sinclaire Buick, where all she had to do was contend with Charles and would no longer be assaulted by such impossible, untenable hurt and humiliation.

Charles helped her in, and she sat silent while they drove down Main Street, past the church, past Kingsland, past the library....

She had lost him.

She had been his for the taking, all of her, but he had declined her offer. The agony of it tore at her heart, halting all other awareness. He can't, she tried to tell herself. He can't just... drop me!

But he had.

"Are you in love with that Bradley fellow," Charles asked crossly. "You were watching him rather intently, it seemed to me."

She said nothing, felt nothing, thought nothing.

"Well?"

"Well, what?"

"I asked if you were in love with that Bradley fellow."

"No."

"Then why were you watching him like a hawk?"

Why, indeed?

It must be explained away, she supposed. "I was watching Alice. Not Tim."

"Quite lower class," Charles grumbled. "I can't imagine why Priscilla's Pater picked her as a duena. And with her being *persona non grata* at your house—I say, Emily, that must have been a bit difficult for you, being at the Warden's when she was there."

It would do. It would account for her obvious unhappiness; it was a better excuse than the truth—the truth she could not bear.

"Yes, it was. I didn't know she'd be there."

He will never love you, she told herself. He's in love with her. And Alice was not lower-class, for all her upbringing. The girl was a Merrick, every bit as much a Merrick as Elizabeth was, and her impact on the lives of others was immense. Her impact on Tim had been lifelong. She had reformed the gang; Pris trailed after her with devotion, and Emily Merrick had lost just about everything that counted, because of her.

"If you're not in love with that fellow, then I'm glad," Charles said. "Because there's something I've been wanting to speak to you about, and I can't very well speak of it if you love another man." He pulled the car to the side of the road. She saw that they had driven as far as the stream where once there had been a ford, and a grist mill, and a fulling mill, and a woolen one. All of them had all burned up or fallen down. Nothing remained of them, and the ford was bridged now, the stream bed dug deeper...

"They're talking pretty seriously about sending me out to Ohio," Charles said, engaging the emergency brake. The motor, still running, hummed on. "They're opening a branch office in Port Huron, Ohio, and they want me to go out there because, of course, men who are already settled in the Boston area are loath to pull up stakes."

"Yes, I suppose they are."

"Now that I've been living on my own, these few weeks, it's become very clear to me that I must put some distance between the Mater and me. Her dependence on me is stifling. And I can do it by accepting this new assignment."

"That makes sense," she agreed, as if she cared.

"And I'm hoping, Emily, that you will do me the honor of coming with me—as my wife."

There it was. Dumbly, she looked at him and felt the start of tears and wished, somehow, that she could sleep, and stay asleep, and not wake up until the sun was setting and the birds were calling in an afternoon far, far removed from this one.

"Emily, darling, what have I done?" Charles, in a twitter of distress, took her cold hand. "Emily," he cajoled, "surely asking you to marry me isn't that bad!"

In her attempt to laugh, a sob escaped, and she covered her burning face to evade the necessity of speaking.

"I didn't realize you were so wrought-up, my dear," Charles said stiffly. "I gather you don't want to discuss marriage just now."

Tired. She was excruciatingly tired. And yet the instinct to preserve herself stirred, reached out, plucked at her consciousness . . . Charles was here. Now. Oh, God, oh God, he was here now and Tim was not and never would be and Ohio was far, far away from this devastation . . .

"Maybe you'd just let me rest here for a while," she choked. "Maybe I'll feel better in a minute." She curled up her knees and rested her head on them and closed her eyes.

"Certainly, Emily, if that's what you need to do, my dear." He reached over the gear shift and patted her shoulder. "You may not know how to answer right away. I'm not suggesting that we get married instantly. I thought I'd set myself up in Port Huron, Ohio, and then come back for you. I was hoping we could, perhaps, get married at Christmas."

She must go home. She must go now. She could not think, she could hardly speak. "College," she stumbled, grasping at the straw closest to hand. "I should finish."

"Well, I suppose so. But the girls all get married when they graduate. You'd just be speeding up the process."

"My parents . . ."

"Of course! Of course! I shall speak to them when you give me the word. But do you think it's a possibility? Do you care about me even a little?"

"You know I do," she made herself say.

"Perhaps you'd show me by allowing me to kiss you?"

"Here? On a public highway?"

He laughed, no doubt feeling rakish and fast. "Maybe your driveway?"

"Better," she nodded, and quickly he engaged the gears, released the brake, and made a U-turn. Again she watched the scenery flow by, but this time she was focused and knew what she must do. She waited for him to come around to her side of the car, once they reached Kingsland; she led him onto the front porch and turned to him. "All right."

Swiftly he bent and kissed her heavily. After a decent, interminable interval she disengaged herself from him. "Thanks for being so considerate, Charles. We'll talk about marriage another day."

In the empty parlor she slid behind a portiere that kept drafts under control in cool weather. It was pulled conveniently out of the way, now providing a nook, a refuge. She slid behind the heavy curtain, and the hot tears that she'd held in were released in the privacy of the musty velvet, running freely down her face and dripping onto her dress, staining it.

"Emily!" exclaimed Cousin Elizabeth, peering in behind the portiere. "Good grief, my dear! What in heaven's name is wrong?"

Brought up short, just before she fell over the brink of hysteria, Emily got herself under control. Cousin Elizabeth led her to the library and placed her in a comfortable chair, poured her a glass of water. "No one's home," she said, drawing up a chair of her own. "You can talk about it, if you want to."

Elizabeth was not the right person! She was absolutely the wrong person, because the Bradleys were never, never supposed to be mentioned in her presence. But Emily's unbearable hurt drove her into the arms of this inappropriate confidant. "I've lost him," she choked.

"From what I saw out the parlor window, I wouldn't judge you'd lost him at all. Why, the look on his face—"

"Not Charles!" she cried. "Tim. And can you guess, Elizabeth, who I lost him to? No, you never will. Never. Not in a million years."

"So tell me," Elizabeth urged indulgently, without realizing who Emily was talking about.

"Alice," she hiccupped. "I've lost Tim Bradley to your sister Alice."

Cousin Elizabeth was ordinarily a handsome woman, tall, imperially beaked, poised of carriage and demeanor. Her inbred sense of dignity did not desert her now, but all the lines in her face, and the creases between her eyes and the parentheses around her mouth tightened and deepened, and made her into a caricature of the woman she'd been a moment before.

"Alice?" Not even her voice was the same. Instead it rasped, as though there were not enough room in her throat for it. She swallowed convulsively, poured a glass of water for herself, her hands shaking. "Could you start at the beginning, Emily?"

There was no point in hiding now, was there? Elizabeth was due for a head-on collision with Alice at the Fall Fest anyway. "I met Tim Bradley earlier this summer," she explained over her pain. "But Mother said he mustn't come here, because it would upset you. So I met him at parties, until I was put under house arrest here because I stayed out all night with him."

"When was that? Refresh my memory."

"A month—no, more like six weeks ago."

"This Tim would be Alice's Bradley cousin?"

"Yes."

"Go on."

"I'd hoped to marry him—I love him so! But . . . but now I discover he was really in love with Alice all the time and only used me in an attempt to forget her."

"The Bradley's were always two faced," Elizabeth said, her voice hard. "Go on."

"They're engaged, is all," she said, her voice thin and whining.

"They're cousins," Elizabeth stated after a short pause, "from a long line of consanguine marriages."

"Apparently that's not stopping them, although I think Alice has put Tim off for a long while because of it."

"Most educated people understand that cousins shouldn't marry." Elizabeth displayed no emotion at all now, and only watched Emily carefully. "Maybe she's not very smart."

Emily shook her head. "She's very smart. She's scheming to take Waterford away from you." Her desolation and despair made her reckless. "Beginning with the Fall Fest."

"Our Fall Festival, here, at the end the month?"

"The very same. Accompanied by her retinue." Cruelly Emily named them, the Shaunessy girl and Amy Stone and the Hall sisters—as well as Pris and the gang, all of them jolly good friends together, blending all aspects of Waterford's population. The expression on Elizabeth's face changed from icy coldness to anger that was white hot, and she was quiet for a long time, her eyes closed. When they opened again, Emily saw that they glowed, like a cat's watching a bird, waiting for it to hop a little closer, a little closer....

"She must be stopped. Both from taking Tim away from you, and from undermining Waterford's traditions."

"And you think you can stop her?"

"Oh, yes," Elizabeth said softly, with malice in her voice. "I believe so, yes. Where do you think she is right now?"

"Now?"

"This moment."

"I... I suppose she's at home."

Unless Tim was taking her someplace for an early dinner, or a cocktail, or a private place where they could park.

Elizabeth opened a desk drawer, took out a piece of Kingsland stationery and an envelope, hunted for a pen. "Wait a bit, dear, while I write a little note. I'd like you to take it to her house."

"Now?"

"Now."

"Cousin Elizabeth, I'm awfully tired."

"I think you'll be glad, once you see that it may help you get the Bradley boy back."

From exhaustion to tentative hope, Emily waited, looking out the window through the trees to the steeple of the church, poking up past them like a finger pointing at God. How ironic it was, she thought, scheming with Cousin Elizabeth to get Tim back!

"Here you are." Elizabeth folded the paper and slid it into an envelope, wrote Alice's name, sealed it. "I think that'll do the trick."

"What did you say to her?"

"That's between my sister and me. Deliver it. I'd like to see her as soon as possible."

"Today? It's a little late."

"It's never too late. Be of good cheer, my dear. Alice may yet decide against marrying her cousin. Then he'd be free for you. Go!"

Hurrying along Main Street's sidewalk, Emily mused on Karma, wondering what she might have done in a previous lifetime that had wrought punishment on her now, and wondering how Elizabeth could undo it. Could anyone? Keeping her mind occupied with this conundrum, the Bradley driveway appeared quickly. Along its edge insects hummed and buzzed in a satisfied undertone, the birds spoke from the bushes, and a rabbit nibbled clover. The peace of the moment caught up with her and lapped at the edges of her awareness, making her even more miserable.

Slowly she moved ahead, and the rabbit, apparently accustomed to people, moved with her for a hop or two before detouring behind a tree; ahead lay the Bradley cottage and further along on the right were some small barns. Spread all around the buildings was a beautifully tended cranberry bog. There were more of them behind the biggest barn, ditched so that the water from the ponds beyond could be delivered as needed.

It was a clean and neat operation, but Emily was in no mood to admire it. As she drew closer she could hear their voices, Alice's and Tim's. Karma, she thought. She's home.

"Alice?"

The voices stopped. Alice came out from one of the sheds and shaded her eyes. "Yes?" she called in response.

"Over here!"

"Emily!" Alice turned to speak over her shoulder to Tim, who appeared beside her in the shed doorway, but made no move to follow her.

"Twice in the same day!" Alice exclaimed. "I'm probably a mess," she laughed. "With cobwebs in my hair and dirt on my nose." In fact, she was looking quite bedraggled. "Everything has to be spankin' clean before we start picking the cranberry crop. We were working on the sorting trays." She brushed off her apron.

"I have something for you."

"Oh?"

Emily held out the Kingsland envelope and Alice inspected the identifying crest and seal without touching it.

"What's in it, do you know?"

"I don't. Elizabeth wouldn't tell me."

"How intriguing."

"I think it has something to do with the Fall Festival."

"Oh?"

"Well, I mentioned to her that you were planning to be there."

Alice laughed. "I'll bet she was pleased to hear about that! Let's go inside and I'll wash my hands so I can open the darned thing without smudging it."

"OK."

"Carry on, Tim," she called to the figure in the shed doorway. "I'll be back when I can."

"OK," he yelled back, and disappeared into the shed.

Alice led the way up to the kitchen door and waved Emily inside. Mr. Bradley was sitting at the table. "It's just me, Dad," she said, "and Miss Emily Merrick." Was he blind? "She brought me a note, and I need to wash my hands before I open it."

"Will you sit down, Miss Emily?" the old man asked, not looking at her.

"Thank you."

He quickly turned his head in the direction of her voice. Yes, he was blind, or nearly so.

Alice poured some warm water into a basin, carried it to the sink and dipped a towel into it to scrub her face and hands.

It was a pleasant room, with a little black iron stove and a soapstone sink and pump, the table in the center taking up all the rest of the space. There were fresh gingham curtains and a gleam and glow that made the place seem warmly loved.

"There." Her hands clean, Alice reached for the envelope. She opened it and took out the stationery, quickly read the message, slipped it back inside. Staring at it, she said, "Do you know what a gauntlet is?"

"A glove, you mean?"

"Yes, a glove that, once flung down, challenges the opposition to a duel."

"Yes, I think I knew that."

"This note, Emily, is a gauntlet, and now it's been flung. I've been waiting for it." As if agreeing with herself, she nodded, then went to a small mirror by the door, took a comb from a nearby shelf and began to struggle with her snarled hair. "I'm going upstreet, Daddy," she told her father.

"To Kingsland?" he asked in a rough old man's voice. Apparently he knew already who would be throwing down a gauntlet.

"Yes. Be back soon. If you need anything, Tim is at the barn."

"Watch your step," Mr. Bradley said.

Alice held the door open, looked expectantly in Emily's direction.

"Goodbye, Mr. Bradley."

"Goodbye, Miss Merrick."

"I'm not going to bother changing my clothes," Alice said and they walked, "because I want Elizabeth to know that there's at least one Merrick who isn't afraid to get dirty. If we leave quietly, Tim won't even know I've gone. I can just sneak out and then sneak back, and he won't be the wiser."

Emily shook her head. "The wiser about what?"

"About Elizabeth. He'd never allow me to brawl with her."

"Brawl?" Emily gulped.

"In a manner of speaking." Alice smiled. "We Merricks never brawl out loud, of course. You're a Merrick. You should know."

"I do." Oh, yes, she knew how much dissention was submerged in Merrick silences. "I'd better warn you, though, that Elizabeth is far from stupid. She has a few preconceived ideas, I'll grant you that—but dumb she is not."

"Nor am I," Alice said firmly. "But my mother—our mother—loved her, Emily. She and my father would have given her everything they had and their hearts too. But no. Dad wasn't good enough. Soon, though, Elizabeth will accept people like my father. I'll see to it."

Emily doubted this possibility, but Alice clearly did not. Her color high, her shoulders straight, she followed Emily into the parlor and then the library where Elizabeth was still seated at the desk, looking Spartan and forbidding.

From the doorway they could see Kingsley Merrick's portrait, the curtains behind him parted to show a Concord Coach on the horizon of an alien country. In his hand was a tome entitled Australian Annals, both the book and the coach designed to let the onlooker know that Merrick had done well down under.

"Hello, Alice," said Elizabeth. Books and papers lay beneath her clasped hands. She neither got to her feet nor smiled in welcome.

"Hello," Alice said, and waited, forcing Elizabeth to show her hand, and Emily was reminded that she was Kingsley Merrick's granddaughter, the same as Elizabeth was, and that both of them shared characteristics of his: swift intelligence, the ineffable stamp of strength that is called presence—and those of his wife, Julia Merrick, a strong and indominable woman, and further back than that, those of great-grandmother Molly Deems, whose green eyes watched from her ancient portrait in the parlor.

"Well!" said Elizabeth. "This is indeed an unexpected addendum to the summer. Will you both be seated?" She gestured to straight-backed wooden chairs already in front of the desk, as though Alice and Emily were pupils—naughty ones who needed talking to.

But Alice rearranged the scene by pulling her chair to the side of the desk, setting it at an angle. No longer was she an erring student, but a guest.

"I hear you're going to the Fall Festival."

"Yes," Alice said, her voice even and strong.

"It's by invitation only."

"I know," Alice answered calmly.

"So you would trespass?"

"No, far from it. If you don't invite us, my friends and I will set up our displays on the roadside, where everyone can see and enjoy them on their way in." She did not mention that Kingsland's young people were among those those displaying a variety of arts and crafts. Perhaps that would come later, Emily thought.

"It could happen that way, I suppose." Icily, Elizabeth appraised Alice. "But it won't, because you and your friends aren't going to display anything at the Fall Fest."

"Tell me why," Alice said softly, "and then I'll tell you why you're wrong."

"Very well." Elizabeth opened one of the books on the desk and pushed it in Alice's direction. Alice did not move or look at it. "This small volume is a record of the burying ground of the First Parish Church of Rockford. It's over by the library, where the original church used to be."

"Yes, I know that." Alice's interruption was deliberate, Emily thought.

Undeterred, Elizabeth continued. "Thirty years ago, when genealogy was so much the rage, Waterford's womenfolk investigated the old cemetery. They divided it into strips, not unlike setting up a cranberry bog for harvest. I believe you also know about such things?"

"I do."

"The first person I'd like to call to your attention is here." Elizabeth pointed to the opened page. "It records a memorial marker, for Captain David Bradley. Died 1818."

She waited until Alice took the book and found the reference. David Bradley was the name of Tim's father, Emily remembered.

"Captain Bradley was trading in Africa when he died. Quite a few ships were anchored off the gold coast, waiting for the coffee crop, when a plague struck. Our esteemed ancestor, Elijah Merrick, was trading there too. So many of his crew were stricken that the Boston Port Authority condemned his ship, *Sweet Charity*, and sank it upon his return, afraid it was carrying the disease. But Captain David Bradley never made it home at all. He died of the plague."

Retrieving the book, Elizabeth flipped expertly through the pages and pointed to another entry for Alice's benefit. "This one, Captain Sears Bradley, is your grandfather, I believe."

"One of them," Alice agreed. Her voice was as cold as Elizabeth's.

"He simply disappeared. Under suspicious circumstances, I might add. He came into Boston, let your Grandmother know he was on the way home, and never got there. His body washed up in Long Island sound. No one knows what happened. They had had four sons, the eldest of whom is your father. Am I correct?"

Alice did not dignify Elizabeth's question with an answer.

"The youngest of them, your uncle, David, is Tim's father. Am I not correct?" Elizabeth's eyes were steady on Alice. This time she waited for an answer.

"Yes, of course you are." Alice looked a little uncomfortable at the mention of Tim.

"Now. To the subject at hand. Your grandmother, Angelina Winslow Bradley. Did you know her well?"

Alice looked puzzled, off guard. "How well does anyone know their grandparents?"

"Well, it doesn't really matter, one way or another. Because I am quite sure you are unaware that she was Kingsley Merrick's mistress."

For an instant Alice neither moved nor breathed. Then she sat back in her chair. "My grandmother was my grandfather's mistress?" Her derisive laugh was genuine.

"There's nothing very amusing about it," Elizabeth said grimly, "as you will see."

"There's nothing very believable about it," Alice said calmly. "It's probably just village gossip."

"It isn't gossip, and I can prove it."

"I don't see why you'd bother. Really, Elizabeth, this is quite grotesque. I can't believe you'd allow yourself..."

Elizabeth slipped a paper from the pile of documents on her desk. "Here's a little something, written by Julia, our Merrick grandmother, yours and mine. Her signature has been witnessed, by the way, and notarized. In it she states unequivocally that out of the liaison between Angelina Winslow Bradley and Kingsley Merrick a bastard son was born. She further states that this information was given her by Angelina Bradley herself—whom Grandmother thought was a rather reliable source, all things considered." Elizabeth smiled. "That, my dear, is why your mother and mine was disowned when she married into the family of Kingsley Merrick's bastard child. Grandmother—Julia—wrote this document because she thought that, one day, someone might need to have this information. I think that day has come."

She impaled Alice with her cold, cruel gaze.

"And you, Elizabeth? What's your excuse for disowning Mama?"

"My loyalty was to our grandmother, who understood me very well. Our mother married John Bradley only three months after my Canadian father died. She would have made me live in that shanty down the road, with a common working man who had no appreciation for life's finer things. I think you ought to read this document, which our grandmother commissioned me to show to whoever required it. Then you'll have a better understanding of the next step I plan to take, if you force my hand."

Silence gathered heavily as Alice read while the sun splashed on the rugs and the gold-lettered book bindings. There was a pause in which Emily was virtually certain that Alice was no longer reading, though her eyes were still glued to the document. "Do you really think anyone would believe this, Elizabeth? Do you really think anyone would credit it?"

Elizabeth said, quietly, "I do. If we were to stand David Bradley and his son, your cousin Tim, beneath the portrait of Kingsley Merrick—" she gestured toward the Great Man "—the truth of it becomes evident." She reached for the document, which Alice returned. "In those Victorian times, illegitimacy was a very serious social handicap."

"All this—even if true—is ancient history, Elizabeth," Alice argued.

"But it is still relevant. I believe that when he learns that he is Kingsley Merrick's bastard, Tim's father, the honorable David Bradley of Worcester and Waterford, will be extremely disturbed and upset. When your own father, leader and moderator of town meeting despite his great age—when he learns of it, his disappointment and distress will be profound—and his health is none too robust these days, I understand. And then there's Tim, David's son, isn't there?" Alice looked up from the damning document. "Not a nice thing to learn about your father, is it?"

"You just cut that out," Alice said fiercely, on her feet by now. "Tim isn't bound by convention like you are, Elizabeth. He understands his father's worth regardless of any rumor that you might spread about him. His devotion won't be altered at all."

"How noble," remarked Elizabeth. "I'll be interested to know how he feels should it turn out that David Bradley can't stand up to the truth. I'd like to know how he'd feel should any harm—self-inflicted or otherwise—occur as a result of public sneers or private qualms. Victorians being so . . . sensitive to such things." Alice was backing toward the library door as one would back away from a snake. "Make no mistake. Should it come to my attention that a marriage between you and Timothy is going forward, I will be compelled to show this document to anyone who has any interest in seeing it. I will be required to stand up at your wedding and explain to the magistrate how it is that that you two are double cousins, and that there's mental difficulty on both sides as a result. And should I see you at any gathering of which I am a part—I would name the Fall Festival specifically—why, I'll show it to all and sundry there, too. It'll make a marvelous exhibit. And don't make the mistake of thinking I wouldn't do such a thing. I would, without a qualm. Emily, would you show Alice out?"

Too stunned and ashamed to speak, Emily did as she was bid, blindly taking the girl back through the parlor and off the porch, out to Main Street.

"I always did oppose the marriage of cousins," Alice said in a tight voice. "Any educated person opposes consanguinity. We were going to use birth control, and adopt children. But I see now that it doesn't matter. Consanguinity isn't the only card in Elizabeth's deck, God damn her to hell." She looked up at Emily. "And I don't mind if you tell her I said so." The tears she was trying to hold back escaped. "Uncle David really is a Victorian, just as Elizabeth says. And so is my father. He waited 16 years for my mother, and through all those years, he was true to her. Trite, isn't it? I mean, who cares?"

Looking up at the tree leaves, dull and drooping now at summer's end, she repeated, "Who cares? They care. Awfully. And so do their contemporaries. It's so important to that generation. All that stuff—virginity and chastity and fidelity and the sacredness of marriage. God knows what it would do to my father and my uncle if they thought their own mother had sported about with the honorable Kingsley Merrick."

Alice's green eyes changed, became cold, hostile. "Please excuse me. I must go home and fix supper. I trust I won't be seeing you again soon, Emily. I hope not, anyway."

She did not look back as she walked away, and Emily watched as she became smaller and then disappeared around a turn in the road.

So, Elizabeth held the whip hand, after all, and had used it not only to prevent Alice from usurping the staid order of the Fall Fest, but also had destroyed her relationship with Tim, freeing him for Emily.

Perhaps he would come to her now. She must wait....

.... until a week later, when she went downstairs to fetch herself a cup of coffee. The cook's daughter, Mariette, was in the pantry talking with her mother. Assuming a privacy she did not have, she said, "Ma, I think there's a bun in the oven again."

A bun? Emily wondered. An oven?

"It's a little soon for another child, don't you think?" Her mother could not conceal concern for her daughter who had produced offspring each year since her marriage four years ago.

"Not much I can do about it, Ma. Not if I don't want my man wanderin'."

There was a great sigh of resignation. Emily could not be sure of its source.

"Maybe you're mistaken."

"I don't think so," Emily heard. "I've missed my monthly three times."

Thoughtfully she crept back upstairs with her coffee, rummaged in her desk for her calendar—a pointless endeavor. Her monthlies were irregular, and she often forgot to note them. The last circled date was four months ago, when she'd been in school. There'd been an event at least once since then, she believed, after school was over for the summer.

Opening her nightgown, standing before the mirror, she examined herself. Her breasts, pert and pretty, were a little fuller than usual—but perhaps she was about due, and they were enlarged because of it. Her oven, as Mariette so quaintly put it, did not look any different at all, firm and flat.

Surely there was nothing to worry about....

6

"'Board!" the conductor bawled. "All abooaard!" The words were drawn out to their fullest, and inside the train Emily watched the milling crowd move even more vigorously, as though stirred with an invisible spoon. Redcaps swam upstream with their baggage carts; passengers tried to get on the train while family members, there to say farewell to the travelers, struggled to get off. Soon The Lakeshore Limited would pull majestically out of Boston's South Station, and she would be separated from Mother, who tearfully reached out to hug her; Daddy's long arms embraced them both. Then everyone switched; Mother embraced Charles and Charles' Mater embraced Emily, and Daddy shook Charles' hand. Blocking the stateroom doorway, a porter appeared with a basket of flowers and a bucket of ice conspicuously devoid of any bottle.

"Anybody here recently married?" he asked, and bowed to their guffaws. "You folks will have to leave now," he said apologetically to those who were obviously parents. His gleaming black visage crinkled up into a smile of subservient joy. Such a happy occasion as the sending off of a newly married couple would result in a considerable tip. Smile firmly affixed, he assisted the ladies in descending the narrow metal steps to the platform, raising his boxy red cap in farewell to each, happily pocketing the five dollar bill that Daddy, who brought up the rear, gave him.

The train shook a little as it further fired up, gave an enormous flatulent blast, rolled an inch, and paused.

There had been an east wind as they'd driven into Boston, smelling of salt and clams and wet pilings and seaweed, and it brought home to Emily the fact that she wouldn't smell an east breeze again, nor see the old, soot-darkened, twisting city, for a long while. Perhaps never.

Desperately she looked out the window, hoping for a last glimpse, but no part of Boston could be seen from the station, only other trains and other platforms. Below stood her parents smiling bravely and Charles's Mater blowing them kiss after kiss in between mopping her eyes with a lace-trimmed hankie. Then the train finally shouldered the yoke, leaned into it and steadily pulled. The home folks, waving frantically, slid to the right, slid, slid, and then they were gone. Charles, watching over her shoulder, breathed moistly down her neck and she was alone with her husband.

A discreet knock at the door, a murmur; Charles went to it and received a package from the porter. Tipping lavishly, he brought it inside and sat beside her on the red plush seat, and withdrew a bottle of champagne. Reaching into the flowers previously delivered, he withdrew two champagne flutes, tapping them together so that they gave a clear ring. Ribbons were tied to the stems of each.

"I thought a bit of the bubbly would hit the spot just about now, even if it hasn't had a chance to get cold."

"Oh, Charles, what a treat!" she exclaimed. The wedding and the reception had been abysmally dry because of Mater's insistence on observing the law, and Emily was as grateful as Charles to have a little something to oil the ways.

"And that's not all!" he crowed. "In my suitcase there's cheese and crackers and anchovy paste and sardines. Just in case lurching around in the dining car doesn't appeal to us on this, our wedding night."

Clearly she was stuck. "I expect if we needed anything more, the red cap would get it," she said bravely. "I think staying here is a fine idea, Charles!"

"Do you think I can get the cork out of the bottle?"

"If not, we'll call the porter!"

"I shall try." He removed the wires and started pushing at the cork with his thumbs, becoming red in the face and grimacing mightily until it exploded out of the bottle neck and boomeranged off the ceiling. The racketing of the train, its squeals and clatters and groans, covered the sound; foam cascaded down the bottle and onto the floor. Charles grabbed for a flute and poured a little, tested it, swishing the champagne around in his mouth before swallowing.

"It would be better chilled," he announced, and filled both glasses. "To you, my dearest. To us." They touched flutes, the ringing muted this time because of the wine, and she drank hers without stopping.

"More?" she asked, holding out her glass, and he poured, and finished off his own, refilling that, too. "To you, Charles." Her flute bumped his. "To the future, the years together." She was beginning to float a little; if she drank the champagne steadily, she'd float as long as she'd need to. She leaned against Charles' shoulder.

"Ah, Emily," he breathed. "At last." He drew her closer, champagne from her glass slopping onto her silk traveling dress. "I can't even begin to tell you what it means to me, that you should be my wife."

"Dear Charles," she murmured, sipping the champagne so he wouldn't kiss her. He's just a boy, she told herself, and eager like a boy. Relax.

"I know you must be tired, Sweeting." He ran a finger down the curve of her breast. "But I've honored this abstinence business just as long as I can. I always thought it was silly—I mean, since we were already lovers . . ."

Yes, the silly fool believed that they'd already Done It! That was why he'd consented to marry her now, in October, instead of waiting until December. Consented? Insisted, because he'd found her naked beside him in the car, weeping with what he'd believed to be desolation at losing her virginity, and manfully he Did the Right Thing. Very pleased, he was, to find himself in such a delectable dilemma.

It had not been difficult to arrange. They'd parked in the woods with a bottle of gin and one of orange juice. They were celebrating their impending engagement, to be announced Saturday evening at the intimate party his Mater was planning. Emily had come up from Bryn Mawr for the occasion, and assented to Charles' plea to go parking.

Figuring that she'd wait until he got a bit tipsy, she'd allow him some of the liberties he'd always clamored for and that she'd always denied him. He would want more, she knew. She'd mixed the drinks, with considerably more gin in his than in hers, assuming that the outcome would take care of the disaster that was now growing in the dark of her womb.

The bun was definitely in the oven, and Tim Bradley had run away. Alice's old father was the only one home when, in desperation, she finally went to the Bradley house. Tim had gone to sea, and Mr. Bradley was proud of the boy, opting for a life on the sea rather than being cooped up inside, making shoes. Following an honored Cape tradition, he was. Clearly the old man was unaware that his daughter had broken the boy's heart, and certainly he was unaware that Tim had broken Emily's.

The pregnancy must be screened by Charles, who would marry her immediately, once he'd had his way with her, because a gentleman always married a lady whom he believed he'd deflowered. And she'd made him believe it!

Her dress and undergarments were down to her hips before the end of the second drink, that night in the woods, and he happily squeezed her breasts while she anesthesized herself with gin and in between maulings poured more, knowing that soon she'd go numb. For she must not hold back.

"Emily, my schweet, my dove," Charles had sighed. "You've ne'r been like this 'fore."

"I've never been engaged to you before," she had said, clenching her fists as he took her nipple between his thumb and finger and pinched. "Why do you think I've been so prim, Charles? Surely not because I didn't like you!"

"Schweetheart," he slurred, "I just ne'r could tell wha' the hell you had in mind." Pressing his lips to hers again, he pinched and fondled because it was his right, after all; they were nearly engaged to be married.

How long should she wait before moving along to more overt intimacy? How much further would he go on his own initiative? She poured him another slug of gin.

"Em'ly." He belched. "Since we're all but en-engaged, dahling, may I take the resht of yer clothes off?" He hiccupped.

"Why, no! she exclaimed coyly, drawing away. "I'd catch cold."

"B-blanket's in the rumble seat."

"The rumble seat is out," she said firmly. "I'd be much too cold, naked in the rumble seat, and that is that."

"I din't h-have in m-mind sitting out there," he chuckled.

"What did you have in mind?"

"I'll show you." Somehow he extricated himself from under the wheel, let himself out into the cool October night, feeling his way to the rumble seat, opening it up, dragging the blanket out. Somehow he staggered around to the passenger side of the car and opened her door.

"Come on. We can both get in the back sheat, dahling."

"All right." Floating freely now, she knew she would need no more gin. It would have been nice to linger in the fresh night air, caressing in a cool, soothing touch, but she had business to attend to.

"I really f-feel that you oughtta take off the rest of your cl-clothes," he slurred. "Then we can wrap up in thish blanket OK?"

Stupidly she looked down at her dress, hanging off her hips. "All right," she agreed, and shucked off everything, stood there stark naked. "What about you?"

Struggling out of his coat and shirt, dropping them in the leaves, he dove into the car. "I'll r-remove the rescht in here. An' make ush a tent." Beneath the blanket, thrashings rocked the car. "Now, dahling."

Climbing in, shutting the door behind her, she was ready for The Event. Charles tucked the blanket around her and wrapped himself up in it, too, so that they were cocooned against the dark. She waited. His breathing became deep and steady.

"Charles?" she whispered.

There was no answer.

"Charles!" She patted his cheek, harder, harder, but there was only a snore, indicating that he was still alive. "Charles!" she called into his ear. The blanket was scratchy against her exposed skin. Pulling it free, she refused to give way to panic, tried to think, tried to consider the situation from all angles.

Given his chance at last, it was just like Charles to flub his lines. But with so much riding on the outcome, it was disastrous, for he must—he must!—have sexual intercourse with her, and he must do it tonight.

Even had her plans gone according to schedule, he well might have passed out, she told herself. If so, he would have no recollection of anything that might, or might not, have transpired between them.

Did she dare?

Did she have a choice?

Gently, she unbuckled his belt, unbuttoned his fly, untucked his shirt. There should be blood, she thought. At least a little. There was when she and Tim made love . . . she put that thought away, far, far away. Easing the car door open, she stepped out and put on her shoes, scuffled about until she found a stick stout enough, sharp enough, to do the job. Gritting her teeth, she poked. Good! There was more than enough blood from the wound to smear on her thighs and even on Charles himself, near his privates.

Crawling back in under the blanket, grateful for his warmth, she busied herself with the blood from her scratch and then waited for him to revive. Everything would be fine, she told herself. Abstinence would prevail until they were married. Just one slip in the height of passion didn't justify indulging themselves whenever they felt like it. They must enter marriage as chastely as possible. That was how It Was Done. Everyone knew that.

"You were right," he said earnestly, swaying gently with the rocking of the train. "It was best to stay chaste until now. But there's no need to put me off any longer, is there."

Rural Massachusetts flashed by.

"Oh, no, Charles, no reason at all," she agreed, finishing the champagne in a gulp. "But perhaps we ought to rest a little," she temporized. "If you're tired, sometimes things are difficult. Particularly if you're nervous."

"Who's nervous," he giggled, his champagne flute shaking in his hand.

"You'd better pull down the shade, then," she instructed, suddenly sweating. "And lock the door."

The compartment became dusky and the rattling room intimate. "Why don't you stand up?" he suggested. "So I can undress you."

Bracing herself against the sway of the train with a hand on one wall, the other on the bulge of the upper bunk, Emily knew the moment had come as Charles fumbled at and peeled off her dress, pulled down her bra, then stopped in dismay at the more complicated fastenings of her girdle and garters. "Perhaps you'd finish the job?"

Her breasts, free from her undergarment, hung free and jiggled a bit with the motion of the train, and she tried not to feel self-conscious as she worked on her girdle and he seated himself to watch, pouring himself more champagne, crossing his legs, studying her.

"You are lovely!" he nodded. "Perfect."

Sliding off the seat and onto his knees, he clasped her hips and buried his face in her crotch. Taking his arms, she pulled him upright. "Let me undress you."

"What?"

"Let me undress you," she repeated more loudly, so he could hear above the busyness of the train, and began unbuckling his belt. He took over, stripping off his suit pants, revealing his thin, white legs with garters that twisted around his calves to hold his stockings up; he kicked the trousers away and took off his undershorts to reveal a limp male member bravely trying to rise.

In wifely fashion she divested him of his shirt and undershirt, then put her hands on either side of his face, drawing his lips to hers and kissing them lightly. The metal door was cold on her back as he pushed her against it, his mouth clamped tightly against hers, his groin grinding harder, harder, as though he could force from her what he wanted and needed. The unyielding metal door hurt, and the hardness of his bony pelvis hurt. She had no idea he was so strong, and knew she would have to tell him he was too rough, even at the risk of wounding his ego, because he was just too vehement, nearly brutal in his eagerness.

Releasing her abruptly, he stepped back, looked down, and she followed his gaze. The flag of his manliness still drooped, swaying with the movement of the train. Transfixed, her mind went blank.

"You've duped me," he said.

She tore her gaze from his disinterested member, to his face, to his burning, blazing eyes.

"You tricked me, didn't you?"

"It's only b-because you've had too much ch-champagne," she stammered. "You just need a good night's sleep. It'll be better in the morning."

His open hand hit her face so violently that her head bounced hard against the door and sparks whirled up, as though a log had been thrown onto a night fire. She shrieked and he hit her again, his lip curled in fury, his face terrible, and he seized her wrist, twisting her arm behind her, forcing to her knees.

"We never did it, did we. That night in the woods." His voice was toneless and terrifying, and she knew she was in trouble, terrible trouble. Her face and lips throbbed where he had struck her, her arm was nearly numb. He wrenched it further and the compartment went black for a moment or two.

"No. We didn't do it," she panted. "Charles, let go!"

He released her, steadying himself against the wall of the car. Clad as he was, in only his stockings and garters, there was no denying what she had never suspected.

Charles Steven Sinclaire was impotent.

Hardly daring to breathe, cradling her arm to ease its aching, she looked up. Hatred was etched on his face and snapped from his pale blue eyes. "It never occurred to me to doubt you. There you were, weeping, deflowered, and there was even blood to prove it. What did you do? Scratch yourself with your fingernails?"

She shook her head. "Stick."

"Stick," he repeated. "While I was passed out."

"Yes. Can I get up now, Charles?"

"You're fine, right where you are." He lowered himself to the seat, stared sightlessly at her while he thought about it, then nodded, as though agreeing with himself. "I've loved you for a long time, Emily. You excited me more than any other girl had ever done, so I always thought that with you things would be different. I was sure, so sure." His despair and disappointment were etched deeply on his face.

"I never meant to hurt your feelings, Charles!" Tears of pain and pity and terror ran freely. "I'll be a good wife to you, I promise. You won't be sorry!"

"Ah. Wonderful. Music to my ears. I take it that you'll do whatever I want?"

"Of course!"

"All right." He stood, braced himself again, offering his flaccid self. "Open your mouth."

Oh, God!

"Open up, and take me in."

She did it, squeezing her eyes shut, refusing to think about this act of prostitution that she had only ever heard about. Endlessly it went on until finally he cried out and fell back onto the seat, moaning happily in the sun of sensuality.

Her knees raw, her thighs trembling, she started to rise but he gestured downward. "Stay there," he commanded, as if she were a trained dog in a nightmare she had never known could happen. His moment of pleasure extended into minutes, and then he sat up straight. "I think I have the right to know why you made such an ass of me, my Sweeting. Don't you?" he asked conversationally.

She stared.

Leaning over, he reached for her near breast and teased its nipple. "Are you going to answer my question?" he asked smoothly. "Or do I need to persuade you?" He squeezed, hard, and she covered his hand with hers.

"Please, Charles. That hurts."

"Go on," he smiled, without releasing his grip.

"I needed you to marry me because . . ."

He twisted.

"Because I'm going to have a baby."

"A baby," he sighed, and thought about it for a while. "Whose baby?" She could not bring herself to answer.

"Who is the father of your baby?" he repeated.

"Please," she whispered, her eyes smarting with hot tears.

"How long do you want to kneel there?" he asked, and reached for the champagne. He poured himself a glass and smacked his lips when it was done. "I'll ask only once more," he said, and she dared not provoke him further.

"Tim Bradley," she said around the obstruction in her throat.

"Ah!" He looked her over slowly. "Didn't you tell him he had fathered a child? Did he reject you? Is that what made you so desperate?"

"I never saw him. Old Mr. Bradley said he ran away to sea."

"Left you high and dry, eh? No wonder you were so desperate, poor thing." Moving over, he motioned her to sit beside him, pouring more champagne for them both as she struggled up. "So you turned to me, because you knew I was more than eager to marry you."

Rinsing her mouth with sips of champagne, she said, "You had already asked me." Her arm and shoulder ached, her lips throbbed, and a headache of searing proportions had started. "I just needed to get you to marry me sooner than you planned."

"So you staged that production in my car." The train lurched around a bend and she was flung against him. Should she move away? Should she lean on him, as if she needed his strength? He decided for her, and pushed her upright, topped off her champagne, waiting while she took a big swallow, poured more. "I'd take as much of this as you can get," he advised. "The evening is young."

In fact it wasn't evening. It was still afternoon behind the window shades, where daylight flickered and leaped.

"What did you plan on doing as your pregnancy advanced and even I, as inexperienced in such matters as I am, would figure out that the little tyke was too far along to be mine?"

"I didn't have a plan," she answered. Her misery was somewhat alleviated by the champagne, and loosened her inhibitions. "I just needed to be far away from everyone, so my friends—our friends—would never know. And my parents—they wouldn't know, either. Or your mater. No one would know. Only you, Charles. I thought I could count on you to help me when the time came. We'd have been married a while and you'd have seen how happy I made you. I hoped it would all work out, somehow."

He said nothing, gazing at the opposite wall where a narrow door disclosed an amazingly small commode and a sink that folded up into the wall.

"I'm sorry I stooped to such shabby behavior," she pleaded. "But I really did believe I could make you a good wife, and I really did need to be married now and not in December."

He nodded. "Yes, of course. And I'm proud to claim you as my wife, Emily."

Was there a chance he would accept her? Forgive her? Let bygones be bygones?

He smiled. "There may be a way we can work things out. I'll claim your child as my own. That's what you want, isn't it?"

"Yes."

"And you can help me." His smile turned salacious, and she felt her eager relief draining away. "I've never had a woman of my own before. One who'd do whatever I asked, who'd explore the possibilities with me. All of them."

All of them. He was virtually unknown to her. All along he'd been disguised as a bumbling adolescent, but he wasn't. He was a man whose temperament and basic makeup were so foreign to her and so alien to her experience that she had no way of predicting what he would want or need or demand.

"Prostitutes have ways of giving people like me a good time. You've already done that. Thank you."

"You're welcome," she said shakily.

"There are other things a woman can do to a man that are pleasurable in the extreme."

"Wh-what kind of things?"

"I don't know, offhand. I haven't had a chance to explore the possibilities, because I haven't had a willing partner. But it looks like now I do. I think that a mutual search for what I need would be a fair exchange for giving Bradley's child my name. Don't you?"

It was hideous, devoid of love or kindness, far from the tender, unfettered sharing she'd known with Tim. It was like being turned out of the Garden and into the desert, to burn and suffer and labor— and perhaps she deserved it.

"Yes?"

Was it possible? Could she live with it? Could she face it day after day, escaping the public judgment and condemnation that surely would follow her if she were found out? If she wanted to keep her baby, she would have to—and she did want the child. It was all she had of Tim, of the night when the stars sang and the wonders of love were revealed to her.

"All right," she heard herself saying.

The corners of Charles' mouth turned up, and his face grew flushed in the anticipation of his every lacivious dream fulfilled in a manner unhurried, enjoyed to the last drop.

"Ah," he breathed. He slid off the couch. "Now it's my turn to kneel." He met her eyes levelly, without apology and shame. "I'd like to see what a female looks like down there".

"What?"

"Open up. Now."

"Charles! Really!"

"Are you refusing my request? When I ask something of you, Emily, I expect your cooperation. Like now. I want you to spread your legs so I can see what's there."

She could hardly believe it.

The smile left his lips. The lust of his fantasies gleamed in his eyes, and his face was lewd. "I'm waiting," he said softly, and she knew he would not wait much longer. She closed her eyes tight and complied. Somehow she would find a way to endure....

Oh, Tim, she thought. See what you have done to me. The child within her stirred.

CHAPTER

The Child

1939

The stock market crash wiped away fortunes of the rich as well as the more modest savings of careful men and women.

A drought, and then wind, lifted the baked soil of the plains in a veil of dust.

Massive unemployment. Long lines at soup kitchens. Homeless men riding the rails, going everywhere and nowhere. The hopeless citizenry were told not to fear.

In Waterford, on Cape Cod, the summer society withered and fell away as one after another of its members were ruined. The townsmen took up the rhythm of life on the land, plied the fields once more, dried herring in the spring, in the summer dug clams and helped to build camps that were opening on the shores of the bay and the inland ponds, catering to offspring of the employed ...

... such as ten year old Steven Sinclaire, in Port Huron, Ohio, who looked forward to the summer season as an oasis in an otherwise untenable landscape.

✢∾ I ∾✢

THE STAIRS turned back on themselves, and he peeked cautiously around the corner, past the banister and through the carved wooden spindles. Father was going through the day's mail, piled upon the mahogany table just inside the front door. He had reached the report card.

Anxiety gnawed like a living creature deep within as Steven watched Father examine the card, then put it back on the pile. He picked up the Camp Quivet brochure that had arrived today, too. His gold framed spectacles flashed as he turned to the window to better see the picture on its cover and Steven ducked around the corner lest Father discover him, and waited until his heart became calm again.

Your life depended on your heart beating, whether you thought about it or not, Steven knew. Nor was there any way, in the year 1939, to make it start again, once it stopped. Sometimes you'd hear about people whose heartbeat disappeared during an operation, then started again, but they said that God had given them their lives back, not the doctors. They had met the Lord while they were dead, they said. They were sorry to leave Him and return to earth....

Father went into the kitchen where Mom was fixing dinner. Their mumbled conversation would screen any noise he might make, and Steven stole back upstairs to his own room, quietly closing the door. The distant murmuring from the kitchen was abruptly stopped as though a radio somewhere had been switched off. It was an old house and more sturdily built than newer ones (Father said) and because it was old and sturdy, when you shut a door, noise on the other side simply went away. A bungalow built today just could not compete with it (Father said) but, of course, if you'd lost all your money in the depression, like some people he knew, you'd be glad of a doghouse to live in.

When he said things like that, he was referring to Grandpa Daniel Merrick, who lost all his money when the stock market fell (did it just topple over?) Steven had never known his grandfather because soon after he was born, Grandpa had jumped out of a window at his office—in a very tall building—and died. But he would not have had to live in a doghouse, even though he had lost all his money. He could have lived at Kingsland, with Cousin Elizabeth, just as Grandmother Merrick did. Was that why he jumped? Cousin Elizabeth was a terror, to be sure, but even so....

Father faithfully sent money to Grandmother Merrick, so she would not be entirely dependent on the family sourpuss, (he said). But Steven suspected that the real reason was to keep Grandmother from coming here to live, in Port Huron, in this large and sturdily built house with its heavy solid noise-stopping doors. Because of them, there was no excuse for not concentrating when you were doing your homework, therefore no excuse for anything less than an 'A' in all subjects. And certainly none whatsoever for a 'B' in arithmetic, let alone a 'B' with a minus sign after it.

The tightrope upon which Steven walked day by day, hour by hour, stretched endlessly into tomorrow and all the days to come. Tonight he would face Father, who would punish him for that B minus. Tomorrow it would be Spike McCloskey, his personal tormenter at school.

Steven Sinclaire was different from the other kids, thus a target. For one thing, he got better grades. For another, he was not allowed to linger on the playground at the end of the school day, like everyone else, but must go home and study. His clothes were too neat, his homework never late. Spike McCloskey assumed the Sinclaire kid was a goody-goody, an easy target. McCloskey's cadre agreed.

Without his quite understanding why, another cadre had formed around Steven himself, composed of three boys who championed him whenever they could and worked diligently to get Spike's gang—and Spike himself, of course—in trouble. They played with Steven at recess and ate lunch with him in the school cafeteria, chose him for their teams and were always on his side. But they could not prevent the inevitable—the McCloskey challenge.

Tomorrow after school Steven would meet Spike at the base of the railroad bridge that spanned the Port Huron River. The kids would watch while he and Spike climbed up the trussed arches, one on each side of the bridge, holding it up. Once at the top, the boys would wait until the afternoon train rolled over, shaking everything. Everyone would enjoy the show. Everyone except Steven Sinclair who was unhappy with heights and who knew what happened to people who fell.

Had Grandpa Merrick, knowing he could not back up, jumped from a window of his own free will?

He tried not to think about Grandpa Merrick. Or the bridge, either. In his room, twenty arithmetic problems waited. Sliding into his desk chair, he hoped they wouldn't be as formidable as they had been when he left them to spy on Father, who was excellent at arithmetic. Anyone could do mathematics, Father declared, if they put their mind to it. Whenever Steven received a 'B', that was proof he was not putting his mind to his work. And a minus sign after the 'B' was evidence that Steven wasn't even trying. Father had a ready remedy for the repair of one's concentration.

In despair, he looked over the multiplication problems he'd done already. Four numbers on top, three on the bottom. He'd done them carefully, but hidden somewhere there would be mistakes, and the remaining ten would contain mistakes, too, once he'd finished them. Of course, he could copy Ed Lamson's homework—but test scores were never improved by this practice.

Perhaps Father was glad that there was a 'B-' on the report card. It would give him a chance to discuss everything very, very carefully, going needlessly over the same old ground, and then the two of them would go upstairs where the broadside of Father's razor strop would be applied to the backside of Steven, and Steven would promise to try harder, keeping his hatred concealed.

You were not supposed to hate anyone. Especially not your father.

Clenching his fists, he tried not to cry. The image of the polar bear in the nearby Toledo Zoo rose up in his mind, pacing back and forth, the same measured three lunges, as though one day it would discover a loose bar that it had overlooked in its frantic haste to be free. Frantic, like himself, because the razor strop cut and burned . . . .

Tomorrow there would be a further infraction of Father's rules, due to Spike's challenge. Steven would not be coming home directly after school. Mom would never tell on him, he knew, so he didn't have to worry about that. But, if it were one of the days Father came home early from the office to make sure Steven really was studying . . . .

Cut it out, he told himself. How long does it take to climb a bridge, anyway? I'll be home before he gets here, even if he does leave the office early....

Steadfastly he bore down on the multiplication until Mom called him for dinner.

It was a very formal dining room, of which Father was especially proud. Its heavy moldings and window trims were dark and shining, its flocked wallpaper matching the maroon of the tasseled drapes. The table was fully set with a glaring white damask table cloth, the sterling silver, fine French china and crystal stemware. The Port Huron Sinclaires did not have supper at the end of the day. They had dinner in accordance with the Merrick and Sinclaire tradition, with supper in the kitchen on Sunday evening, giving Mom a day of rest from the labors of elegance.

Father wanted Steven to be acclimated to gracious living so that when he visited Cousin Elizabeth on Cape Cod, he'd know which fork to use, which spoon, which knife. It would not do to have Elizabeth believe that just because the Sinclaires lived in the cultural wasteland of Ohio, their son would inevitably be a barbarian. No, indeed! Father could raise a cultivated and cultured child wherever he had to, preserving the traditions important to the Merricks, a child who would, one day in the distant future, inherit Kingsland. It would come to Mom after Elizabeth died, and Father would be the executor. (Was that like being a manager?) When Mom died, on a day far from this one, it would be Steven's, according to Elizabeth's will, and he would, by then, be well enough trained to carry its traditions into the next generation.

Because of this insistence on training, Steven never, ever invited any of his friends to come to his house unless Father were away in Boston, doing whatever went on in the main offices of his company. Upon these occasions, "supper" was served in the kitchen, like it was everywhere else in Port Huron, and his three friends came to the house and ate meat-loaf and home fried potatoes and canned vegetables and chocolate pudding and afterwards everyone played gin rummy on the cleared-off kitchen table and drank Coca-Cola out of the bottle.

Steven was quite sure Father was unaware of these Sinclaire "suppers". They were a carefully guarded secret which Mom, he knew, would never betray. But they were very important in taking the curse off his Boston-born parents, both of whom, as far as his friends and Port Huron children in general knew, attended the Boston Tea Party where baked beans were served, and who spoke in a peculiar manner, removing R's from some words, adding them to others where they did not belong, and doing something strange to the sound of "a".

The silent dinner progressed: roast lamb with mint jelly, mashed potatoes and gravy, carrots and Parker-house rolls. "If you're through, Charles, I'll clear," said Mom, and waited for Father to indicate that she should. Taking the plates to the kitchen, she set them down on a towel she spread on the enamel drain board to muffle their clatter.

"You spilled something," Father observed when Steven's butter plate was removed.

The stain was green. "Mint jelly?" he suggested, although he had not dropped any. It was an old stain, perhaps from the relish that Mom had served yesterday.

"Emily, there's a spot here, under Steven's plate."

"Why, yes," Mom admitted. "I noticed it when I was setting the table, but there wasn't enough time to get out a fresh cloth." Probably untrue, Steven thought; Mom wanted to get another night's use out of it. Ironing table linens was a time-consuming project.

"Perhaps we'd better devise a report card for Mother," Father said jovially. "After all, Steven has them. It doesn't seem fair that he's the only one."

Here it came. The crab that lived in his belly reached out with its claw and pinched. He clasped his hands in his lap and pushed against the cramp to keep it under control.

Mom brought the spotless and gleaming percolator from the kitchen and poured Father's coffee. "Bring me the card and the Quivet brochure, Emily, if you please," he instructed. Mom complied and Father pretended to study the card, as though he had not seen it before, while Mom slid into her chair and poured coffee for herself. Father turned the card over, inspected the deportment marks, turned it back again. "What seems to be the trouble with your arithmetic?"

"I don't know," Steven answered, his words carefully enunciated. Father hated mumbling. "I always seem to have a lower grade in it than everything else."

"Your teacher remarks," Father turned the card over again—"that you seem not to like math."

"I don't like getting lower grades in it," Steven declared with what he hoped sounded like strength and determination. "I want to do as well in it as I do in science and social studies." Hopefully this would please Father.

"Indeed. And I'd like to see that, too. I want to see you go to Harvard, as I did, but the standards at Harvard are very, very high. 'B-' would be regarded askance there. So, what is the problem?"

What was a 'skance'? "We've been doing long division," Steven offered. "It's especially hard."

"Do you check the answer by multiplying?"

"There's never enough time."

"That," said Father, "rather depends on whether you're using your time well or not. Doesn't it?"

This, Steven knew, was the prelude to a strapping. He looked down at the damask cloth, the pattern woven into it, the shining of some threads, the muted finish of others, and did battle with his rising tears. Father would belittle him further if he cried.

A stone-cold silence filled the dining room.

"Let's postpone the grade card discussion momentarily and talk about camp," Father said, opening the Quivet brochure. "I assume you'd like to attend again this year?"

Quivet. Eternally in an uproar over merit points, earned in the pursuit of the bronze, silver or gold arrow. Bustling with activities that were squeezed in a every turn. And a bone-deep loneliness he recognized as a need for the quiet, sustaining presence of his mother. Nonetheless, Steven desperately wanted to go.

For besides Camp Quivet there was Kingsland, with its huge old trees and its high-ceilinged cool rooms and its four-story tower with windows all around. From there you could see the curving north shore holding Cape Cod Bay like a great cup, and the bay so beautiful it hurt just to look at it, dancing in the sun and sulking in the rain, breathing deeply, creating the tides, calling to him . . . .

"Quivet's a kind of reward, don't you think?" Father was saying, "for a job well-done at school. I don't see that you've earned it when all you can do is get a 'B minus' in math."

"Charles," Mom said, her hands clasped tightly in her lap just as Steven's were. "Are you really thinking about taking camp away from him because of a B minus?"

"Are you questioning my judgement, Emily?"

"I guess I am," she said meekly. "I'm sorry if that offends you. But maybe the fault lies with the teacher."

"I doubt it," Father said. "I think the fault lies right here, with Steven."

"But we won't really know unless we at least try to find out," Mom persisted—surprisingly, for she rarely confronted Father on any issue. "Perhaps I should go to school tomorrow and speak with Miss Meagher."

Oh, gosh. That would get the teacher down on him! She'd turn other teachers against him; she'd keep him in at recess for the least reason . . . His child's distrust of authority made him say, "Miss Meagher might not like it, Mom."

"If I came in to speak with her?"

"I mean, if you said it was her fault."

"Oh, Sweetheart, I'd never say that, believe me! I'll only ask if we should be doing something more to help you."

"Well, now, that's a point," Father concurred. "We might find out if we should get Steven a tutor, or if he should be staying after school with the teacher a few times a week until he's more comfortable with arithmetic. Or if, in her opinion, he's simply lazy and needs stronger discipline here at home."

The whole thing was going from bad to worse. Steven despaired.

"I'll call the school and arrange a time to see Miss Meagher, tomorrow if possible." Mom pushed her chair back. "Don't bother to fold your napkins. I'll wash them with the cloth. Steven, please clear the table."

Well! That ended that. At least she had promised not to make Miss Meagher mad. Steven replaced the unused silverware in its proper slotted, allotted place in the buffet, bundled up the table cloth and folded the silence cloth beneath it, and wondered how it was that Mom had outright argued with Father.

"I'll excuse you from helping tonight," she said as he picked up a dishtowel. "If you haven't finished your homework, go on up."

"Sure!"

"I think it would be a good idea to stay upstairs, honey. Out of the line of fire."

"O.K." he grinned, and then said, "I really do try, Mom."

"I know you do," she smiled sympathetically. "Don't worry about it now. We'll see what happens tomorrow."

Kissing her cheek, which he could easily reach now that he was ten years old and getting tall, he crept upstairs, soundlessly closing his bedroom door.

Would Father really take Quivet away because of a B minus?

It was possible, he knew. With a sigh, he again approached his homework.

✢∾ 2 ∾✢

The sky behind the high classroom windows was uniformly overcast, arranged into ordered segments by the metal mullioned panes of glass. The wind was rising; Steven could see the bare treetops dip, rise, and dip again.

Climbing the bridge would be bad enough without a breeze trying to blow him off it. Maybe he would become sick—too sick to climb. In fact the fear and dread deep in his stomach, where the crab lived, were riling up his lunch. Maybe he'd throw up soon, and have to go to the nurse's office....

At the front of the room Miss Meagher was talking about something; two rows over and a seat behind him McCloskey was watching, he knew, trying to make him nervous. Ed Lamson, who occupied the seat in front, furtively dropped a note onto Steven's desk.

Don't do it 2 day. 2 cold. Wind 2 high.

He smiled to himself. No matter what he did or didn't do, Ed would be his pal. Not every kid had the patience to befriend someone who was hardly ever available. But Ed always had.

The clock over Miss Meagher's desk told them all that in ten minutes the school day would end. In ten minutes he and Ed would get their coats from the cloak room, put the books they needed in their book bags, meet Sam and Robbie in the hall (they occupied the adjacent fourth grade classroom) and along with Spike and his gang, go down to the river. There would be other kids, too, there to witness what was by now a well-known contest, carefully kept secret because if adults found out, they would put a stop to it. Adults always broke up anything that was fun or exciting or dangerous.

By this time Steven would have been relieved if someone did break it up, because he didn't want to climb the arching truss that held up the bridge, and was beginning to doubt whether he even could. But going over and over the problem of the bridge wouldn't make it any easier. Better to think about something else.

The sails bellied and snapped in the gale-force wind, and the little craft rode the waves joyfully. Salt spray, clean and cold, was flung up and over the bow....

The bell shrilled and the students instantly closed their books and waited expectantly to be dismissed, row by row. Steven was propelled into the hall by the pack of kids pushing from behind like stampeding cattle. Waiting outside the door was Mom, her smile bright and cheerful, as though she were confident that everything would be all right.

"Hi," he faltered.

"Hi, honey. See you at home."

"Um, OK."

"What's your Mother doing here?" Ed asked.

"She's going to ask Miss Meagher if I should have a math tutor."

"Huh," Ed commented, and said no more out of respect for Mrs. Sinclaire, whom he liked and, when he was really on his game, could beat at gin rummy. "Are you going to do it? The bridge?"

"I guess I am."

"There's Sam and Robbie. We'll stick by you, Steve, if you want to just go home and forget the whole thing. We wouldn't climb it on a day like this, either."

"Well, I guess I'll at least try."

"Hey," Robbie greeted them. "The bridge?"

"Yup."

"Too bad you can't use pistols at 30 paces," Sam remarked. All three of his friends knew Steven was afraid of heights. "Well, let's get it over with."

A failure to climb was bad, but a failure to show up was worse. Unobtrusively Spike and his gang, Steven and his, along with those who wished to watch, eased over the edge of the sidewalk and down onto the path that would lead to the river and the bridge, out of sight from the road.

They arrived all too soon.

Casually Steven gave his book bag and jacket to Robbie. Ed, like a spear-bearer, followed him to the river's edge where the bridge crossed, its twin metal arches bounding over the water in a large leap. The river was high, Steven noted, and certainly very cold now at winter's end.

"Well, look who's here," Spike McCloskey grinned. "I was afraid you wouldn't be able to make it, Sinclaire. I saw your Mommy at school. I figured you'd hide behind her skirts."

"You figured wrong." Steven returned. "I did make it."

"We'd better hurry," Spike said. "Or we'll miss the three-thirty. Unless that's what you had in mind?"

Of all the trains in the whole of America, the three-thirty was almost always on time because it started in Toledo, only thirty miles away.

"Dry up," called Ed, and went with Steven to the farthest pylon.

A casual wave of the hand was required. "Call the fire department if it looks like I'm stuck," he told the waiting group. "Tell 'em to bring the ladder." The girls laughed and clapped and the boys whistled—even Spike's gang.

The top of the arch seemed endlessly far away, like Jack's beanstalk that just kept growing and growing. Complete with a giant at the top in the form of a train.

The river was probably deep enough with snow-melt to be able to jump into without being pounded to a pulp on the bottom. Steven knew how to do the life-saving leap, with arms and legs spread wide. Too young yet to take the junior life-saving course at camp, he had watched the classes and read the manual and practiced what the older boys did. Maybe he would have to jump today, if he got half way up and could go no further. Unless he was too cowardly to do that, either. His need for the fire truck with its ladder might become a reality, and soon.

The truss consisted of rusted steel that left dark marks on his hands as, putting his left foot in the angle of the lowest X, right hand in the highest he swung himself up.

"Looking good!" Ed cheered. Sam and Robbie hollered encouragement. Some of the other kids did, too.

Across from him Spike mounted the corresponding arch and climbed the X's like a monkey clambering up a palm tree, pulling himself ten feet up in a single go. Never could Steven do that, no matter how hard he tried. No clambering for him. One X at a time; if you had three appendages firmly planted, you could move the fourth. They taught him that at camp. A useful trick, as long as you knew what an appendage was.

Doggedly he placed his right hand in the highest X he could reach, his knees touching the lift of the arch. Right foot up. Left hand a little higher than the right, left foot in the X below his left hand, lift up a notch with the right, reach. Slowly, slowly, another step up. Even though he wasn't a good climber, if he didn't give up and was willing to meet Spike's challenge, his reputation would be salvaged. Duelling pistols would have been easier, he thought, like Aaron Burr and Alexander Hamilton. Why had they challenged each other?

His hands were so cold he couldn't even feel them as he reached, lifted himself up, reached again, thought about Burr and Hamilton. . . .

Spike, higher than ever, was laughing. From the sound of his voice, he might be two thirds of the way up. Steven dared not risk taking a look to find out.

"Having a little trouble, Stevie-boy?" Spike jeered from his perch. "You'll miss the train if you don't hurry."

Left foot, right hand. Right foot, left hand. Below him, tin cans and trash winked up from the bottom of the river; the small upturned faces of the kids all looked alike. The breeze picked up and sang in the spans; the bridge seemed to sway.

Yes. It did sway.

His left foot refused to move—or was it his leg that refused, locked at the knee? His hands were unresponsive to his will. There was no power on earth that could loosen their grip.

Spike's voice floated down. "I think you're chicken, Stevie. I think you're a little yellow around the edges. You're Barton Elementary School's gutless wonder!"

Could the kids on the ground hear Spike's taunting? It began to look as if they really would have to call the fire department to come and rescue him . . . and then he was horribly aware of the distant, then closer roaring of the train. Releasing one hand, he wrapped his arm around the span, then the other, his body pressed tight against the truss.

Oh, God, oh God, here it came, the train's ponderous entrance onto the bridge that shook the arch vigorously. Soot came pouring down; the horrendous crashing burst over him and he squeezed his eyes shut and clenched his teeth and held his breath.

The train crashed and roared and rushed off the bridge. The shaking and quivering stopped, and then screams and shouts came from below. Opening his eyes, blinking the shards of soot away, Steven looked.

Spike was in the water, floating face down.

Was he good enough? Could he do that life-saving jump right? No time to decide. He leaped as he'd done from the high board at camp, hitting the water so fast he had no sense of falling, snapping his legs together, pushing down with his arms. His head and face stayed on at the surface, just the way they were supposed to, the breath nearly squeezed out of him by the shock of the cold water.

Spike's inert body was right beside him. It was hard to turn the kid over, grab his shirt collar and pull him to shore with hands so frozen that his fingers could hardly move. Ed and Robbie and Sam waded in and took over dragging McCloskey to the river bank while the spectators gathered around.

"Roll him over, onto his stomach," Steven told them breathlessly.

The pages of the life-saving manual seemed to flutter before his eyes as though ruffled by the breeze, men in black bathing suits with tops like underwear, straddling the victim, pushing on its back to the count of three, releasing to the count of three. Or was it four?

Spike coughed and threw up river water, followed by his lunch. Gasping, he threw up more. Everyone who had crowded around politely looked away. When they looked back it was to observe the wet and shivering Steven Sinclaire, the boy who saved Spike McCloskey's life. No one remembered whether he made it to the top of his arch or not. Arch-climbing was kid stuff. What Steven Sinclaire had done was not.

At his feet Spike retched and groaned and shivered.

"Someone call his folks, wherever they are," Steven said. "They need to come and get him."

"What about you?" Ed asked.

"I can walk, if you help me." The shock and cold were getting to him now, and it was hard to control the shaking. Robbie held his coat open and stuffed his arms into the sleeves. Ed grabbed him on one side, Robbie took the other, Sam pushed from behind and the little cadre passed through the crowd of admirers.

"Did you see that jump?"

"Great jump!"

"Wonderful, Steve. You were wonderful."

"Spike owes his life to him!"

Smiling, his lips blue, he waved modestly. "Hurry!" he urged his friends. If he got home fast, he could change his clothes and pretend to be studying if Father arrived early, and he'd never guess that Steven hadn't come right home after school.

He faltered and stumbled.

"You OK?" Ed asked. You're shaking bad."

"You guys are wet to the knees. You're probably pretty cold, too," he grunted.

"It'd be better if we ran," Robbie urged, and without breaking formation, the boys jogged lockstep to the back of the Sinclaire's house. And there was Father, opening the kitchen door. The small squad abruptly halted.

Mom pushed forward. "Good heavens!" she exclaimed.

"Steve probably ought to get in a hot bath right away," Sam said, his teeth chattering. "He's been in the river."

"Come in, all of you! Quickly! You boys, go stand on that register. Mr. Sinclaire will turn the heat up. Charles? More coal? Steven, run upstairs right now and draw a bath. The boys can tell us what happened. I'll fix hot chocolate for everyone."

Despite his misery, Steven grinned as he took the stairs two at a time, thinking about Father having to squander extra coal for the furnace. Steam from the bath rose and curled upward; stripping off his clothes, he lay gratefully in the tub as the water got higher and higher, higher than he'd ever been allowed to draw it before. Oh, the blessing of it! He soaked there until the bath cooled. Dressing in the warmest clothes he owned, he became aware that the house was quiet. Where was everybody?

Father was waiting for him in the kitchen. "Your mother took your friends home," he said. "She'll be back presently. There's hot chocolate on the stove."

Being alone with Father was usually an unpleasant experience, involving the razor strop. Stirring the chocolate, Steven asked, "Did Ed and Robbie and Sam tell you what happened?"

"Yes. How is it that you let yourself get snared into a challenge with a ruffian like this McCloskey boy?"

How much could he tell Father? How much would he understand? Pouring the chocolate, Steven sat at the table, too. "I'm a lot different from the other kids. Spike takes advantage of that."

"Different in what way?"

"I'm the only one who comes home right after school. And my grades are good. Kids like Spike McCloskey figure I must be a sissy."

"About your grades," Father said. "Miss Meagher apparently thinks you're far from stupid. That's what your Mother tells me, anyway. I came home early today to hear what your teacher had to say about your report card."

Steam from the chocolate rose up to his face; Steven closed his eyes and reveled in it and tried to shut Father out.

"Since it appears that you're not stupid after all, we needn't discuss that possibility." Father went on. "But I'd like to find out how the McCloskey boy lured you into climbing the bridge. To me, that sounds like sheer stupidity."

"If I didn't at least try, he'd be able to prove I was a sissy, and get more kids on his side. I'd be worse off than before. So I said I would."

"Despite the fact that you are forbidden to stay after school."

"Yes, sir."

The car door slammed in the driveway and Mom hurried in. "Well!" she chirped, hanging her coat in the kitchen closet. "They're all delivered home. I hope they don't catch cold, wading into the river to help you. And you, honey? Are you warm enough? I see you found the chocolate—that ought to help. If you're chilly, I can get a pan of hot water for your feet. It may be old fashioned, but it's a sure-fire way to get body temperature rising."

It must be she was nervous, Steven thought, rattling on like that.

"Have a seat, Emily," Father said coolly. "It looks like Steven will survive. He tells me that we have isolated him to such an extent that he must prove himself in order not to be molested by this McCloskey person."

"*You* have isolated him," Mom said firmly, taking her chair. She was different, somehow. Steven, finely attuned to her, sensed the change. "There's no 'we' about it."

Father was clearly surprised at this combative stance. "Would you repeat that?" he asked, trying to stare her down.

"I think you heard me very well. It's you who have isolated him. You alone." Turning to Steven, she said, "My conference with Miss Meagher was great, honey. She says you're the best student in the class, better than any she's had for a long time, and getting a slightly lower grade in arithmetic only means that you need more time to grow with math concepts."

"Grow?" Father asked skeptically.

"She explained that for some people, reading takes longer to pick up, for others math. She says Steven's doing fine, and soon enough he'll be able to get answers quicker. The important thing is that you understand why numbers are carried from one column to the next," she told Steven. "And you do. She's not in the least worried. So now that we don't have to worry about his grades, we can decide which sessions of Camp he'd like to attend," she went on. "I thought he might prefer the four weeks of August, when it's so hot here."

"When did we decide he was going?" Father asked. "The last thing I heard was that the boy hung around after school in defiance of our request that he come straight home."

"Your request." Mom was really pushing now.

"I probably won't have to do it again," Steven said quickly, filling the pause. "I think Spike has been put in his place."

"When I tell you I want you home, young man, I mean right after school. You chose to disregard that rule, and perhaps as your punishment, Quivet ought to be forfeited."

Forfeited. Did that mean Father would not allow him to go?

"His application has been sent in already," Mom said. "I put down August, but I'm sure it can be changed to July, Steven, if you'd prefer that."

"What did you say, Emily?" Father was clearly dumbfounded. "You sent in his application?"

"Yes," said Mom. "I put it in the mail this morning."

"You mailed it already? Without my authorization?"

"I did. And in case you're wondering, I took care of the cost, too."

"Did you, now?" Father's face was getting quite red. "How did you manage that, if I may be so bold as to ask?"

"Cousin Elizabeth is going to see to it."

For once, Father seemed at a loss.

"I called her this morning about it."

"You called her."

Despite the danger inherent in the situation, Steven had to fight a smile over Father's shock.

"I did. On the telephone."

"You've had a busy day," Father observed, glaring. "And what did Elizabeth have to say?"

"Oh," Mom said lightly, "she said she'd be glad to cover expenses and even the train fare. She hopes your financial troubles will clear up."

"You've lost your mind, my dear. I'll call her and let her know you misunderstood the state of our finances."

"And tell her that you can easily manage tuition and train fare?" Mom smiled, and her expression wasn't so pleasant, either. "That's marvelous, Charles. A good decision, I think. Much better than letting her know you plan to deprive the boy of his summer at camp and his visit to Kingsland."

Father took a deep breath. "Steven, please excuse us." It was a command.

Glancing at Mom, Steven left the kitchen slowly, then hurried through the living room and up the stairs to his bed room, firmly shutting the door without going in. Quietly he crept back down to listen.

"Shall I tell Elizabeth that you terrorize the boy?" Mom was saying. "That you're likely to withhold camp as a punishment for his breaking an arbitrary rule you made up in order to be in control?"

"I think you've forgotten who's in charge here."

"You may be in charge of me, Charles, and our house. But from now on, I will be in charge of my son, not you."

"Really," Father exclaimed in false amazement. "Whatever makes you think so?"

"Because I don't think you want me to tell Elizabeth that you've been abusing the heir of Kingsland."

"Steven's not the heir. You are."

"Exactly. I don't want to tell her or anyone else what you do when no one's around to see it. But I'll tell now if I have to, and I'll talk to a lawyer about your abuse of Steven, which I think would provide grounds for my having sole custody of him and a show that a court order should be put in force that would keep you away from both of us."

A chair scraped against the linoleum floor. Father must be on his feet now. "Is that a threat?"

"It is. I'm your key to Kingsland, Charles. I've always been. I haven't pressed my advantage before, but you've gone too far, threatening the boy with Camp Quivet, the very thing he loves most."

"Really, Emily, you are quite hysterical. Perhaps I'd better explain a few things that you may have lost sight of."

"Perhaps you'd better sit down, so I can remind you of a few things you may have lost sight of, yourself."

Father must be complying, because there was a short silence and a bit of rustling around. "Very well, what have I lost sight of?"

Mom's voice was strong now. "Elizabeth believes you're in financial difficulty. She's offered to send money for me to come East with Steven and visit her and Mother while he's at camp. I'm thinking that perhaps I should, and that perhaps Steven and I should just stay in Waterford, once camp is over."

In the silence that followed, Steven could imagine Father's face, frozen, betraying nothing, because when he was angry, he became like an icicle. Probably Father was trying to stare Mom down. Usually he succeeded.

"And you think Elizabeth would support such a thing?"

"I don't know, Charles. Probably she couldn't afford to feed and house us both indefinitely. But if I were to get an allowance, maybe it would work."

"An allowance! You have lost your mind, dearest."

"It's called alimony, if we get a divorce. An allowance if we're legally separated."

There was a floor-shaking crash. China shattered. Chairs fell over. Mom cried out. Terrified, Steven burst into the kitchen where his mother cowered on the far side of the upturned table.

"Get out!" Father raised his hand to strike, his face scarlet. "Get out, you bastard!" he snarled.

Steven ducked and circled around to Mom, who was cradling her arm. "Are you hurt?"

She shook her head. "I'm fine, honey."

Father, rapidly regaining self-control, was already lifting the table up again. "Pick up the crockery," he ordered. He took his chair and watched while they scooped up shards and threw them away, finally seating themselves, Steven and Mom on one side of the table, Father on the other.

"Let's begin over," Father said, his voice steady and authoritative. "We've let this camp thing get out of all proportion."

"Oh?" Mom querried. "Did you or did you not threaten to withhold it from Steven in order to punish him?"

Was she taunting Father?

"I believe I was suggesting that since the boy did not come home directly after school, as he has been told to do, there ought to be a consequence. And I'm not willing to let you visit Kingsland by yourself, by the way. I'd miss you too much, my love."

"And if I decide to go, anyway?"

"I think you know what I'd do, should that unfortunate event occur. I don't think you want your mother, or Cousin Elizabeth, to know who Steven really is." Father smiled wickedly. "Do you?"

Looking to his mother for clarification of this mysterious statement, Steven saw her go pale.

"I don't think you'd want anyone to know you beat your son and abuse your wife, either." Her voice shook. "I don't think the fellows at Sommerset and Troy would think much of it."

A long silence followed, during which Mom did not look away. "Well, then, it looks like a stalemate. Let's compromise." Father grew expansive, stretching and clasping his hands behind his head. "I'll say nothing to anyone. I'll call Elizabeth and assure her that my finances are in good shape. That I can pay for camp and Steven's transportation myself. That you will not be coming east to visit this summer."

They locked eyes. Mom was the first to look away. "Very well." She took a deep breath, as though steadying herself.

"Perhaps we might have supper here in the kitchen," Father suggested. "It's getting a little late."

"Yes. Supper. It's nearly ready."

Father watched as she took cold chicken slices from the ice-box and opened a can of peas, heated them while Steven hastily put out kitchen flatware, bread and butter, filled water glasses for his parents and milk for himself.

Father forked two chicken slices onto his plate. "Well, then," he said jovially, passing the platter. There was a look in his eye Steven didn't like. "I take it that the math grade isn't an issue, as far as the boy's teacher's concerned."

The peas in their serving dish came next, pale and awful.

"Miss Meagher thinks that by the time his grades matter, he'll be as good in math as he is in reading," Mom told him.

"Gratifying, to say the least. Well, then, I suppose the only issue remaining is the boy's decision not to come home from school this afternoon."

"I explained why I had to stay," Steven dared to put in, given courage by Mom's unbelievable performance.

"You did, and I do understand. And since your mother is much closer to the day-to-day situation than I am, I have decided that what you do after school will be up to her. The criteria will be your grades. Right, Emily?"

"Naturally," Mom agreed.

"Now, then, about Quivet. Perhaps the boy would like to go for four sessions, instead of two. All of July and August."

Puzzled, Steven looked at his mother and saw despair in her eyes. Despair. It began to dawn on him that whatever went on between his parents, it happened when he was gone. This summer—all of it—she'd be the one to pay in coinage he knew nothing about.

"Two sessions would be fine," he said quickly. "Or maybe one."

"No, no. I know how much you enjoy camp! Up until now you really haven't been old enough to leave home for two months, but I think you are, now. I'll call Quivet in the morning, and reserve the extra time. From the office, where it will cost us nothing." Pointedly, he glanced at Mom to remind her that she had incurred a bill without his permission. "And let me congratulate you, Steven, on Miss Meagher's assessment of your abilities. The probability of your being admitted to Harvard is nearly assured." Father looked pleased with himself. "I'd like some bread and butter."

Steven passed it, and tried to come to terms with what had just happened. Mom had traded her freedom for his. It was too much to take in. There were things going on here too deep for him, and suddenly he was exhausted.

"I'd like to go to bed," he told them. "May I be excused?"

✢∞ 3 ∞✢

Cousin Elizabeth glared up at the smudged train windows, waiting with her arms folded, her foot tapping impatiently as though she'd been at the depot all morning. Her hat's veil was tied so tightly that her nose appeared to be flattened somewhat by it; her dress was dark and too long, hanging just above thick-heeled shoes with laces like teachers and librarians wore. Clutched under her arm was her pocketbook, held tightly as though she were afraid someone would snatch it, and she did not flinch as the train stuttered to a stop, spraying soot and ashes.

Steven retrieved his overnight bag from beneath the seat where he'd stowed it. The conductor hauled the rest of his stuff out onto the platform. "Camp Quivet!" he called with a grin.

Of course it was not Quivet at all; it was Waterford depot, but Steven had held a long conversation with the conductor on the connecting trip down from Boston's South Station, where the train from Ohio stopped and the one to Cape Cod began. He'd told the conductor all about Quivet, the bronze, silver and gold arrowheads, earned by merit points, and the swimming and sailing, crafts and tennis.

"Welcome, stranger," Cousin Elizabeth exclaimed, hugging Steven briskly. "You can put his things in my car, just over there, redcap," she told the conductor.

"Afraid not, Ma'am," the man said. "The train's about to leave."

Cousin Elizabeth was not looking into her pocket book, and perhaps had no plan to tip the conductor. But Mom had told Steven that good service deserved a tip, and had given him envelopes with dollar bills in them to use along the way. He gave two of them to the conductor now. "Nice to meet you," he said politely.

The conductor tipped his cap as the train huffed and began to roll. Cousin Elizabeth disappeared into the depot, to persuade the station agent to put Steven's camp gear into her Model T. Should he be tipped too, Steven wondered as the train pulled away and his conductor, with a wave, disappeared inside. But the agent appeared happy to help, called Cousin Elizabeth by name and shook Steven's hand.

"Nice to see you again, young man!" he exclaimed. Elisha Pollard had run the depot forever, and knew everybody.

Steven climbed up onto the slippery upholstery of Cousin Elizabeth's car, watched her do those wonderful things with levers on the steering post and pedals on the floor. "Hold on!" she called as the motor caught and she aimed the car toward Main Street.

"How was the trip?" she asked.

"Fine."

"I hope you aren't too tired. Did you sleep at all last night?"

"Well, no."

"I've got your room in the tower all aired out and ready for you," she assured him. "If you feel like lying down for a while this afternoon, please do so. And your parents? How are they?" she asked quickly so that he would not have time to thank her. Cousin Elizabeth hated sentiment.

"They're fine."

"Your grandmother and I had hoped your mother could come East with you."

"I guess she couldn't."

"Do you know why?"

"No."

Without looking to see if any cars were coming, she turned onto Main Street, as though the road had been constructed expressly for her use. "I believe they're both coming East to pick you up at the end of August."

Would Mom be safe while he was gone?

"Yes. They'll come on the train and we'll all go back together."

The old captain's houses lining the road passed briskly by as the Model T picked up speed, hit thirty miles an hour, and stayed there. Behind the gracious old New England elms, Cape Cod bay spread out with gentle power to the straight, limitless horizon, omniscient and calm, just as he remembered it.

They turned again, abruptly crossing the road and causing an oncoming car to stop with a flurry of dust. The Model T drove up to the house tall and regal, pillared and towered and porched, waiting for him. He could not slow the beating of his heart, which raced and ran and jumped for joy at the thrill of seeing it again.

Yes, it was the same as it had always been, steadfast since the last time. A rising, flooding benediction stilled him and gave him peace.

It was still there, and it was his.

CHAPTER

The Allies

1944

The nation was dragged out of the Great Depression by war. At first only the president of the United States was in favor of it. Understanding what a boon to the stifled economy war would be, Roosevelt, treading carefully, gave aid to a desperate England in its war with Germany, and waited for the right moment to take America into battle.

The Japanese obliged, bombing the naval fleet at Pearl Harbor, and the war machine began to grind, slowly at first, then faster and faster as women went to work in the factories and American boys died in far away places and men too old to fight managed the home front. Tin cans and old tires, cooking pots and newspapers were collected to aid the war effort. Food, gasoline, and clothing were rationed.

Otherwise, life in America went along as it always had, despite shortages and losses and fear. The National Anthem brought tears to the eyes of those who sang it; the pledge of allegiance was recited as fervently as a prayer. Older schoolboys waited for their turn to fight, while the younger ones pursued the interests of early adolescence, free from the shadows that overhung the civilized world.

❋∞ I ∞❋

STOOP-SHOULDERED and long-armed, their knees jabbing the students in front of them, Steven and his friends watched the girls with feigned disinterest. The afternoon air was crisp on their faces; the clarity of the sky bespoke autumn. On the football field the drum-majorettes of Morrison High School strutted, their batons twirling, the gold buttons on their dark blue uniforms flashing in the sun.

Steven had not paid much attention to girls until this year, but now, going on fifteen and large for his age—now, with his body changing fast and his voice sliding down and his daydreams fluctuating between enemy aircraft which he shot down single-handed and the models on the calendars at the local filling station which he admired at an inarticulate distance—now Steven Sinclaire was well aware of female persons. All this past summer he and Ed Lamson had discussed their merits and drawbacks and had gone so far as to take one or two to the movies, double-dating for safety. At this very moment, he knew, Ed was admiring the second majorette from the left, whose curves were very apparent even at this distance.

The band thumped to a halt and filed into the two rows of bleachers allotted for it behind the goalpost; the loudspeaker at the opposite end of the field echoed incomprehensibly. A roar from the whole stadium went up as the teams spilled out from their respective lairs beneath the grandstands where they hid before the game and at half-time, and the cheerleaders lined up in front of the student section. Instantly he and Ed and Shakey and Sam and Rob were focused on the large letter M's on the front of their bulky white sweaters.

"Morrison!" the cheerleaders called through their megaphones. "Morrison!" They sank to their knees, their arms outstretched as though worshiping the sun and the students obediently yelled and clapped in unison.

"M! M! M-M-M!"

Clap, clap. Clap-clap-clap.

The cheerleaders rose a little.

"O! O! O-O-O!"

Clap, Clap. Clap-clap-clap.

They rose a little more with each letter, then threw themselves sideways in a cartwheel on the full yell "MORRISON!" and happily the gang watched the leg display.

The cheerleaders ran back to their bench just below the student section as the teams lined up on the field. The referee's whistle blew and the spectators hooted and shouted and cheered. Steven yawned. Football was not his favorite game.

No, it was basketball that claimed his attention. And Ed's. And Robbie's and Sam's. They had recruited Shakey, and the five of them practiced continually on the Lamson's driveway, which was concrete and smooth. On rainy days, when Father was away in Boston or Washington, they practiced in the Sinclair's basement. Next year the graduating seniors would be gone, and they'd be varsity! In the manner of boys everywhere, Steven pictured himself scoring spectacularly, playing wisely, the model of sportsmanship conduct, admired, emulated, trailed after by girls, sought out by men . . .

"Want to get some popcorn?" asked Ed.

"Sure," he said, relinquishing his daydream. "Let's go. You guys want any popcorn?" he asked the rest of the gang.

Shakey and Sam and Robbie did.

Down in the bowels of the stadium, an ascending howl from the spectators told them that the kicker was running to the ball. The bass drum bumped and there was a muffled cheer. The sounds of life above were muted and remote, as though he and Ed were under water. They ordered popcorn, waited for the bags to be filled. A crowd of Negro boys came down, and Steven's stomach tightened in an instinctive defense against something alien to himself. Deliberately he did not look at those boys, whose teeth flashed as they laughed, whose voices were slurred and soft as they slid snide jokes back and forth between themselves, their contemptuous glances, their mocking falsetto laughter an indictment that he only vaguely understood.

Carrying the popcorn carefully, he and Ed made their way back. In the tiered student section the social makeup of Morrison High was laid out before them like a huge Dagwood sandwich: the Negroes at the top, without a chance to succeed; the tough white kids of Port Huron in the rows just below, both boys and girls whose expectations in life were not much higher and who had no interest in school. Below them sat kids not unlike Steven and his own gang, kids who might, if life were kind, amount to something. In front of them were the golden ones—the ones who were sure to succeed, who led clubs and who participated in school activities like the yearbook and the newspaper, and who were smart and whose parents were well-to-do, whose fathers worked for Sommerset and Troy, Port Huron's largest business, and who were bound for great things when they grew up, assuming the war didn't get them first.

One of these days, Father was going to discover that Steven was not part of that golden group. If Father were home instead of representing Sommerset and Troy at the Pentagon, he'd complain that Ed and Shakey and Sam and Rob weren't good enough, not smart enough, not suitable companions for Steven. He'd disdain Ed, whose father was a supervisor at the glass plant and whose mother was an Ohio farm girl brought belatedly to the city; he'd make Sam and Shakey and Robbie feel so small and uncomfortable they'd scatter like leaves in a hurricane, and that would be the end of his friends and the hall of fame.

Until now, World War II had been on the horizon of their lives for so long it seemed permanent, like a movie perpetually playing at the Paramount Theater. But one day—perhaps soon—the announcement on the marquee would change. It would read "ALLIES VICTORIOUS" and Father would come home to stay and Steven would once again have to toe the mark—an obligation nearly forgotten since the start of the war, when Father spent so much time in Washington DC overseeing S & T's lucrative war-time contracts.

Steven did not look forward to his return.

The opposition scored another touchdown and the grown-up spectators, losing interest, began to leave. The students stuck it out because there was going to be a record hop after the game. As he watched and waited, along with the rest, Steven wondered about the dance and whether or not Pam Thompson, who was sitting behind him, higher up in the bleachers, really meant what she'd said in study hall.

She'd approached him at the pencil sharpener.

"Going to the hop Saturday, after the game?" she had asked softly, so the teacher monitoring the hall wouldn't hear.

"I don't know," he'd answered, self-conscious and stupid.

Perhaps she wanted to be friends? He gambled on it. "I might go if you'd dance with me."

"Maybe I will." She smiled seductively, and he smiled back, trying not to glance down at her little breasts that pointed up at him from under her tight sweater. Stumbling back to his seat, he considered it all. Any jackass could see that she was wise in the ways of the world. This past summer he'd seen her at the movies with Spike McCloskey, who was also wise and probably a lot more interesting than he was. And she was a good dancer—he'd watched her at other hops. Steven was not especially light on his feet unless he was on the basketball court. Probably he'd step on her.

Yet if he could somehow make a good impression, get her to go out with him, probably she'd let him kiss her—and maybe more. At fifteen, having dated a little and thought a lot, he was ready for more!

The score was 48-12 when the final gun popped and the crowd dispersed, the student section surging toward the school building and the gym. In the crowded foyer everyone milled around, waiting for the members of Philodendron, the girls's literary society who sponsored the hop, to finish arranging the records, to station themselves at the door for the collection of the twenty-five-cent admission charge. The girls who were not members of Philodendron (the majority) clustered in the ladies' room, peeking around the doorway every now and then to see how many boys were there. When a Glenn Miller record began, they moved out en masse, Pam Thompson among them.

Then Steven and his gang went in, and it was now or never. Marching up to her was unfortunately similar to diving off the high board at the YMCA, because once you were airborne, you could not turn back.

"Would you like to dance?" he asked hoarsely.

Glancing around, as though hoping there would be an alternative, she said, "All right." Her voice revealed neither pleasure nor eagerness.

As he'd feared, she was a better dancer than he. But since she knew what a girl should do and did it without waiting for his lead, twirling herself at every provocation so that her skirt swooshed out and up, revealing pretty legs, they looked good as a couple. When the record stopped, he was winded and wondering what to do next. Should he take her back to the girls' side? Turn and walk away before she beat him to it?

"Thanks for the dance," he managed to say.

"Sure thing."

"I hope I wasn't too bad at it," he apologized.

Glancing around again, then looking up at him, she smiled at last. "Oh, you were fine." Did he dare to ask for another dance?

The introductory measures of "Heart and Soul" blatted from the loudspeakers high in the corners of the gym, and behind him, Spike McCloskey said, "Can I have this dance, Sweetheart?"

Steven froze.

"No," Pam said rudely. "This one is definitely taken." She held her arms out in dance position.

"By him?" Spike's voice broke with incredulity, as though he did not believe Steven Sinclaire could even walk, let alone dance.

"Who'd ja think?" she drawled. Spike threw them both a menacing glare and stalked away while Steven put an arm around Pam's waist and cradled her hand in his.

Her smile was warmer now. "I hope you don't mind, Steve. That I forced you into dancing with me again, I mean."

Mom and he had practiced ballroom dancing a lot. "Heart and Soul" was just perfect for what he knew how to do; he executed a quick turn and Pam followed him, easily, through another, and another.

"I don't mind at all." He smiled. "Especially since you dance so well." That sounded good, he thought, confident, suave.

"Gee, so do you!" she exclaimed, obviously impressed.

Now what should he say?

"I guess you don't like Spike much, huh," he commented inelegantly.

"He's a creep." From the pack of tough kids in the corner of the gym the enemy was watching. Steven danced her to the opposite end, where they couldn't be so closely observed. "Do you know him? McCloskey?" she asked. "Because if you do, you know yourself what a creep he is."

"We both went to Barton Elementary," he told her. "I know him better than I want to."

"Ohhhh!" she exclaimed. "You're the one!" She laughed. "The one who pulled him out of the river! I heard about that!"

"It was a long time ago," he admitted modestly. "You used to go with him, didn't you?"

"I've gone out with him," she said disdainfully, as though it were a mistake of immaturity that she did not intend to repeat. "But not anymore."

"Heart and Soul" abruptly stopped with a tearing sound as the needle scraped across the record, and he walked Pam back to the girl's side.

"Thanks again."

A new record was started.

"You're welcome. Any time," she added, and they turned from one another simultaneously. To do anything else would be an expression of too much interest for so new a friendship.

Eager to find Ed, Steven nearly mowed Spike McCloskey down. "Oh!" he exclaimed. He moved to the left, to go around, but Spike moved that way, too.

"That's my girl you were dancing with," he said unpleasantly.

Steven stopped, no longer attempting to avoid Spike or get away from him, a move that McCloskey would take as cowardice, he knew.

"That's not the story I heard." At a distance, Pam Thompson watched.

"Let's discuss it outside," Spike said.

"Go outside? With you? Forget it, boy! I can't be bothered." Hopefully his tone of scorn and derision would be sufficient to get Spike to back off. But with Pam watching, Spike could not afford to lose face.

"We can talk here, if you'd rather," Spike challenged. His fists were balled up and he was ready.

But Steven was ready, too. "Go ahead. Do it. I dare you. Right here. Right now."

Several teachers, alerted to the possibility of trouble, came hustling over. Spike took one look and backed away, then casually left the gym. There was nothing for the teachers to see, and nothing they needed to say to Steven Sinclaire who had never been a problem to anyone.

The kids nearby returned to their conversations, which were not nearly as interesting as the promise of an impending fight. Pam was still watching, waiting. Spike, after all, had yielded the field. An especially loud jitterbug blasted from the speakers and Steven beckoned to her; she grabbed his hand and they backed away from one another, then jived forward. Ducking under his arm, she twirled to face him.

"Perhaps you'd like to come home with me after the dance," she shouted as she zipped past in the next move. "I can fix you a sandwich or something."

He'd made it! He'd scored! He was sure of it! Taking her hand, he led her off the floor. "That's real nice of you," he said when they reached a corner sufficiently removed from the loudspeakers that they could make themselves heard. "But I'd rather take you to the movies tomorrow. And come back for a sandwich after that. John Wayne is at the Paramount."

"Yeah. I heard he was."

"Would you like to go?"

"Sure," she said.

"I'll stop for you at one-thirty," he said. "The next bus will get us there in time."

"The bus?"

"Well, I'm pretty sure my mother would take us, if you'd rather."

"Your mother?"

Strength and manliness were required now. "I didn't know you were deaf," he said daringly.

"I'm not," she laughed. "It's just that I've never dated a boy who didn't have a car."

He risked it all. "You can change your mind, if you want."

"No," she said, looking him over. "It might be fun to go on the bus." She turned and walked off to the girl's end of the gym, and Steven searched out Ed and the others, hiding in the shadows of a far corner.

"What did McCloskey want?" Ed asked. Shakey and Sam and Neil came close to hear the answer.

"I think he wanted to claim his girl. Since that wasn't working so well, he wanted to meet me outside and discuss it."

"Discuss it!" Ed snorted. "Is she worth it?"

"I don't know yet," Steven laughed with what he hoped sounded like John Wayne bravado. "I'll find out soon, because I'm going to take her to the movies."

"When?"

"Tomorrow afternoon."

"Hey!" Ed grinned and turned to the others. "Can you beat that? He's going to take her to the movies."

"Whew!" Sam salamed in admiration.

"Hubba! Hubba!" Robbie and Shakey crowed.

And thus was Steven Sinclaire launched into the pursuit of womankind.

✦∞ 2 ∞✦

News of the week flickered across the screen, and then a cartoon with Bugs Bunny. Everyone seemed to think it was hilarious, and perhaps it was. Steven was too nervous to notice.

At what point was he expected to put his arm over the back of the theater seat, preparatory to draping it over Pam's shoulder? Should he settle for just holding hands, he wondered, considering that they had never dated?

Well, he didn't have to worry about it right away, at least. They had both dived into the huge bag of popcorn he'd bought, and now were watching and munching in unison. The feature began with trumpets and the roaring lion, the listing of the stars, and then John Wayne and his horse and his little bunch of good guys galloped into the center of the screen, looking for desperados who had robbed a bank somewhere.

John Wayne spoke a little oddly, as though something hot was in his mouth, but Steven loved him—and there! There was Deanna Durbin, cute as anything, all dressed up in ruffles and flounces and a little bonnet and gloves, looking up admiringly at the hero.

Pam was forgotten. As the movie ended, Steven was suddenly aware that he had a girl with him, and that he had not thought about her at all in the last hour.

"That was great!" she exclaimed, apparently as involved in the plot as he had been. Thank goodness!

They followed the crowd out into the sunshine, shocking as it always was after a daytime movie. Now for the bus. They had the movie to talk about, the ride was pleasant enough. On her street, houses stood close together and front yards were little scraps of grass. Narrow driveways separated one home from the other.

"I'll show you our victory garden," she announced, and led him up the driveway, past the garage and around to the back door. A high fence closed off the Thompson property from the people next door. A gate opened onto an alley that ran behind all the houses on the block; the Thompson back yard was entirely taken up by their victory garden, dug up now and ready for planting next year.

"That's my father's pet project," Pam said. "Do you have a victory garden at your house, too?"

"Not yet," he said. "My father is always out of town and doesn't have much time."

"Maybe my Dad can help him, next spring. He can break the ground for him with his tractor." She pointed to a shrouded hump on the far side of the garage.

"I'll remember that," Steven promised, wondering what "Dad" would think of a tractor rolling into the yard.

Pam looked under a loose clapboard by the back door and took out a key. "Just a sec," she told him. "I'll have the door unlocked in a jiffy."

"Is anyone home?"

"They're visiting my grandmother in Detroit." Pam said, replacing the key.

No boy spent time in an unoccupied house with a girl. Even he, in his inexperience, knew that. But she seemed to have no hesitation. "Come on in."

"Well—OK, for a minute," he temporized.

"What's your hurry?" Pam asked. "You just got here."

"Um . . ." There was no graceful way out. No matter what she thought of it, he'd have to bite the bullet. "I can't stay inside with you, Pam. Not if your mother or father aren't here."

"Why not?"

"It's just not the way it's supposed to be done, is all."

"Huh!" she exclaimed. "Not the way you la-de-da folks with your English accents do it, you mean."

Was she was referring to Father's deliberate British drawl, or Mom's New England mannerisms of speech? "We aren't la-de-da folks," he said patiently. "The reason I can't spend time in here with you is because it might damage your reputation."

"Oh! My reputation." She seemed astonished at the very idea. "It's very nice of you, Steven, to care about that. How about taking cookies and milk out to the garage? Since our family doesn't have a car, we fixed it up like a den. Would that be all right?"

Was there a difference between an unoccupied house and an unoccupied garage?

"Sure. That would be fine. Can I help carry something?"

Pouring two glasses of milk, she loaded up a plate with cookies stored in a canister on top of the icebox. Carrying them carefully, they entered the garage by virtue of a small side door. The large doors on the front, the ones that would normally be open to accept Mr. Thompson's car if he had one, were securely fastened and locked from the inside. The little door closed firmly, and he noticed that Pam locked that, too.

It was dark in there, but wired for electricity. Pam turned on an old floor lamp with a battered shade to reveal a table with crooked, unmatched chairs around it, and a derelict couch on the far wall. In a corner were rakes and shovels, along with a rusted lawnmower and a heap of old leaves that had, no doubt, crept in on the crest of last autumn's wind.

Pam spread a blanket over the sofa so its leaking innards wouldn't get lint on their clothes. Sitting down, she patted the space beside her. Like a glad lamb he followed, sat, crunched on a cookie and wished he knew what to say next.

"You're on the basketball team, aren't you?" she asked.

"Junior varsity. I keep the bench warm."

"But the team's all seniors, just about. You'll probably be varsity next year."

"Probably."

They consumed cookies silently for a while until it occurred to him that she was probably waiting for him to kiss her. Nearly swallowing his cookie whole, he quickly washed it down with milk and took her hand in his. She did not resist.

"You're so little," he said, comparing her fingers to his. He felt large and strong in comparison.

"I haven't really had a chance to thank you for taking me to see John Wayne," she smiled.

"Oh, you're welcome." A drop of sweat rolled down his ribs as he waited for her to give him a clue about his next move.

"I could show you how much I enjoyed it."

Ah! At last! "How would you do that?"

She put the cookie dish on the table, pulled him toward herself and pressed her lips against his, softly, gently. And then her mouth opened slightly, an invitation for more if he dared. He felt the faint moisture of her tongue, and touched it tentatively with his own, just a little. Suddenly a yawning emptiness opened up, and then her tongue twined with his.

Releasing her before he made a fool of himself, he hoped she didn't know how deeply she'd stirred him. "I-I have to go," he faltered.

"Not if you don't want to."

"I'd sooner catch the bus before it gets dark."

"O.K." Glancing down to see if she had aroused him, she nodded, satisfied. Unlocking the little side door, she waited considerately for his erection to subside.

By the time the back door was reached, he was able to think. "Well, thanks again," he said, "Maybe I'll see you Monday."

"Sure thing. Meet me at my locker? After school?"

An invitation! "If you like," he said, as though he could take it or leave it.

"I like," she laughed, and turned away.

Almost certainly this invitation contained within it the possibility of walking home with her, visiting the garage again, kissing again, and who knew what else.

He ran to the bus stop and rode home, rejoicing.

∾ 3 ∾

Her hand was warm, insistent; he burrowed his burning face into the curve of her neck and hoped he would not unman himself by crying out when he reached climax.

Kissing his sweating forehead, she whispered, "You like that, don't you."

For three weeks now he'd walked her home; for fifteen school days she'd taught him the progressions of petting, and she could bring him to this point now almost without preliminaries.

"You know I do," he whispered back, and kissed her small, pointed breasts which, by now, were always accessible to him once the privacy of the garage was reached.

"Do you know what comes next?" she asked.

"Sure. The Fall Frolic. Will you go with me?" More formal than a hop, no girl would be there without a date, and most boys would have partners, too.

"Maybe. How would we get there? I'd rather not take the bus."

"I don't blame you, sweetheart, but the alternative is my mother."

"Your mother?"

"Can you think of an alternative?"

"Taxi?" she suggested.

"Well—sure." It would put a hole in his savings. If he continued to take her to dances and she continued to want cabs, it would put an even bigger hole in them. But he could straighten that out in time. She must be secured first. "A cab is a great idea. I'll take the bus and a taxi can pick us up here. We'll take one back, and I'll catch the last bus home."

"And we can even come back early," she said. "Early enough to make sure we have a little extra time here. It would be fun. We wouldn't be able to turn on a light or my parents would know we were out here. It'd be interesting that way, don't you think?"

He went hot and cold all over. They kissed again, touched again....

"I have to leave, or else I'll be home late for supper." Mom had not been told that he'd walked Pam home from school every day for past the three weeks. While it was true that the Thompsons were not the same kind of people as the Sinclaires, and while it was true that Pam wasn't exactly his type, either, it was not the awareness of these rather intangible differences that had stopped him from saying anything. More realistically, he knew, it was because his aspirations with regard to Pam were not the most straightforward, and you couldn't very well say so to your own mother, could you?

In any case, he did not correct Mom's impression that he was going to the dance stag, an impression she could hardly avoid, since Ed and Shakey called at the door and the three of them went off together. He told himself that he did not mention it because Mom had received a telegram from Father, that day, with the disappointing information that he was on the way home. It had not escaped Steven's notice that Mom was usually testy and high-strung at the impending presence of Father. Much as he was, himself.

But he did not let himself dwell on this unfortunate prospect. For once he was so absorbed with the possibilities that lay ahead he was able to relegate Father to the a small corner of his mind. Setting off with Ed and Shakey, he'd call a cab from a payphone nearby the Thompson house while his friends would continue on into town, catch a 9:00 movie and meet him at the bus stop near Pam's afterward, in case Spike McCloskey happened to be loitering nearby.

By the time he reached the Thompsons', the cab was waiting. Pam, at the door, called goodbye to her parents (whom Steven had never met) ensconced herself like royalty in the taxi, allowing him to hold her hand all the way to school.

In a moment to be savored, they walked grandly into the gym. The place was decorated with streamers and flowers made of Kleenex, and a disc jockey made sure the music flowed smoothly, one record to the other.

With a heady sense of well-being, Steven curled Pam's hand into his own and (he had practiced this with a broom handle) twined her arm beneath his so that she was pressed close to his chest. *Stardust* played over the loud speaker. As the evening progressed, they danced with more and more clandestine intimacy in a manner that escaped the notice of the chaperons. Would he ever, ever get enough?

"McCloskey's here," advised a boy from the basketball team who crossed their path with his date. Glancing over Pam's head, he saw Spike near the door.

"Who's here?" Pam asked.

"Santa Claus." He grinned crookedly, much as John Wayne might have done.

"You must mean Spike," she said.

"Yuh."

Her face was impassive. "He'll probably ask me to dance."

"Probably."

"What should I do?"

"Whatever you want, Pam."

"Don't you care?"

"You bet I do. But if I tell you what I want and you do it, I'll never know if *you* care."

"You think you're so clever," she mocked, delighted to be the focus of so much attention; everyone in the gym was watching now. The record ended, but instead of the hum of conversation and laughter that usually rose up after each set, the whole place was silent as Spike walked across the floor. Several of the male chaperones moved tentatively toward the center of the room.

"I'm cutting in. Scram, Sinclaire."

"Get lost," Steven said, stepping in front of Pam.

"Listen, buddy. Pam's my girl, and I want to dance with her."

"Sorry, Mac. She isn't your girl. If you want to dance with her, you'll have to ask."

For a moment Spike just stood there and looked hungrily at Pam in her pretty pink dress. "Well?" His voice was rough.

Staring back, her head held high, she said nothing, and the moment lengthened.

"Don't say I didn't warn you," McCloskey said to Steven, and swaggered out of the gym as the clarion call of *In the Mood* blasted from the loud speakers. The gym became noisy again as everyone backed and filled according to the requirement of the beat.

What did it mean, that she had not said yes or no, Steven asked himself. Did she still like Spike, and had left the door open for future encounters?

The dance was ruined for thinking about it. When the set was done, she went to the powder room while he called a cab from a payphone in the school lobby. They waited at the curb.

"Do you want to go home by yourself?"

"What? Without you?"

"Maybe you wish you had accepted McCloskey's invitation to dance. Maybe he'll be waiting at your door, hoping for your attention."

"Why should I pay attention to him, or even answer him back there on the dance floor!" she exclaimed. "Gosh, Steven, here we are with a little extra time on our hands. Why not take advantage of it?"

"Let's go!" The taxi arrived and he handed her in, raced around to the other side, and held her tight until they got out a block from her house where they could access the alley behind the Thompson garage. The gate was unlocked, as was the side door. They felt around in the dark for the couch, found it.

"I'm sure glad I had a fight with Spike, back then when I first danced with you at the football hop," she said close to his ear as they embraced. "Because if I hadn't, I'd have missed the chance to get to know you."

"What did you and Spike fight about?"

"He wanted to go steady," she said. "And I just wasn't sure. Now I'm glad I didn't take his ring! He's not like you, Steve. You're going to amount to something. Pretty soon you'll be on the basketball team, and I'll bet you're even going to college—and Spike McCloskey isn't going anywhere, and he never will."

His pride swelled. In the darkness she kissed his ear and then his mouth, and something else swelled, too.

"I think a lot of you, too," he managed to say.

"Enough to go steady?"

"Go steady!" Never had he dreamed she'd want to do such a thing—though now as he thought about it, perhaps it was what she'd been suggesting for quite a while, and he'd been too stupid to understand it, too insecure to believe that a girl like Pam would take such a novice as himself seriously.

Yet there was still an insurmountable problem. Father. "Well, Yes, I would—like to go steady—but I haven't had a chance to tell you that my Dad's coming back, and I'll be expected to be home all the time until he leaves again. We won't be able to see each other, except at school, until he leaves. Maybe now's not a good time . . ."

"Back from where?"

"Washington, D.C. He works in the Pentagon. With the army."

Patriotic as they all were, she was impressed. "Well, of course, you should be there while he's home. I'll wait, Steven. It's my duty as an American!"

"Well, do you want to go steady now, or wait until he leaves?"

"Why wait? I won't change my mind. Will you?"

"No!" He ducked down to kiss her, but she held him off.

"Usually people who go steady exchange jewelry or something."

"Here's my class ring," he said, taking it off and folding her hand around it. "I'd be real pleased if you'd take it."

"It fits my thumb." She laughed. "I'll wind thread around it and seal it with nail polish and then I can wear it."

Wow!

"And I'll give you something of mine." She took off one earring. "I'll keep the other under my pillow. You do the same, with this one."

What a wonderful token of love! Pocketing the earring, he drew her close, and she offered herself up, helping him to loosen her clothing and his own, her breast soft against his lips, her fingers searching and finding him. The prelude to climax gathered and soon she would reach for the handkerchief she seemed always to have handy. But instead, she pushed him to one side and divested herself of her panty girdle and stockings, hiking up her whispery skirts, and it was very, very clear what going steady entitled him to—and enormously clear to him that he would be able to deliver. Like a migrating bird, he knew where to go without even thinking, knew to peel off his pants and shorts, spread her legs and crawl on top of her. Beneath him she thrust up her hips, presenting the best possible entry to her hot threshold, and when he tentatively prodded, she gasped and guided him into herself, moaning as though deeply in pain. The beating, throbbing, hotness of his groin stretched him taut on the rack of his body's imperative and he could hardly breathe . . . .

"Lover," she murmured, "have you got a safe?"

"What?"

"A safe. A condom. So I don't get pregnant, Sweetheart."

When he opened his eyes, he could see only the vague outlines of her face as he struggled to understand. A condom. Yes, a condom. That was what she'd said.

There was only one way she could have learned about condoms. For an instant he hovered, his attention diverted to the probability that there was a lineup of boys going back into her still-brief past, the last of whom had been Spike McCloskey. A lineup which no doubt would extend into her much longer future, the first of whom was himself.

In this moment, the urgency of his lust let up long enough to give him a chance to choose. He drew back.

"Lover?"

He climbed off the couch and found his discarded clothing.

"Steven, what's wrong? What are you doing?"

Putting his trousers back on, tucking in his shirt, he could not speak for the pent-up needs that raced and scrambled within.

"Are you leaving?" she asked, incredulous.

"I'd better, or I'll miss the bus."

"Why did you pull out like that?" she demanded.

"I don't have a condom." An answer that would satisfy her, he thought—but he was wrong.

"Well, then, you can pull out just before you come."

"I have to go, Pam," he said, firmly as he could. "I have to go now."

"Okay," she said, clearly mystified.

"We'll walk around to the front of the house, as though we were just coming back from the dance. Then your parents won't think anything's going on."

"Okay," she said submissively, and without saying anything more he opened the side door, then the gate to the alley, down it to the street, around the next corner to her house. Abruptly leaving her there in its bright light with only a light farewell kiss on the cheek, he started off toward the bus stop, his thoughts mercilessly flaying him.

The answers to his questions were clear. Pam knew he would be on the varsity basketball team next year. For the next two years he would be important, and he was going to college. And he'd stood up to Spike, right from the beginning and again tonight, making a prize out of her, a trophy. How gratifying, when the gym hushed and everyone watched McCloskey walk up to them!

Possibly, when she'd been at the pencil sharpener a month ago, she was only fishing in untapped waters, without knowing what she'd catch until Steve Sinclaire nibbled at the bait. The school was small enough that she must have known he came from the better end of town.

In the night he blushed. Yes, sir, he'd let her hook him! And got McCloskey mad at him besides. A person it didn't pay to have as an enemy. Spike had promised revenge: *don't say I didn't warn you.*

Oh, Jesus! Why hadn't he arranged for Ed and Shakey to take the early bus, just to be on the safe side?

Because you wanted your chance with Pam, he answered himself. And God knows who might be following you now.

Instantly he was alert, his hearing more acute, every sense tingling as he walked rapidly from one pool of streetlight to the next. Then, from behind, running footsteps approached like summer-swept rain. A car pulled alongside; he was pushed into the back seat. The pusher followed him in, pinning him to the floor. Someone else in the back seat knelt on his shoulders. The door slammed; vaguely he heard the voices of Ed and Shakey shouting somewhere in the darkness as the car roared away.

There was, for a moment, only the smell of old carpeting, and motor oil, and sweat from his captors, then the panic of not being able to breathe. Desperately he tried to move; the car threw itself around a corner, and the weight of his captor shifted a little. Breathing was easier, and he could think.

Beneath his ear the tires on the road hummed and small stones were flung up, pinging against the undercarriage. When the car stopped, he would be at the mercy of Spike McCloskey and his gang. Prisoners in the camps of the Germans and Japanese had torture done to them. This wouldn't be much different. He would have to take what was coming, without outcry if possible. Not only would there be no one around to hear him, but screaming his head off would diminish him, take away his pride. He knew a lot about that. After all, for years he'd been on the receiving end of punishment, deserved or otherwise.

But Spike was not really any stronger than Steven himself. None of these boys were any larger than he was. And he could fight back, unlike his confrontations with Father. Now—this night—he didn't have to take it without giving as good as he got.

A vestige of strength stirred. There were, of course, four kids in the car, as far as he could determine. Four-to-one odds weren't so good, and there was little hope he could escape into the blackness of the night. But he sure as hell could break a nose or two before they overpowered him!

When the car stopped, he went slack. The boys, featureless in the shadows, dragged him from the car and toward a patch of woods, and were unprepared when he wrenched himself loose, rolled over, and leaped up quick as cat. Doubling his fist as he'd seen John Wayne do, he drove it into the face of the nearest adversary, his whole hand in the grip of sudden agony as it connected with something both spongy and hard. Blood spurted, and he turned to the next kid, in a frenzy to reach him, and the one after that, and then Spike himself. The giving of pain fed on itself, and he was no longer the person he'd known all his life, but a stranger doing alien things. He hit and kneed and kicked and did not stop until they had him pinned against a tree, forcing his arms back and around it so that his shoulders were wrenched in their joints and he was immobilized. They were breathing hard, their faces bloody, even Spike's, and he guessed he was bleeding too, but just now the agony of his shoulders was the most important event on his limited horizon.

"I guess we've all got a score to settle now," said Spike. "Who wants to go first."

"I might as well," said one of them. "And then I'll take an arm and Joe will be free, and Joe can take Art's place..."

"Okay, okay," Spike said impatiently. "I get the picture. Go ahead."

The boy hesitated.

"Afraid?" Spike jeered.

"I might hurt my hand," the kid complained.

"Get out of the way, then."

"Hell, no." The boy approached Steven's helplessly exposed self and punched him, just below his ribs, and then again, and again. "Your turn," the boy said to someone, and Steven's shoulders were further wrenched in their sockets as the new shift tightened its hold.

The next tormentor did not hesitate, but hit hard, ramming agony deeply, sharply, unmercifully into his innermost self, and then sent a crashing blow to his face. The world narrowed down to a black, soundless hollow where everyone, everything, receded and he was unaware of who hurt him or even how until he heard Spike say, "Turn him around."

The pain in his shoulders as they lowered his arms and turned him was abrupt, and the world exploded in bright light and he heard himself scream.

"I knew we could get him bawling," he heard Spike say. "When I'm through, he'll be bawling plenty."

His cheek was pressed against the rough, scratchy tree bark. Then there was the slapping of leather against the palm of a hand, and then the too-familiar whistle of the belt whipping through the air. He locked his teeth to prepare himself for what was coming next, and heard himself scream again as the buckle of Spike's belt ripped into his back. And again. And again.

There was a distant high-pitched moaning which was not himself. The boys dropped him where he stood, the tree bark scraping his entire length as he crumpled to the ground, alone with his agony as they ran for their car, the gravel thrown by its wheels spraying him in a final spitting insult.

There were spinning lights. There were people in the night. A blanket was tucked around him where he lay, unable to breathe because of the obstruction that was his nose and because his ribs refused to expand. His wounds throbbed and pounded as though the beating were still going endlessly on, on, on.

Ed's voice called. "Steve! Steve!" but he did not answer, because he could not. Everyone else did things, everyone else made the decisions and someone jabbed him with a needle, and then he coasted, suspended over them all as he was lifted into the back of an ambulance that arrived from an unknown source, and then . . .

. . . the ceiling of the ambulance disappeared.

∞ 4 ∞

His interrogation by the police moved forward without interruption the following day when, well fortified with pain killer, he was able to speak through a hole in the bandages covering his face.

Ed and Shakey told everyone that when they came back from the 10:00 movie on the bus, planning to connect with Steven after the dance, they saw him being forced into a car, saw it make a right turn. They'd run to Pam's nearby house, pounded on the door and used the Thompson telephone to call the police, describing the direction the car was headed in and, with Pam's help, the probable places it would go. No doubt places where she and McCloskey had gone for privacy.

Spike and his pals were in custody, all of them admitting complicity—difficult to deny with their broken noses and blackened eyes and rumpled clothing that looked as though they'd rolled in the dirt. Now it was Monday. Ed and Robbie and Sam and Shakey had bumbled in after school, shuffling and poking around the room.

"They're all on probation now," Ed said cheerfully, inspecting the bedpan hidden in the bottom of the bedside table. "They can't drive anymore, and they have a curfew, and the next time they get in trouble, they'll go to reform school."

"McCloskey won't be getting in your way for quite a while," Sam said, playing with the cord that controlled the venetian blind. The room slowly grew dark, then slowly bright. "You and your girlfriend are free to pursue whatever it was you were after."

Blushing beneath his bandages, he mumbled, "Not my girl." It was hard to move his jaw.

"Did you say she's not your girl? Speak up, man!"

"She's got your ring," said Sam. "Do you remember giving it to her?"

No. He'd forgotten. He must get it back! But how?

Shakey looked at the chart hanging from the foot of the bed. "It says here you died, Sinclaire."

"Feels like it." Tears came to the surface. He'd been very moody—a normal response to shock, the doctor said. It would pass, given time. The only thing left would be a slight off-centering on his nose—nothing to be alarmed about—and some scarring on his back. Trying not to clench his teeth because it hurt too much, he worked at making the tears go away. His bandages effectively disguised the trouble he was having.

There was a stir by the door, and the atmosphere of the room changed, like the surface of a pond ruffled by a sudden breeze. The boys turned, all at the same time, to see Father standing there, his coat over his arm, fedora in hand, his hard, pale blue eyes appraising them.

Mom came breezing by him, her smile broad as she tried to put everyone at their ease. "Well, boys!" she said cheerfully, perching on the edge of Steven's bed, sending a ferocious knife blade through him. It took all of his concentration not to cry out, and for a moment he forgot that everyone was there, that Mom was thanking his friends for coming to see him, and reminding Father what their names were. The lacerations on his back wept; his ribs complained.

Uneasily the gang shuffled its collective feet.

"We were just leaving," Ed mumbled.

"Well, thanks again!" Mom rose from the edge of the bed to see the kids out, and sparks flashed across the back of his brain as the mattress changed shape. In the corridor the voices of Steven's pals got farther and farther away until their exodus was only an echo; the elevator doors opened and shut again, swallowing them up.

And then there were just the three of them, a little group that should have been close-knit and was not, that should have belonged to one another in the special ways of families, and did not. Thankfully, Mom did not return to the bed, but leaned instead against the dresser.

"Well then, hello," said Father finally, coming close to look down at the wounded warrior.

"Hi, Father," Steven said through the hole in the bandages. "Welcome home."

Because his voice was muffled, Father had to tip his ear toward the place where the words came out, and it occurred to Steven that Father, for once, was at a disadvantage. For the first time ever, he could confront Charles Sinclaire with something to hide behind, with the advantage of being able to take his time to think about his answers to the inevitable questions.

"How in heaven's name did this happen, Steven?"

Much as he hated to do it, he had to bring Pam Thompson into the equation, because that's where it started, wasn't it? Besides, Father probably knew about her already, but in his usual manner was baiting the trap to see if Steven would perjure himself.

"I was leaving a girl's house..."

"A girl! I see things have been moving right along in my absence. So there you were, leaving a house..."

"And this guy and his pals jumped me."

"I'm having trouble understanding you, Steven. Speak up!"

"He's doing the best he can, Charles," Mom said, moving to the foot of the bed.

"What person did you encounter?"

"Spike McCloskey."

"McCloskey. The same barbarian that gave you trouble in elementary school?"

Steven nodded cautiously, thought the better of it as Father appeared to slide up and then down. "Yes. Ed and Sam and I planned to meet on the last bus."

"Why?"

"In case Spike McCloskey was planning to jump me. Like he did."

Talking was getting easier, with the extra practice.

"Your friends weren't much use, were they?"

"They called the police from the girl's house. She knew where they'd most likely take me, and she was right."

"They're really nice kids," Mom put in.

"They don't look nice," Father said. "They don't look even presentable—not by a long shot. Why in heaven's name are you associated with such riffraff, boy?"

Beneath the bandages, Steven grew hot and sweaty. "Ed Lamson is my best friend," he said. "And next year the other three are going to play varsity basketball with us."

"Did you know about this, Emily?" Father turned to her, frowning.

"Of course I did. He needs recreation, Charles. Exercise is good for adolescent boys."

"But must he recreate with those boys? The ones who just left? That down-at-the-heels, shambling example of manhood that recently walked out of here?" The expression on Father's face was similar to one he would wear at the monkey house at the Toledo Zoo, trying to be tolerant of the odor of the inmates and their occasionally gross behavior. "It's a good thing I found out about this, I can see that! Perhaps I'd better arrange for a replacement for me in Washington, so I can get things better organized here in Port Huron!"

Behind the protection of the bandages, Steven assessed this horrible possibility. Surely Father did not want to be replaced at the Pentagon. He gloried in his importance as Sommerset and Troy's representative there. It was an empty threat.

But one day, perhaps soon, the war would be over and Father would be home for good, and he would do nothing but diminish Ed and Shakey, Sam and Rob. He'd pressure Steven into doing what he decided was right to do, and this battle would have to be fought without the screen of bandages behind which he could come out fighting, rather than whimpering and hoping for the best.

Taking as deep a breath as his bruised ribs would allow, Steven said, "The boys who just shambled out of here—and I—may be able to take the state championship, next year or the one after."

Mom repeated it, so Father was sure to understand, but he was unimpressed. "It would be difficult to maintain a top-flight grade average if you're playing games at the same time. And you must have good grades to secure your admission to Harvard. You know that. It's important to order your values, Steven. I didn't realize that your mother had allowed you to get so badly off-track."

"Hardly off track!" Mom protested. "If Steven has no chance to do at least some of the things he likes—especially sports, which uses so much male energy—his grades would suffer more than if his schedule were too full. He needs to tire himself in a healthy way. The Dean of Boys told me that."

"Dean of Boys!" Father scoffed. "Does this person know what it takes to get into Harvard?"

"This person knows more about adolescent boys than either you or I do!" Mom retorted. "Steven's grades might slip if he were bottled up, without an outlet for his energy." Urgently her eyes sought his, commanding his attention.

"Not if he . . ." Father began.

"And his motivation would be badly compromised," she barreled on. "Don't you agree, Honey?"

Suddenly Steven understood that she had thrown him a life-line.

"Well, I guess that's true," he said behind his mask, trying to form his words clearly at great cost to himself. "Without being motivated, a person doesn't get good grades. A person might not be able to get into any college." He managed to turn slightly toward Father and met his gaze squarely, unflinchingly. "Especially a person doesn't get into Harvard."

The room was filled with stunned silence. It was a standoff; permission to see his friends, play ball, lead his own life at Morrison, in exchange for grades good enough to get into Harvard—an accomplishment well within his reach. Here was his chance to manipulate Father instead of letting Father manipulate him. Willing himself not to look away, he did not hide his hatred.

Father brushed at his suit coat as though the room had contaminated him.

"Well, we certainly wouldn't want to see your grades slip! I see you're quite fatigued, my boy," he said smoothly, as though nothing at all bothered him. "And since I've only just this day come back to Port Huron, riding the train for more hours than I care to say, I'm a little tired, myself. Perhaps it's time to go home, Emily."

Reaching for her coat, he held it out and slipped it over her shoulders, ushering her out of the room without saying goodbye, an indication of his frustration and aggravation. Their footsteps faded as they moved down the hall and to the elevator.

Well, he'd won, hadn't he? The right to freely choose his friends? To play ball? He should be glad, shouldn't he? But dominating his mind was concern about Mom, who would have to bear the brunt of Father's anger. The joy of victory was lost and the pain of his injuries came back with a vengeance, now that there was no energy—adrenalin, he would learn later—to deal with them.

Don't! he urged himself. Don't let him win like this! Concentrate on the things Father can't take away.

Think.

Think.

And then it was there, blessing him, soothing him, restoring him—Kingsland in its fastness behind the maples in the yard—Kingsland with its tower that he'd claimed for his own, before the war made attending camp impossible. And there was the sun setting across the bay, upon which he would sail again, once the war was over and he could get back to Camp Quivet and salt breeze, and the tide. It all would be his again. These were the important things.

These were the things that not even Father could destroy.

CHAPTER

Waterford

1947

World War Two ended with a bang, one in Hiroshima and one in Nagasaki. Germany had already surrendered when America's atom bombs fell. The nation's war machine slowed down, but soon enough was changed over to peacetime use, meeting the needs of returning soldiers and a population that had been deprived of necessities and luxuries for four years. The specter of the Great Depression was vanquished.

Europe was not so fortunate. There was nothing left; the cities were reduced to piles of rubble. A dazed and stricken citizenry had nowhere to turn. Communism looked like a reasonable solution, but America staved off this threat with the Marshall Plan, funneling amazing amounts of money into clothing and feeding the multitude, rebuilding the cities and repairing the infrastructure.

But money alone was not the answer to Communism, which used the weapons of ideology, small diverting wars, subterfuge and a constant undermining of the democracy America had paid so dearly to defend. The Cold War was on.

The first of the Nuremburg trials began, and the atrocities committed by physicians and scientists were made known. An atomic bomb was set off on the Bikini Atoll, to explore the possibilities of using this power for the public good as well as for a whole new level of weaponry, should such be needed, while in every-day America, a new social and economic order began to rise.

"JULIUS THAYER'S Last Will and Testament provided money for the town," Cousin Elizabeth declared with ice in her voice. Samuel Hall, chairman of the Waterford Selectmen, sat across the parlor from her, perspiring and uncomfortable in his Sunday suit.

"Ay-yuh," Sam nodded. "To use in the best way possible. For the good of the town."

"I'm quite sure that Mr. Thayer meant to provide funding for the arts, Mr. Hall. Culture, to edify the townspeople." Beside her, Grandmother Merrick nodded in confirmation.

"Well, them arts is good, for sure," Hall plugged along, doggedly defending his position. "But Waterford's dump is runnin' out of room, ma'am. There's more than one way to interpert the public good."

Everyone in the room noticed how Sam pronounced this word. Naturally he would not know the proper way to say it, being a local man, without much education.

"Apparently the public good is being interpreted in more than one way," Cousin Elizabeth told everyone. "And I think it's up to me to preserve the intent of an old gentleman who loved Waterford dearly and whose concept of the public good embraced more elevated concerns than the disposal of garbage."

"Oh, good one!" crowed Father. "Score for you, Elizabeth!"

Steven cringed at Father's drooling over their cousin. Don't pay attention, he told himself. Ignoring Father was not always easy, but he'd gotten a lot of practice since the end of the war and Father's return to Port Huron. Now, thank goodness, he was about to enter Harvard, and could leave Father behind.

On the maroon velvet chair with gold fringe and curving legs, Mom chain smoked.

This denigrating of Mr. Hall had to stop. "The arts were fine in Julius Thayer's day, Cousin Elizabeth," he pointed out. "But the depression and the war put an end to his day." Father's face became red. "The town isn't as well off as it used to be," Steven forged on.

"If Mr. Thayer's bequest can be used to take away some financial pressure on the local folks, he would certainly be well remembered."

"Indeed," Father snorted. "We could carve a stone in Mr. Thayer's honor and plant flowers around it, right outside the gate to the dump. With a box in which to leave an offering. For maintenance of the Julius Thayer Memorial Garden."

"Very likely we'll have to start chargin' for the dump, whether we get a new one or not," Sam Hall responded patiently, acknowledging neither by expression nor body language his understanding that he had been mocked by Mr. Sinclaire, whom everyone in town knew to be an asshole. Turning to Cousin Elizabeth, he said, "The land we want is one of old Barney Stone's woodlots. What with a willin' buyer and all, Barney could pay someone to help him take care of Mrs. Stone instead of having to send her to the county home, an' the town would get a new place for its trash."

"In view of such a worthy cause, Waterford's town meeting will, I am sure, vote to purchase the land out of tax revenue. Then Mr. Stone will be as well off as he would have been if Julius Thayer's money had bought it, and the town would have its dump, would it not?" Elizabeth rose grandly from her chair. Father, too, got up, as did Steven. Gentlemen did not remain seated when a lady was standing.

Sam Hall finally figured out that he was being dismissed and rose also.

"So pleasant of you to have called, Mr. Hall." Cousin Elizabeth extended her hand, which Hall took and then dropped quickly as possible. "Steven, you may show Mr. Hall to the door." She waved in that direction and then rudely turned away. "I'd like to see Julius' money used to purchase my grandfather's mill site and put a museum on it," she said to the family.

Sam Hall knew when he was beaten. The money had been left to the discretion of the Historical Society, and everyone knew that old Miss Edgarton, its president, ran the society to suit herself.

Steven walked with Hall out to his ramshackle car. "Will town meeting vote to buy Mr. Stone's land, like Miss Edgarton thinks?"

"No," said Sam Hall. "I don't believe it will. Barney hasn't paid taxes on that woodlot for years, and can't start now, so the town will just take it. The selectmen and me was tryin' to stop it from comin' to that, is all."

"Then Mr. Blake will have to put Mrs. Blake in a nursing home."

"Looks like it."

"I'm so sorry."

Sam Hall saw the distress in the youngster's face. "Somethin' will work out," he smiled, climbing into the car. "Somethin' always does." The engine started amid a plume of blue smoke and a series of backfires. "Sorry about that," he grinned cheerfully at this mechanical fart. "Sorta says everything, don't it?"

Waving, he roared away down the circular driveway, and the sound of the unmuffled motor gradually died. Loath to return to the stuffy, impossible parlor and the people in it, Steven lingered, giving himself a chance to figure out his next move.

For he badly needed to be in East Waterford. The family of his counselor-in-training was waiting for him to play Canasta. Already half an hour late, he must somehow get Mom to take him there. She'd want him all to herself after his summer at Quivet, especially in view of his departure tomorrow for Harvard, but there was a compelling reason by the name of Diana Harrison that outweighed his obligation to his mother.

"Why are you loitering out there?" Father called from the parlor window. "We travel halfway across the country to see you, and you aren't even here."

"Just catching some fresh air," he called back. "After all that wholesome living at camp, it's hard to be confined to a smoky room with a ceiling."

Father chuckled, pleased with this evidence of the Sinclaire way with words, and its implied disparagement of Mom which Steven had not intended and for which he was instantly sorry. "Come in anyway," Father commanded. "You're being impolite to our hostess."

He must get away! He must see Diana one more time before he left for Harvard and she returned to her home in Worcester.

Diana! Her hair was shoulder-length and curved gently and held the sun with golden lights. Her eyes were a brown-and-green mixture (mundanely called hazel, a name that did not convey their loveliness. Her voice was rich and vibrant, her laughter contagious, and when they embraced, it seemed as though he could feel every pleasant curve she had, perfectly fitting the contours of his own body.

If he asked for the car, Father would want to know where he would be going, and Steven would never tell him because everything Father touched turned to ash. Camp Quivet was officially closed, but perhaps he could invent something he'd left behind there and needed to fetch, requiring use of the car. But Father might come along, or everyone else might decide to come along, too—Cousin Elizabeth and Grandmother dearly loved to ride around town, viewing places that were only ceremonial markers now, commemorating a life that was gone. The depression had wiped out the summer society, and the war had made travel impossible. None of the previously wealthy folks had been back to Waterford for more than fifteen years, and their old, empty houses were slowly sinking into dereliction.

Except for Kingsland. It stood proudly among the ruins of Waterford, its comparison to its shabby neighbors honing its grandeur to an even finer edge and, unless Steven was very much mistaken, whetting Father's appetite for it more and more acutely. It would be Mom's, one day, with Father appointed to run it. Once retired, he'd probably take up residence, a feudal baron.

Reluctantly, Steven slunk back inside.

Mrs. Archie Stone, wearing a maid's uniform that she probably hated, was passing a tray with cups of coffee on it, and cream and sugar. Glancing up at him, she smiled.

"Now, Elizabeth," Father fawned, "now that you've belabored Sam Hall with it, what do you know about your grandfather's Civil War woolen mill?"

"Almost nothing," Cousin Elizabeth acknowledged. "The point is, Charles, that hardly anyone else knows anything about it, either. But the mill can be reconstructed, and I think it should be, along with a means of describing a whole way of life that has disappeared without a trace."

If he could help it, Father never did anything to contradict Cousin Elizabeth. Scornfully Steven watched him fall all over himself in order to please her. Now that he had a means of comparison—Diana's Dad—Father was particularly odious. Her brother, Steven's C.I.T. at Quivet, had invited him to the cottage on the first change-over Saturday, and their father had been welcoming, their mother cordial. Three younger sisters completed the family, and they'd all had a picnic on the beach, with cookies and Kool-Aid and a more adult refreshment for those old enough to take advantage of it.

"Do you like beer, Steve?" her father had asked. "I'm about to run out and get some."

"Sure," he'd answered.

"Let's go, then."

So easily had the man offered companionship right from the start! It was as though he considered Steven equal to himself, an individual, therefore worth knowing. So unlike Charles Sinclaire! "You're the swimming instructor, right?" he asked as they rode to the nearest package store.

"I am," Steven confirmed.

"Doug thinks you walk on water. He talks about nothing else. He wants to be a swimming teacher, like you."

"Actually, I'd really rather be the sailing instructor, but I didn't have the chance to get good enough. The war stopped me from coming back to Quivet after I was eleven."

"Oh. No gasoline. No room on the trains either, I expect."

"Right. Were you in the war, sir?"

"Yes."

"Can I ask where you served?" He knew that often men did not like discussing their war experience. It must have been very bad, and he respected their need to leave it alone, like a wound that never healed but didn't hurt if you stopped pressing on it.

"Italy," he answered. "I like sailing best, too."

Yes, the war was going to be avoided. "Have you done much? Sailing, I mean?"

"I used to. Right here, on Cape Cod." They pulled up in front of the store, went in to fetch a couple of cold six-packs and returned to the car. "Help yourself, if you want. There's a church key in the glove compartment."

Steven did.

"One for me, too."

Quickly he handed over the one intended for himself, made holes in the lid of another. It was freedom such as he had never known as they rode along, beer in hand, the wind blowing through the car and the sun high and warm overhead. Pulling into a small landing, they parked and watched the bay and drank beer companionably. How strange it was, and wonderful too, to feel so comfortable with a grown-up. This is what it should have been like....

And then there was Diana. After that first meeting, all Saturdays off, and even Sunday mornings, were spent in East Waterford with her; he came to Kingsland only to sleep and share breakfast the next morning with Cousin Elizabeth and Grandmother Merrick. Neither of them had ever mentioned his absences or questioned where he'd gone, for which he was thankful. He disliked lying.

Now Diana, a senior in high school, would go back home; he planned to visit her this winter, and would write to her, but just now he needed to kiss her one more time.

His urgency increased.

On the change-over weekend after he'd first met her, he'd taken a Quivet rowboat down to the cottage on an incoming tide. The family was on the beach. Doug and his father were some distance away, fishing, the little sisters were busy with an enormous sand castle. Diana and her mother greeted him, fed him and chatted until he turned to her and asked, "Would you like a rowboat lesson?"

"Who? Me?" she querried.

"Unless your mother..."

"No," her mother laughed. "Thanks anyway."

"Well..." Diana squinted at him doubtfully. "I would if you're not too bossy."

"I am, a little. I have to tell you what to do, if I'm going to teach you anything. Come on." He pushed the boat out, held it steady while she climbed in, then hopped over the stern. "First of all, you have to face me."

"Oh!" She looked around. "That would be more convenient, when you get right down to it. Since the paddles are positioned behind me."

"We call them oars," he said as the boat lifted and sank and grated on bottom, making a wrenching sound.

"I'd just like to remind you," said Diana's mother, coming to the rescue, "that this boat is private property, and does its owners no good if it doesn't have a bottom." She gave them a push.

"Turn around, take the oars, and give it a try," he suggested.

She did, and the boat moved. Quickly she took another stroke, splashing him.

"Sorry!"

"It's OK."

"Since I'm facing you, how do I know where I'm going?"

"It's within the rules to look over your shoulder."

"It seems hard to row and look at the same time."

"Once you're satisfied that you're pointed where you want to go, then you set up a landmark, relative to the stern. In this case, with me. If you keep the landmark in the same relative place, you'll stay on course. What's your landmark?"

"A tree."

"O.K., then, keep it lined up on one side of me or the other."

She tried a stroke and giggled. "I seem to be going somewhere else."

"Line it up again."

She tried, without success.

"Two people are always better than one," he told her. "You could move over and take the oar on your side, and I'll move up and take the other."

Doubtfully she looked at the oars and then at the seat. "There's enough room?"

"Sure. In the old days, when you chased a whale you nearly always had two rowers to a seat."

"OK, then," she agreed. "Let's chase a whale."

Carefully she moved, and the boat sank a little on her side. Carefully he moved, his weight counterbalancing hers, so the boat was level again. They settled, thigh to thigh. The sun's accumulated warmth seemed to emanate from her, and on the beach he could see that the whole family had joined the little girls in their sand-castle building, Doug and his father lugging nearby stones to reinforce the fortifications, their mother helping with embellishments to the castle itself.

"It must be nice to have so many people in your family," he remarked a little wistfully.

"Are you an only child or something?"

"Yes," he admitted.

"When families are good, it's wonderful. When they aren't, it's awful." How well he knew that! "A while ago, Doug and I had a different father, who wasn't too nice."

"Mine's not so great, either," he offered. "But it sounds like your own father isn't in the picture now."

"No, thank goodness. My Mom married my new dad five years ago, and he's great."

"He sure is," Steven agreed.

"Do you think we could turn around? The shore looks awfully small, to me."

"Sure. Hold your oar steady and deep."

She did, while he continued to work the oar on his side, and instantly they reversed directions.

"How about that!" she exclaimed. "You really do know how!"

"She doubted me!" he complained to a passing gull.

"Sorry! I didn't mean it quite the way it sounded. You earned a golden arrow when you were a camper, didn't you! And no one wins a gold arrow at Quivet without being proficient at everything Quivet has to offer."

"True. Proficient as we can be, anyway."

"And you must have a bronze one too, and a silver one, because Doug says you can't earn a gold unless you've already got the others."

"It's not real bronze or silver, you know," he said modestly.

"What difference does that make?" she demanded. "They stand for something. Something you achieved."

"They stand for carrots," he grinned. "They're dangled in front of campers to keep them ever striving, onward and upward forever. I have mine tacked up on the wall where my bunk is, to serve as an inspiration to the campers in my cabin."

"Does it work?"

"Oh, yes, the boys are very inspired." There was a scrunching, and then a jolt as the boat ran up on the beach. "If you like, I could show them to you, and you could get inspired too," he said in a sudden surge of boldness.

"I'd loved to be inspired," she responded, equally bold.

Elizabeth was still going on about overshot wheels and undershot wheels and ones with little buckets attached to them, and turbines, too, although she was not certain just which of these Kingsley Merrick had used in West Waterford. "A museum would be a fine contribution to the town," she was saying. "The locals have very little appreciation for history. They're so very..."

"Local," contributed Father, and they all laughed.

"A practical group, to say the least," Grandmother Merrick said.

"I'm sure the Marshalls—the ones who have the old Merrick house—would be happy to contribute to building a museum at the mill site."

"Emily and I met them years ago, when they'd just taken the house over as a summer place. Tell you what," Father proposed, "I'll match whatever you can squeeze out of them." It was his bid for Cousin Elizabeth's favor.

"Fairly said," she approved. "And fairly done."

"You and I can do fund-raising projects, too, Elizabeth," Grandmother Merrick suggested. "We can get a few like-minded souls together and have bake sales."

"Well," Cousin Elizabeth grimaced. "You and your friends could." Cooking was not her forte. "That would be very sweet of you."

"And now tell us about the Sunday dinners you three have shared while Steven's been at camp. I'm sure you've had a grand time," Father beamed.

Steven held his breath. If Cousin Elizabeth wanted to complain about the free time he had not spent at Kingsland this summer, here was her opportunity to do it.

"Why, we've had lots of fun." She smiled blandly and moved on. "And now we'll have even more, with the Marshalls here. Elvira and I can play bridge all year 'round."

"Indeed we can!" Grandmother agreed.

Relieved, Steven sank back as the conversation veered away to the subject of Goren bridge, a craze that had erupted fairly recently. The adults would sit around interminably, finding endless uninteresting things to talk about while the afternoon waned and his chance to see Diana waned, too....

He'd come back the morning after her rowing lesson, and she had walked all the way up to Quivet with him. On the camp waterfront, canoes were stacked like firewood, the rowboats overturned, one leaning against the other like spoons in a drawer. The gulls keened, and sandpipers chattered; the waterfront was empty because all of the boys were gone. The new ones would not arrive until this afternoon.

"About those carrots," he began.

"Oh, yes! The carrots!"

"I could show 'em to you, if you like."

"Sure," she agreed.

Hoping he wasn't in violation of a rule, he led her up the path and into his cabin. Bunks lined the rough wooden walls, a light bulb hung, unadorned, from the rafters. The counselor's bunk was closest to the door so that in the night he'd be more likely to hear a camper leaving for the latrine, and be listening for his return.

The bronze, silver, and gold trophies were visible if you stooped slightly, so that you could see beneath the bunk above.

"There!" He pointed and she crouched down to see them, and his heart began to pound because he knew what he was going to do next. Putting a hand on the rail of the top bunk, he was waiting for her as she straightened up again. Their eyes met and neither of them looked away. She waited as slowly he leaned toward her. Their lips met softly, without haste or demand. When he drew back, he saw her eyes were still closed, her lashes long and dark against her cheek, her face peaceful.

"I didn't plan on doing that when I brought you here," he lied, and when she looked up, the green and brown in her eyes were intense, a quick smile lighting them.

"You must be purer than me. I had it in mind all along." Her smile deepened, and his body felt weightless, as though it were joyfully taking off in a striped and brilliantly colored balloon, lifting and soaring, free in the breeze. They stood a moment longer. Into the essential quiet of the moment the sound of sneakered feet patted by on the path outside the cabin. The camp was coming to life.

"I guess we'd better get going."

"I guess we had." She waited for him to take his hand away, but he slipped it around her waist instead, pulling her in close. Sure enough, he could feel her delicate bones and the muscles of her thigh and the softness of her breasts against his chest, just as he had imagined, and he kissed her again, carefully because she was young yet, but fully, so that she would know how he felt.

Then they left the cabin and at their leisure walked back to East Waterford and her family and had a game of canasta before he was due at camp for the start of the next session.

"Old days and old ways are all well and good," Father was saying, "but many modern improvements really are superior—for instance, oil heat as contrasted to coal." It was not the first time this topic had come up for discussion. "An oil burner wouldn't take up as much room in the cellar, either," he persisted.

"I don't live in the basement," Elizabeth pointed out. "So I don't care how much room the heating plant takes. But since it's a capital improvement and since you might stand to benefit by it, Charles, in time to come, perhaps we should take a look at the best place to install one—if I decide to do it someday."

"How about the far corner, where the coal bin is now?" Grandmother suggested.

"That might work. Come along, Charles. Let's take a look. But I'm warning you, I don't intend to buy one. Not now, anyway." They started down the cellar stairs.

"How about if I helped you with the expense?" Father's voice offered.

"Even with Harvard board and tuition?"

"Yes, even with that."

Father was doing well at Sommerset and Troy.

The door leading to the cellar closed, and their voices changed to murmurs.

"Well!" sighed Mom, putting down her cigarette. "How are you, honey?"

There was a gentleness and warmth in her voice that was never there when Father was present. Mom did not want Father to know that a bond existed between herself and her son that did not include him.

Grandmother Merrick picked up her crochet and busied herself with it, giving them a moment for each other. Steven smiled genuinely for the first time that afternoon. "It was a good season at camp. I did fine as swimming director." His instructor's certificate, earned at Port Huron's YMCA, had stood him in good stead. "Mom." Leaning forward, hoping his grandmother wouldn't hear, he spoke quietly. "I have a date in East Waterford. Could you take me over there?"

"East Waterford?"

"Now? Before they come back upstairs?"

The light in her face faded as she realized he had not lingered simply to be near her. "Of course," she said, reaching for her purse. Well did she understand that Father would massacre a request for the family car.

With a finger over their lips, they gestured for Grandmother Merrick to say nothing. She nodded and smiled conspiratorially; they hastened to the Pontiac with its Ohio plates. Mom slid in behind the wheel while Steven hurled himself into the passenger seat. Once the engine caught and they were already moving, both of them slammed their doors simultaneously. Even if he heard, it would be too late for Father to interfere.

"Grandmother's a good egg, letting us sneak out like that."

"She is," Mom agreed. "And far from stupid. She'll never tell your Father anything. Speaking of Father, how do you feel about going to Harvard tomorrow?" she asked, continuing the perpetually ongoing discussion about it. "Does it feel OK, now that the time has nearly come?"

"I guess." He was supposed to be elated to be going to Harvard, he knew, proud to be accepted there, confident that it would open any door to him that he chose. "Turn here," he directed, pointing to a sandy, bumpy lane on the bay side of the road. As soon as they bounced up to the front of the cottage, Doug and the younger girls came running. Diana followed slowly.

"Gee, we were afraid you wouldn't be able to make it," Doug exclaimed.

"This is my favorite camper," Steven told Mom.

"I'm Doug Harrison." The boy extended his hand to Mom as she climbed out of the car. "And these pests are my sisters."

The little girls smiled widely in acknowledgement. "We're in charge of making Kool Aid. In the kitchen. Do you like cherry? It'll be ready in a minute." They charged off.

"And this is Diana," Steven told his mother. "How pretty she was!

"My sister, Diana Harrison," Doug explained unnecessarily.

"Hi." Diana's smile was shy. "Please come in, Mrs. Sinclaire. Our folks would love to meet you."

"Thank you. I'd love to meet them."

"Our aunt is visiting, too," Diana said as she led them onto the porch, through the door. "She's a lot of fun."

"She can beat me at cribbage—and I'm pretty good," Doug added for clarification. In the tiny living room a card table was set up for the anticipated Canasta game, an extra chair in place, occupied by the visiting auntie.

Diana's parents came in from the kitchen to greet the visitors. Her father stopped abruptly, his handsome face awry with shock and amazement. From her chair at the table the aunt struggled to her feet, staring. When he turned, Steven saw that Mom was staring, too, looking incredibly old and incredibly young, all at once, her face white, white, white.

Diana's mom was the only adult capable of speech. "This must be your mother, Steven," she prompted.

"Um, yes!" His voice was louder than he intended, magnified in the presence of so much tension. "Mom, I'd like you to meet Mrs. Bradley."

Mom's smile was wooden.

"We're so glad to meet you, Mrs. Sinclaire," Diana's Mom said warmly. "We've enjoyed having Steven with us this summer. Thanks for bringing him tonight."

"You're welcome," Mom said without inflection.

"This is my husband, Tim," Mrs. Bradley continued valiantly in the utter silence into which the stirring sounds in the kitchen filtered. "And his cousin, Alice."

"Hi, Alice," Mom said wearily. "Hello, Tim."

"Hello, Emily," said the aunt. "It's nothing short of amazing to see you."

"You know one another already!" Mrs. Bradley exclaimed.

Doug's father, who so far had said nothing, suddenly came to life. "Emily!" He hugged Mom quickly, placed a chaste kiss on her cheek. "After all these years! The Sinclaire name threw me off."

"Probably you remember Charles," Mom said. "He ran around with our gang."

"His family had the old Denning place in the summer, isn't that right?" asked the aunt. "The boy with the English accent—or what passed for one." She tried not to stare at Steven, while Mr. Bradley tried not to stare at Mom, and Mom concentrated intently on Mrs. Bradley.

"Us kids can drink Kool Aid in the kitchen," Diana suggested. "In case you all would like to visit a little."

"Oh, no!" Mom moved toward the door as she spoke. "No, I must be running along."

"We'll bring Steven home later," said Mr. Bradley.

"Thanks. 'By." The car started up, backed into the sandy road, disappeared.

Aunt Bradley extended a hand to Steven. "I'm so happy to get acquainted with you. Your family and mine have known each other for a long time."

That was true for a lot of old timers from Waterford.

"Well!" Mr. Bradley challenged. "Who wants to get whipped at Canasta?"

The game over, the rest of the family discreetly consuming snacks in the kitchen, Steven and Diana walked out onto the beach and up to the next point.

Pulling her to a halt beside him, he put his arms around her. "End of the line," he murmured, and they stood together, clinging.

"In more ways than one," she sighed.

"I'll visit you in Worcester," he told her desperately. "I can take a train from Boston."

"Yes."

"When you do want me to come?"

"Tomorrow."

Sorrowing, they laughed.

"How about the first weekend in October?" His allowance from Father would have arrived by then.

"First weekend in October would be great," she agreed. "If I last that long."

"And I'll write you."

"Yes."

"And you'll write me."

"Yes. Yes, you know I will." Her voice shook, and he was close to tears himself; he kissed her, the aching, trembling kiss of departure that they prolonged hopelessly.

Her face was lovely in the moonlight.

"Soon, then. Right?"

"Right!" She willed her tears away, and they slowly, sadly, went back to the cottage where he said good bye to the little sisters and to Mrs. Bradley, and Aunt Bradley, and to Doug.

"See you all next summer." He left them on the porch and climbed into the Bradley car without looking back.

"Well, I won't go into a song and dance about how nice it's been," Mr. Bradley said as they negotiated the ruts and turned onto Main Street. "But you know it has."

"Yeah," he agreed awkwardly. "I'd like to visit you folks in Worcester. I hope that's all right with you and Mrs. Bradley."

"Renewing your acquaintance with Doug, no doubt."

"Um, no doubt."

"Diana, of course, has nothing to do with it," he teased, and then laughed. "It'd be great, Steven, to have you with us."

The ache of parting eased in anticipation of a continued friendship with this wonderful man. Mr. Bradley pulled into Kingsland's driveway, waited until Steven got out and waved. The car moved away, taking Mr. Bradley with it, and Steven was lonely for him even before it turned onto Main Street.

The house waited, a looming hulk silhouetted by the risen harvest moon that scattered blue and insubstantial light everywhere. In the tower a lamp was lit, and one in the downstairs hall to help him see his way.

Mom was waiting for him.

"Hi!" he exclaimed softly, so that no one would wake up. "What are you doing up here?"

"I had to talk to you."

"Was Father upset that I snuck away?"

"He might have been. I didn't ask."

Sitting on the edge of the bed beside her, he waited to find out what was on her mind.

"You enjoy the Bradleys very much, don't you?" Mom asked finally.

"I do, yes."

"All of them."

"Sure."

"The boy, Doug?"

"Yes."

"The daughter, Diana?"

"Very much so."

"Have you gotten to know her well?"

"Pretty well," he hedged. "I expect to get to know her better this winter, because she and her family have invited me to come to their house in Worcester whenever I can make it. Do you think you could send me train fare, Mom? Or bus fare, if I can't save enough out of my allowance?"

Staring at the floor, she gave no indication that she had heard him.

"What about Mr. Bradley?" she asked strangely.

"Mr. Bradley?" In the region of his heart something fluttered briefly, downward, like an autumn leaf swirling to the ground. "I like him a lot. He's a nice change from you-know-who. He says I can visit them any time this winter; I think he really likes me, too."

Mom covered her eyes. To his horror, Steven heard her voice trembling. "Oh, God! Oh, my God."

Paralyzed by her display of distress, her loss of control, he put his arm around her. "Mom! Should I have not said that? About how Mr. Bradley's a nice change?"

She shook her head, her eyes still covered. "It's worse than that, Honey. Oh, God," she keened. "Oh, God, oh God."

Within rose the recognition of catastrophe.

"Steven," she wept. "Steven, this has got to stop. Tim Bradley is your father."

No dog bayed at the moon. The night was silent beyond the open window, and within, the house made no sound, no groans or snaps of aging wood. Between himself and his mother a distance grew exponentially, even though neither had moved.

It was clearly a mistake—a monstrous mistake—clearly he had heard it wrong. Cold sweat gathered as he waited, waited because there was nothing else he could do.

"I don't know how to tell you," Mom struggled. "I've never known how—but I always meant to, someday. I owed it to you. Now... now, of all the freakish things that could have happened, you've met him. The old families always seem to come back, one generation or another, but this! This is..."

At a loss for words, she stared at their reflection in the opposite tower window. It was as though the room were a stage setting and the two of them, the actors, were playing out their parts.

"Perhaps you'd better tell me everything," he said, his throat dry, his voice hoarse.

"Yes. Yes, I'd better." She took a deep, shuddering breath. "I met him nineteen years ago, right here in Waterford. "I was crazy about him. The friendship got a little ahead of us, is all, and I'm afraid I—I behaved badly. I got pregnant. But, of course, you never know you're pregnant when first you get that way." Her weeping overcame her, and she looked away.

"Go on." Within himself the boy he had been withdrew into an inner corner from whence he looked out at the world, and the consequences of his mother's foolishness.

"I didn't know I was pregnant until after Tim had left Waterford. He'd gone to sea, and I couldn't reach him. I'm sure he'd have married me, if he'd known about you. He was a decent person, he really was."

"Yes," he managed to say. Mr. Bradley was, after all, decent still. Pain started to build as he realized what he had missed, in that terrible turn of fate that had put Tim Bradley beyond his mother's reach when she needed him.

And now? Now he was filled with senseless protest—against abandonment, against injustice, against the dying of innocence.

He was Tim Bradley's bastard.

And Father knew it. Had always known it. He'd even called Steven "bastard" once...

"So I was on my own," Mom went on, her voice steady now that she'd gotten past the hard part. "There was no question, of course, about bearing a child out of wedlock. Not by a respectable girl, from a respectable family." It was true. Nice people did not beget children out of wedlock. Nice people did not associate with women who did that sort of thing, either.

"I didn't know what to do. I could have gone away and delivered my baby and put it up for adoption without ever seeing it. But I'd have needed my family's help for such a thing, and telling them was unthinkable. And I didn't want to give Tim Bradley's child away. I wanted to keep it if I could. It was all of Tim Bradley I was going to get."

A bastard. He was the result of a sweaty, secret, panting liaison such as he'd known with Pam Thompson. He was a mistake, the consequence of the insatiable lust of male-kind. Turning away from his mother, he went to the window, seeing only his own alien reflection and hers behind him. His gut had cramped without his even being aware of the pain as he slowly came to realize that he had labored under the heavy hand of

Charles Sinclaire all these years, and his mother had allowed it to happen.

"I'd known Father's family forever," Mom was saying. "He wanted me to marry him, so I did, a little earlier than planned."

"What happened when he found out?"

"I think you can guess."

"So he rescued your reputation and provided for you, and in exchange you let him do whatever he wanted. To me."

"And to myself."

"Was it worth the price?"

"Steven," she pleaded. "I loved Tim Bradley, and you are his child. I certainly never regretted the chance to keep you close to me—you've been a wonderful son."

"How swell for you." Coldness pervaded him.

"Isn't it better than being adopted?" she cried.

"You've got to be kidding." His sarcasm was brutal, and he regretted the hurt that it inflicted. But it was too late to take it back, too late to care, too late for a lot of things. In the window he stared at her tormented face.

The pain was getting worse and worse as the enormity of this disaster grew on him. Mr. Bradley, whom he'd enjoyed so much this summer, was untouchable now. So decent a person, if he ever learned the truth and the tragedy of his desertion, it would tear him apart, perhaps tear the Bradley family apart.

And there was more. Now he, Steven Sinclaire, would have to hide the truth about himself, always and forever, because few people would be able to accept him if they knew. Illegitimacy made him inferior. That was how people thought; they always had. As Father's attitude so clearly proved. To him, Steven was a bastard worth nothing, a piece of humanity without value, a mere mote in the eye.

And the crowning disaster, as if he needed more—was Diana. He would never be able to see her again.

"I don't want to talk about this anymore," he said to his mother. "Please go."

"Steven..."

"Now," he commanded over and above the impossible begging of the boy within to be comforted. Coldly he turned to face her and her overwhelming sadness, meeting her eye mercilessly, hatefully, and watched her stumbling exit from the room without a shred of compassion. Turning off the bedside lamp, he stared out at the land lit in the moon-blue night, wrestling with what he'd been told.

What difference would it have made if he'd always known? Would it have mattered?

Father would not have been any different, and Mom would probably have been the same, passively sustaining abuse he could only imagine, so that Charles Sinclaire would keep her secret. Maybe there was a God after all, Steven thought, who had seen to it that Father was in Washington during the war so that the adolescent boy could grow in peace.

He leaned his hot forehead against the piercing coolness of the window and simply suffered. Thought of Diana, of her clear, honest face and body that fit his so well, now out of reach forever, along with Doug, who admired him, looked up to him. Thought of Mr. Bradley himself, whose praise had kindled bonfires in the barren spaces of his heart. His father! His father! What could he have been and done with a father like that!

Good Christ, he must turn away from this before it destroyed him with its rage and frenzied railing against such injustice. Turn away and, instead, concentrate on what was possible, on what he could do to reinvent himself. Unless he did that, this pain and twisting hatred and unfulfilled longing for the father he never had would submerge him and he would be lost forever in it.

Maybe the God that had given him breathing room during the war was still in operation, for there was plenty of space, now, in which to start over. He would begin tomorrow. Once Mom and Charles drove him up to Boston and Harvard, and then left for Port Huron, then he would be in charge. He did not owe his mother anything, and certainly had no obligation to remain in the proximity of Charles Shithead Sinclaire.

And he would not, for there was Kingsland.

CHAPTER

The Bastard

THE MAPLES lining the curved driveway were beginning to turn gold. Basking in the noonday sun, Kingsland glowed, as though it had inner light. Steven paused on the steps of Snow's Store, looking across the street at it and listening to the sounds of Waterford crisp in the September air: the call of a child; the honk of a distant horn; a dog barking. The usually continuous passing of traffic had disappeared with the Labor Day exodus of summer visitors. An unhurried quiet had reasserted itself.

This morning, after Charles and Mom left him at his dormitory, he had returned his books to the campus bookstore and pocketed the refund. Hustling his duffel bags from Cambridge to the bus station in Boston, he rearranged their contents and loaded his book bag with a change of clothes and a razor. Leaving the rest in the luggage room, he bought a bus ticket and returned to Waterford.

It was a gamble. He understood that. If Cousin Elizabeth and Grandmother Merrick sided with Charles and refused to give him sanctuary, he'd have to go back to Boston and find work of some kind, enough to keep body and soul together, and wait to see what came his way. But he was never, ever going to let Charles Sinclaire have the upper hand again. So determined, he had not even been nervous or anxious until now. But standing there, face to face with his immediate future, the crab in his gut was getting restless. And he was hungry, having only consumed Cracker Jacks and Coca-Cola since leaving Harvard. It was time for a box of Oreos and a quart of milk.

Bert Snow was stocking shelves, arranging, rearranging, marking prices. In his own good time he took his place behind the counter and nodded a greeting.

"Hi, Mr. Snow." Steven placed the milk and cookies by the cash register.

"Afternoon." Snow had seen the Sinclaires leave that morning, their car loaded with the boy's college stuff. He did not indicate that Steven's return now was in any way unusual. Eyeing the book bag, he made change. "Back from college a little early," he observed.

"A little early," Steven agreed, "You wouldn't happen to know of any jobs around town, would you, Mr. Snow?"

"You looking for work?"

"Yes."

"Changed your mind about going to school, I guess."

"Yes."

"Hummm." Mr. Snow left the cash register and resumed his shelf work. Steven followed. "What kind of job do you have in mind?"

"Any kind."

"Like carpentry or painting or some such?"

"Like that, yes."

"Probably wouldn't pay much."

"No. But I wouldn't need much." If Cousin Elizabeth gave him refuge, his needs would be modest.

"Bob Casey's just starting out on his own. Probably he'd be happy to know where he could get cheap labor."

"I don't think I know Bob Casey."

"Comes from Harwich. Married the Benson girl. You know where the old Pollard place is, down-street?"

"Sure."

"He's putting on a new roof. You could talk to him right now, I expect."

The crab clutched tightly. The moment had come. "Would it be OK with you if I left my bag behind the counter?"

"Expect so," Snow agreed.

The pavings of the sidewalk were uneven, like teeth that needed straightening. The lovely old trees dappled the dust on the road's edge as he approached the Pollards' house, square and hip roofed as so many of the older captain's houses in Waterford were. It had a pretty fan of glass over the front door and a lilac bush on either side of the steps. But between the Depression and the war, the house had deteriorated, its paint old and dull, the bushes along the sidewalk scraggy and unkempt, the front lawn a riot of weeds.

At the rear of the place was the sound of pounding, ripping and shattering as the old, weathered, and mossy slate roofing hit the ground. Brittle bits of tar paper and bent, rusted nails littered the back yard, along with the slates. Surely they needed to be picked up. By someone.

By me, Steven thought.

"Mr. Casey?"

Up on the roof, one of two men paused and looked around. "You callin' me?" He had not raised his voice, but Steven had no trouble hearing him.

"Can I come up and talk to you?" Surely it would not do to ask the older man to come down. "Sure." Casey turned to his companion and said something Steven couldn't hear as he gripped the sides of the ladder and started up. It bounced and rattled with each step, unlike steel trusses on a railroad bridge.

"I'm Steven Sinclaire. Mr. Snow, at the store, said you might be interested in hiring help. I'm willing to do whatever you need."

Casey sized him up. "He says he'll do anything, Hubie," he said to his co-worker, an old and wizened man.

"That mean he'll tote shingles?" the old fellow asked.

"Hubie wants to know if you can carry shingles up to us."

"Sure."

"And pick up the old slates and take them to the dump?"

"Sure."

"And collect all the old nails that might be laying about?"

"Yup."

Bob Casey smiled. His face was the kindest that Steven had ever seen, his eyes crinkling at the corners and twinkling as he spoke. "Ever done any carpentry work before?"

"No, sir. I delivered newspapers when I was in high school, and worked as a counselor at Camp Quivet the last two summers. I wouldn't need any money right away, Mr. Casey. You can find out first if I'm good enough." It would take a long time to get anywhere, working for nothing, but he had to get started, and he liked this man. "I can clean up the stuff on the ground right now."

Casey turned to his cohort. "Says he'll start right now, Hubie."

"Now would be good," Hubie agreed.

"OK, youngster. Let's see your stuff."

"Thanks, Mr. Casey!"

"Bob. The name is Bob."

"OK, Bob!" Hurrying down the ladder, Steven slung the shingles and tar paper into the truck, then took a nearby rake to clear away the scraps and splinters, then set to collecting the nails. The Oreos and milk disappeared and he worked steadily until Casey and Hubie stiffly climbed down the ladder. They stretched appreciatively, grunting and grimacing, glancing around at Steven's efforts.

"By the Jesus, it won't hurt my feelin's none to have someone else totin' shingles up to the roof tomorrow," the old fellow remarked.

"Know what you mean," Casey agreed.

"It don't hurt my feelin's none to have this junk all raked up and in the truck already, neither. Think he's any good at scraping?"

"We're supposed to paint the house trim," Casey told Steven. "If you want, you could start on that in between bringin' us shingles."

"Bitch of a job, scraping," Hubie said. "Wouldn't hurt my feelin's none to have someone younger than me doin' it."

Steven's throat had mysteriously closed up.

"Hubie's right. That's tough work. I can't pay you much. Would seventy-five cents an hour be all right?" Casey asked.

Steven nodded. "You bet."

"When it rains, we don't work on roofs, and we can't paint, and you're not going to be able to help with carpentry until you learn how. So it's not like there'll be steady work."

"It'll be fine, honest."

"Good." Casey held out his hand, and they shook on it. "Be here tomorrow at 7:00."

"Right! And thanks."

He hurried back to the store to fetch his bag. "You were right, Mr. Snow!" he exclaimed as he burst in, then saw the man was busy with a customer. "Oh—sorry."

"This here's a good brand," Snow said to the customer. "I sell a lot of it." He picked a can off a nearby shelf. "Miss Edgarton has your bag," he said over his shoulder. "She was in earlier, so I gave it to her." He turned back to the customer. "But some folks like this one," he went on without missing a beat.

"Um, thanks." At least he was spared having to tell Cousin Elizabeth that he had defected. And since she'd taken his bag to Kingsland, she probably expected him to stay the night. What she might agree to after that remained to be seen. He was too tired to even care about it right now.

The old house seemed monumentally large as he crossed the street and went around to the kitchen door, knocking loudly before letting himself in.

She was at the sink, scraping carrots.

"Where've you been?" she demanded without looking up. "Your grandmother and I expected you long before this."

"Working."

She looked up. "Working?"

"As a carpenter's helper. With Bob Casey. Do you know him?"

"No. I never heard of him. How much will he pay you?"

"Seventy-five cents an hour, when it doesn't rain."

"And when it does?"

"There'll be nothing for me to do until I learn enough carpentry to be able to work indoors."

Filling the saucepan with water, she put the carrots on the stove, turned one of the knobs and struck a match. Blue flame popped up. "And you propose to support yourself on seventy-five cents an hour?" she asked.

"I, um, hoped you would let me stay here. If I could, I wouldn't need more than that."

"Here at Kingsland."

"Yes, until I've earned enough money to go to college."

"I must be getting senile. Could have sworn you were already on your way to Harvard. Let's join your grandmother in the parlor." She led him there. "Look, Elvira."

Grandmother Merrick was knitting. "Well, here you are!" She held her cheek up for a kiss. "We were wondering where you'd disappeared to."

"He's been working."

"Really! As in, having a job?"

"Yes. Picking trash up in the Pollard's back yard," Steven told her.

"Ah," she nodded. "We wondered what was going on over there."

"New roof," he explained.

Cousin Elizabeth sat down in her favorite chair, waved him toward another. "Why are you here at all, Steven?"

He'd rehearsed this part all afternoon. "I don't want to go to Harvard. I want to go to college in Ohio."

"Why ever would you want to do a thing like that? An unknown school in Ohio rather than Harvard?" Grandmother asked.

"I grew up there, and I like the people. They're friendly."

"Unlike New Englanders, I suppose," Elizabeth snipped.

Ignoring this, he pushed on. "Father wants me to be like him. That's why he wants me to go to Harvard. But I don't want to be like him. I want to be myself."

"Well, I can understand that," Grandmother declared. "If you'll remember, Elizabeth, your mother wanted you to be something quite different than you were."

"True, true," Cousin Elizabeth nodded. "Somewhat in reverse, but true. Good observation, Elvira."

"And your mother?" Grandmother asked. "What does she think?"

"I didn't have a chance to talk about it with her." Or about anything else after their confrontation in the tower last night, aside from the usual and expected remarks riders in cars make. "I wouldn't be an expense to you," he said to Cousin Elizabeth. "You can have the money I make. It ought to pay for my food."

"That would certainly be a help," she said. "I'm not made of money, though I believe your father thinks I am."

"You offered once to pay for a season at Camp, as I remember," Steven said. "Both of them probably think you can afford whatever you want."

"Not true," Grandmother Merrick put in. "She spent everything paying off your grandfather's debts."

The conversation halted, no doubt in deference to Grandfather Merrick's memory. Grandmother knitted on, her lips trembling.

"So this fellow Casey has given you work, and you propose to stay here, which puts your grandmother and me square in the middle of a family problem. Is that right?" Elizabeth asked.

"I'm afraid so."

"Sinclaire has always been a problem," Grandmother said, having recovered from the passing moment of mourning. "He's never let your mother come here by herself for a visit. We think he may be trying to control her."

Again there was silence, and Steven looked at his filthy fingernails. What could he say?

"It looks a little as though he's trying to control you, too," Elizabeth observed. "What do you think, Elvira?"

"I think you're right." Grandmother watched Steven closely. "When will they get back to Port Huron?"

"Probably sometime tomorrow."

"Perhaps you'd better clean up," Elizabeth suggested, "and get ready for supper. Those carrots are going to boil dry unless we do something about them."

Fetching his book bag, Steven climbed up to the tower, dropped the bag, went back down two flights and fetched a towel from the linen closet. Bark and tar paper bits and grit poured onto the bathroom floor as he peeled off his T-shirt and jeans. Somewhere there was a dust pan. He'd have to ask, and clean up his mess after supper. Or was it really dinner, with a properly set table?

Changing into the extra clothes he'd brought along, he went downstairs where the meal was on the kitchen table, already served. Apparently Cousin Elizabeth and Grandmother did not dine off china and crystal and sterling. Nor was dinner the repast that Charles Sinclaire always insisted it should be. Soggy carrots, cold sliced ham, some left-over clam chowder, crackers, a pot of tea.

From habit he held his Grandmother's chair and tucked her in, went around to his own while Cousin Elizabeth seated herself.

"If you're planning on staying here, you can't take such long showers," she said as they helped themselves to the chowder. "Uses up all the hot water."

Had they decided he could stay? "Sorry," he said. "The chowder is delicious. Did you make it?"

"I did," said Grandmother. "Elizabeth isn't much of a cook."

"I'm good at scraping carrots though."

"Indeed you are," Grandmother nodded.

He could wait no longer. "Then can I stay here, Cousin Elizabeth?"

"May. 'May I stay here.'"

"May I?"

"We're thinking that if you're willing to do a little work around the place, then I wouldn't have to hire help to do what needs to be done. I might even be better off."

"Anything you want—or need. I'll do it, if I can."

"But there's one stipulation that we're going to make," she rolled on. "It's about college. We don't care which one. We just want you to promise that you'll go, somewhere, some time."

"Meanwhile," Grandmother said, "there's a lot of work to be done here. When it rains."

"You might see if you can get this Mr. Casey to show you how to reputty storm windows," Cousin Elizabeth said, pouring tea into three mugs. "That could be one of your jobs around this place, come fall. If you agree."

Agree! Dare he thank her? She was odd about things like that, and he didn't want to annoy her. "Repaying you for your kindness is the least I can do." That was pretty close, he thought.

"I don't want to take all the money you earn," she said. "In the first place, you won't earn very much. In the second place, you've got to have something of your own, or you'll be begging me for nickels and quarters continuously."

His ears burned as his irritation began to rise.

"When can you get your things? The bags you left at the bus station?"

"Sunday, I expect. I think Mr. Casey works on Saturdays."

"Carpenters work in cold weather, too. It'll give me a lot to knit about," said his grandmother. Her smile was a deep one, her eyes tender. Would she really have disowned her illegitimately pregnant daughter 18 years ago?

"You may take the garbage out now," Elizabeth instructed. "It's under the sink."

"Father will probably be calling tomorrow night, after the rates change."

"Probably."

"He may be upset with you, for letting me stay here."

"He may."

"So what will you say?"

"Me?" She smiled wickedly. "I'm not going to say anything. It's you who'll have to deal with him."

"Well, that's a problem," he confessed. "I really don't know how."

"I'd say you already have," Grandmother observed.

"She's right. You're here, aren't you? I'd suggest you advise him to call the college and get his money back." The prospect was very agreeable. "Once you're acclimated to your new job, you can start learning to play bridge. Then we can be a foursome, you and your grandmother and Mr. Snow and I," she dictated. So, old man Snow was a friend. No doubt he had told her he'd sent Steven to talk with Bob Casey. Probably she'd figured everything all out long before he walked through the door.

"I'll be glad to learn bridge," he declared. "What else would you like?"

She actually chuckled. "We'll start with digging a hole for an oil tank. It's time we got a new furnace. But for now, bridge will do."

The old ladies set themselves to clearing the table and washing up the dishes while he took the garbage out to the pail set into the ground, with an iron lid and a step-on lever to open it. The evening was a lovely one, and he walked to the edge of the yard, looked up. Clouds in the western sky hurried to witness the setting of the September sun, their underbellies flushing, their tops darkened. The sky became deep and lustrous as the sun touched the rim of the world; the breeze of the fall season, coming now from the northwest, whispered its winter warning in the trees. A line of descending ducks was stitched in the sky and he watched as they reversed themselves and dropped closer to the earth, and heard them calling, calling until they coasted to their nighttime destination beyond his vision.

And then the sun was gone.

The clouds, having seen what they came to see, dispersed and the bright star of evening watched now from the cool, clear sky, and Steven, also watching, was somehow made pure, emptied for that moment of his angers and hurts and poisons, an empty vessel into which the peace and benediction of the evening and of the season was poured.

Cousin Elizabeth was going to help.

He could ask no more. For now.

✦❈ 2 ❈✦

The winter, with its odd jobs for Bob Casey and many tasks for Cousin Elizabeth, had passed. Now, early in May, Howard Ware from Camp Quivet pulled into the driveway of the old Blake place, got out of his truck and wandered over to the ladder, at the top of which Steven was waiting for Bob Casey's instructions.

"Can you hold the flashin' right here?"

"I think so," Steven grunted, pressing the copper strip against the bricks of the chimney.

He couldn't look at Howard Ware from this position, and hoped the man wouldn't call to him at this delicate point. Focus and concentration were needed; Ware seemed to understand that and was quiet.

The flat-head nail pierced the soft copper and sank its length in one stroke.

"All right!" Bob said. He moved down a bit, again sinking another nail perfectly. "Better find out what Ware wants," he said. "And bring up another bundle of shingles with you when you come back."

"Hope I'm not interrupting you," Ware called up.

"Nope," Bob called back. "We need more shingles anyway."

"Well, hello," Mr. Ware said heartily when Steven reached the ground, and held his hand out to be shaken. "How's the carpentry going?"

"Pretty good," Steven said. "Mr. Casey's a great teacher."

Ware smiled. "Glad to hear it. How about we sit in my car and talk?"

"I can't," Steven said. "I'm working."

"It looks like hard work, too, up there on the roof. Do you plan to do carpentry this summer?"

"I hope so. When it's raining, I'll help Miss Edgarton, my cousin, with some projects around her house." This past Sunday he had removed the seaweed from Kingsland's foundation, a time-honored though largely unsuccessful Cape Cod solution to drafts. The house had been impossibly frigid all winter, despite the new furnace. But all of its woodwork had been freshly sanded and painted, its many windows reputtied.

Howard Ware looked him straight in the eye. "I was hoping you'd want to work at camp again. You can teach sailing, if you want."

"I already have a job, Mr. Ware." Steven moved toward the stack of bundled shingles. "And I plan to stick with it." Up on the roof Bob hammered steadily.

"I'd pay you well, Steve. You're very valuable to us, and enrollment is rising."

"No, thanks."

"How about sailing clinics on Saturdays. You're not working as a carpenter on Saturday, are you?"

"During the summer I expect we'll work seven days a week." He picked up a bundle of shingles. "Thanks anyway."

"You're such a good sailor," Howard Ware persisted. "Won't you miss it?"

"Mr. Casey's a good sailor too, and he has his own boat. We go out in it sometimes." He started for the ladder and rested the corner of the bundle on a rung. "I have to make my own way now, Mr. Ware. I have to earn my living all year, not just in the summer."

"Your father hopes that you'll take the Quivet job and go to Harvard in the fall. He's willing to double whatever I'm able to pay."

Steven disliked being rude. He had been taught to treat adults with respect, and besides, he had always liked Mr. Ware. But his anger flared at the very mention of Charles Sinclaire, and he put the shingles down. Bob Casey looked over the edge of the scaffolding, put his hammer in the loop of his nail pocket. "Time for lunch," he announced loudly as the ladder rattled and bounced with his rapid descent. Any comment Steven might had been about to make was interrupted.

"I hope you're not tryin' to hire this boy away from me," Bob said to Ware when he got to the bottom.

"I was only thinking about what would be best for him," Ware said stiffly. "Higher education is important."

"Yes, it is," Steven said. "And I'll get it. But not now, and not at Harvard. You might mention that when you speak to Mr. Sinclaire next. Please excuse us; like Mr. Casey said, it's lunch time."

In unison they turned away from Ware, walked over to Bob's truck where their lunch buckets waited. Usually they ate right where they were parked, but this time Bob drove onto the low road, past the Marshalls' place, then past Kingsland and down to the parking lot at the old packet landing. Several other workmen sat in trucks with their lunch, drinking coffee, smoking.

"No point loiterin'," Bob explained the hasty departure. "He might think of something more to say."

"He might at that," Steven's anger had dissipated. The turkey sandwich—one of three—that Grandmother had packed was skimpy, more bread than meat, but liberally spread with mayonnaise. Cousin Elizabeth had baked some cookies, an endeavor she continually tried to master, without success. Maybe he could persuade Bob to take one or two.

"I'm goin' to bid on the old mill project," Casey said between bites of meat loaf sandwich, full and luscious. "This spring, the town passed a proposal to reconstruct the original buildin'. It'll give me work all next winter, and be a good chance to start teachin' you carpentry, if you're still interested." It was Bob's way of asking what Steven was planning.

"I had hoped to go to college in the fall, but I won't have saved enough money. So I'll be right here, and I'd like it if I could learn carpentry."

"I can probably raise your pay to a dollar an hour. That might help."

"Sure would! Thanks!" What a decent man Bob was! But it would not do to say so. "What would help the most is if you took a cookie or two."

"OK. There's a hole out back of my house. They'd make good fill." Bob had sampled Elizabeth's wares before. "And since now you're permanently employed by me, how about we go to the Ace-High when we're done today."

"That'd be good," he remarked, trying to sound casual. Waterford's tradesmen gathered at the Ace-High at the end of each work day, and going there with Bob meant that he'd be considered one of them.

"I'll buy. It's called a fringe benefit, I think."

"I think it is," Steven agreed with inward rejoicing.

At 5:00 they drove to the roadhouse after a long afternoon on the roof. The interior of the Ace-High was not elaborate; booths on one wall, bar on the other, just inside the door. A pool table dominated the far end, with stools and chairs scattered nearby for observers. There were restrooms and a jukebox and that was all, but it was enough.

The place was well-populated with men in work-worn overalls, pungent shirts, their sweat-stained caps still in place, their quiet voices mumbling and rumbling and occasionally breaking out in a rash of laughter. A few were at the bar, some were standing around while they talked and finished a bottle of beer. Several were leaving.

"Casey!" they acknowledged without looking at Steven.

"Hey." Bob took a place at the bar and gestured to the stool next to his. "Draft?" he asked.

Gratefully Steven nodded and drank half when it arrived.

"You're a good worker, Steve," Bob said.

"I try. And I appreciate the chance," Steven assured him.

"No, I mean that a lot of city kids would have quit after the first week," Bob insisted, more talkative with the aid of his quickly consumed beer. After so much work, a little beer went a long way at the end of the day; a bit of a buzz was not hard to achieve. "You were no different than them. Your hands weren't calloused, your back not used to carrying a lot of stuff up and down ladders, yourself not used to sweating, I expect."

"I was never quite that spoiled," Steven said. "My friends and I lifted weights in the basement and did yard work in the summers. With so many men gone during the war, there were a lot of folks who needed someone to clean out gutters and mow lawns and stuff. In winter we shoveled snow and even after the war we had work." What Charles

Sinclaire thought of such demeaning activities he never learned, and now he did not have to care.

"Good thing for me," Bob remarked.

The bartender came by. "Another?"

"Sure," Bob said. "We're celebrating."

"Celebratin' what?" asked the bartender.

"This boy," Bob gestured, "is going to work with me this coming winter. He's going to help renovate the mill sites for the town, him and Hubie and me."

"You got the contract already?"

"Not yet. But as soon as the biddin' opens, I'll put mine in."

"Well, I'll drink to that!" From under the bar the man took a glass half full of amber liquid, waved it toward Bob while carefully not waving it at Steven.

Nodding toward the bar keeper, Bob said, "This here is Ed Pollard."

Ed Pollard reached across the bar to shake hands, in the manner of countrymen looking elsewhere as he did so.

"Steve is old lady Edgerton's cousin," Bob continued.

"I thought he was her nephew," Ed said.

"I thought he was her kid," interjected the drinker to Bob's left.

"I'm not, thank goodness," Steven told him, bringing laughter all around.

"We're at the Blake's old place now," Bob said. "Hubie and Steve and me."

"That so?" Ed remarked, as though he did not believe anyone related to old lady Edgerton would work with his hands. He turned to another customer who, from what Steven could gather, was asking who the new young fellow with Bob Casey was. Bob spoke unintelligibly to the man on his other side and Steven waited patiently while everyone ignored him. The second beer was going to put him over the edge, he knew. He was much too tired to down two of them. But it was pleasant, sitting here in the midst of rough but honest men who might accept him, in time, despite the handicap of being a Merrick.

"This here is Arnie Stone," Bob said at last, leaning back a bit so that Steven could see the fellow on his far side. Apparently introductions were performed selectively in Waterford.

"Casey here went on his own just last year," Stone said to Steven. "In case he didn't tell you."

"He didn't. Mr. Snow did," Steven said. He suspected that Mr. Snow's indirect endorsement had done him no harm.

"It takes guts to go it alone," Stone continued. "But we all have to do it sometime."

"I'd rather you didn't say that to the boy," Bob interjected. "I've just got done procurin' his services for the foreseeable future, and I don't want him getting ideas."

They laughed. "Bob worked for me," Arnie Stone said. "'Til last year." It would seem this caused no resentment on Stone's part, although Bob was now a competitor. "Plenty of work for all of us. I think soon there's going to be more than we can handle. Lots of new places to put up, not just repairin' the old ones."

"I think you're right." Bob stood, gesturing in farewell. "We gotta go."

They went, walking back to the truck a little unevenly—the parking lot was rough, after all! Steven hung onto the dashboard as Bob bumped over potholes to Main Street and on to Kingsland.

"7:00 tomorrow."

"Right." Steven waved him off with the small unobtrusive gesture countrymen used on such occasions, went around to the kitchen door to let himself in, called to Cousin Elizabeth and Grandmother, promising to join them soon, and mounted the back stairs to take a shower—a quick one. Wrapped up in a towel, he went on up to the tower to put on fresh clothes, sat for a few moments to look out. It was nearly full dark now, the sky only a bit brighter than the land, the occasional lights on Main Street doing little to penetrate the evening but indicating the town was there.

This was his place. He had work for as long as he needed it; he was beginning to gain acceptance by the townsmen despite being the nephew or cousin or god-knew-what to Elizabeth Edgerton. If he believed in the Almighty, he'd be on his knees now, giving thanks. Since he no longer did, he gave thanks to the earth, instead, and the sky, and the sea.

He was free.

∞ 3 ∞

"Hi! So you're the guy who's fixing our house. I'm Janet Crawford."

The girl, hand on hip, loitered at the foot of the ladder with her friends, all of them looking up at Steven who was painting trim on the second story windows. Propped up against trees in the yard were the shutters for all the windows, to be scraped and sanded and painted by Hubie. They would be a deep blue when he finished, but since he only worked half days, finishing anything was apt to be a prolonged process.

The Crawfords had bought the old Warden house west of town during the depression, paid Waterford tradesmen to maintain it during the war, and now used it to entertain their extended family and city friends during the halcyon months. The Crawford girl's college pals stood with her at the bottom of the ladder, holding tennis raquets. They were all pretty, bronzed delicately, their hair bleached by the sun. One of them called up. "Are you going to come with us tonight?"

"It depends where you're going." No longer worried by height, Steven descended. He'd done a lot of painting and shingling by now; he was getting good at ladders.

"The Ace-High," Janet said. "We want to hang out at the Ace-High, like bad girls. We'd feel a lot better about it if a person who knows his way around Waterford came with us."

"A local," one of the girls put in. "Are you local?"

"Can you protect us against lewd and lascivious males?" asked another.

"I don't know. It depends on what lewd and lascivious means," he answered, playing the expected role of uneducated workman.

"Shall we tell him?" they conferred with one another.

"No," they agreed. "Not yet."

"Are you local?" the first questioner persisted.

"A little," he smiled. "Enough to know the guys who might be there. What time?"

"Oh—eight or nine o'clock."

Of course. They didn't have to be on a ladder at 7:00 in the morning, working through the heat of an August day. They could start partying late and get in late, sleeping until noon, if need be.

"OK," he agreed. He could tough it out if he had to. Probably there would be a few local young men at the Ace-High; hobnobbing with the summer visitors could yield interesting results, they'd all found. Refilling his paint can, he nodded. "I'll see you later."

They departed to the tennis court, and he heard the hollow "thwock" of the ball back and forth, heard them laughing, jeering at each other when a shot was missed, a little louder than necessary, he thought, probably wanting to keep his attention on them. Well, it worked. He hadn't had a date since he'd arrived in Waterford, so exhausted at the end of the day that the thought of girls seemed hardly to matter. But with real girls in the offing—not just the thought of them—well, now, that seemed like a good place to start.

Bob drove in at the end of the day, helping with the paint brushes and empty cans and sealing up the partially used ones. "The shutters?" he asked.

"Hubie didn't show up," Steven explained.

"OK. How long do you think the windows will take?"

"I wish I knew," Steven said. "I'm sorry. Finishing just one seems to take forever."

"I'll work on the shutters tomorrow, then," Bob said, appearing unperturbed by the length of time it took a neophyte to complete painting colonial-style windows, 12 over 12. In fact, it was a time consuming job, and no one knew it better than Bob himself. "If Hubie comes by, I'll help with the windows. It'll go that much faster. Come on. I'll take you home."

There was little to say on the ride to Kingsland, but silences with Bob Casey were comfortable, and Steven had learned to enjoy them. Once home, he showered briskly and had dinner with Grandmother and Cousin Elizabeth, taking out the garbage as was their bargain. It was unusual for him to go out in the evening, but neither lady asked questions. They were not his parents; they did not stand *in loco parentis.* Nor did they ask him how late he'd be, for which he was grateful.

The Ace-High was a couple of miles down on Main Street, a bit of a hike after all day on a ladder, but he did not allow complaints, even to himself. A girl was a girl, after all! Arriving before Janet Crawford and her friends did, he slid onto a bar stool and ordered beer. Gus Pollard and Phil Sears were there already. They were older than he was, and would buy his beer themselves. He would pay them back; thus Gus's uncle, the bar-tender, would not be guilty of selling to a minor.

"Evening," Steven greeted the boys.

"Evenin'," they chorused, looking at themselves and him in the mirror behind the bar. They were hardworking kids who had been willing to accept him—provisionally, he knew. After all, he was a Merrick.

After another round, Gus said, "Take you on at billiards."

"You sure you want to do that?" Steven asked with the usual jockeying around for position. "I might beat your ass."

"Did ya' hear that, Philly?" Gus asked his friend.

"Sounds like he thinks he's better than you," Phil Sears nodded. "I'll bet on him." In this way they included him. He would never be one of them, but he was a pretty good shot and understood their ways. Never were they uncomfortable because he was a Merrick. "Shall the meetin' come to order at the pool table?" Phil asked.

"I so move," Steven said, picking up his beer and selecting a cue.

They had just racked the balls when Janet Crawford and her friends arrived. Though there were only four of them, they seemed to fill up the place with their high-pitched chatter and excited giggles.

Steven waved them over. "You're just in time," he told them. "The match is about to begin. Pull up a chair."

Janet dragged one to a position at the middle of the table. "I'll be the referee," she said. She was a live wire, Steven thought, unlike the other three who went to the juke box and poured over the selections, then sat in a booth and languidly chattered while they drank ginger ale and Coca-Cola, sizing up Philly and Gus.

A pleasant, non-competitive game went forward, one that Gus won easily.

"Sinclaire's just warmin' up." Ronnie Tabor, recently arrived, pulled up a chair opposite Janet, beer in hand. "I'll play you, Gus, and then I'll take him on."

Two young men from out of town appeared from nowhere. Steven wasn't sure of their names. They were college kids with summer jobs, and the girls left the booth and pulled bar stools closer to the pool table, the better to be on display.

Steven finished his beer while Ronnie beat Gus; now it was time for a play-off. Chalking their cues, they stalked around the table like cats preparing for encounter. Ronnie, as winner of the previous match, broke the balls, dropped one in the pocket.

"Stripes it is," he declared, and put two in before he missed and it was Steven's turn.

"Come on, Sinclaire!" one of the college kids called, clapping his hands while the other stomped his feet. "Our money's on you."

"I'm betting on the other kid," one of Janet Crawford's friends called. "Come on, Other Kid!"

"His name is Ron," Steven told her, while circling the table. Ronnie would never have introduced himself. You could sit at the Ace-High all night and no one would tell you their name. They'd talk to you, maybe. But it took an intermediary to do the introducing.

"I'm Mari."

"Her name is Mary," he said to Ronnie, and sank a solid.

"No, it's Mari," she corrected.

He glanced at Philly, who shrugged. He missed the next shot because his concentration was broken, trying to understand what she was saying.

"Mary?" he asked as Ronnie readied himself for his shot.

"Mari."

"What's the difference?" Gus asked.

The ball dropped into the pocket. And another.

"How do you pronounce the name of the mother of Jesus?" she asked Gus.

"Mary."

"What do you call it when two people are in a ceremony that make them husband and wife?"

"They get married. Marry!"

"And how do you say it when you bang up a piece of furniture and ruin the finish?"

"I say, Oh, damn," offered one of the college boys. "Damn, I banged up that piece of furniture."

The group laughed happily

"Mar. To mar the piece of furniture," Steven said, without noticing that Ronnie had sunk all the striped balls, but had missed the eight. "You mean, Mar-ee?"

"Mari. Right. Mari Crawford. I'm Janet's cousin."

"I'm Steve Sinclaire."

"I'm winnin'," Ronnie grinned.

Steven nodded to Mar-ee Crawford. "Please excuse me."

"Sure thing," she smiled prettily.

"Any bets?" he called. "Place your bets now or forever hold your peace."

They booed. "We already bet on you," cried one of the college kids. "Do something! Please!"

He refocused, circled the table, lining up his shot and sinking the eight.

"Nuts," said Ronnie. "I'm goin' home. You comin' Philly? Gus?"

"Not yet," Phil said, standing beside one of Janet's pretty friends. "You play Gus a game, while I buy Little Miss Sunshine, here, a beer."

The out-of-towners drifted away. Ronnie bought another pitcher for the group; the girls took on the boys, losing with gusto, then the boys teamed up and played more rounds until the bar closed at 1:00.

It was decided that the pool players were too inebriated to drive, let alone find their way home. Everyone discussed it in the parking lot, draped over Janet Crawford's car.

"I'd be glad to take anyone wherever they need to go," said Mari Crawford. She had drunk nothing alcoholic, and was more than capable of driving.

"Sounds good to me," said Janet, whose car the girls were using. "But there are too many of us to fit in."

"Not if we squeeze real tight," said Phil. "I'd really druther not go home. My Mom hates it when I drink. My Dad's an alcoholic. Did I ever tell you that?" he asked Steven.

"Tell me what?" Steven asked, looking up at the star spangled sky, falling over backward. Ronnie and Phil reached for him. All three went down.

"About my old man."

"No. You never did," he replied, stargazing more easily from this position.

"The problem is my mother."

"Well, look," Steven told him, "there's a storage shed at the back of my place. It's got hay bales in it. We can break them open, and all of us can sleep there. Together."

"What fun!" one of the girls exclaimed.

"And what do we tell my parents in the morning?" Janet asked crossly.

"You drive everyone home at sunrise, before your folks are even out of bed. You slip into the house..."

"Yeah," said Ronnie, nuzzling one of the girls, "as long as we leave before Miss Edgarton is out of bed, so she don't see us and call the cops."

"Who is she?" Mari Crawford asked.

"She owns the shed. A lady of the old school. Hard as nails."

"You don't want to run into her in the dark," Philly agreed. "You'd get a black and blue spot even just looking at her." They laughed loud at this non-witticism as only drunken fools will do, and climbed into Janet's car which filled instantly with alcoholic fumes.

"I'll get tipsy just breathing in here," Mari Crawford complained, winding down her window. "Tell me where to go."

Steven sat beside her in the passenger seat with two of the girls on his lap. "Left," he directed.

Shortly, the car headlights lit up the circular driveway. "Kill the lights," Steven instructed, "and turn right."

Very, very slowly they cruised carefully past the house and into the yard beyond, up to Kingsland's tool shed.

"We're trespassing," Janet observed. "This is a private estate."

"You mean we're breaking and entering?" Mar-ee asked.

"Not if you have a key," Steven assured her.

"Do you have one?"

"I do."

"Are you the caretaker here, or something?"

The boys laughed, quietly so as not to wake a nearby sleeper.

"Good Christ," Philly whispered loudly. "He's the fuckin' heir."

The old Warden place was very similar to the Elijah Merrick house (now belonging to the Marshalls). In its back yard the Crawfords had built tennis courts and a cottage where guests might stay for a week or a month or a summer. It was perfect for parties, like the one planned for tonight.

Waterford was a relatively quiet place—quite inadequate to meet the social needs of young college girls, but since Janet had a car of her own, this posed no problem. Much more was going on in Hyannis, and she drove her friends there often. They had met numerous other vacationing collegians in bars, some of whom were coming up to Waterford tonight for the party.

Frank Sinatra was crooning loudly on the radio when Steven arrived, and the Crawford's driveway was crowded with parked cars. This posed no problem for him, since he had walked. And he could walk back to Kingsland any time he chose, if he didn't like what he found.

College kids were apt to be overbearing, automatically assuming that the workers of the world were dull and slow-witted. He expected to be ignored by them, since he had neither a college nor a fraternity to talk about.

Ordinarily he would never have considered attending such a party. But he had spent a night in the hay with Mari Crawford; they had lain together chastely, and in the dawn-light they had snuggled and kept each other warm. He would welcome more. Much more.

Besides, he found her interesting—the way she held herself separate from the drinkers while appearing to enjoy them, the way she had efficiently ferried them to the tool shed, the way she'd helped Steven break the hay bales and spread them, the way she gathered him to herself, once they laid down, and pillowed his head. The way she helped him repack everyone into Joan's car in the morning, herself behind the wheel. He had walked beside her, guiding the car along an access path that ran behind the old carriage barn to the Rockford Road. It had seemed like a good idea not to pass by the house; Cousin Elizabeth was an early riser.

Mari had invited him to the party as they were leaving, careful to keep her voice low so that it wouldn't carry in the early morning stillness, and he had been happy to accept. With misgivings, since he knew he wouldn't fit in (did he fit anywhere, he wondered?) But he wouldn't be able to see her again unless he did—she was leaving tomorrow—and so here he was, skirting the main house that was well lit, signaling the presence of adults, letting the party-goers know they were being monitored, albeit from a distance.

"Hi!" she welcomed him. "I've been watching for you."

There was a small front porch at the cottage and she was on it, watching through the screens. Inside, a few couples swayed to "All of Me" in the livingroom, while more young people leaned against the counters in the kitchen and chatted. The tone of the party was low-key and pleasant, and he began to relax. Two bottles of beer were found in the ice-filled bathtub, and he followed Mari back to the porch where she had arranged two chairs and a small wrought iron table with a candle.

"So you do drink," he observed, opening the bottles.

"A little."

"But not the other night, at the Ace High."

"Usually stay sober when I'm with my cousin."

"Smart."

"You bet."

They clinked bottles in an unspoken, unspecific toast, and the candle was lit.

"Tell me about yourself, please," he said, taking her off guard. Usually the girl's job was to get the boy talking, but he didn't want to disclose much of himself at this point.

"Well, I live in Arlington, Indiana, near Indianapolis. I go to college in Ohio."

"Where?"

"At a school in Delphi. Athens College. I'll bet you don't go to college at all."

"Not yet. I'm trying to earn enough money to cover the first year, at least. And learning a trade, in case I need one."

"Well, now, I am confused." Her skin was flawless in the glow of candlelight. "I heard the other night that you are going to inherit that magnificent house in the middle of town."

"At present I'm the handyman. My cousin owns the house. I believe my mother will inherit it, and then me, so it'll be quite a while before I'm lord of the manor."

"Still, you'd best get yourself educated so you can make a lot of money. You might need quite a bit for maintenance, one day."

"Probably," he agreed.

"Everyone is hoping to work for a big company now. That's where the money is."

"I'm not opposed to making a bundle." They drank another toast to that prospect. Then a commotion—a small, muffled one—went on just outside the porch. Someone knocked on the screened door and a low voice—a young man's voice—called, "Janet?"

Mari looked up quizzically. "Who is it?"

"A friend."

"Lots of friends!"

More shapes congregated around the door now.

"Janet, Janet darling come here, baby!"

It looked like trouble. "We'll find her," Steven told them, and took Mari's arm as he slid to his feet, pulling her along.

"Aren't you going to invite us in?"

"There's mosquitos out here."

"We'll let ourselves in."

They shuffled onto the porch and followed Steven and Mari into the cottage.

"Ohhh! Look who's here!" Janet squealed. "I'm so glad you could make it, you guys. We're nearly out of beer."

"We brought more, like we promised," they told her, and Steven saw that each of them carried a paper bag. "We have some good stuff, too." In the kitchen the contents of the bags were laid out on the counter. Varieties of beer, whiskey, mixers, a bag of Krystal Klear Ice. Steven signed Mari back onto the porch where the candle guttered.

"I'm not going to stay," he told her. "I think there's going to be trouble, and I don't want my relatives to think I'm out carousing."

"You're just going to leave me here?" she asked plaintively.

"Not unless you'll come with me. But it's a long walk to Kingsland."

"You walked!"

"I don't have a car."

"Wow!" She thought for a moment. "I can use Janet's car. We could ride around a little, and then I can take you home."

"You know where her keys are?"

"I sure do."

"It beats walking," he grinned, and waited while she went inside to find them, came back onto the porch and blew out the candle.

"I don't think I'd trust those kids with fire," she remarked matter-of-factly, and once their eyes adjusted, led him off the porch and to the side of the cottage where the car was parked.

"Janet's parents are bound to be a little upset if the party gets out of control. What will they do about it?" He opened the door for her, went around to the passenger side.

"Call the police, I suppose."

Probably the Crawfords thought Waterford had a regular force, instead of only Roly Hall, police chief and dog officer. Waterford was ill-equipped in the face of any emergency save fire, but that was, no doubt, how Roly would manage a crowd of drunken college boys. The Crawfords would probably not be too happy to have the town's fire truck chewing up their lawn, but the kids would disperse soon enough in the presence of the volunteer fire force.

"In the meantime, what'll we do?" Mari asked.

"The hay is still spread out in the tool shed, just as we left it. We could hide out in there and talk."

"The tool shed is out," she declared.

"We could see if the tide is high," he offered regretfully. "I could take you for a sail." Safer, no doubt about it.

"There's no wind."

"Or for a ride in my dingy. I can row you around."

"I think we ought to go down to the beach and just talk."

"You don't trust my skill as an oarsman?" he scoffed.

"I do," she assured him. "But it sounds kind of damp, riding around in a rowboat in the dark."

"OK. We'll go down to the West Waterford fisherman's access." It had a small beach and parking lot of its own. Judging from the cluster of cars already there, mostly old ones, as well as a truck or two, quite a few seekers of privacy had arrived before them. Mari pulled over.

"Now this," she gestured at the congregation of neckers and petters, "is common."

"This? Finding a place where people can get to know each other?"

"All the cars in the same place, doing the same thing. That's what's common."

This did not bode well for his plans. "Well, then, how would young folks, who have nowhere else to go, get acquainted?"

Wrinkling up her nose, she thought about it. "Maybe in the woods, where no one can see."

"Would you go into the woods with me, if I knew of a good place?" He took her hand. It was small, and very soft.

Turning toward him, she said, "I might, if I knew you better. But I don't know you well enough for that. Until I do, I won't. You'd think I was fast and loose with boys. And I'm not."

"Is Janet?"

Mari paused. "I'm not sure. She's pretty wild, as you've probably guessed—but rich people are never common, no matter what they do."

"And Janet is rich."

"Oh, yes."

He moved in then, his face close to hers. "You're her family. So if we kissed each other, you wouldn't be common, because rich people never are. Even though we're in a parking lot filled with common-type people."

"I'm only a poor relation." She laughed quietly. "But maybe it rubs off—the rich part, I mean."

Her lips were lovely, warm and inviting. They had only snuggled before, in the hay, but had not as yet kissed. He'd forgotten how nice a woman's mouth could be. Putting Diana Harrison—and all girls—out of mind had included this aspect of friendship.

Now here was Mari Crawford. She seemed fairly conventional in certain ways. Further pursuit of kissing might be a mistake. Instead, conversation seemed required.

"Tell me about Athens College. I'm from Ohio, and I want to go back. Maybe Athens would be a good place to try for."

"I didn't know you were a mid-westerner!"

"We didn't have much time to talk last night."

"True," she laughed. "But we do now. What would you like to know? Maybe you should come to visit me later in the fall, after school's been in session for a while. I could show you around and you could talk to the admissions people."

Pretending to listen to what she was saying, he slipped a hand slowly over her breast, so soft, so lovely.

Pulling back, she took his hand away. "I really have to know you better, Steven."

"Sorry."

"Me, too. I'd like to know you better—but I'm leaving tomorrow; my parents will pick me up at noon and I'll go home and get packed and ready for school."

"I guess we'll have to wait until next year."

"Unless you visit me at Athens."

"Probably no privacy there, though."

"I'll arrange some." She turned the motor on, turned the car around, turned the lights on. Their dashboard glow illuminated the little smile on her face, and he rather thought that if he made the effort to visit her, she might indeed find them some privacy. After all, he'd have come all that way just to see her. He'd deserve special consideration, wouldn't he?

Maybe he could hitch-hike. It would save money....

CHAPTER

The Annhilation of Charles Sinclaire

*W**ar was the last thing on everyone's mind. While it was true that the communists in far-away Russia seemed hell-bent on a totalitarian course, and an expansionist one, too, the Marshall Plan showed Europe how fine and generous the American people were, reinforcing the superiority of democracy supported by capitalist enterprise.*

Indeed, capitalistic enterprise was filling the American marketplace with goods of all kinds. The G.I.'s, most of whom had grown up in the Depression, easily secured work. Along with their wives, they swore their children would never know the hardships they had faced in the thirties. Then arrangements were made in Levittown, New York, to sell its tiny tract houses rather than renting them. Home ownership became the fulfillment of the American dream, and making enough money to buy one became the goal of the middle-class family.

It was during this time that Alfred Kinsey made public his study of male sexuality. The domination of North Korea by Communists was not thought to be of much importance in comparison to the facts that Dr. Kinsey presented about promiscuity before marriage and infidelity after, sabotaging Americans' belief in in their own innocence.

But commercial television was on the rise, and this disturbing information could be easily forgotten by watching Hopalong Cassidy and I Love Lucy and by reading the comic strips, whose latest star was Charlie Brown. The shmoo, created by L'il Abner's author, was the national hero.

What was the point in worrying about a non-descript place like Korea, anyway?

June 25, 1950

"I'LL MISS THIS BOY, I really will," said A. Lincoln Sears. His voice was loud, and everyone at the Ace-High, embarrassed by this display of sentiment, looked away.

Steven lightened the moment. "I haven't left yet. You can miss me tomorrow."

"You really got to go?"

"I think I'd better."

"I thought you was leavin' in the fall," Hubie remarked.

"Changed my mind," he said briefly. Indeed, the plan had been to go in September, after working with Bob's crew this summer. But Elizabeth's death had made change necessary.

"Well, I'd like to toast Sinclaire's success," said Don Slater. "As long as success'll make him rich enough to retire to Waterford when he's old like us." Don was all of thirty.

"I'll drink to that," said Bob Casey.

"And we'll do all your repairs for you, Steve, because you'll have forgotten everything you ever knew, and be too fat and lazy to do them for yourself," Greenleaf Stone said. "And we'll charge you a fortune."

"Hear! Hear!" cried Ed Slater.

"Thanks," Steven laughed. "What pals you are." Most of them were older than he—some by quite a bit—but by God they *were* pals: they'd been good to him; they'd made him one of their own.

"He'll be able to afford it," Linc Sears assured the group. "Educated people always end up rich."

"That'd be nice," Steven agreed. Although they were only kidding around, he knew that they admired his determination to go to college. And they understood that he would never consider himself better than they were, no matter how rich he got. Nor would they consider him a failure if he never got rich at all.

Working shoulder to shoulder with them this past two and a half years, he had learned as much of their trade as could be expected in that time, had been accepted at Athens College with a full scholarship and had saved enough money to pay his room and board for the first year. Of course, some of this would be used up by the time the fall term started, because his scholarship wouldn't be available until the start of the academic year in September. Room, board and tuition would come out of his own pocket until then. But it was a sacrifice he was determined to make. He was not going to stay at Kingsland, because Charles Sinclaire would be living there. As executor of Elizabeth's will, he'd commute to Boston where Sommerset and Troy had offered him a position. True to his own style, Charles had started making these plans when Elizabeth had her first heart attack a month ago, counting on her death and finally, three days ago, attaining his longed-for position as manager of Kingsland.

Roly Hall appeared, pulled up a chair while declining a beer. "Can't drink on duty," he explained. "I might get relieved of my situation if I had alcohol on my breath whilst telling off them summer people." For years Roly had been Waterford's policeman and dog officer; since neither of these positions was full-time, he comfortably managed them from the office of his gas station, where he smoked cigars, gossiped with his cronies, and listened to his police radio, pride of his life. "Wanted to tell you that we're at war again."

"We're at war?" asked Bob Casey.

"We just got done with one," grumbled Ed Pollard.

"I heard about it on the police scanner."

"Where?"

"Someplace near Japan."

"Korea, maybe?" Steven asked.

"Yup. That's the place. So you're leavin' soon, Steve. Wanted to wish you luck."

"Thanks!"

"And if you ever want a job pumping gas, you come talk to me, hear?"

"Sure thing."

"Wanted to offer my condolences, too."

There was a pause—a counterpart of foot shuffling. "Thanks, Roly."

"This boy's going to be rich," Linc said quickly, so that more comments about Elizabeth's death would be unnecessary. "He won't need you, Roly, or your gas station."

"Wrong," declared Steven, forcing his voice past the tensing that had suddenly clutched at his throat. "One of these days I might forget myself and drive too fast. I'd need him then, wouldn't I? To fix my traffic ticket?"

They guffawed, because they could not remember Chief Hall ever fining a Waterford native for speeding through town. Stopping them, maybe. Asking them to keep it down, so no one would get hurt, if need be. But a ticket? It was against his principles. It was the summer folks who got the tickets.

They drank a toast to their policeman and dog-officer, and Steven watched them fondly. He would miss them.

"Here's a funny story," Arnie Stone said. "Today I was diggin' out at the edge of the marsh to see if a septic tank could be put in. I'd taken this heap of dirt out of the hole, an' it was between me and the far edge of the property. I hear voices. I look over the top of the dirt pile—I see 'em. A whole clutch of 'em."

"Clutch of what?" Steven asked.

"Of bird-watchers!" Arnie crowed. "Like a damned Boy Scout troop, only there was ladies there, too. They had binoculars hung around their necks, books under their arms, all slicked up in their best city bird-watchin' clothes, sneakin' along the edge of the swamp, listenin', lookin'. I couldn't stop myself, boys. I just couldn't."

"Well?" they urged.

"I call. Hidden behind my dirt pile, I call. Like this . . ." Fingers cupped around his mouth, Arnie melodiously whistled a bird-song, full and rich and beautiful.

"Gosh," said Steven. "Maybe you should go on the Ted Mack Original Amateur Hour."

"Never heard of it," Arnie said. Television had yet to come to Cape Cod.

Steven had seen it, when he visited Mari Crawford this spring. "It's great," he told Arnie. "Everybody watching gets to vote. They write in about who they want to win. Ted Mack counts up the votes and announces the winner a week later."

"I seen a TV once," Ed Pollard put in. "All snow. But I'd vote for ya, Arnie. Did the city people think you was a bird?"

"Sure did. They dropped their books and whipped out the binoculars, pointed this way, that way, all directions, whispering, excited as hell. I made their day. Last I seen, they was still thrashin' around in the bull rushes."

City people were always a good subject of Waterford humor. Steven would miss this lampooning, but there were things to do, things to learn that could not be done or learned here (although he didn't know, yet, what they were). But he would start his doing and learning now, a little earlier than he planned, since there was no possibility of staying, even to the end of the summer. Not with Sinclaire at the house.

"To bird watchers," Ed Slater proposed, his stein high.

They drank with gusto and prepared to leave. Each one shook Steven's hand a final time, a few of them clapping his shoulder, pointedly not saying how nice it had been but, instead, muttering that they hoped to see him when he came to Cape Cod next.

They were men who made no apologies for themselves, who accepted the rhythm of life close to the soil and sea and who lived with it peacefully. Men who weighed one another's worth in a balance of their own devising, to whom it would have made no difference should they learn how it was that Steven Sinclaire came into the world. They'd ask: is he any good with a hammer? Is he willin' to learn? Is he willin' to work a full day in the sun and drink beer when it's done? Those were the standards valuable to them, and by which they lived.

Only Bob Casey remained at the bar now; Ed Slater resumed his vigil behind it.

"You can level with me," Bob said. "What's goin' on? Why are you leavin' now?"

He had not seen Bob since Cousin Elizabeth's fatal heart attack, since he'd called Port Huron, since Mom had told him about Charles Sinclaire's relocation to the Boston office and his plan to live at Kingsland.

"Starting early seemed like a good idea, is all."

"I wondered . . . if you're leaving because you're not going to be welcome at your house . . . now that Miss Edgarton is gone." Bob looked down at his beer, embarrassed at what appeared to be prying. "If you want to hang around for the summer, you're welcome to stay with Barbara and me."

Not for the world would he embarrass Bob further by letting him know the strength of his gratitude. "Thanks. But I'm all set to go. I shipped my stuff to Ohio this morning. I'll leave tomorrow."

"Before the funeral?"

A funeral Alice Bradley might attend.

"Yes. I don't think Elizabeth would care, one way or the other. Would it be OK if stayed with you folks just for tonight?"

"Sure. I can take you up to Boston in the morning, if you want."

"That would be great."

They sat in silence until Bob put down his empty stein. "If you're goin' back to the house, I'll drop you off."

"OK," he sighed.

They did not speak until the truck stopped by the front door. "I'll be at the Ace-High at nine o'clock," Bob said. "Come by whenever you're ready."

"OK."

After nine o'clock Bob would loiter until Steven arrived, and then take him back to his house right away, if he wanted, or drink until closing time if he preferred, or walk on the beach if that's what he needed to do.

That was the way friends handled one another's problems—with definitive action and a minimum of words.

At Kingsland, Charles was in the library going through Cousin Elizabeth's papers. Grandmother and some friends were in the kitchen making sandwiches, their subdued chatter weaving a counterpoint with the Attwater Kent radio that was full of chatter about the impending Korean conflict.

Sitting with Mom, Steven held her hand so that she would know he still loved her, that he had forgiven her, that she was precious to him beyond the telling even though he would not live here with her, in the presence of Charles Sinclaire. Beyond the parlor window Elizabeth's rose garden was coming into bloom. He'd tended it carefully, under her supervision, and was glad she'd lived long enough to see its first blossoms. She could be difficult, sometimes, and demanding, but he'd grown fond of her and would miss her ascerbic wit.

"If this Korean thing's as bad as it sounds," Mom was saying, "I'm very worried you'll be drafted, Honey."

The young, unmarried, and nonessential were draft-bait. "After you told me that Charles was planning to transfer to Boston and live here, I enrolled at Delphi. That should defer me."

"Oh, yes. I understand," she sighed.

"It's your house, Mom. Maybe you should think about living here with Grandmother, and arranging for Charles to live somewhere else."

"He'd just love that, wouldn't he!"

He shrugged. "Think about it, why not?"

"And who would pay the bills?"

"You had a plan once. A long time ago. I don't know if you remember..."

Like a bad smell, Charles drifted noiselessly into the room. Stopping by the radio, he listened for an update, then came down to their end of the parlor.

"So you decided to join us, Steven. I was wondering when you would." Steven stood. He had not laid eyes on Charles for two years, and did not want to be at the disadvantage of looking up to him. "I'd like to see you privately, if you don't mind. Estate business."

Now it was time to match wits with Sinclaire, a scenario Steven had envisioned often. How pleasant it would be; he needn't give a damn about what the man said or how he said it, so would be able to think clearly.

"I'll be there in a minute," he answered, just for the hell of it. Sitting down again with Mom, he waited silently with her until Charles returned to the library.

"Is that called 'asserting' yourself?" she asked.

"I believe so," he grinned. "Think a little about asserting yourself too, Mom." Kissing her cheek, he left her and wandered down the hall to the library.

"Close the door." Charles was sitting behind Cousin Elizabeth's desk.

"I'd rather leave it open," Steven said, and drew up a chair for himself.

"Very well." Charles arranged the pencils on the desk into a meticulous row, signaling his annoyance at being defied before he'd even begun the interview. "You're planning to go to school in Ohio, I understand."

"Yes."

"And what do you plan to study?"

"History."

"Ah, history." Charles contemplated it for a while. A choice very far from the math major he'd insisted on two and a half years ago, when Steven was slated to attend Harvard. "Indeed, history is being made even as we speak."

Steven did not respond, but only watched.

"Unpleasant news, this business in Korea."

Another silence, a skill Steven was good at by now, schooled by his Waterford mentors.

"Hard to study history in Korea, don't you think?" Charles asked eventually.

"I won't be in Korea. I'll be in Delphi, with a college deferment."

"You may be drafted before you even get there," Charles smiled.

"I enrolled in summer school. I'm deferred already."

Charles did not move so much as a muscle, studying Steven's face minutely. "That was very wise of you, moving on it so quickly." He nodded, and turned in the swivel chair so that he was looking toward the fireplace and the portrait of Kingsley Merrick that hung above it. "I'm sure you remember that I worked in the Pentagon during the late lamented war."

Steven waited.

"I know a lot of people in Washington, especially in the military. It's possible that a college deferment won't work for you, especially considering that your enrollment was originally scheduled for this fall. It might be considered draft dodging."

Steven continued to wait, well connected to that private place where Charles Sinclaire could not touch him no matter what he did.

"Should the draft board take that position—that you're draft dodging—I can arrange a deferment for you."

Steven remarked, "How very fortunate."

Charles glanced at him sharply, recognizing the use of his own stuffy style. "Likewise, I can make sure your name comes up immediately, so that very soon you'll get a letter from the President of the United States. Probably by the end of July. What I choose to do depends on your decision about certain choices."

"I've already made my choice."

"There are others, ones you don't know about yet." Charles turned back and studied him as a cat would watch a mouse.

Suddenly he knew. Yes, with a certainty.

"I've just gotten through reviewing Elizabeth's papers," Charles announced. "Incredible as it seems—unbelievable, actually—she has left Kingsland to you."

Distantly a dish clattered; a car horn honked somewhere on Main Street.

He could not think. He could not speak.

Charles scowled. "The fact is that I've always assumed that Cousin Elizabeth was going to leave the house to your mother, and put me in charge of it."

Kingsland. This absurd house, with its ridiculous tower, its drafty rooms, enormous lawns that required endless care (who should know better than himself?) An albatross, if ever one existed, yet it somehow legitimized him, and Cousin Elizabeth trusted him with its care.

"It's extremely unfair of her to simply ignore all my contributions to maintenance," Charles complained, "but she could be unpredictable."

"Are you the executor?" Steven asked.

Upon the answer everything hinged.

"No," Charles scowled. "Your mother has been named executrix, and will be the guardian of the estate until you're twenty five. Obviously a house this size, and this old, needs to be monitored constantly. To that end, we are prepared to take full responsibility for it while you're gone—either to college or to Korea, depending on your choice."

"You mean you'll leave Port Huron."

"Yes. We'll move in this summer. I'll commute to Sommerset and Troy in Boston—an arrangement I've already made. Naturally I must insist on a legal document that gives us the right to live here as long as we wish, even after you turn 25. I've always wanted to own this house, and I thought I'd be able to, through your mother. But I can be satisfied with an irrevocable right to live here."

The thought was untenable.

"No."

Father's customary pallor brightened to pink.

"I don't want you living here. I have a trade now. I can support myself and maintain Kingsland with my own hands." He had never planned to stay here his whole life. He was not like a young person born here, who would be married by now and staking his claim right here, on the Narrow Land. But if keeping Sinclaire out meant staying, he would.

Father cleared his throat. "Let me clarify your situation," he said. "You have a trade, which seems to please you, Lord only knows why. But you will be unable to ply it from a foxhole in Korea. And I can guarantee you that Korea is where you'll find yourself, without that document." He smiled again.

The man was insidious. Steven felt his control slipping, his anger rising with his frustration. How much he wanted to smash that smile! Unable to contain himself, he jumped to his feet, tipping over his chair. Turning to retrieve it, he saw that Mom was standing in the open doorway.

"This is a private conversation, Emily. I'll thank you to leave," Sinclaire snapped.

"It's not very private," she said. "I've been listening out here in the hall ever since you began toying with the boy."

"Then you're aware that Elizabeth hasn't left Kingsland to you after all."

"Yes, I heard that."

"I'm sorry," Father said. "I'm sure you're disappointed."

Mom laughed. "I think there's a way around my disappointment."

"By our living here, you must mean," Father said. "Yes, I quite agree."

"Well, actually, Charles, I had something a little different in mind. May I come in?"

"Ask Steven," Father said brusquely. "It's his house."

"By God, you're right!" Steven laughed at the sheer absurdity of it all, the hopelessness of it all. "In fact, she ought to sit behind the desk, Charles, since she's the executrix."

Father did not miss the use of his first name, but he let it pass. "A fine idea," he said, coming out from behind the desk to take his place in front of the fireplace while Mom took Elizabeth's chair and Steven righted his own.

"The meeting will come to order," Mom chuckled. She, too, must be seeing the absurdity. "I move that the Executrix, Emily Merrick Sinclaire, remove herself from Port Huron, Ohio, and occupy the house of the late Elizabeth Edgarton."

"Seconded," Father crowed, seating himself beside the fireplace. "Definitely a good plan. Bravo, Emily!"

"Let's vote," Mom said. "All in favor?"

"Aye," the three of them chorused. It was the first time in Steven's memory that all three of them had ever willingly agreed on anything.

"Second, I move that Emily Merrick Sinclaire be the sole occupant of the house commonly referred to as Kingsland."

"What do you mean?" demanded Father.

"I mean that I will live here by myself, executing Elizabeth's estate."

"And, of course, you know how to do that."

"I expect I can find out," she nodded. "Perhaps from Elizabeth's lawyer."

"It's most unusual for a woman to do such a thing, Emily," Father pointed out. "Finance and management are the purview of men. You may find yourself beyond your depth if you embark on such a harebrained scheme."

"I'll chance it." Mom smiled beatifically. "Moreover, I move that the executrix be maintained by contributions of Charles Sinclaire, of Port Huron, Ohio, or Boston if he prefers, to be mailed the first of every month."

Father's bark of laughter resembled that of a seal. "Be serious!"

"Sometimes, it's called alimony," Mom went on. "But if a divorce is something the party of the second part—you, Charles—would rather avoid, then it would be called an allowance."

"And why would I want to avoid it, may I ask?"

"Well, if I commit adultery, or you do, those are nearly automatic grounds for divorce. Short of that, I would have to appeal to the mercy of the court to rescue me from an abusive situation—I think it's called mental cruelty—and I think you might have some reason to hope that the details of said mental cruelty remain out of the public eye."

"I should think you would, too," Father said coldly. "After all, you've been a willing participant for these twenty years. I've given you and your son a hearth and home and shelter for all that time. The court might see that as positively gentlemanly. And local knowledge would mean you'd not only be shunned, you'd be a pariah. As would Steven."

A long silence filled the room as they waited each other out.

Steven made himself speak quietly, his voice steady. "If you're referring to the fact that Tim Bradley is my father, you're a little behind the times, Charles. I've known it for several years."

"Two and half, I gather," Father said, putting the pieces together with his usual rapidity.

"Yes."

"Since you've chosen a course of discreet silence, I must gather that you are very much aware of the difficulty you would experience, trying to make your way with the known fact of your bastardy dragging along behind you. And since the two of you force my hand, I shall tell you outright that if you balk me, any man you interview for any job higher than ditch digger shall get this information, though he will not know its source."

"How do you think your career at Sommerset and Troy would fare if your habits and pleasures—and deficiencies—were known, Charles?" Mom countered. "Which would be the case if you and I end up in a Massachusetts divorce court."

"But your own reputation would be ruined too, Emily," Charles said, a bit of a whine in his tone. "Pregnant out of wedlock at the age of nineteen."

"It's a funny thing," Mom said evenly, "what you do to people, Charles. I've just heard Steven tell you that life is literally not worth living under your thumb. You've backed him into such a corner that you can't bluff him anymore."

"Believe me, Em, I'm not bluffing."

"Nor am I. I want a legal separation, an allowance, and a deferment for Steven if he needs one." Coldly she settled back in Elizabeth's chair, playing her cards without hesitation as only twenty years of living with such a man could teach a person to play. "If I hear so much as a whisper about my reputation or his, yours is down the drain. I will sue you for divorce, citing mental cruelty, and I'll do it as publically as I can. Whether I'm successful or not is beside the point, because you'll be ruined as surely as we will."

Charles turned. "I'd like to hear from you, Steven. How do you feel about your illegitimacy becoming public knowledge?"

It was like jumping off the bridge. "I don't think you'll do it." He held his breath. "I don't think you'll risk your own reputation."

"Are you willing to gamble on it?" Charles asked.

He listened to the voice of his heart. "Yes. I am."

They waited while Charles weighed it; they waited while he stared at them, assessing the strength of their resolve. Then he stood up and walked out of the library without looking back.

Mom sighed. "Well." She smiled shakily. "That, I expect, is that. I hope I've done the right thing, picked the right time, so that he's gone for good."

It was hard to know what to feel, having seesawed back and forth between such extremes. Steven wondered if he would cry as he stared at his mother who had done so much for him over the years, in so many unobtrusive ways. He saw now that her love for him had been kept inviolate even though he had not allowed contact these past months, and he wondered what she had endured, alone in the Port Huron house with Charles Sinclaire.

Pulling his chair up close to hers, he made himself speak despite the aching in his throat. "I should have written you, Mom, once I started living here with Elizabeth. I'm sorry."

"I know, I know," she whispered. They sat silently. Then she said, "If there's anything you want me to tell you... about your father..."

"There's nothing."

"If it troubles you, though, if you think about it a lot..."

"Believe me, Mom, I don't think about it at all. I'm not the boy I was two and a half years ago. I've had to start over, and my new life doesn't include him. It never will. Ever."

"All right," she said hastily. "We'll consider the subject closed."

"I'm going to Delphi in the morning," he said. "I need to get some stuff together, and then I'll be on my way. I'll be at the Casey's tonight."

"OK," she nodded. "I can mail the rest of your clothes. Have you got a way to get up to the Boston bus station?"

"Bob will take me."

"Just so we're clear, tell me what you'd like to do with the house."

"This house?"

"Yes," she giggled. "I think it's the only one in question. Do you think it'd be alright if I stayed here by myself?"

"Someone needs to take care of Grandmother. Who better than you? She'll be old soon."

"She's old now."

"Then as legal owner of Kingsland, I decree you stay now."

They hugged one another and he climbed up to his tower room, looked out each window, to the bay, to the town, up Main Street and down, at the newly leafed trees below, abundantly green. As heir to Kingsland, it was up to him to keep the house safe. Along with it was the town, spread out below, and the friends he had made here, whose well-being was somehow his responsibility too, somehow part of his inheritance.

It was time to celebrate, not meditate! It was time to get drunk at the Ace High, totally stoned, a free fall into relief. Charles Sinclaire was as good as dead! Damn! Life was good!

Tomorrow he would leave for college. One day he would get a job, a good one that would allow him to support Kingsland and his mother, too. And, perhaps, a family.

He would see Mari Crawford, when she returned to campus this fall. She was a good girl, that Mari, and smart. And she liked him, he knew. They'd been in regular contact since first meeting. Perhaps she was exactly the girl he needed, level-headed and firm of purpose, to help him with a future he could only barely discern.

He would find out.

CHAPTER

The Nomads

✦✧ I ✧✦

ATHENS COLLEGE. It looked classical, with pillars and pediments and all. That the college was located in the town of Delphi added to the Grecian ambience. AC's roots reached back to the Northwest Ordinance of 1787, when admiration for ancient Greece and its republican government was high. It was a mini-Harvard, with its quadrangle of ivy-covered brick buildings and huge trees overhanging everything and its library the finest among schools of comparable size.

Not that Steven would ever, ever speak of its similarity to Harvard! Although Ohio people didn't know one end of Massachusetts from the other, everyone had heard about Hah-vahd. There was a certain reverence attached to it, in fact to "The East" in general, as well as a lot of resentment. The East had a longer history than Ohio, and it was the cradle of whatever culture America could boast about.

That culture had not yet crossed the Appalachian Mountains. Places like Delphi, where the college provided a venue for academia and its attendant intellectual attractions, was as good as it got. Otherwise, the Midwest was a cultural wasteland, just as Charles Sinclair had said, and it was unlikely to change any time soon. As far as mid-westerners were concerned, Massachusetts may have been in America longer, but there was nothing wrong with the good ol' Ohio!

Steven Sinclaire would be seen as alien, for he had a strange accent, an "eastern" one overlying his Port Huron patois. In addition, he was Older. Only veterans entered college after the age of 18. If you had not committed yourself to higher education by then, or if you could not afford to, then you were on an entirely different track—most likely a menial one. And you would probably stay there.

Riding west on the bus from Boston, Steven thought about these things and dismissed them. Being different was nothing new. He had always been an anomaly. Illegitimacy tended to make you that way. But thanks to Mom and her standoff with Charles Sinclaire, no one would ever find out—including Mari Crawford.

What little he knew about Athens College was acquired from his infrequent visits to her there. The first time, in fall just after they'd first met, she arranged a bed for him in the men's dorm and showed him around, as she'd promised—not just the campus but the recreational spots as well. Notably Smokey Joe's, a subterranean hangout that the college kids loved.

"They only serve 3.2 beer. It might taste pretty watery to you."

"I don't drink all that much," he assured her. "I only went to Ace-High that night because you girls invited me."

"Pretty forward of us, huh?"

"You were on vacation. Everyone's forward on Cape Cod in the summer. It's the party place."

"It certainly is!" she laughed, her white, even teeth flashing in the light of a candle thrust into the neck of a picturesque Chianti bottle provided by Smokey Joe himself.

They corresponded throughout the winter that year, and the summer too, when it turned out that her waitressing job in Arlington, Indiana, didn't allow for time off for a junket to Cape Cod. Steven's job with Bob Casey didn't allow for time off during the summer, either, and so a return trip to Delphi didn't happen until the following fall.

Because he'd arrived later in the season than the year before, he was witness to the uproar over sorority and fraternity rushing. Crowds of dressed-up young people roamed the campus, dropping into this

Greek house or that, introducing themselves, showing their wares to the best advantage. Within the week, bids would go out. "Last year I decided not to pledge a sorority," Mari told him over a pitcher of 3.2 beer at Smokey Joe's.

"Why not?" he asked. This was something she hadn't written about. "It looks like everybody is doing it."

"I found out, during last year's rush, that the houses I was interested in weren't interested in me." She said it almost proudly, though it could not have been an easy situation. Like most small schools, the sororities and fraternities eased the housing needs of upper classmen. Living in a dormitory as a junior, she would be badly out of touch with the most sought-after social element of college life.

"How could they not be interested in you?" he asked incredulously. Smart and cute as a button, with her pixie-style haircut and wonderful smile, she'd be an asset to any sorority.

"They don't want girls who are working their way through school," she told him.

"What's working got to do with it?"

"Bad for their image, I guess. If they are the house of rich girls, I don't fit the description. If they are the house of the sophisticated and glamorous, a server in the cafeteria line doesn't exactly live up to that image, either."

"How about the sororities that don't find your working a problem? There must be some of those."

"Oh, yes, but those girls are totally Out Of It. I got bids from all of them, but if I joined, then I'd be Out Of It, too. So I didn't," she explained. "Remember I wrote you about the church youth group I help to run? That, and other stuff at the church, fills in time when I might be at loose ends."

"Good for you!" The girl had a mind of her own, despite the pressure of campus expectation. She made no apologies for her exclusion, and his admiration for her grew.

He described the Mill Site project that he'd worked on with Bob Casey and his crew last winter. The shell of the building was up by

November, providing him work every day because rain or sleet or snow didn't matter if there was shelter. They'd built a water wheel this summer, in between repairing old houses for the influx of new people who'd bought them, and would finish the interior of the mill itself over the upcoming winter.

Curfew was midnight; Smokey Joe's began to empty at 11:45. Floating out on its receding tide, they had followed the throng to Mari's dormitory. All over the front yard pairs of students were locked together in farewell embraces. He drew her close. "When in Rome," he murmured.

She reached up and wound her arms around his neck, raised up on her tiptoes and touched his mouth with hers. "Like that?"

"Something like that," he approved. "Unless you're worried that it's common."

"Maybe there's something to it—being common, I mean." Unaccustomed to kissing in a crowd with all the lights on, he nearly laughed aloud, but decided instead to do as all Romans were then doing; the porch lights started blinking, a signal there was only one minute left. The young women turned away from their dates and stampeded through the front door, needing to get in before midnight or they'd get a demerit—shades of camp! But Mari seemed not to care about demerits. Her kiss deepened as the yard emptied and finally she pushed away. "They'll lock the door in a minute," she explained, and ran.

Avoiding his assigned dormitory filled with raucous juvenile males, he went back to Smokey Joe's, happy and filled with good will. He had not been especially happy or glad until then.

But the situation wasn't cut-and-fried, he told himself after several more beers.

Dried, he corrected himself. Cut-and-dried. But he like "fried" better, because it described an ongoing process, in this instance a decision on what kind of new world he wanted to create for himself, and whether or not he wanted Mari Crawford to be part of it.

That was last fall. A whole winter of correspondence had gone on since, while the interior of the mill was finished up. Once the academic session started this fall, and Mari returned to campus, they would be together quite a lot, if they chose to be. What would that be like, he wondered.

Upon arriving at Delphi, he was assigned a room in the nearly empty men's dormitory, and started his summer classes—English comp and world history. Letting Mari know that he was on campus already, he settled down to work. Few students were taking summer classes and the dorm was quiet. But his concentration was nil, his study habits totally annihilated by the passing of so long a time without classroom pressure. World History was a jumble of facts and names; composition was labored, and when the assignment was his own choice, no ideas, not a single one, came to him. Perhaps it was an impossible plan, going to college. Perhaps he ought to think about going back to work with Bob Casey.

But then he'd be draft bait. He must try harder.

The message arrived from the administration the following week.

"Well, Mr. Sinclaire," the distinguished Dean of Men began affably. "It begins to look like you might fail your courses."

Fail! "I didn't know that. Neither of my professors has said so."

"I am always notified at the first indication that one of our students is having difficulty. They tell me that you seem to be having trouble concentrating, and your homework assignments are rarely complete. Needless to say, this isn't college level performance, though I'm not surprised. After three years of being out of school, you've lost momentum."

"I'm afraid that's true," he agreed ruefully.

"I checked your transcript, and you certainly were a good student once. On that basis we accepted you, and gave you a scholarship besides. But I'm going to have to change your status to probation and hope we can somehow get you back on track."

Probation! "What would you suggest, sir?" he asked weakly.

"A tutor, to begin with. Weekly conferences with your professors, so you'll know if the tutoring is succeeding. We may have to reconsider whether or not you should work in the cafeteria, come fall, if you need more time to complete your assignments."

"I'm obliged to work, I'm afraid."

"You're obliged to pass," the Dean reminded him. "Clearly you're smart enough, Mr. Sinclaire. Successful course work must be your first priority."

There was only one place he could turn. At the end of his hall was a pay phone, and he used it that very afternoon, calling collect.

"Steven!" Mari exclaimed. "Is something wrong?"

He had never called her collect before, let alone on daytime rates. "I'm flunking out."

"Flunking! I don't believe it!"

"I'm on academic probation."

"Golly, Steven!" she commiserated.

"I'm hoping you can help."

"How?"

"If it would be O.K. with your folks, I'd come there on weekends, and you could tutor me. Starting tomorrow. I could take the bus after my last class." She was studying to be a teacher. Surely she'd know how to get him back on track!

There was a longish silence on the other end of the line as she thought about it. Not that she wouldn't be willing to tutor him, he was sure. But it was a little unusual for a young man to come to a girl's house for the weekend—for a number of weekends—unless there was an understanding between them. Not only were there her parents to consider, there were the neighbors, too. What would they think? In Ohio, where everyone knew everybody else's business, public opinion mattered a lot. He was sure that the same was true out there in Indiana.

"Let me find out what my Mom and Dad have to say," she offered. "I think we'll have to start there. Of course I'd be glad to help, if I can. Perhaps you could just withdraw from the summer session, and then in the fall—"

"I'd lose my deferment."

"We'll think of something, then," she said firmly. "Can I call you back? Where are you?"

"The dorm." He gave her the number.

"I'll talk to my parents at supper. In the meantime, there are probably study questions in the back of each chapter in the history book. Start answering them, in writing. Thoroughly. I'll call around 7:00 or so."

He tried. He truly did. By 7:00, he was half-crazy with waiting, and the shrill bell on the telephone caused him so jump so high that he tipped over his desk chair.

"They think it would be fine for you to come, as long as we're engaged," she reported. "Otherwise, it just wouldn't look right for you to be staying here overnight every weekend."

Engaged!

"I know we haven't talked about that, or anything like it. But if we got engaged, so that your being here would look right, we wouldn't necessarily be stuck with it." She hurried on. "We can always break it off if we need to. I mean, if we aren't as compatible as we seem to have been up to now."

It was like the high diving board, or the Port Huron bridge.

"I'll bet Cousin Elizabeth had a diamond ring that we could use," he said, leaping off. "You might have to resize it."

"That can be done easily enough." Pleasure rang clearly in her voice. "And I'll arrange to get our pictures taken."

"Pictures?"

"For the Society Page. Announcing our engagement."

"Ummmm. Of course."

"Did you work on your history like I told you to?"

"I did," he lied. "And I'll work more on it tonight." And he would, in between thinking about being engaged.

"I'll meet you at the bus station tomorrow afternoon, then."

"Can't thank you enough, Mari!"

"I'm a tough teacher. You may not be thanking me for long." She was chuckling as she hung up.

It was time to assess the situation. Her companionship just now would be welcome; the empty dormitory was beginning to get on his nerves. Certainly she'd be able to get him through his summer courses.

This winter, while she worked on her teaching certification, she could continue to tutor him, if he needed it. If she could find a teaching job near Delphi, once she graduated, they could get an apartment and he could cram all the requirements in and graduate a year later. Hopefully.

Did he want to marry her? Well, maybe. He would not commit himself to a girl he didn't love, but Mari was loveable, and that issue would probably take care of itself. Then there was the reconfiguration of Steven Sinclaire, of the person he would become now that his non-father was no longer a threat. Perhaps Mari Crawford was destined to be part of that, too.

He'd call Mom, ask her to find a ring, mail it, and let the future take care of itself while he wrote out the answers to the questions in the back of the history chapters and outlined composition papers he'd write with Mari's help.

The reconfiguration would begin there.

∾ 2 ∾

Consumerism captured everyone, with television leading the way, showing ideal families, ideal fathers and mothers, ideal children. Americans raced for the suburbs, where the ideal décor could be displayed in the ideal house.

A wall was built in Berlin, separating east from west; a man orbited the earth; a catholic was elected president; a black minister redefined the American dream. The number of military advisors in South Vietnam increased, but few people worried about that. Instead, corporate wives vied with each other for leadership in their suburban world, paying little attention to the "feminine mystique", while their husbands competed with one another in the corporate climb and the status that success conferred.

1963

"And then we joined up with O.T." (This was Oliver Thaddeus Brown, president of Tri-State Construction.) Ron Howland smiled proudly, pleased to be so well connected that he could use this stuffy epithet. "O.T. plays a great game of golf," Howland went on. "He beat me, of course, but F.A. held his own." (This was Franklin Algernon Sattiswaite, president of Bronner Fiberglass and Insulation.)

Howland finished his martini, tapping the cocktail glass gently to dislodge the olive at the bottom. Around the table eddied the clink and clatter of Newton's Restaurant and Lounge. Steven swirled the contents of his own martini in a gentle whirlpool around his own olive, listening to the rising and falling of voices and an occasional eruption of laughter, felt the gentle breeze of hustling staff as they barreled by. An older waitress approached with an armload of hamburgers and French fries. Steven watched, pretending an absorption in her expertise while evaluating Ron Howland's game with Bronner's president and O.T. Brown, a large-quantity consumer of fiberglass insulation.

They dug into their burgers as the waitress poured coffee and left.

If he got promoted to being chief of Bronner's insulation division, would he be known as S.C.? Apparently importance generated the use of initials. The lower echelons, like himself and his companions at Newton's, only ever called themselves by their initials in jest. They were not important enough for it to be anything other than a joke. Yet.

"I really like the fries here," Wade Roper said, dipping one in the pool of ketchup on his plate.

"You can take mine, if you like," Howland said, wolfing down his burger.

Steven wondered what Howland's middle name was, and if he would use initials when he became a corporate higher up at Bronner. The fact that he was playing golf with men who were so important might indicate this event was not far in the future.

Across the table Wade Roper happily accepted the bonus load of French fries. "What do you guys think of Bronner getting into fiberglass fishing rods? Seems pretty risky to me."

"Hah!" Ron Howland laughed derisively. "You'll never get anywhere thinking that way, Wade! Promotion-wise, I mean. You know how much F.A. likes fishing!"

"What's that got to do with it?" Wade demanded. "Will fiberglass make a good rod or not?"

"F.A. knows what's good and what isn't." Howland's company-man mask did not slip even fractionally. "The man's remarkable, believe me! Fiberglass will make a hell of a good fishing rod, if he thinks so. Just as it's going to make a good canoe."

Canoes were the latest company foray into the marketplace, causing the most recent chance for promotion to arise. The present head of insulation had been appointed to lead the new canoe division. Now insulation was up for grabs and two of the men in contention for it were sitting right here, at this table.

Well, soon it would be all over. The new organization would be announced anytime now, and Steven, due to leave for his annual vacation starting this afternoon at five o'clock, was determined to have an answer by then, even if he had to go to Mr. Sattiswaite and ask for it. Only a dunce would leave town with everything up in the air, the competition free to cut Sinclaire's throat while the selfsame Sinclaire was enjoying life in his hammock at Kingsland.

Good ol' Ron Howland, on the other hand, was out on the golf links with Mr. Sattiswaite every Saturday, fishing with him on Sunday, licking F.A.'s boots Monday through Friday. At first Steven had lugged his golf clubs out to the club, too, thinking that he should join the corporate game. F.A. certainly liked it, but in fact Steven did not. Saturdays could be used to mow the lawn, help Mari with house projects, take his kids to a matinee. After a session on the green, he opted out in favor of his family. Mari was worried about that decision, knowing that promotions were often earned on the golf course.

But there were other ways to curry favor. On Sunday was church. Kathy, now twelve years old, and Rick, ten, attended Congregational Sunday School while Steven and Mari joined Bronner's upper echelon in the sanctuary. Also included in The Sinclaire Plan was Steven's membership in the Rotary; Mari was president of the PTA and played bridge with the Bronner wives. The goal of The Plan was to put Steven at the head of insulation. With plenty of experience in building, he understood specifications and inspection requirements, and related comfortably to men in trade. And it would pay well. Very well.

The waitress reappeared. "Coffee?" she asked.

"Yes, please," Wade Roper smiled.

"Me, too." Steven finished the last of his burger and gestured to the plate so she'd take it and the table would have elbow room.

"Well, then, I hope you'll excuse me." Howland pushed his chair back. "There's some things I want to finish up before the weekend."

They waited for him to leave.

"I think he's got it," Wade said.

"Insulation?" Steven asked needlessly. He knew exactly what Wade was talking about. "What makes you think so? The golf game with O.T.?"

"Miss Hastings. She says she heard it in the girl's room." Miss Hastings was Wade's secretary, a Bronner employee for twenty years. If she'd heard it, probably it was true.

Steven's lunch turned to lead. "Maybe Miss Hastings is wrong."

"Maybe. But I'll tell you this, Steve. If Bronner has come to the point that a brown-noser like Howland can take the prize, instead of the guy who knows the job best—well, I think it's time I began looking for another company."

"Let me know what you find," Steven said grimly. It was supposed to be a joke, and Wade obliged him with a chuckle, but both of them knew there wasn't much funny about it. Wade would never leave Bronner. A man was as good as married to his company. It was understood that the corporation would arrange for a generous retirement in exchange for a lifetime of loyal labor. Any other company to which Wade might apply for work would look askance at his coming to them half way through his career. Was he a trouble-maker? A slacker? Why take a chance on him where there were so many well-qualified men available?

Finishing their coffee, they crossed the street to the Bronner Building. Wade clapped Steven on the shoulder as they parted. "A toast to your vacation later on?"

"Sounds good," he agreed. His friend took the elevator while he started climbing the stairs, his daily offering to the goddess of fitness. Eight flights were good for something!

So, Howland would probably get insulation. Slowing down at a landing where the small window looked over the Pennsylvania countryside, out beyond the ever-creeping suburban sprawl to the gentle rise of the Allegheny Mountains, Steven stared out, seeing nothing. The insulation division was the corporate Golden Arrow, as far as he was concerned. A link to home building, and to Bob Casey in particular, as though, in an unexplained way, they still worked together. It seemed possible to live with being a corporation man, if he were the head of insulation. Would he be able to live with it if Ron Howland were the head?

He'd have to.

Clearing his desk in preparation for his vacation was the order of the afternoon; he sorted through unfinished business, made notes to help his secretary if certain customers called about certain specs, or certain difficulties presented themselves before he could get back to attend them.

"Mr. Sinclaire?" Miss Thurston peeked around the door. "Mr. Sattiswaite is on two-three. Do you want to take it, or call him back?" Rather than buzzing his phone from her desk in the secretarial pool, where the others might hear that F.A. had summoned him, she'd notified him quietly and unobtrusively. A good secretary if there ever was one.

"I'll take it," he said, "in a minute. Tell him you'll put him through and then leave him on hold."

Knowingly, she nodded and went back to her desk to switch the call. The men often played this game, so the boss would believe them to be slaving so madly at their work that they couldn't take a call the instant it came through. Steven let the phone ring. F.A. would not hear it; the phone would be effectively dead until Steven picked up the receiver and pushed the blinking button.

It did not accomplish much, letting it ring like this. But it was satisfying. Finally he connected. "Sinclaire."

"Hello, Steven!" Mr. Sattiswaite boomed. Use of the phone was unnecessary; he could hear F.A.'s voice both in the ear piece and echoing down the hall from his office.

"Sorry to keep you waiting," Steven lied. "I'm in the process of getting ready to leave for vacation, and I was in the middle of a file drawer. What can I do for you, sir?"

"If it won't interfere with your shutting up shop, I wonder if you could drop by."

"Glad to."

Strolling out, he walked through the secretarial pool as casually as he could, to the corridor at the far end and on down to the corner office. There F.A. Sattiswaite had the best, biggest, and most impressive suite in the building, complete with floor to ceiling windows, decadent plush furniture, a lush carpet and an adjoining office for his secretary. No pool for her!

"Go right on in," she smiled.

"Well, Steve!" F.A., a heavy man, heaved himself out of his immense chair, gestured grandly toward an overstuffed lounger. "Sit down, my boy."

Steven settled into the chair and in its soothing, comforting depths realized he was very, very tired.

"Well, sir!" F.A. cleared his throat, as he always did after well-sir-ing. "We've been very pleased at the way you've dug right in and helped to fill in the recent gap at the top of the insulation pyramid." F.A. paused for a moment in silent admiration for his hyperbole, playing with the array of pens on his desk. "Insulation sales are humming, and I think your efforts—and those of Ron Howland—have a lot to do with that."

"Thanks," he said. "It helps that there's a building boom, too."

Ron Howland would have claimed full credit. Modesty does not pay, Steven reminded himself, yet it would not matter in this case. Sattiswaite had his mind made up already.

"The boom in construction has certainly been a factor." F.A. nodded. "And I think your rather intimate knowledge of building and construction has stood us in good stead. Howland tells me you actually built houses once."

"That's right. I worked with a carpenter, earning money to go to college."

F.A. beamed. "I earned my own way, too."

Steven began to feel heartened; predictably, Sattiswaite would look approvingly on a man with enough gumption to put himself through school.

"Boise or Denver or Portland, Oregon," Sattiswaite mused importantly. "What I'm toying with, Sinclaire, is sending you to manage the Bronner office in one of those districts. I can't think of a man better suited to dealing with contractors than you, and frankly the men we have there now have lost touch with the company. We'll bring them back to the home office and give them a refresher course. If they don't catch on, requirement-wise, well, they can't complain they weren't given an opportunity."

"The home office is certainly the place to learn," Steven remarked, knowing he was dead in the water.

"I'm going to name Ron Howland head of the insulation department. I'll be doing that next week, but you'll be on vacation and I wanted to tell you about it before you left. It was his suggestion to put you in charge of a district office."

Steven Sinclaire had been outmaneouvred, outclassed, outdone, and he couldn't think of a word to say. He could only stare at F.A. Sattiswaite, a deer in the headlights.

"I'd rather you didn't mention this to anyone. There's at least five people in line waiting for each district I've mentioned, and I'd hate to have them know you can take your pick." Bullshit, Steven almost said aloud. "Why don't you talk it over with Mrs. Sinclaire and see what she'd like?" Sattiswait suggested. "Think it over, yourself, and check in with me as soon as you get back from your vacation, if you will."

Sattiswaite heaved himself up again, terminating the interview. Steven shook the required hand and let himself out, down the hall and through the pool, where the girls were surreptitiously getting ready to leave for the weekend, their hair combed and their lipstick freshened, busily working at their typewriters so they'd appear too hard-pressed to take anyone's last-minute dictation.

His secretary looked up as she saw him coming. "Mr. Roper called," she told him, glancing at her notepad. "And Inventory Control, wondering where your estimates for the Dallas Office are."

He noticed that she carefully avoided mentioning his meeting with Mr. Sattiswaite, and her eyes, when they met his, were filled with concern. Most likely she, too, had privileged information from the grapevine.

It took fifteen minutes to straighten out Inventory Control; his desk was clear by five minutes before five. Even higher-ups such as himself did not leave Bronner before closing time. He called Wade Roper back.

"Want to celebrate my vacation now?"

"I'm on my way."

Wade was in high spirits, and entertaining too, helping to keep Steven's mind off his troubles until the empty office echoed and it was time to come to terms with the fact that he had lost out to Ron Howland.

With another finger of bourbon he answered Wade's vacation toast, saw his friend out the door, and settled back into his chair.

Why in hell hadn't he stood up for himself, demanded to know why Howland had got head of Insulation, when he, S. C. Sinclaire, had demonstrated his expertise time and time again? Most aggravating of all was himself sitting there silently, listening to that crap about the boys in the district offices. He was the skinny kid on the beach who had just gotten sand sprayed in his eyes by the big guy running past.

Slinking lower in his swivel chair with another finger of bourbon, he tried to edge away from the inalterable fact that Ron Howland had gotten rid of him. For now, at least. Maybe one day he'd be called back and given a position that required the use of initials, and that's what he'd tell Mari. But there was no point kidding himself. If you were out in the field too long, you lost your leverage in the home office. And in this case, Ron would make sure it happened. Steve Sinclaire was competition he could do without.

Take things one at a time, he advised himself.

Primary among them was the fact the Sinclaires were going to pack up their tents and load their camels and move on to another oasis. They'd done so, a half-dozen times, working up to this present position at the main office.

Mari would be awfully disappointed.

Boise, Idaho. Portland, Oregon. Denver, Colorado.

Unless he missed his bet, the family would enjoy Denver. Terrific weather, nice little city, and closer to the East Coast and to Cape Cod than Oregon or Idaho.

The phone at his elbow rang; he knew who it would be. "Hi, honey," he enunciated clearly.

"Steve? Are you okay?"

"Yes, I'm fine."

"I thought you'd be home by now."

"Just clearing my desk, getting everything ready for vacation. Loose ends to tie up and all."

"I wanted to remind you that the Stanley barbecue is tonight," she said. "Don't be too late."

"Okay," he agreed, tucking the bottle back into its customary hiding place, the bottom right-hand drawer. "Be there as soon as I can." Hanging up, he swiveled around to look out his window and tried to work up some zest for his impending holiday, now dampened by his non-promotion. Tried not to think about the discouraging discussion he must have with Mari.

She'd take it like a trooper, of course—the transfer part, at least. As a good corporate wife, she heroically set up the family domicile in one place, and then, on signal, dismantled it and set up in another, finding new doctors and new dentists, meeting new teachers, serving on new committees.

No, the transfer she could handle, no matter what she thought about moving. But that Ron Howland had beat Steven Sinclaire out of the promotion he deserved—that was something else.

Perhaps another dram of bourbon? No, Sinclaire, he admonished himself. You can face her without being stoned. Party at the Stanleys'? Probably that would take some alcoholic propulsion, but first things first.

You are in the wrong business, Sinclaire, his inner voice stated. It was the obvious choice fourteen years ago, when the post-war economy was expanding without limit, businesses vying for college graduates, and himself married already and eager to get on with life. It was not a choice he'd questioned at the time. Besides, it was a forgone conclusion that history majors, along with the rest of the liberal arts crowd, would join the business community after graduation unless they intended to get a Ph.D and teach.

It was a little late for questioning his decision now.

He sat a moment longer, wondering if he'd miss this office, if he'd like the one in Denver better, or Boise, or Portland. Then he took the elevator down to the lobby of the building and slipped around the corner to Maxie's Grill, where he could grab a spot of coffee to fortify himself for the drive home, for the Stanley barbecue, for the complications of vacation and transporting suitcases, boxes, and bags to Waterford. And for the inevitable confrontation with his wife.

As he approached his split level house (a style repeated often in Wildwood Estates) Steven could see, even before he got out of the car, that a problem had arisen. Ricky's bike was propped upside down near the front door, its back wheel lying on the grass next to his father's open toolbox, wrenches of varying sizes arranged on the front steps. The carcass of the bike and the clutter on the steps was sure to irritate Mrs. White across the street, who was probably glaring at them right now. Steven often wondered if planned communities that limited themselves exclusively to older people wouldn't be a bad idea. It would avoid unhappiness like this. No kids, no mess.

The front bumper of his Buick came to rest ever so gently against the back wall of the garage. The houses here had been built early in the fifties when designers were unaware that the automobile would ever be so long. Now hardly anybody's vehicle could comfortably fit in any garage in Wildwood or any other sub-division of its vintage.

Along the walls were rakes and shovels. In a small attached shed resided the Sinclaire power lawn mower, a suburban symbol of success.

Ron Howland had a terrific power mower.

Steven opened the car door carefully, so it wouldn't bang into the concrete wall, took his briefcase out of the backseat, pulled the garage door down (it barely cleared the tail fins), and entered the family room that lay adjacent to the garage. The Pennsylvania split level had a lot going for it, including the partially subterranean family room, cool just as the garage was. It was carpeted wall to wall, with built-in bookcases and closets for toys and puzzles in which the kids were fast losing interest as they grew up. At its far end were two lounge chairs for the viewing of television. Presently each was stacked with the things the family would take to Waterford. As a division manager out west, he'd probably get three weeks of vacation instead of two. He'd need them, just to get to Waterford and back. And he'd need a trailer to tow enough family baggage to last them that long.

His daughter Kathy sat cross-legged on the rug in front of the television set. On the screen Della Street handed a paper to Perry Mason, who reached for it without taking his penetrating gaze off the man in the witness box.

"Hi, Dad," said Kathy cheerfully. Still watching, she offered her cheek to be kissed. "You smell," she observed.

Mason, without even pausing, trapped and utterly demolished the guilty party who had been sitting in the courtroom's spectator gallery. The culprit now leaped up, confessing his hatred for the deceased.

"Of booze. You smell of booze. Celebrating your vacation?" she asked, holding a hairbrush in her hand. She'd read that a girl ought to brush her hair vigorously every day. Magazines carried a lot of articles about how girls-in-the-know should groom themselves, and the youngsters Kathy ran around with all read the same ones. At twelve years old, his daughter was preparing herself for Life.

They both watched until Perry Mason told Della Street how the culprit had committed his deed. The closing commercial began.

"Patio party tonight," Kathy said.

"So your mother told me."

"At the Stanleys' house."

"What will you do for fun there?"

"Play Ping-Pong in the rec room, stuff like that."

A rerun of "I love Lucy" began. Kathy settled in for another half-hour that would be happily spent, requiring nothing of her.

Steven went up half a flight of stairs to the second level, through the living room and dining room and into the kitchen, where a pot of something in the oven was bubbling over. Turning the temperature down, he mixed himself a highball, took off his coat and tie, loosened his collar. In the backyard, the slates of the patio were soft in the gathering evening, and the potted plants that defined its periphery glowed. In this light the lawn was taking on a velvet texture, the whole scene, no doubt, very nearly approximating the picture in a ladies' magazine that had inspired it. Mari had worked long and hard out there. Yet another cause for anguish at having to move. Again.

The kitchen window was placed in exactly the right spot for the happy housewife to have a nice view while she did whatever needed doing in the sink. He mixed another drink for himself and one for Mari and, juggling them along with his coat and tie, crossed the well-kept, dustless living room, up another half flight of steps to the level over the garage and family room, where the kids had their bedrooms. A third was reserved for Mom when she came to visit at Christmas, used just now as a holding pen for winter curtains which had been changed for summer ones and had yet to be put away.

Then on up to the master bedroom over the living room, complete with its own bath, his-and-hers closets, and sundeck overlooking the side yard. The room was immaculate, carpeted and noiseless, and he felt very far away from Kathy, down there watching "I Love Lucy".

"Hi, honey," he called. A sudden roar of water from the bathroom told him that Mari was rising from the tub.

"Hi, Steve! I didn't know you were home!" Clouds of vapor preceded her as she came into the bedroom, wrapped in a towel but still wringing wet. "How are you?" she asked—a well-intentioned question that needed no answer. Pecking his cheek, she took the drink he'd brought. "Thanks. And thanks for getting home in time for the cookout, too. You smell of liquor," she complained as she slipped into her closet, which was large enough to serve as a dressing room. In there she dried herself and slipped into her seersucker bathrobe and took off the ugly plastic hat that looked like a pot cover used to keep leftovers fresh in the refrigerator.

"I have been celebrating my vacation." Shoes removed, he stretched out on the bed, stuffed a pillow behind himself and leaned against the headboard, watching Mari arrange her hair.

At thirty-five, his wife was probably approaching her prime. Her skin glowed and had not yet acquired crows' feet or laugh lines or whatever the hell it was that caused women to be depressed when they looked in the mirror. Her breasts did not yet sag. Maturity had made her lovely instead of just pretty.

"In a way I wish we weren't going to the Stanleys'," she sighed. "Sometimes Rosalie annoys me, just a little."

"Let's not, then."

"If we don't go, Rosalie will be mad."

"And if she is?"

"She might not ask us next time. And then the next time when the Murchisons or someone else has a cocktail party, we won't be invited because everyone will think we had a fight with the Stanleys and won't want to get in the middle of it, and pretty soon no one will sit with us at the club and no one will serve on my committee at the PTA..."

Should he tell her now? That she need not worry about these repercussions, because she wouldn't be here to call a committee meeting in the fall or have dinner at the club?

"So I think we'd better go," she was saying, "because Rosalie is talking about starting a bridge group in September, when the kids go back to school. I'd hate to be left out."

No better moment would present itself. "I'm sorry to tell you that we'll be gone by September, Mari, so it won't matter." There was a long silence while he miserably inspected the melting ice in the bottom of his now-empty glass. "This time we have a choice. Boise, or Portland, or Denver. Seems that the fellows in those offices need to be brought back for a refresher."

"You're being transferred? But honey, you'll die on the vine," she protested. "If you aren't here, in the home office, they'll just forget you!"

"Probably."

"You'll never get to be head of Insulation."

"I never will anyway. Ron got it."

"Oh, Steve!" she wailed, her face screwed up in anguish and disappointment. "You mean after all this time..."

"That's what I mean."

"But you're twice as good as Ron Howland. And I'll bet you never told Mr. Sattiswaite so. I'll bet you just sat back and let Ron Howland tromp all over you!"

"I sat at my desk and did the best job I knew how to do," he said tightly.

"But it's not enough!" she cried. "I've told you and told you, Steve, it's not enough. Why, if you knew what *other* men do to get promotions! I listen to their wives! I know!"

"I know, too, honey. But it's not the way I operate."

"Then maybe you shouldn't be in business," she yelled. "If it's too hot in the kitchen..."

"You'd better get out," he chorused glibly, sliding off the bed. "I'll be in our kitchen if you want me. Which I think is relatively cool this time of day."

"Oh, Steve, I'm sorry," she cried, but he didn't look back. She may not have meant to hurt, but she hadn't thought to spare him, either. This was a hell of a time to point out that her husband was a failure, when failure glared and stared and laughed in his face.

Well, perhaps he'd be happier in a branch office. There'd be no one's ass to kiss there, and he'd be left alone, to pursue sales of insulation and write up specs. Meet with builders and architects, go out to look over sites. Actually, it would suit his temperament a hell of a lot better than the home office.

But would Boise, Portland, or Denver offer his family anything different? They would end up in the suburbs, as they were now, and they'd belong to a club, and the kids would belong to scouts and complain about homework and avoid as many chores as possible, and there'd be social conclaves in backyards, like the one they'd attend this evening. Was this what they wanted, he and Mari? She had thought so, once. Would she choose it now?

With another highball, he watched the flowers out on the patio grow dim, the shadows lengthen. Mari came in, her makeup in place, a determined look beneath it.

"Well," she said, looking at the casserole through the oven's glass door. "Since I've got our contribution already made, we might as well go."

"No," he said.

"Just because you're mad at me, there's no reason not to join the neighborhood fun."

"It's not because I'm mad at you. It's because these parties are dull as dust. You know it, and I know it, and since we won't be living here anymore, there's no reason on God's green earth why we should go to another one. Besides, we won't have any fun; we never do. Bill Hughes will complain about the pro shop, and Rosalie will work the conversation around to her sorority and her sister, whose husband is the mayor of whatever godforsaken city they live in." And Ellen Hughes would make another attempt to seduce him, as she did every male.

"Steve, we can't just sit here while a party we've been invited to is going on over there!" As though to add credibility to her words, the distant bleat of men's laughter from the direction of the Stanleys' patio reminded them—unnecessarily—that the guests were gathering. "Rosalie will be crushed if we don't go," Mari coaxed, swamped by threat of being left out. She'd been excluded once before, in college, and did everything she could to prevent its happening again. Apparently, Steven guessed, her sorority problems had been more difficult for her than she'd let on.

Kathy came up from the family room. "Isn't it time to go to the Stanleys'?"

"We thought we'd relax for a while first, sweetie," said Mari, hastily covering up the problems of the present. "Run on over, if you want to. We'll get there sometime."

"I'd better," Kathy said. "I hate having a party start without me."

"Can you take the casserole over with you? Will it be too heavy?"

"Let's find out."

Mari loaded her up and opened the back screen door.

"It's fine, Mom," Kathy said.

"Tell Rosalie we'll be along soon."

"Okay." Kathy started off, the casserole dish held out like an offering to the gods, mulling over so unusual an event as her parents deliberately being late to a neighborhood get-together. Something must be going on. Probably another argument—not an uncommon occurrence. But to be late to a party on account of it?

She hurried away.

The decorator harvest-gold phone jangled from its place on the wall, and Steven reached for it. "Hello?"

"This is Mrs. White, across the street," came a strained and tense voice. "And I'm looking at the bike in your front yard. I've been looking at it all day. It doesn't do much for your yard, Mr. Sinclaire, and it doesn't do much for my view."

"We'll take care of it, Mrs. White," he said with the politeness he was trained to use on elderly ladies, hung up with uncharacteristic abruptness.

"Who was it?"

"Mrs. Goddamn White."

"I'll go move the bike," Mari said wearily. "Unless you're volunteering."

"I think Ricky ought to move it and pick up my tools."

"That would be nice, of course. But he's already at the Stanley's. I hate to make Mrs. White wait," she said, putting down her drink and picking up a cover-all apron in preparation for removing the bike. "She's old and unwell, and even if it's not important to you, it is to her."

Across the greensward of three adjacent and neatly mowed back lawns, smoke rose in dense spirals from the Stanley patio. The drink was beginning to make inroads in his tensions, added to the alcohol he'd consumed at the office. The walls of the kitchen spun a little, the bricks behind the stove blurred in their neatly grouted lines. The birch cabinetry and the harvest gold Formica-sheathed countertops seemed to lurch a little. He considered another bourbon highball before picking up Rick's mess, which clearly he'd have to do, sooner or later.

"Let's not tell the kids until the end of vacation," Mari went on softly. "They enjoy Waterford so much—why spoil it for them." Her eyes filled; she reached for a paper napkin from the harvest gold holder in the center of the table, blotting carefully so as not to smear her mascara. "I'm terribly sorry for what I said, Steve."

Realizing he'd been too wrapped up in his disappointment to consider hers, he was ashamed. "It's okay, honey," he consoled. "Don't think about it anymore. Why don't we let Mrs. White stew in her own juice a while longer? It'll be dark eventually, and she won't be able to see a thing."

Mari laughed and held out her hand, and they cut through the three backyards.

"Here come the Sinclaires!" called Rosalie Stanley.

"We thought you'd never arrive!" Bill Hughes waved a barbeque fork.

"Of course we were coming!" Mari called back gaily. "Didn't Kathy tell you we were coming, Rosalie?"

"Oh, she told me, she told me." Rosalie had placed a tossed salad on the Stanley picnic table and was covering it with a net umbrella to discourage the flies. Lined up around the edges of the table were casserole dishes on metal holders with candles beneath to keep them warm, and buckets of potato salad, heaps of chips, and assorted desserts.

"Hi, Dad!" It was Ricky, appearing out of the Stanley recreation room, from which the record player and the plinking of Ping-Pong balls could be heard.

"Hey, Pal!" Rick was still young enough to appreciate touch, and Steven hugged him briefly. "We gotta talk about doing bike repairs on the front lawn."

"Mrs. White?" the boy asked with a doleful grin.

"Mrs. White," Steven confirmed. "Go on, now. Have fun!"

"O.K." Rick's departure was instant.

"Let me make you a drink, Steve!" Jeff Stanley said. "Sit right here, on this chaise. Put your feet up. I hear you're officially on vacation."

"I am." Steven stretched out, clasped his hands behind his head. "Thanks."

"Lucky dog," said Dave Cameron pleasantly.

"Every dog shall have his day," Steven pronounced. "My day is now."

"The Potters want to paint their house pink," John McClaine told the party. "How in the name of God can I sell my house if the one next door is pink?"

"Don't worry about it," said Jeff Stanley. "No one in Wildwood paints their house pink. We'll all see to it, old man."

"I shall sleep at last." John raised his glass in appreciation.

"You're going to move?" asked Jeff Stanley. "Is that why you're worried about selling?"

"You're moving?" Rosalie cried.

"Selling?"

"Transferred?"

"Transferred!" It echoed around the party, the counterpoint to all their lives. Steven flicked a meaningful look at Mari, reminding her that they had decided to keep quiet.

"No, not transferred," John McClaine said. "Though I'm ready for it."

"We could use a nice promotion right about now," said John's wife. "Pay for the orthodontist."

"Oh, you can't leave now!" Rosalie said exuberantly. "We need you for the bridge club."

"Well, then, we'll reconsider. I'm really looking forward to that."

"Me too. I haven't played seriously since my sorority won our college tournament," Rosalie agreed. "My sister—the one whose husband is the mayor—her bridge club is really going places, and here I sit, my game getting rustier and rustier."

"I don't like the way the pro shop is being run these days," Bob Hughes was saying. "It's getting cliquey. Group-wise, the club is great. But you ought to be comfortable with any of the members, and soon you won't be."

Dave Cameron smiled complacently. "Like always gravitates to like."

"I think I'll gravitate to the picnic table," Steven said, struggling out of the of lounge chair. "It's a shame to ignore such good food."

"I'll join you," declared Ellen Hughes. Approaching the table, they picked up plastic utensils and paper plates. "Bob's right," Ellen said, putting a small mound of everything in spaced dollops on her plate. "The club is getting to be unfun. Don't you think so?"

"I haven't been over for quite a while," he said, dumping some potato salad into a paper bowl.

"So that's why I haven't seen you."

"Unfun, like you said."

"But don't you get bored, just sitting at home?" Behind her smile was a suggestion he ignored. You had to be careful around Ellen Hughes.

Everyone decided to eat, right then. The kids poured out of the Stanleys' rec room, heaped their plates, quickly returning to the house so they'd avoid having to eat with the boring grown-ups. The adults settled back, ate, drank, watched the fireflies beyond the patio lights.

Jeff Stanley got Dave Cameron into a debate on professional football, to which Steven listened while drifting far, far from sobriety. Ellen Hughes pulled up a chair. "Well, you and Mari must be about ready to take off for your vacation," she said, turning a little to talk. Her blouse was buttoned lower than even casual summer fashion dictated, and a generous portion of her breast was exposed. Instantly he was stirred, and looked away. "You're going to Cape Cod?" she asked, her voice husky and intimate.

"Yesh. To my family place."

"I seem to remember that it's old."

"Yesh. Positively hishtorical."

"I wish you had a picture of it."

"I do, of coursh."

"Well? Let me see."

"Itcsh at home. In a photo album."

"That's too bad. You must bring it with you next time. Or you and I could just slip over to your house and take a look."

"That'd be fun," he said, his face straight.

One eyebrow went up, and she smiled suggestively. "Now or later?"

"Later," he told her, and watched her stroll away. Did she expect him to follow?

Rosalie brought him another drink; following anybody just now was not an option. Probably getting out the chaise wasn't, either. Nor had he any intention of following Ellen Hughes. There was a woman like her in every suburb, bored and restless, unclear about the origin of her malaise, seeking a way around it with a man. Any man.

The party faded for a while. In time Mari materialized out of the fog of alcohol with an empty casserole dish in her hand. "I thought perhaps we ought to be on our way," she said, "since we have a long day tomorrow."

"I'll get the kids." Yes, he could rise from the chair now, after his snooze. Heading steadfastly for the Stanley rec room, he heard Mari saying insincerely, "Thank you, Rosalie, for such a nice evening." It had not been nice; it had been dull and exactly the same as all Wildwood parties, with variety in neither the guests nor the conversation nor even the food.

Wildwood was, indeed, in a rut, and would more than likely remain in one.

The kids were extracted and the four of them crossed the three backyards to the Sinclaire door. Ricky and Kathy disappeared into their third level bedrooms without protest. Steven mixed two more highballs, then followed Mari up to the fourth.

"Not another!" she protested.

"We're on vacation, after all," he told her, enunciating carefully. "Besides, how'm I going to seduce you if I don't get you drunk?" He watched her with an intensity that notified her sexual intimacy was next on the agenda tonight unless she had a strenuous objection.

"I saw you talking with Ellen Hughes," Mari said, as though this limited infidelity was sufficient to excuse her.

Too inebriated for caution, he protested. "But Mar! I turned her down!"

"You mean she... propositioned you?"

"Honey, she always does. She'll give it away to whoever will take it."

"Disgusting," Mari sniffed.

"But I didn't buy. Honest. If you don't believe it, just try me," he grinned.

Glancing at the evidence, she laughed humorlessly. "You're impossible." She kissed him in acquiescence and disappeared into the bathroom, no doubt to do whatever needed to be done with her diaphragm. Then she'd putter about, hoping to outlast him. But this time he wouldn't fall asleep, alcohol or no alcohol. It had been two and a half weeks since he'd had intercourse with his wife, and Ellen Hughes had whetted his appetite. Mari escaped this aspect of marriage whenever possible—yet she'd never turned him down outright. Just played a waiting game, as now, peeking around the bathroom door to see what state he was in.

Pleasantly he smiled, waved, and she came out, slipped into a sexy nightie which she believed disguised her lack of interest. Indeed, it went a long way! Against its ephemeral sheerness her nipples pressed like the noses of two eager puppies, and the darker mat of her crotch was seductively suggested beneath the filmy nylon cloud.

"I hate Rosalie Stanley," she said, reaching for the drink he'd brought her.

"Don't think about Rosalie Stanley."

"I can't help it."

"You could practice not thinking," he encouraged her. "In Denver or Boise or Portland. And if you get lonely, I could take care of you."

She giggled. "Poor Steve! You've been waiting all night!"

"I sure have."

Putting her drink on the bedside table, she slid down beneath the covers, patted the space beside her. "Come on, then," she said in gentle resignation. "What are you waiting for?"

"Just an invitation."

His clothes were instantly shed, the light extinguished. He would touch his wife tenderly, and he would roll on top of her and penetrate her and come to climax, quickly or slowly, depending on what he believed she wanted him to do. But he knew she would not truly enjoy it, despite her compliance and expressions of pleasure; he knew Mari believed she must fool him, that in doing so her wifely duty to him was discharged.

It could have been better, yes. But it could be worse, too. Accepting it as he always had, he came to rest beside her, the soporific of sex providing respite from that day. The loneliness within receded, and he slept.

❖∾ 3 ∾❖

The portrait's gold-leafed frame caught the afternoon sun. Steven contented himself with observing its brilliance as he listened to Mari, sitting beside him in her pocket on the velvet couch. It's time to get this thing reupholstered, he thought, before we hit the floor butt-first. Nearby, Mom occupied a tassled chair; the Marshalls had settled themselves on the horsehair settee. Cousin Elizabeth's furnishings were Victorian, to say the least! But usable, fortunately, since Charles Sinclaire had claimed the contents of the Port Huron house.

"So you're going to move to Elijah Merrick's place?" Mari asked Claudia Marshall.

"We're thinking about it," Claudia assented. "We've been a little upset about the tax rate at home. It's a lot lower here."

"We thought we'd modernize the plumbing now," J. Barry Marshall said. His parents, who had owned the old house, had passed on some years ago. Now it was his, to do with as he wished. The family had used it for summer vacations, until now. "We came down this weekend to arrange it. Just in case we do decide to move. Then it would be ready for us."

"Wouldn't you miss all the activities you're involved with at home?" Mari asked, for Claudia had impressed on them her importance in the suburban Boston scheme of things. The girl was another Rosalie Stanley if ever there was one, Steven mused, but it was a comparison that Mari had yet to make.

Claudia's smile was orthodontically perfect. "One reason we wanted to talk with you today was to find out if there's enough activity here to keep us from going stir-crazy. We've been going at it hammer and tongs, Barry and I."

"That makes it sound as though we'd had a knock-down, drag-out fight, dear," J. Barry protested.

"Well, that's not the way I meant it, of course!" Claudia exclaimed, patting her top-heavy bee-hive hairdo to make sure its swirls were still properly in place. "I'm sure they know that, Barry!"

"What it amounts to is that we think living here year 'round might have a lot of advantages," her husband said to Mom. "I keep telling Claudia that she won't have time to be bored—and then I said, let's go over and ask Mrs. Sinclaire instead of arguing about it." J. Barry nodded deferentially in Mom's direction. "Do you get bored, Mrs. Sinclaire?"

Steven wondered if Mom found the Marshalls objectionable, or if it was only some quirk of his own that made him wish they'd go home.

But she only laughed, and he couldn't tell. "You may have noticed that I rent rooms to tourists during the summer. We business people don't have time to be bored."

"I guess I didn't realize Kingsland was a boarding house in the high season." Claudia's lip upcurled a trifle. Was it disdain? Mari would be mortified if that was the case.

"It's called a Tourist Accommodation."

"How about in the winter, without the tourists around? Isn't that a little boring?" J. Barry persisted.

"Hardly. We're too busy relaxing. But there are quite a few new people coming into Waterford now, and not just retired ones. People like yourselves, sick of the suburbs. I haven't any doubt that sooner or later you'd find pleasant friends to keep you company."

"Barry could work from home," Claudia explained to Mari and Steven. "He thought if we moved down he could make one of the back bedrooms over into his office." Marshall was an architectural consultant, flexible, virtually self-employed. "He plans to work on restoring the place to its original décor in his spare time."

"What a fascinating idea, Claudia!" Mari exclaimed, impressed. "Its history is very well documented. You could show it, if you wanted to, as an example of the Cape's Colonial Georgian architecture."

"Federal," Claudia corrected. "It was built after the Revolution, so it can't be called colonial. We weren't colonies any more."

"You could start a historical society," Mari suggested, undaunted.

"Actually, we already have one," said Mom. "But its membership is mostly ladies over the age of 80. I've never paid much attention to it."

"Well, we're not even close to a decision about moving," said Barry.

"I worry about the details," said Claudia. "I mean, who would teach Junior his clarinet? He's really doing very well. We could send him to private school, I suppose, where they'd have a good music program. Still, it'd be good for him to learn the country way of life. It's the drug thing that scares me," she went on, switching topics back and forth like a hot potato. "And the black people. And the crime rate."

"We're pretty good about crime," Mom said. "And black people aren't an issue yet, since there aren't any."

Steven had a hard time picturing the Marshalls camping out in the old Merrick house. Sure as hell the place didn't have a shred of insulation in it! He cast himself out over the sea of his expertise: remove the clapboards (probably there was nothing between them and the inner plaster walls), install fiberglass bats . . . perhaps a vapor barrier? Sure as hell that house could never be so tightly sealed that condensation would develop as a result.

"The tax rate here is certainly favorable," Barry said to Mom as the back door rattled and the sound of knocking came faintly to them.

"I'll get it," Steven said to Mari. Upstairs he could hear Ricky squabbling with Junior Marshall. Kathy's record player crooned from somewhere in the house, probably the billiard room.

"Bob!" he shouted joyfully as Casey's bulk and breadth came into view through the screen door. "Son-of-a-gun, it's good to see you! Come in!"

"Thought I'd stop and see what you were up to." Casey's handshake was as warm as his smile.

Steven gestured toward the east lawn. "I'm sure you can tell." The grass was freckled with chips of faded green; shutters scraped and freshly painted, leaned against every available tree, tilted one way or another like old tombstones.

"Bitch of a job," Bob remarked amiably.

"That's for sure. But a nice change from the desk at Bronner." The shutters had taken nearly the whole vacation.

"How's the world of big business?"

"Not so good," he said shortly, "and life in the living room isn't much better. You'd be doing me a favor if you stayed and had a beer."

"I'll do better than that. I'll take you with me, and you can have a beer on the way. Matter of fact, that's why I stopped."

"Oh?"

"I'm going to Hobbes Hole. Want to come along?"

"What's going on at Hobbes Hole?"

"A surprise." Bob grinned. His leathery weathered skin was ruddy and tanned, crinkles around his eyes and grooves around his mouth deep. Very likely he was approaching fifty by now.

He's probably in a lot better shape than I am, Steven thought, whisking back to the parlor to tell Mari where he was going, excusing his departure with a wink at Mom and a wave to the Marshalls, who were still mulling over the feasibility of moving to Waterford (which they would never do, he thought, being too firmly attached to the amenities of city and suburban life).

Feeling like a boy again, setting off on an adventure, he climbed into Bob's truck just as he had in bygone years, listened to his friend's description of Waterford's building boom as they barreled down the mid-Cape highway, beer in hand, and then cut south toward Falmouth and on to the harbor at Hobbes Hole.

The outskirts of the village modestly appeared: a smattering of cottages, a restaurant, a Creem-Mee Freeze and a fish market, and then, the town itself, silver-shingled in the afternoon sunshine, the white-painted trim of its buildings hiding the shabbiness of their old age. Between them was the wink of water; the road plunged down to the harbor, where the masts of small and tall sailboats created a little forest.

Bob parked by the main wharf, which jutted into the cloudy water with a floating dock attached to the end of it at right angles, forming a T. Along the wharf were pleasure craft, the owners of which lolled on deck chairs, entertained guests, drank early-in-the-day cocktails. On the T itself, a group of tourists and townsmen watched the approach of the largest sailing vessel Steven had ever seen, her twin masts towering over everything else in the harbor. Bob moved quickly to the right end of the T, at which the ship was aimed. Steven followed, unable to take his eyes off the old schooner that clearly belonged to another age, another time, her height and breadth becoming more and more impressive as she approached, like a juggernaut. Was she under control?

His heart quickened; then the ship jibed smoothly, the sails spilling the breeze. She coasted parallel to the T; at her stern a crew member threw a weight with a thin line attached. It bounced on the splintered gray boards of the dock like a meteorite from another dimension. Quickly Bob snatched it, towed in the heavier line to which it was tied and wound it around a cleat. The sailor who'd thrown the line ran his end around a belaying pin. There was a tensing, a tightening, and water sprayed from the rope as it twanged and groaned and, abruptly, the ship, all one hundred feet of her, stopped, neatly parallel to the T.

"Christ," Steven swore reverently.

"Monkey's fist," Bob explained of the rope-wrapped lead weight that had been thrown. A belatedly-arrived harbor hand secured the other line tossed from the bow.

Along the side of the ship was her quarterboard with her name: *Jenny H. Lawrence*. She was no longer beautiful because she was old. Her years in the coasting trade, for which she was initially built, had spread her shape as a woman's body is broadened with childbearing. Her black paint was scabby and her brightwork dull, her gaff-rigged sails streaked with age, but none of these things diminished her. They made her even more compelling than if she had been young and slim because of the vastness of her experience, the mystery of her past.

As a crew member furled the immense sails, the captain poured drinks for his passengers, using the waist-high roof of the after-cabin as a bar. Lifting his glass in a toast, his words raucously boomed over the harbor, indistinguishable.

"Would you like to go aboard?" Bob asked.

"I sure would," Steven sighed. To behold it: the world of ropes and cleats and canvas and all the special and precise paraphernalia needed for the sailing of a ship, unique and not to be found anywhere else than on the deck of a vessel rigged for business.

"Casey! You old son of a bitch! How the hell are you!" The captain yelled from the midst of his party. "Thank God you were there to catch the monkey's fist!"

"Glad to oblige. There's someone I want you to meet," Bob replied as they joined the festive group.

"Grab a brew. I'll be free soon." The captain nodded at Steven and then turned back to his passengers. Having been part of something larger than themselves, something a mere sightseer could not be expected to understand, they paid no attention to the newcomers. Another round of drinks was had, more reminiscing about the past week, and then the pull of their lives onshore compelled them to pick up their bags and reluctantly disembark. The captain helped them when they needed it, bid them hearty farewell and accepted the gratuities pressed into his palm.

"Jesus! And to think you're wasting your time building houses for fat-assed suburbanites, Casey, when you could be sailing with me." The captain, surprisingly young, was startlingly drunk.

Undaunted, Bob pressed forward. "I brought a friend with me. Steve Sinclaire, meet Eric Larsen."

Larsen extended his large hand. "Good to meet you, Steve. Let's get out of the sun. It's too fuckin' bright out here." Three steps led down into the after-cabin, where there was full headroom. Along its sides were built-in benches; a plank-topped table took up the center, bolted to the floor.

"I thought Steve would like to see the ship," Bob told him. "He used to do a lot of sailing."

"Not on ships like this, though," Steven said quickly. "Only little ones like summer camps have."

Larsen reached behind a bench cushion and came up with a bottle, helped himself to a slug and passed it over.

"Steven's great-great-grandfather was one of those old merchant captains," Bob said, taking a swallow.

"No kidding! So do you still sail, Sinclaire?"

"When I can," he said, swelling foolishly with the pride of belonging, yet eager to steer the conversation elsewhere than his own insignificant nautical past. "How did you ever learn to handle a vessel this size?"

"Not at any goddamned camp," Larsen laughed.

"Eric, here, is licensed to sail on the seven seas," Bob bragged. "Not just everyone can say that!"

"How did you do it?" Steven asked again. Surely Larsen was not old enough to have had time for all seven seas!

"I quit school when I was fourteen," the captain said. "Worked on tramp streamers and along the way I found guys who could teach me what I wanted to know."

"*Jenny* has been sailing in Maine," Bob said. "Barbara and I went on one of her windjammer cruises a year ago. That's how we met Eric, here."

"Why's *Jenny* on Cape Cod now?" Steven asked. "Instead of Maine."

"She got sold," Larsen said. "Her new owner moved her down here early this spring. It's a longer season, and warmer. We could even go out in October, if anyone had the guts to do it."

"Warm on land, but cold on the water then," Steven remarked, reaching for the bottle.

"That's what the owner thinks. The city dudes would be miserable. Bad publicity. He figures to sail her around here as her own advertisement this summer, and sell her to the first reasonable bidder. Which there are more of here than in Maine."

"Any bids yet?" Bob asked.

Larsen held his hand out for the bottle. "Not yet. But we're booked for the rest of the season. The ship's reputation is spreading fast. The wharf is filled to the brim with spectators when we arrive back on Saturdays, like it was today. The tourists always try to catch the lines when we throw them. It's the truth," he said affably to Steven. "The minute a man looks at *Jenny*, he becomes a seafarer. Or claims his great-grandfather was."

"I didn't claim that. Bob did."

Larson laughed. "It shows, anyway. I mean, that you like ships and sailing. It's something a man can't hide. Take him around, Casey, if you want." He yawned. "If anyone asks for the captain, tell 'em you don't know where I am."

With a jaunty wave he left.

"Where's he going?" Steven asked.

"There's two forward berths, one for the captain, the other for the mate. He probably hasn't slept much this week."

The old ship sighed and shifted at her berth as the tide rustled past her hull. The voices of the departing passengers and onlookers on the wharf, their shouts and calls, sounded distant and happy, like the cries of children playing at dusk. All the worries Steven had been carrying fell away, along with his dread at the impending move to Boise or Portland or Denver.

"Ready to take the tour?" Bob asked after a long period of companionable silence.

"Sure."

They mounted the steps to the deck, moved forward to the middle of the ship and climbed down a ladder. To the left was the galley, with a wood stove on one wall, compartments for storage on the other, and a sink with a pump adjacent to the after-cabin. High above it a sliding window could be seen, through which food could be passed up to the screwed-down table. Further on, beside the galley, were lavatories with pedals for pumping water into the closet and flushing it out again; down the center of the vessel ran a narrow passageway with several enormous beams bridging it, forehead-high. On both sides were cabins, inside of which were bunks and just enough space to get into them.

"And that is that," Bob said. "Except for the captain's and first mate's berths in the bow. You have to hope for decent weather, because sure as hell there's no place to go and nothing to do unless it's topside." Patting one of the bridging beams, he looked about affectionately.

"When I can, I come along. Help out. Take the ferry back after a day or two. Probably Larsen wouldn't mind if you came, too."

A chance to sail in such a ship!

"Will you find out? If I can?"

"Sure."

"Can you ask Larsen before we go?"

"I'm sure he's sleeping; I'll ask him later. I doubt he spends much time in the sack when there's a voyage in progress. Or, if he's in the sack, I doubt he's there alone."

Larsen, large and rugged and capable, was doubtless attractive to the opposite gender. "I can believe that." Good God, every female for miles around must be lined up at his door!

"Very moody, actually. Up one minute, down the next. But he can sail," Bob said affectionately. "There's nothing he can't do with a ship. I'm going to meet *Jenny* in Nantucket later this week. I'll ask him then."

"I've only got this week left of my vacation. The only chance I'll have is to go with you to Nantucket."

"Sure. I'll find out, and call you later today or tomorrow. We can take the ferry over."

The truck climbed up to the main street in first gear. Behind them in the harbor the small boats bobbed like ducks riding the swells, and the towering masts of the *Jenny H. Lawrence* became short and squat from the heightened perspective of the town's elevation.

Far out past the jetty were channel lights and flashers and blinkers and bells and horns. Hobbes Hole was preparing for the night of revelry to come, the evening Mardi Gras of summer in the sixties. Opening fresh cans of beer, purchased at a local bar, they set out for Waterford.

"Where were you?" Mari frowned. "I thought you'd be back before this."

"Hobbes Hole isn't exactly next door."

She gnawed on her lower lip, said nothing.

"What's wrong?"

"Nothing."

"Come on, tell me," he coaxed, and sat down with her at the kitchen table.

"Well, once the Marshalls left, I got to thinking about packing and moving and getting school records and things like that," she admitted. "It just got me down a little, is all."

"Don't blame you a bit, Honey. Let's have a beer and forget about it for a while."

"I'd say you were well ahead of me on that score. But I'll take you up on it." Her smile was only a partial success. "I don't think we can forget about it, though. Vacation's nearly over. It's time we told the kids."

"I guess you're right," he agreed slowly. "And my mother."

"Tell me what?" Mom asked as she entered the kitchen.

"We'll talk about it when the kids come in."

"Oh." Mom looked from one to the other. "I think I can guess." She shrugged. "Onward and upward, right?"

"Onward, anyway," Steven said wryly.

"Onward?" Kathy asked, popping in suddenly from the billiard room.

"Get your brother," Mari ordered. "We have something to tell you."

Just as Mom had done, Kathy looked from one adult face to the other. Quickly she ran outside, and Steven heard her voice, thin and wavering. Rick-ee. Rick-ee. She was close to tears already.

Pulling a chair out for Mom, getting two bottles of beer out of the refrigerator, Steven tried to arrange his face into lines of calm confidence. The children appeared, looking cautiously through the kitchen's screen door.

"Come on in," he instructed them. "We have some things to talk about, and we might as well do it now."

Wary, they watched him as they joined the adults at the table.

"I'm being transferred," he said, his voice calm, without apology, applying the church key to the bottle caps so he wouldn't have to look at the assembled family.

"You mean we're moving again," Ricky said, stating the case clearly, as he always did.

"Yes. But this time we have a choice. We can go to Oregon, way out on the Pacific Ocean, or Idaho where there's a salt-water port—the largest—maybe the only—inland seaport in the country. Or Colorado, where the Grand Canyon is." He smiled with determination. "I don't have a preference. Do you?"

"Do we have to go, Daddy?" Kathy asked.

"To one of those places, yes."

"Do you really want to?"

"No." His discouraging setback at Bronner, now like a prison sentence, had to be faced. "But I don't have much to say about it."

"When are we supposed to leave?" his daughter asked.

"I'll tell Mr. Sattiswaite which territory I'll take when we get back. We'll move in a few weeks."

"Why can't we just stay here?" Rick asked.

For an instant no one moved.

"Here?" Kathy turned to her brother. "In Waterford?"

"Yes, here," Rick said stoutly. "At least we know where everything is already. Where the school is. Who our neighbors are. We don't have to learn that stuff all over again. We belong here."

Here.

Here, Steve repeated to himself. Here. At Kingsland. Here, on Cape Cod.

The masts and sails, the bowsprit and transom, passenger cabin and galley of the *Jenny H. Lawrence* instantly became real and present—as real and as present as his own family right here in the kitchen. Longing rose up, poignant, sweet, strong.

Hastily he worked on his beer, poured more for himself and Mari. After the booze already in his system, it took very little to cause him to float.

"I think I need a drink," Mom said. "Maybe a gin and tonic."

"Shall I get you one?" he asked.

"I'm not sure you can navigate just now," she said, trying to lighten the moment. "I don't know where you've been, but I know what you've been doing."

"Could we stay here with you, Grandma?" he heard Ricky ask as Mom lined up bottles of gin and tonic at the kitchen sink. "We could help you, couldn't we? With your tourist business?"

"Let's see first what your Mom and Dad have to say," Mom said as she stirred her drink, put ice in it, a slice of lemon, and joined them at the table again.

"I say it's a crazy idea," Mari said definitively.

"What's so crazy about it?" Ricky asked.

"Yeah," Steven said to her. "What's so crazy about it?"

"Don't tell me you'd even consider it!" Mari exclaimed. "It's only the whim of a pre-adolescent boy!"

"It's not a whim," the pre-adolescent boy insisted. "Whatever that means."

The whole thing was impossible. Yet Kingsland was his own, free and clear. There'd be no mortgage to worry about. If they sold the house in Pennsylvania, there'd be plenty to support them for quite a while.

"We could all help run the house in the tourist season," Kathy said. "That'd be nice for you, don't you think, Grandma?"

Grandma did not get a chance to answer.

"Look, Kathy," Steven told his daughter, "there are no big department stores or malls where you can hang around with the gang. There's no bowling alley or movie theater. The kids here aren't like the ones at home," he went on reasonably, though there was no reason in the world why he should be arguing the point, particularly with Kathy, whose present friends he did not like. "The kids here will be uncool."

"To tell the truth," his daughter said, "I'd sooner not have to be cool. It's a drag. If everyone is doing it, you kind of have to go along. But if no one is—why, you can be yourself, can't you?"

There was a tightening somewhere inside, a little quiver. "Why, yes, baby. You can." He glanced at Mari.

"I don't believe this!" she protested. "You *are* taking it seriously!"

Their little girl might remain a child a bit longer, here on Cape Cod. His wife might lay claim to her own personality here, shrugging off the Rosalee Stanleys of the world, making her own way. And Ricky might grow straight and strong and more true to himself than would be the case elsewhere.

"This seems like a good time to share something that I haven't mentioned so far," Mom put in. "If you came here to live, it would be perfect for me."

"Why is that, Mother Sinclaire?" Mari asked.

"Well, an old friend of mine who lives in Philadelphia has been recently widowed. We were roommates at Bryn Mawr, and she wants me to be her roommate again. Between my allowance from Charles, and some kind of part-time job to augment that, like the tourist business here does, I could get along. As far as I'm concerned, you can move in tomorrow. And if you're interested in a business of your own, the tourist industry is growing by leaps and bounds."

She'd been happy here, Steven knew. But after 16 years, certainly she deserved a change.

Mari was trying it on for size, envisioning herself busily directing her own destiny, managing the myriad details of the boarding house business. Actually earning money, which suburban women seldom had a chance to do.

"If you did a little work on the space right over the kitchen here, you all could sleep up there and then the rest of second floor would be available to rent. You could use the billiard room for yourselves. You'd have privacy that way. And the third floor attics haven't been finished at all."

"When you rent rooms, how much do you charge?" he asked Mom.

"Astounding amounts." Mom smiled in wry amusement. "Sometimes fifty dollars a week for the front rooms. Twenty five for the smaller ones."

"If we made a couple more rooms and a bath on the third floor," Steven asked, "could we get twenty five dollars for them?"

"Probably," his mother said, her eyes sparkling. "And when you're done, I'm sure you can get work with Bob Casey. He's always asking when you're coming back, Honey."

Nowhere else, he thought. Nowhere else can you get what there is to be had here; if you're ready for it, you can learn to live as Waterford people do, able to take what life offers and make the best of it. He had been too young, once, to join them—but now, now he needed what they had. And perhaps his children did, too.

"Let's do it," Ricky urged.

"If we run a tourist house here at Kingsland, you kids would have to help," Steven said. "We couldn't do it without you."

"Sure," Rick agreed. "I'll take out the garbage."

"I'll make beds," Kathy offered.

"We could raise chickens," Rick said. "I'd build a house for them."

"A pig!" Kathy shouted. "A horse! A cow!"

To never, ever, sit at a desk in an office. To wear blue jeans in the middle of the week. Shave only when necessary. To once again see the elms fuzz up greenly in the spring and reach across Main Street to each other in the summer. To watch the coming of the little black ducks in the fall and their going again once winter was done....

"You're all crazy," Mari insisted. "We are not going to run a guest house. We are going to move to Denver or Boise or Portland."

"Must be time for Hogan's Heroes, kids," Steven said. "Go watch. We won't make any decisions while you're gone. Promise."

Dubiously they left, and he sat with his mother and his wife and his malleable future, his to shape, his to decide, his to risk if he could but persuade his wife to venture out of the safety of the known.

"Tell you what," he proposed, forcing himself to speak calmly, nonchalantly. "Let's just go off by ourselves, Mari, you and me, tomorrow. No hurry. No rush. Think about it without kids hanging around."

"Or your mother." Mom grinned. "Pressuring you to let her off the hook."

"There's an art gallery in Barnstable I'd sort of like to see," Mari said. "As long as we're just cruising around."

"Then we shall see it. And there's something I'd like you to see, too. In Hobbes Hole."

"If you don't mind, Mother?" Mari asked. "Watching the kids?"

"Who? Me?" Mom waved any inconvenience that a day of keeping track of Kathy and Rick might cause her. "Far be it from me to impede the onward and upward march of the Sinclaires!"

"I'll drink to that," Steven smiled, and Mari did, too.

CHAPTER

The Heir

SPRING HESITATED with its usual reluctance; the wind off the bay was still shrill around the edges and the water was still gray; herring had not begun to come up the mill stream. Steven wiped his hands on the greasy rag that Roly Hall always left on the gas pump, and turned up his coat collar, shivering a little. But he did not bother to go into the shelter of the station, because another car was pulling up to the pumps. Without enthusiasm he saw that its driver was Claudia Marshall in her Ford station wagon, wearing slacks and a sweater and heavy gold bracelets. Her daytime makeup was meticulously right so that she looked like a fashion model in the Sears, Roebuck catalog, sporty but utterly feminine. She and J. Barry were camped out in the old Merrick captain's house, living in one room after the other as the rennovations they required progressed.

She rolled down her window, and the hot air from the car heater warmed his face. "Hi, Steve!"

"Hi. Fill it?"

"Yes, please." He prepared himself for the conversation that was sure to take place while the meter clanked and whirred and the pump delivered gas at thirty-five cents a gallon. "All set for the meeting this afternoon?" she asked.

"At the rate Mari's going, we'll never be ready. We've moved every stick of furniture five times, trying to get it right."

"Really, Steve," Claudia said earnestly. "I was so glad when she told me that you two were able to take a little time out, at last. It must mean you're on top of your renovations. Everyone is dying to see what you've done to the house."

"Mari's looking forward to showing you," he assured her. "She had all the old furniture reupholstered and resprung and refinished for the parlor and dining room, and she's been digging up artifacts and portraits that have been stored in the barn. We look like something from a museum."

Their own furniture filled the library and billiard room and the second floor maid's quarters over the kitchen. What they couldn't use they sold along with the Pennsylvania house.

"Can't wait to see it," Claudia assured him.

He edged the meter over to three dollars and hung up the nozzle. Claudia gave him a five dollar bill and he took it into the station, where Roly Hall and Linc Sears watched without offering comment. If she were aware of the observation by the old men, she gave no sign of it, waiting with an untroubled brow, listening to the radio in her car, a woman without worries who watched while the tradesmen of Waterford did her work for her.

He took the change out, and she smiled prettily. "Thanks!"

"Right."

"See you later."

Waving, he turned away, working hard not to resent her because it was not her fault that she and Barry were fresh and perky while the Sinclaires were exhausted. Keeping their savings in tact, Steven worked on Kingsland nights and the days he had off from the Texaco station; Mari had painted every window and papered every wall. They'd done everything themselves except the upstairs plumbing, which Harry Mayo had finished in December. The man had charged so much that the whole first summer of income would be needed to offset it.

No other car was approaching. He went inside the station and sat down in the chair nearest the desk.

Roly Hall grinned and winked. "We was just sayin' that's a nice-lookin' car."

"Nice-lookin' girl, too," said Linc. "Nice tits. You could just about see 'em from here."

"Linc," Steven chided. "You were looking."

"If a woman rides around in this weather with a tight sweater on and no coat," observed Linc, "it appears to me that she wants someone to look. Glad to accommodate her." He waved his pint in accolade.

"Help yourself," Roly said, nodding toward the pan of Mrs. Hall's cinnamon rolls which she'd sent in with him.

"Thanks," said Steven, scooping out a morsel. The discussion which, no doubt, had started some time before, continued.

"They have all the signatures they need to put it in the warrant, you know." Link gestured widely as he was apt to do, having been drinking since this time yesterday.

"Put what in the warrant?" Steven asked.

"That damn article about that damn Lyceum Hall in Truro."

Steven shrugged. Thirty years ago, during the depression, Waterford's Lyceum Hall had been bought cheaply from the town and floated over to Truro on a barge. Since that time it had served as a private residence. Now certain elements of Waterford's citizenry wanted it back, to be refurbished and turned into headquarters for the recently expanded Historical Society. "Why doesn't the society use the museum we built at the mill site?" he asked. "It has quite a lot of room, as I remember."

"No heat."

"Putting in a furnace sounds cheaper than bringing the Lyceum Hall back. It'll have to be heated, too."

"Trust you're goin' to town meetin'," Roly said. "Trust you'll bring those points to the attention of the folks there."

"I'm going, sure." He wouldn't miss it. A real town meeting, like New England had used since very the beginning. He'd never been to one, though he remembered the men at the Ace-High talking about it.

The little office was quiet as each man settled into the unoccupied conversational space, thinking about the dislocations being caused by Waterford's real-estate boom.

"Did you hear about the fella from New Jersey who bought an old shack on the beach," Linc asked. "He found this date on one of the cellar timbers—1760. Goin' to have one of them little signs put by the front door."

"They might want to check that carving," Steven suggested. "I don't think any shack would have lasted this long if it was on the beach."

"He's right," Roly remarked. "It would have been washed away years ago."

"This fellow insists it's historic, and he's going to—whatever it's called."

"Restore it?"

"Ay yuh."

"Good for the carpentry business," Roly remarked. "Who got the job?"

"A fella from Connecticut. Moved in a year ago; specializes in old places."

Roly shook his head in resignation. "I dunno. Maybe the town's gettin' ahead of us."

The bell rang, and Steven ran out to fill the tank of an out-of-state car—rarely seen during the raw spring of Cape Cod and almost never during winter. Indeed, winter brought work nearly to a stop, and only the long-standing relationship he'd had with Roly kept him employed now.

He checked his watch: good. Eleven-thirty. Quitting time for him. He'd been on the job since six, when Roly opened up, but his day was far from over. This afternoon he'd work on the last of the newly created third floor bedrooms. He'd made three up there, and a bathroom, and now he was taping and sanding sheet-rock, a laborious, time-consuming, and not always successful job for an amateur like himself, who'd done so little of it.

"I'll be leaving now, Roly," he said, ducking back into the office momentarily. "See you in the morning. Tell Mrs. Hall the rolls are great."

"Right."

"So long, Linc."

"So long, Steve. Take it easy. I think we just shouldn't take it layin' down, is all," Linc said to Roly. "Pretty soon they'll be wantin' a regular police chief, instead of an old war horse like you."

Steven shut the door on the amiable protest from the present chief, and jogged downstreet to his house. He'd finished the bedroom to the right of the stairs yesterday, and hopefully it was ready for Mari's assault with paper and paste. An old house, they agreed, should be papered, even if the job was done badly by beginners. It would add to the charm and cover irregularly plastered sheet rock seams. Transients would never notice them. He'd take another look this afternoon, in the harsh cruel light of the March day, and hopefully find it satisfactory.

"Hi, honey!" Mari called from the parlor. "There's chowder on the stove."

"Great!" He helped himself. "Kids coming home for lunch today?"

"Nope. They took sandwiches and an apple to school." She bustled into the kitchen. "I'd like to bring Kingsley and Julia out of the library and put them on the wall by the piano, if you don't mind, honey," she added. "They're your ancestors, after all."

"Of course I don't mind," he reassured her, stirring his chowder. "I'd sooner they were out of the library." He'd have preferred to store all of the portraits in the barn, but they had become very important to his wife.

Letting his chowder cool, he followed her into the library, lifted the heavy portrait of Kingsley Merrick off the wall. Together they carried it into the parlor, and he held it in an approximate place and waited for her confirmation.

"A little to the left. I hope you'll come downstairs for the program, and meet everybody."

It was important to her, he knew. He'd been too busy with the house to care much about the recently burgeoning Historical Society, and his dislike of Claudia was part of not wanting to be involved, too.

Yet, judging from what he'd heard at Roly's today, he should have been paying more attention.

The nail sank deeply into the plaster and seemed fairly firm. They went back for Julia, hung her portrait next to Kingsley. From her gold encrusted frame on the other side of the room, Molly Deems Merrick watched the goings-on with interest. Stepping back, it seemed like the parlor, for all its size, was very heavily populated.

"So you'll come downstairs for the program?" Mari asked as he went back to the kitchen to fetch his well-cooled chowder.

"Sure. I might be dirty and sweaty, though."

"The last time I looked, there was a new shower on the third floor," she remarked brightly.

Dumping the chowder back into the pot, he stirred and served himself again. Just right. "If I can clean up, I will. Around 2:30?"

"Make it 2:15."

"OK. But tell me—is it true that the society wants the town to buy the Lyceum Hall?"

"Yes. Though I doubt the town will. Until there's more newcomers than locals, anyway. Then just watch our smoke!"

"What else does the society have in mind?" he asked casually as he continued to eat.

"They're interested in creating a historical district on Main Street someday," Mari said slowly, as though thinking carefully. "But I don't know what else." She laughed lightly, and he suspected she knew every plan very well. "Will we be ready to take on the last room tomorrow?"

"I think so."

"Great. I'm supposed to pick up the paper today. I'll be back by one thirty." Perkily she kissed his cheek and sped off, her mind on the details of the gathering. Uneasily he watched from the parlor window as she whipped out of the driveway, spraying clamshells as she went, happy as an adolescent girl preparing for the senior prom.

Rinsing his chowder bowl, he picked up the trowel where he'd left it on the kitchen counter, climbed the back stairs which had been used in more affluent times by servants, past the second floor where the Sinclaires would sleep in the summer, on to the third.

The room he'd finished yesterday wasn't bad, he thought, running his hand along a seam. Moving to the next bedroom, he opened the can of plaster and rolled out a length of tape.

A commotion on the back porch drew him to the window. Prying it open was a major accomplishment. "Who's there?"

The person who'd been knocking backed into the yard and looked up. It was old Eben Gray.

"You busy, Mr. Sinclaire?" he called.

"Wait a minute." The tape curled back up into its original shape as he replaced the lid on the plaster (it would dry out if you didn't keep it tight closed when you weren't using it), and clattered down the stairs, opened the kitchen door. "Won't you come in, Mr. Gray?"

"Thanks," Eben said, looking around as he entered. The kitchen had not changed much over the years, and the old man visibly relaxed as he saw the black iron stove and the cracked linoleum on the floor. "I'm awful sorry to bother you," he apologized.

"No trouble. Won't you sit down?"

"All right. I won't be long." It would be hard for Eben Gray to come to the point, trained as he had been to pass pleasantries for an indefinite amount of time before getting down to business. Patiently Steven waited him out until the man outright asked, "Have you heard about town meetin' next week?"

"Yes, I've heard."

"Read the warrant?"

"No, but Linc Sears told me that there was something about the old Lyceum Hall."

"Eh yuh." The old man's face did not indicate his opinion about it. Clearly this was not the object of this visit.

"I'm afraid I don't know about anything else," Steven confessed.

"Well, actually, that's why I'm here," Eben said hesitantly. "You see . . . it seems like they want a clam warden."

"Clam warden?"

"Yup."

"What does this clam warden do?"

"Well, I'm glad you asked that, Mr. Sinclaire," Eben said, relieved of having to come to the point unassisted. "It seems there's this idea goin' around that the town can cultivate them clams. They plan to section off the Waterford flats like we used to divide cranberry bogs—make it eight parts and close all but one each summer, a different one every year. That way there'll always be a nice clam supply. They'll charge money for permits, the town will make enough to pay for the clam warden, and we'll have more clams than we ever had before."

"Yes?" he asked, unsure of the drift of Eben's conversation, mindful of the work that waited for him upstairs.

Eben Gray fidgeted a moment. "To tell the truth, Mr. Sinclaire, me and the Mrs. depend a lot on those clams. We certainly don't aim to go on welfare—no, sir!" Gray drew himself up proudly. "But without them clams, I don't know how we'll make out. We sell 'em to restaurants in the summer. Lots of 'em."

"You can dig in one part of the flats, can't you?"

"Yes. But there's going to be a charge to dig 'em, and a limit for each person that's a good deal less than what me and the Mrs. generally take. And if the clams don't look so good to the warden, he can close the flats altogether, so the population will grow. But Mr. Sinclaire, the fact is, only the Lord knows what makes a clam decide to grow, and where."

"Yes, Eben, I see your point." But why was the old fellow telling him about it?

"I don't mean to take too much of your time, Mr. Sinclaire. What I meant to do ... what I wanted to do ... is ask you if you'd speak at town meeting against the clam warden."

"Huh?"

"Well, it's all about whether or not the town votes the money to pay a clam warden. They'll argue that it's only temporary—that the town won't have to pay for the warden very long, because in time the clams will pay for him. But Mr. Sinclaire, them clams won't pay, and by the time the conservation people have seen it won't work, the Mrs. and I'll have to take welfare whether we want to or not. I'll speak against it, too," Eben Gray said earnestly. "But all I can do is say that from my years of clammin' I don't truly think they can be regulated like that. And somehow, Mr. Sinclaire, I don't think the conservation people will believe me. They'll take one look, and they'll say: what does this old man know about it?" Steven looked through the eyes of the 'conservation people' and, indeed, saw an old man whose scrawny neck extended through a frayed collar too large for it. There were patches on his knees and elbows, safety pins where his buttons should have been, clumsy boots, and stubble on his chin....

"I'd be glad to tell the meeting what you've told me—about the clams, if you think it would help."

"I don't think it'd hurt, that's for sure," Eben Gray said. "And thanks."

Steven watched the old fellow shamble down the driveway, and climbed the stairs again, smearing goo onto a seam, then covering it with the tape and another light coat of spackle, smoothing it, spreading it, feathering its edges so that it would eventually be unnoticeable.

There was another commotion on the back porch, and again he opened the window which moved more freely than before, now that it was getting use.

"Yes?" he called. "Who is it?"

This time two men moved backwards and into the yard. "Don Slater," yelled one.

"And Greenleaf Stone," yelled the other.

"Wait a minute." Replacing the putty lid and trotting back downstairs, he threw the trowel into the sink and opened the door.

"Hi, Don. Hi, 'Leaf." He'd known them both from days gone by at the Ace-High. "What can I do for you?"

"It's about the warrant for town meeting next week," Slater said. "Hate to bother you, Steve, but could we take a minute of your time?"

"Sure," he said, momentarily giving up on the third-floor bedroom. "Come on in. Have a beer?"

"Sure," they chorused, and accepted a seat at the kitchen table.

"Seems there's a problem come up," Slater began, "and neither 'Leaf or me knows what to do about it."

Steven was beginning to get the picture now. Because he had lived here, not so long ago, as a tradesmen like themselves despite the fact of belonging here at Kingsland, he was accessible to people who had nowhere else to turn.

No good can come of this, he thought. No good at all.

"Actually, 'Leaf and me—the problems we're running into are a little like two sides of one coin," Don explained. "'Leaf's the building inspector now. I'm on the Plannin' Board, so between us we get a pretty good idea of what's goin' on."

"The new folks on the board want to make buildin' here in town harder and harder," 'Leaf said. "They keep addin' more and more regulations to the code so people won't want to build here. Especially young ones, with children. They're afraid we'll need a new school, and taxes will go up."

"And they want to slow down the growth of business." Don said. "There's goin' to be an article that says no one can operate a trade from home. But what about our young folks? How are they going to get started?"

"You can see what's happenin'," Greenleaf Stone said. "The new people want tradesmen to live somewheres else. Do business somewheres else. Raise their kids somewheres else, too. And somehow, Steve, it sticks in our craw."

"Yes, I can see that it would."

"So we came to ask you to speak against that zoning article. You ...well, hell, you talk like they do, and they'll listen to you. And whilst they listen, the rest of the folks at the meetin' who haven't figured out yet what's goin' on—maybe they'll understand better what's at stake, and they'll vote against the article, too."

They were men with large, work-scarred hands and weathered faces the texture of old wood. Men yet in their prime who would age quickly because their work made such enormous demands on their bodies. Men who had managed their own lives, in their own way. Men he had admired for years, who had accepted him. Now they were asking for help.

"Sure. I'll do what I can," he agreed unhappily.

"There!" Don beamed at 'Leaf. "I told you!" He thrust out a hand to shake. 'Leaf Stone shook hands too, and they finished up their beers and disappeared around the corner of the house. Soon the roar of an inadequately muffled engine soared and they took off in a cloud of blue smoke.

Troubled, he cleaned the plaster off of the trowel and climbed back up to the third floor and began working again. Mari returned, and he labored on while Historical Society cars pulled into the driveway, people got out and greeted each other, then went inside where he couldn't hear them any more. Good! The guests using this room wouldn't be disturbed by anything going on downstairs; probably all of the rooms up here would be quiet.

"It's time for the program, Steven," Mari called up the stairwell.

And him without a shower or change of clothes! He picked up his mess as fast as he could and went down to again rinse the trowel in the kitchen sink.

"You're still in work clothes!" She was waiting for him.

"I'm sorry, honey. But I finished the first coat of plaster, and the other room is ready for papering."

"Great!" She forgave him with a smile and he followed her into the parlor where the guests, mostly unknown to him, were chatting and waiting for the program to start. Their chairs were arranged in a semicircle in front of an easel. An attractive young woman, standing nearby, was also waiting. Quickly he sat down at the edge of the group, hoping he didn't smell like a ditch digger.

"This is Wendy Lane," Mari said to the society members. "She's going to tell us about her book, which has some interesting history in it."

Miss Lane set a charcoal sketch on the easel. "An interesting feature of our really old houses—particularly the small ones, the Cape

Coddy ones—are the chimneys. The bricks are set in unique patterns, and often the shapes are different, too. Each has a distinct personality." She set another chimney sketch alongside the one on the easel, and sure enough, it was different. "My book will be about the houses, and will be illustrated by these sketches."

Actually they were both artistic and interesting, and Steven found himself wondering why he had never noticed such craftsmanship on the old houses before. It was like the window in a cathedral he'd read about years ago—a little, insignificant window that made its church famous.... He thought about the little perfect window and then about other small attainments and achievements that could approach perfection if you were good enough, like shingling a house well, or plastering a sheet rock seam.

The presenter continued to the end of her sketches. At the conclusion was an open forum for the discussion of historical, Cape Coddy things.

"We've discovered a formal garden laid out on the west side of our house," Claudia announced. "We uncovered old flagstones beneath quite an accumulation of soil. I never realized that Cape Cod colonial people lived so graciously!"

"They must have," said someone else. "We found a sundial top, a bronze one."

"We're going to rejuvenate the garden come summer," said J. Barry. "Put in a fountain, plant flowerbeds."

"How charming," cried Mari.

"We're getting a quarterboard carved, too," said Claudia.

"Quarterboard?" someone asked.

"You know. One of those long pieces of wood with with a ship's name carved on it. People have been buying new ones and hanging them on their houses. You can use a ship's name, of course, or one that you've made up yourself. Ours shall be inscribed 'Kaptainsholme'," she announced proudly, "because that's what our house was."

"Kaptainsholme?"

"Spelled with a K," Claudia said. "Like they do in Vermont. When they name a ski chalet or something."

"It's darling, Claudia," Mari fawned. "A darling name."

"And this house—Kingsland? Who named it, I wonder," the speaker asked the group.

"This gentleman." Mari gestured toward the grand piano over which Kingsley Merrick's portrait hung.

"Well, Elijah Merrick was a sea captain," Claudia persisted. "I think that's very romantic! Much more romantic than being a coach driver. And Elijah's house has far more character than this one. Colonial houses are much more pure than Victorian ones."

"I don't know about that." Karen Jackson, president of the Society, protested. "They're each so different that I'm not sure you can compare them. Both your house and this one are jewels, in my opinion, each in their own way." She smiled and nodded to Steven, as though to reassure him that Kingsland was not a white elephant.

"Perhaps you're right," Claudia reversed herself and changed the subject quickly to one that suited her better. "But it's not as old as ours."

"Beneath this one is the foundation of the original Merrick house." Courageously, Mari pressed forward. "Built in 1725. Where Elijah Merrick was born."

"Ours is—"

"Maybe driving a coach isn't as romantic as sailing a ship," Mari went on, willing now to compete with Claudia while the whole Historical Society was listening. "But Kingsley Merrick made a fortune running them to the gold fields in Australia, and another fortune right here in Waterford when he set up the woolen mill on the stream west of town, to make cloth for the Union Army."

Steven watched her, laughing and happy.

"Kingsley Merrick was an extraordinary man," Mari was explaining to the group. "He made two fortunes while he lived, and was close to a third, in South Africa, when he died. He promoted the library, here in town, and strengthened the district schools, and he even got the two principal Protestant churches to unite. And you know how fussy people were about religion then!"

"Oh, yes!" They laughed as they considered the antiquated notions of the Puritans in pursuit of the Almighty.

"I think Elijah met his nemesis in South Africa too, didn't he, Steve? Like Kingsley Merrick did?" Claudia asked.

He disliked the position of oracle, dispenser of information. "I think so, yes," he admitted.

"You must really know a lot!" exclaimed Karen Jackson. "I'll bet you have information about that old Lyceum Hall."

"The one that was floated across the bay to Truro?"

"That's it!" she exclaimed. "The very one!"

"No," he answered. "They'd taken it away by the time I remember Waterford."

"There's a lot about it in the old records," Claudia said. "The town voted, after the War of 1812, to build a hall because they'd gotten into the habit of debates. A lyceum of sorts was held at our house all through the war."

"Your house?"

"Kaptainsholme," she said loftily. "And it was so successful that the town voted to put up a building just to use for debates and lectures and the like."

"The Historical Society hopes that the town meeting will vote to move the old Lyceum Hall back," said Karen.

"So I hear," he remarked laconically.

"Do you know what the locals think about it?"

"You mean whether they're willing to pay for moving it out of tax money?"

"Yes."

"Why should the town foot the bill for the use of a private society?" he asked, as pleasantly as he could.

"The society is open to anyone, and the building would benefit the town and everyone in it," Karen asserted.

"It would benefit people who are interested in history, and that's all."

"The Bicentennial will be here in a few years. It might get us government money..."

"It's not a Revolutionary object," he argued. "Claudia just said it was built after 1812."

"But money aside," Claudia interrupted, growing agitated, "it would be good for people to get stirred up a little about their heritage. If they don't care about it, they ought to." It appeared that the Marshalls deeply enjoyed enlightening the masses. Probably everyone in the society did.

"I think the question was about local feeling. I believe it isn't favorable."

"We need at least fifty natives on our side," Karen said. "Would you be willing to speak for it at town meeting?"

Everyone was watching.

"No."

Mari's dismay was nearly palpable. Probably she had assured everyone that her husband, scion of the house of Merrick, would work in behalf of history.

"Why not, Steve?" Claudia's voice rose in her disappointment.

"Because if the Historical Society thinks the building's so important, it should raise the money itself, instead of making everyone else pay whether they want to or not."

"Oh, shoot, Steve," Karen Holmes said persuasively. "The society tried raising money for a building of its own years ago—but they never seemed to get as much as they needed. Why, it'd take forever for us to raise enough—and with costs being what they are today, it's just about impossible. Besides, that wonderful building won't always be available. We have to act! We have to act now! You aren't as alien to the natives as we are. You could persuade them, I'm sure. And if we could muster up one hundred total votes, we'd have it."

"Look," he urged, "Waterford folks don't always agree with each other. But they argue things out on the floor of town meeting and made decisions then and there, either on the basis of what they've just heard, or their gut response. Not a little pushy group packing the meeting."

"Nonsense," Claudia said briskly. "There's only one way to get things done, and that's to organize."

He was quite sure that Waterford's meeting had been packed before. But by Waterford people, who had lived there since the beginning of time. Not newly arrived strangers. "You folks can install heat in the museum at the mill site, and run the society from there. Maybe the town would be willing to help with that, if you ask for just part of the expense. You don't need the Lyceum Hall."

They stared, as though he had descended into their midst from another planet.

Into the awkward silence came knocking on the kitchen door.

"Excuse me. I'll answer it," he said, escaping. It was Bob Casey.

"Ol' sport!" he cried in relief. "Come in and have a beer."

They settled themselves at the kitchen table.

"How's everything?" Bob asked, his manner casual, but beneath it Steven could sense a careful excitement. "I'm here on business, in case you're wondering."

"I was. You're supposed to be at work."

"Finished early so I could meet with a fellow about the *Jenny Lawrence*."

"Oh?"

"He's willing to put up some money so we can buy her."

"Buy her!" He remembered now that *Jenny* was up for sale.

"You and me and Eric Larsen. And this guy. He's willing to split the price four ways. Each of us would put in $4500. Eric says he can borrow that much, and he'd be in charge of repairs. Dominic Bruno—the new fellow—would be supercargo and take care of the finances and when he can, come aboard to help keep everything ship-shape."

"How do you know it's not Mafia money?"

"Talk about stereotyping!"

"I'm ashamed."

"You ought to be. He's a dentist. From New Jersey. He's wanted to go to sea forever, and *Jenny* is his chance."

"What would you and I do?"

"Job share—all the rage with the younger set, I believe. I'll order supplies and manage the laundry on weekends. You'll sail with the tour and take the guests ashore and bring them back and make sure the galley's running properly, supervise the liquor supply and do whatever needs doing to make everyone happy. And come home on the weekend to help out here while I go to Hobbes Hole and get the ship ready for the next tour."

"That doesn't sound like you're going to have any fun."

"I have a business to run. You don't. And I'm sure somehow there'll be some fun. Later in the season, perhaps."

Sail with the tour. Every week. All summer.

Could he persuade Mari to go along with it? Would they make $4500 back in the first season, let alone see a profit?

Suddenly he didn't care. He, too, along with Dominic Bruno, God bless him, could realize a boyhood dream.

Mari had her historical society.

He would have *Jenny Lawrence*.

He would go to sea.

CHAPTER

Jenny

THE SUN WAS BENEVOLENT, reflecting off the water in countless prisms. Its indolent warmth drew a saltiness from the muck and grasses along the shore. In the bow of *Jenny Lawrence,* Steven stood with a knife in his hand, ready to cut the anchor rope if necessity called for it. Nearby, Jerry Ferris, first mate, was poised to throw the monkey's fist; at the stern Bob Casey watched Eric Larsen intently, ready to do his bidding whatever it was.

Mari and Barbara Casey watched the hostess/cook whom Eric had hired—a young woman who was entirely too good-looking to suit them. They had come along on this test voyage to Fair Haven, sleeping aboard last night and sailing back again to Hobbes Hole this morning, and they sardonically watched the girl posing at the bow, the wind pasting her T-shirt tight to her breasts, her hair streaming behind her.

"Maybe there's a figurehead contest going on," Barbara remarked. "Maybe she's auditioning."

"Do they have such things here on Cape Cod?" Mari asked.

"Not that I know of," Barbara snickered.

Ricky and Kathy leaned on the starboard rail, waving to cars that honked and people who waved back vigorously, welcoming *Jenny's* well-publicized initial outing.

Proudly the ship approached the wharf. Her new paint shone, her brass fittings were polished and little colored flags fluttered from her stays. *Jenny* was as a middle-aged bride who had become young again, in a new gown with attendants holding her train and admirers throwing flowers. Her following of last summer, clients scheduled to sail this week, and tourists who'd read the local papers or the Boston ones—all of them waited to welcome *Jenny*.

"Eric," called Jerry Ferris from the bow. "I can't throw this damn monkey's fist without braining someone. It's too crowded on the wharf."

"Maybe they'll move back," Eric suggested calmly from the wheel. He turned to Bob and said something that Steven could not hear. Bob instantly disappeared over the stern; moments later the motor of the freshly tuned-up yawl boat roared.

The wharf drew near—too near—too fast. The crowd cheered and grew even larger, moved yet closer to the edge, unable to hear the harbor-hand calling, "Make way! Make way!" The fellow struggled and pushed aside one person, then another in hope of getting to the front and catching the fist when Jerry threw it. But the crowd was oblivious. Young and old, in shorts and sundresses, wearing odd hats and carrying peculiar parcels, they had no intention of giving way.

Eric called to Jerry now, his words unintelligible, but his voice urgent.

Jerry dropped the fist and went to the donkey engine, turned it on.

"Ready about!"

"Ready!" they called back.

Steven saw Eric nod at him; with a sinking heart and an instant loss of faith, he obeyed and cut the rope. The anchor chain tore through its hole, sudden and violent like a load of gravel sliding off a dump truck, the anchor itself plunging down and into the water.

"Helms alee," Eric called, and *Jenny* jibed, turning on her own axis. Her enormous spread of canvas traveled from left to right and stopped with a lethal crack. Now parallel to the wharf, she began to edge toward it, while all around them the pale worried faces of yacht owners watched, and on the wharf, the cheering became wilder. The donkey engine, sputtering, tightened the anchor chain, and Bob in the yawl boat herded the ship to the dock. *Jenny* snuggled up to the old tires that hung there as bumpers, and the harbor-hand, who had made it to the front of the crowd at last, tied her fast.

Blithely unaware that the *Lawrence* had survived her first near-catastrophe, everyone cheered and reluctantly allowed the passengers to stand at the front with their luggage. Hard on their heels were the press and the camera-men.

"Ready for them, folks?" Eric made a sweeping gesture toward the wharf. To the figurehead, he said, "Only the guests and press get liquor, Arlene. If anyone else asks, give them a paper cup and direct them to the water bucket and dipper. Mari and Barbara, you hang out looking beautiful and fill the press in on background material—family stuff, where the crew comes from; I'll tell them about the ship. Bob and Steve, you help with the luggage. And you kids"—he waved at Rick and Kathy—"direct the passengers to the after-cabin so Bruno can collect their money, and pass brochures out to anybody who wants one. Jerry, check on the ice and get more if we need it. At one-thirty we'll be ready to clear. Hopefully."

"Hopefully?" Bob asked.

"Weather permitting." Eric nodded. "Now, move!"

The passengers came in all sizes and shapes, but in only one color: white. They entered eagerly, paid their money, listened while Dominick Bruno described the table sittings for supper, the routine of the ship when at sea and when in port, the location of the toilets (call them "heads", please) and the limitations of the generator, hence the request that flashlights be used when reading in bed at night.

Jerry fetched more ice and brought chilled beer back from a nearby bar; Arlene poured highballs into paper cups with a friendly smile. She'd brewed coffee, too, for anyone who wanted it. In the cockpit, Eric recounted *Jenny's* history for the benefit of the press. "The *Lawrence* is one hundred years old. She was designed for use in the coast trade, taking goods up and down the Atlantic seaboard. Potatoes from Maine, shellfish from Maryland, iron from Pennsylvania, bullshit from New York."

Laughter, joy, scribbling of notes by the press.

Bruno assigned bunk spaces, calling the cubicles below staterooms; explained that the "head" was extremely delicate, so would *everyone* refrain from putting *anything* extraneous down them? Steven and Bob formed a luggage brigade; Mari and Barbara Casey talked knowledgeably to visitors while Arlene made sure the press had all the alcohol it wanted.

At one o'clock all visitors were urged to leave so that the passengers and crew could begin their week at sea. The weather and the tide would determine the tempo of their lives, and contemporary civilization would be left behind, which meant not only the press and the curious, but also the Caseys and the rest of the Merrick family. Bob would return next Saturday to help ready the ship for the following week, while Steven would return to Waterford and Kingsland for the day and night, coming back to Hobbes Hole in time for Sunday's departure. In the after-cabin Eric spread out charts, explaining their hieroglyphics to Bruno and a half-dozen passengers. It was one-thirty now, the hour of expected departure.

Steven slipped into the group. "Well, Sinclaire!" Eric acknowledged his presence affably.

"Well, Skipper," he boomed back with equal affability, as though they were on a stage. "How's it going?"

"Yes. When *are* we going, Captain?" asked a spectacled man with a nautical cap. Carelessly Eric looked through the small cabin windows to the land, over the wharves and sheds and the town.

"Not yet," he said, rolling up a chart. "Why don't you folks have another drink?" Pleasantly he looked in Steven's direction.

"Sure, folks," he was bound to say. "There's a whole section in the forward bulkhead full of ice and beer and setups, and cases of scotch and gin and bourbon near the foot of the ladder. I regret to announce that since the press is off the vessel, spirits are not supplied by the house.

That happens only for truly spectacular occasions, such as a visit from the staff of the Boston *Herald*—as happened today—or the ramming of another ship at sea. There's a clipboard hanging by the bulkhead door, where you can sign for whatever you take. We'll keep a running tab and settle up at the end of the week."

"But since we're not on the high seas yet," Eric put in, surprising him, "help yourselves. Don't bother to sign. Enjoy yourselves while we wait."

Quickly the guests flocked to the hold.

"Why did you offer them our private liquor supply?" Steven asked. "They haven't paid to sit here in Hobbes Hole and drink themselves blind."

Again Eric glanced landward. "According to the flag flying over the post office, the wind is still steady from the wrong quarter. We can't buck the wind and the tide, too, Steve. Either we wait until the tide's strong on its way out, or the wind dies."

"How long will it be before the tide is right?"

"About two hours. But I think the wind will drop before then, and when it does, the yawl boat can push us to the other side of the jetty. Then we can pick up a sea breeze and sail wherever we want. Just be sure no one goes ashore."

"That might be more easily said than done, if they have to sit on their hands much longer," he protested. "They'll want to do something to fill the time, like shop for souvenirs and stuff."

"If they're farting around Hobbes Hole we might miss our chance. We'd have to wait for them to come back, and we'd be late reaching Edgartown harbor. Mooring is tricky enough without doing it in the dark; we'd have to wait until morning to leave."

"We've got to sail today," Steven agonized. "We said we would."

"Sailor," Eric said severely, "nobody argues with the tide. You ought to know that."

"But—"

"The charm of a wind-driven vessel is that you're driven by the wind—isn't that right? Keep the booze flowing. If they're having a nice cocktail party, they won't care whether they're moving or not. Find Arleen and tell her to cook something. Cornbread or those little hot dogs in a jar that you eat with a toothpick."

"Okay," he assented grudgingly. It was true; the arrival of a hot snack would reassure the passengers their welfare was in good hands, even if the elements were uncooperative. And food might offset the tremendous amount of liquor being consumed.

Down below, he ducked the beams running from one side of the vessel to the other and made his way to Arleen's berth near the bow, knocked on the door. No answer; he shouted her name, without result. Peeked in. No Arlene.

Hurrying back again, passing the lavatory in which the flushing mechanism sloshed and moaned as its occupant furiously worked the foot pump, he waited to see if its inhabitant were Arleen. It wasn't; he went topside to look into the captain's berth on the port bow. Empty. That left the mate's; when he opened its hatch cover, Jerry Ferris looked up, his hands cupping the fair whiteness of Arleen Patterson's spectacular breasts. Unable to take his eyes off them, Steven tried to speak.

"We need you in the galley," he croaked at last.

"Who? Me?" Jerry asked.

"Her."

"Who needs me in the galley?" the girl called up, and laughed; she was very drunk.

Summoning what he hoped was a commanding tone, Steven said, "Ferris, get your ass up here!"

Reluctantly Jerry came, scowling, dropped the hatch cover as Arleen snuggled herself into his bunk for an unworried snooze.

"I don't care a damn about who you fuck and who you don't," Steven explained as reasonably as he was able. "But I care about this ship and the tour. We're due to sail soon. Arleen's supposed to fix a hot snack and she can't, thanks to you. Stay topside, Jerry."

"Okay, okay." Jerry waved away his offense. "But she was pretty well boozed up to begin with. It's not all my fault." He went off to pump the bilge while Steven hurried back to the galley and dumped munchables onto platters, handed them through the window to Bruno in the cabin, started the stove, fanning the flames until the dial read four hundred degrees, mixed cornbread according to the directions Mari had printed out for the serving of thirty people.

Up on deck the party progressed, Eric moving among the merrymakers, his voice joyful above theirs. Then he began calling instructions to Jerry and the passengers erupted into cheers. *Jenny* was going out!

Steven slipped up to the deck to help cast off the lines, raise the sails, watch the shore slowly, slowly slide away, pushed by the yawl boat with Jerry at the helm, until the jetties were left behind and the breeze drew *Jenny* outward and dispersed the smoke pouring from the galley.

Clearly the cook was in no position to enjoy sailing, much as he'd have liked to! Mixing himself a drink, he dumped the burnt cornbread over the side and got another batch going, piled salad by the handfuls on plates, handing them up to Bruno, who took them and flung them onto the table. There was chowder already made by Barbara and only needed heating; somehow Steven managed not to scorch it, filled ten soup bowls, handed up another platter of cornbread. He hadn't felt so competent in years, so entirely capable, serenely facing the tasks that lay ahead, strong, confident.

"We'd like some butter up here, for the cornbread," a passenger said through the window.

"Sure." He handed it up, heated water for dishes and started on them, bracing himself against the surge of the ship, joining the third sitting himself, lingering happily over his supper, talking to passengers while, in the galley, Bruno washed dishes. It was a well-fed, content, and cheery load that cruised into Edgartown at dusk, descending on the yacht-filled harbor like a great bird coming in to feed.

"Ready about," Eric called. Steven cut the anchor rope and into an incredibly small pocket near shore the *Lawrence* dived and wheeled, her sails crackling, her bowsprit swooping above the deck of a nearby yacht, barely clearing it while its owner cowered.

The sails sagged as the *Lawrence* quietly drifted to the end of her tether. All around them power-driven craft coughed to life, lifted anchor, and moved away.

Night was falling and the passengers would be ferried to shore where they would play, shop at the tourist traps awaiting them, sample the bars, walk around the tiny picturesque town where whaling captains had built their houses more than a hundred years ago. Laughter and music were already emanating from a restaurant that hung out on pilings over the water.

"Couldn't Jerry have pushed us in slowly, with the yawl boat, so we wouldn't be tearing into the harbor at sixty miles an hour?" Steven asked Erik.

"We weren't going sixty." Eric chuckled. "Besides, I like to see all those worried faces, watching us from their million-dollar Chris Crafts, wondering if we're going to spare them."

"What if the wind shifts? What if the anchor chain snags? We'd never survive the lawsuits."

"We have no power," Eric reminded him, "so we have the right of way. But nothing will go wrong. With a vessel this large, it'd take more than a wind shift in a sheltered harbor to alter her direction. She'll go where I tell her to go. Jerry will take ferry duty tonight. You'll take it tomorrow, Sinclaire."

"Should we furl the sails?" asked Dominic Bruno. "Since we're here for the night?"

"Christ, no," said Eric. "We'd just have to raise 'em again in the morning."

"We just leave them as they are?"

"Standard practice, believe me. We're all set."

Jerry brought the yawl boat around to the ladder and the passengers began their descent.

"Mr. Sinclaire," smiled a pretty woman, "I'm afraid the bathroom is plugged up."

"The head, you mean," chided Eric playfully.

"Oh, yes, the head." She giggled.

"There are nice restrooms at the Sunoco station in town," Eric told her. "We'll fix up the toilet while you're ashore. The ferry's loading now."

"Oh, thanks." She looked dubious as she climbed over the side and into the yawl, but whether she was worried about the Sunoco station or the crew's ability to repair the facilities aboard, there was no way of telling.

"She probably plugged up the goddam head herself," Eric said scornfully. "No matter how big a sign you put up, they'll try to flush sanitary napkins down every time. Well, old fellow, once everyone's ashore, it's your baby."

"I know," Steven said gamely. "And after I unplug the head, I'll finish the dishes."

"No. Bruno's finishing them now. If you have extra time, you can pump the bilge."

"Since Arlene's not conscious," Steven said, "I'd better locate pancake fixin's and be ready to make breakfast."

"No, don't. The ship sinks unless everyone does their part," Eric said seriously. "Breakfast is Arlene's job."

"But . . ."

"She can get up early. If she doesn't, and we'll all have to cook breakfast ourselves, she's out of here. We'll find someone else. There's plenty of girls looking for something to do on the Cape in summer." He turned to help the last of the passengers onto the yawl, which, despite the calmness of the evening, pitched to a different rhythm than the *Jenny Lawrence*. Gallant with the girls, well-met with the men, gracious, charming, Eric Larsen was truly spectacular in his role.

They leaned together on the rail, watching as the yawl roared toward the town wharf. "If the passengers are happy, and feel they've gotten their money's worth, they'll talk about the *Lawrence* for the rest of their lives," Eric said, waving at the departing passengers. "They'll talk about her to their neighbors, and their friends, and their business associates, and they'll throw more business our way than any advertising could possibly scare up."

"Certainly they'll be happy, the way you're treating them," Steven observed. "You can tell me now, Eric, and I won't breathe a word of it—but isn't that why you made such a spectacular entrance into the harbor? To please them? Give them something to talk about?"

Eric laughed. "With a ship like *Jenny*, anything she does is spectacular. She's a spectacular lady." He patted her old scarred side. "She has an image to live up to, and so do I. Just now I shall go ashore and polish my image as a man who knows how to hold his liquor. I'd offer to help with the head"—Eric grinned—"but it's bad for my reputation. You understand."

"Oh. Yes, indeedy."

"A bent coat hanger will probably do the job. And don't forget the bilge. The planking works when we're under sail, and she takes on more water then. We'll need to keep ahead of it."

It took forty-five minutes to unplug the toilet, a half-hour to pump the bilge, and more time to help Bruno who was still struggling with the dishes. Exhausted, fully clothed, Steven fell into his bunk.

At dawn he was wakened by the pounding of sneakered feet as Jerry Ferris ran along the deck, rinsing it off with seawater. A new, soft clean day awaited, full of expectation: a day with horrendous amounts of work in it and the prospect of joy, a short sail over to Vineyard Haven and after that a long sail to Nantucket, the open sea and its vastness, its release.

A salt water shower from the barrel suspended for that purpose gave him the tremendous lift that came—and only ever came—with the prospect of success wrested from the sea. Yes, *Jenny's* promise would be fulfilled, because he and Eric and Bob and Jerry and Dominick Bruno and even Arleen Ferris would make it happen!

It was on the next week's tour that the first mishap occurred. "Hell and damnation! You should have called me! You knew the wind had changed, for Chrissake! You entered it in the fuckin' log." Eric jabbed at the entry: "1750: Wind SW," and the entry that followed it, "0100: Wind shift to NNE."

The breeze had reversed itself, and *Jenny* was stuck in the mud due to her 180-degree change of position around her anchor.

Jerry stood his ground. "If you hadn't been so busy screwing around, Skipper, you'd have done something about it yourself, and we wouldn't be aground now."

"Bull shit!" Eric shouted. "You just leave my screwing out of it. Read this, instead." Insistently he pushed the logbook into Jerry's unwilling hands. "Go ahead. Here. The notice posted on the front cover."

"Night orders," Jerry read in an elaborately bored voice. "'Call me for any shift in the wind that requires a course change.' But we couldn't change course." Jerry pointed out stubbornly, "because we weren't under sail."

Belaboring Jerry further was nonproductive. Eric waited for calm to overtake him. "We'll just have to hope that she floats on high tide, is all. The passengers'll have to fend for themselves this morning."

"Let's take them for a tour," Arleen suggested. Any relationship she had, intimate or otherwise, with either the captain or his first mate, was forgotten in view of the present challenge. "Bikes," she said. "We'll rent bikes and we'll ride to the beach. The Vineyard's mostly flat. Even city people can manage it. Anyone who doesn't want to go can spend the day right here in Vineyard Haven. Their choice." Vineyard Haven offered only limited entertainment and it had already been explored yesterday afternoon, when *Jenny* sailed in from Edgartown. "I'll get breakfast ready, and we'll all make sandwiches afterwards," Arlene continued.

The three men, all of whom had seen her in varying degrees of nakedness, admired her as she climbed up the after cabin stairs. All of them sighed, her transgressions forgiven. The girl was enough to awaken the lust in any man.

While she fed the crew and the passengers, Steven and Dominic Bruno constructed a picnic for thirty people. Loving the idea of a Vineyard tour, the passengers clambered into the yawl boat and mounted the bikes that Jerry had rented for them in town. Waving happily at the captain and crew, they took off like a flock of gaily colored geese.

As the tide rose, the men took turns with the yawl boat in an attempt to haul, push, and coax the *Jenny Lawrence* out of the mud, but the breeze was still blowing toward shore and held her fast. The motor on the yawl began to stutter under the strain, and finally quit altogether, casting a pall of silence on the scene.

Jenny Lawrence had not moved.

"You know," Steven said to Eric, "a man could get discouraged under these conditions."

"Oh, hell! Don't let this get you down!" Eric waved it all away. "We'll hire the harbor tug. No problem, Steve."

"What about that?" He pointed at the yawl, where Jerry was poking at the motor.

"I'll go ashore now and find someone who can fix it. Have yourself a snooze until I get back."

"A snooze!" he exploded. "Goddamm it, Eric, we just paid to have that engine overhauled. If we have to keep tinkering with it . . ."

"Relax, partner." Eric's voice became very firm. "It needs a new motor—and new motors are very expensive. I'm sure we can get through the summer on this one. Not without difficulty, but we'll make it. Then we'll know how much profit there is, and what kind of new engine we can afford. Nothing ever goes *right* when you sail. Come on! Loosen up. We'll make it fine. We just have to roll with it."

Eric was right, Steven told himself, watching him and Jerry row to shore in the dinghy. You had to measure yourself by your ability to handle whatever it was the sea threw at you, and you had to know when to lie back and let the situation develop. Well, it would take a little while, he consoled himself. After all, he hadn't lived aboard a seventy-ton schooner very long. Naturally he had to condition himself.

He opened a can of beer.

Eric brought back a mechanic; a tug chugged alongside; the *Lawrence* was dragged out of the mud, the tug (*Harriet R.*, Captain Holms) paid, the yawl repaired. The ship was theirs again.

"I suppose I should check the bilge," Jerry said finally. He made no move to do so. "I kind of hate to find out how bad it is," he confessed. "Stuck like that, with the tide rising and all, her calking is bound to have loosened up."

It was bad. All three of them took turns pumping for the rest of the afternoon until the passengers returned from Arleen's picnic. The girl was good at her job, and worked like a Trojan when she worked at all.

"Oh, it was fun!" She waved off her accomplishment negligently. "Did you get us unstuck?"

"Were we stuck?" asked a sunburned lady nearby. "I didn't know that!" She did not seem unduly alarmed.

"We have been stuck, madam," Steven confirmed, bowing, "but no longer."

"Well, I expect we'll be on our way sometime." The passenger turned away and did not even bother to spread the news that the *Lawrence* had been earthbound all day. After all, when you were nautical, time and schedules had to be put away. That was why everyone was here—wasn't it? You had to roll with it, didn't you? And if the following day's sail to Nantucket proved tedious because fog blanketed everything, why—who cared? Not the thirty passengers of the *Jenny Lawrence*, toughened by the sea and succored by endless highballs and beer.

It was, just as advertised, a week away from worry.

Nantucket.

Jerry's running feet on the deck above dragged Steven into consciousness; over and around Jerry's swabbing of the deck was the sound of the wind, and on the other side of the hull the waves lapped against his ear.

Wind! Wind, and they had a long day's sail ahead, back to Hobbes Hole! With a breeze like this, they'd be able to leave Nantucket's harbor in style. *Jenny* would raise an impressive wake and fly free as she was meant to fly! He had yet to watch her in a heavy sea, and eagerly squirmed out of his bunk. From the galley came bacon and coffee and baking-bread smells, and in the after-cabin the tableware gleamed, ready for the first sitting. The breeze made the rigging buzz and whine and raised whitecaps at sea; Eric was drinking coffee, moodily looking at charts held down on the after cabin roof by stones.

"I don't like it," he scowled. "*Jenny's* too old."

"Too old for what?"

"The damned wind. It's at fifteen to twenty knots, and I'll bet my balls it's going to get stronger. Then it gets too rough for her planking. More leaking. Much more. I'm not sure we should leave at all."

"Eric," Steven exclaimed, "we have to leave. It's Saturday. We're due back to the mainland this afternoon!" Dissatisfied passengers would definitely not generate good publicity.

"I know we have to leave, for Christ's sake," Eric grumbled. "And *Jenny* needs wind, but we're in trouble if it rises to thirty. Well, we'll have to chance it, I suppose. We'll weigh anchor after breakfast. Go ring the son-of-a-bitchin' bell. Let's get these lazy assholes on their feet."

It took no genius to understand that Eric was upset and worried.

Steven hammered the bell furiously so that anyone silly enough to still be asleep would awaken. He helped Arleen in the galley, then left her to manage the dishes and presented himself on deck to help cast off. *Jenny Lawrence* would be leaving Nantucket in style!

Jerry started the donkey engine. The sails, which they had furled last night on the prediction of wind, slowly climbed the mast as the engine inched them up. Then the anchor was brought in and *Jenny* leaned into the wind, her sails taut, and rode out to sea, gulls shrieking their praise and the other ships in the harbor tooting and whistling.

Oh, wonderful ship!

The breeze tore at him, and he laughed at it; *Jenny's* rigging sang as she raced, and spray flew up, catching in the sun and falling back onto the listing deck. Nantucket dropped away and only open water surrounded them, wide as the sky, bright as the clouds that raced with them. Never would he get enough! Happily Steven accepted the beer that Arleen opened and thrust into his hand, and leaned on the rail and dreamed himself into the days when sailing ships were the fastest conveyances known to man.

They were abeam turning buoy number seven when Eric ordered the jib to be set. Instantly alert, Steven helped Jerry unfurl and raise it and felt the ship leap forward. Eric was drunk by now, he guessed—knew it for a fact—because the captain should not have set the jib if he was worried about the wind....

But no one needed to worry for long: the jib let go almost at once, its tatters flying out over the water like banners. There was nothing they could do about it while the ship was moving.

Twenty minutes later, abeam the cross-rip light house, the wind rose yet higher, but *Jenny* settled into it comfortably as the passengers settled into tequilas. The whole party was wonderfully happy, cheering, singing, exhilarated by the elements of *Jenny's* drama without understanding the details. Proud and happy, Steven watched them from the helm where he stood with Eric.

"Enter abeam gong number fifteen. Compass 295 degrees," Eric ordered, and Steven set it down in the log, pleased that he'd been trusted to write in it. "Hold the wheel steady. I want to check the sails."

He left the cockpit to take a closer look.

"Head her up into the wind!" he shouted. "Head her up!"

Obediently Steven spun the wheel, and *Jenny* heeled. There was a sound similar to lightning hitting a tree, and a cracking, and a ripping as the mainsail split and the gaff splintered. The ship paused, without power, and backed down on the trailing yawl boat. The passengers, too surprised and full of alcohol to realize the severity of their situation, remained exactly where they were, thereby sparing themselves injury.

"Well, I guess we aren't going to make it to Hobbes Hole," Eric observed, calmly inspecting the tangle of lines, sails, and splinters that lay heaving up and down in the water beside them. In the face of disaster, he had lost the power to think up the appropriate four-letter words. "Bail out the yawl. We'll put out extra lines and tow her."

The passengers watched, discussing it all in unconcerned voices.

"Why did you have me head into the wind?" Steven asked.

"Squash Meadow shoals are nearer than I thought," Eric said. "I saw bottom, for God's sake. We'd have gone aground again, at a full clip. God only knows if we'd have ever gotten her off. Get the sail and the gaff out of the water if you can; cut us loose if you can't. We'll try a port tack under the staysail."

They limped.

They wallowed.

Steven was closer to weeping than he'd been in years when they accepted a tow back to Vineyard Haven, the closest port.

"How'll we get home?" asked the little bitch who'd plugged up the head.

Steven stopped himself from snarling just in time. It was a logical question, after all, and most certainly was the first he'd have asked in her place. She'd left from Hobbes Hole; she expected to be returned there.

"I'm afraid we'll have to put you on the ferry," he apologized. "Wasn't exactly what we planned—but the ferry it is."

"Do things like this happen often?" she asked innocently, gesturing at the wreckage. "It's so exciting! And interesting, too, watching you all cope."

"Oh, we're very good at coping," he assured her. "Part of seafaring is knowing how to cope! Let me assure you, by the way, that we'll be responsible for your passage to the mainland. And we'll talk to the harbor master at Hobbes Hole, so that he can notify anyone who's planning to meet you."

"I may sue," grumbled another passenger. "I'm going to miss my train."

But nobody commiserated or sympathized with the fellow who would miss his train. When you sailed right out of the twentieth century and back again, a paltry thing like a train schedule was beneath the notice of all but the most obtuse.

To the last passenger, even the one concerned with schedules, they refused reimbursement for the ferry and left with hearty handshakes and embraces, taking with them more than they had brought aboard. For them, at least, the cruise had been an overwhelming success.

For the crew, the owners, it was a near-disaster. It would take a week, at least, to fix the damage, a week they could earn nothing but would pile up indebtedness—indebtedness that would require a good part of the summer to repay, with little left for maintenance....

We'll do it, Steven thought doggedly. We'll make it, damned if we won't. It'll be a long haul, but we'll do it. And to that, he and Eric, Domenic Bruno and Arlene drank well into the evening and beyond.

CHAPTER

The Runaway

HE TURNED onto the mid-Cape highway. It was Saturday afternoon and the rush of weekend visitors had subsided. The pace was leisurely, traffic minimal, and he was glad of it. *Jenny* and her complement had been late arriving at Hobbes Hole. Running a windjammer was a lot of work, he reflected. Even now Bob was hustling to get everything cleaned up, new supplies on board, fresh sheets on the bunks, laundry delivered to the cleaner, but *Jenny* was going to make it. Bookings were running high, every berth taken since they'd launched in June and half the berths were reserved well into September. If nothing broke—the yawl boat's motor being the most worrisome—his share of the summer's profit would refill the hole in the Sinclaire savings account.

His head wobbled, and he shook himself awake, turned on the radio of Bob's truck which he would bring back to Hobbes Hole tomorrow afternoon. Bob would party with Dominic Bruno and Eric tonight, Steven was sure. They were celebrations, those parties, and he'd thoroughly enjoyed this bonus. Bruno had hidden his copious liquor supply somewhere on board, refusing to reveal where, and everyone spent a good part of their free time looking for it, the rest drinking it. Bruno himself never left the ship. His home away from home, he said, bucking himself up for his return and his dentist's drill, his office, his telephone, his wife.

Steven pulled off the highway and took a right onto 6A, the old Main Street which would be called the King's Highway one day, he supposed.

Low tide on the bay, he noticed, easily visible now because some of the elms that once lined the road had died and been taken away, opening the view. West Waterford wandered out to meet him, sparsely populated and as rural a spot as the Cape's North Shore could boast. And there was the mill stream, so narrow that a man could jump across it, and the mill itself, built by Bob Casey and Steven Sinclaire and a lot of men so long ago. The historical society was opening the museum inside, and today Mari was hosting a meeting to organize the grand event. Kingsland, itself open for business, was not the most logical place for such a meeting, but it was her chance, she insisted, to undo the harm that Steven had done in the spring at town meeting when he had spoken for the townsmen in opposition to the society.

He sighed. She'd been furious. He decided not to think about it.

The library came into view now, and then the driveway of Kingsland, into which he turned, carefully avoiding all the cars parked for Mari's meeting and stopping the truck by the back door.

"Hi, Dad!" Kathy was sitting on the steps of the kitchen porch, fanning herself with last week's edition of the local paper. "How was the trip?"

"Good." He stretched, working out the kinks collected from his drive, sat beside her in the cool afternoon shade. "How are things here?"

"All rooms rented," she reported. "And all guests at the beach, just like Mom wanted. We've been making little bitty sandwiches with all the crusts cut off, and deviled eggs, till they come out our ears. And then I passed them around and listened to ladies ooh and aah over me. And now I'm resting."

He laughed. "Where's your brother?"

"Hiding." She grinned. "He moved chairs this morning and then disappeared so he wouldn't have to make deviled eggs."

"Steve!" It was Mari at the back door.

"Hi, honey." He stood and waited for her to welcome him or complain about something that had gone wrong in his absence. "I'm so glad you got back in time!" she exclaimed. "I was worried you wouldn't! There's someone here you've just got to meet. She's been telling us details about the West Waterford mills, and she's fascinating! Come on!"

She opened the screen door to usher him in, led him through the kitchen. "How was the voyage?"

"Fine. Just fine."

"No catastrophes?"

"Not a one."

"Thank God!" She dragged him through the hall and into the parlor, where the guest of honor sat in front of the flower-filled fireplace, teacup in hand, nodding attentively as an old geezer filled her ear earnestly and probably repetitively. The room was in a state of pleasant disorder, with chairs scattered here and there; people were picking up their belongings, wandering one way and another as they made their farewells. Everyone was speaking at the same time, and their words and voices drifted by him, remote and disconnected as he walked with Mari toward that day's fascinating speaker, Alice Bradley.

She was nearly old now, wearing gloves and a hat, which gave her vintage away, and a skirt too long for a short-skirted age but appropriate for hers.

Alice Bradley.

About whom he had not thought in years. She had not entered his mind even once in all the time he and Mari and the kids formed a family and made their way through life. Now the circumstances under which he'd first met her were rising from the grave in which he'd buried them, rising in all their untenable, unbearable impossibility.

She knew. He was sure she did, in a way he could not have described. Sitting there calmly, without noticeable reaction, she knew who he was. She had known since that evening eighteen years ago, when he'd played canasta with the Bradleys in their summer cottage. Beneath his belt the crab that so long ago had lived in his vitals stirred, rolled over, came to life.

"Steve, this is Miss Alice Bradley," Mari murmured reverently.

"Hello, Steven," Alice Bradley said. Her voice wasn't old at all, but was the same steady, even, unhurried one he remembered. He was suddenly aware that he smelled of sweat and low tide and was unshaven and looked disreputable in his well-worn blue jeans and T-shirt with holes in it that positively reeked now with the rise of his body temperature.

Nearby, Claudia waved the Historical Society program in front of her nose. "Whew!" she exclaimed. "The mariner returns!"

Alice held out her hand, and he shook it. "Nice to see you again, Miss Alice," he managed.

Her green eyes were deep, and he was trapped in them, unable to look away.

"Do you already know each other?" asked Karen Jackson, standing next to Alice Bradley's chair.

"Old Cape people always know one another," Alice said. "They're always bumping into each other, in the most unexpected places."

"We were trying to find everything we could about Kingsley Merrick's mill," Mari said to him as he listened without comprehension and without caring. "That was when we discovered Miss Bradley. The titles to some of the property out there were passed to her through her mother, who was Kingsley Merrick's daughter."

"And here you are, a Merrick," Claudia crowed. "You could have told us all about her."

"Not necessarily." Although her words were unhurried, Alice Bradley broke in quickly and firmly. "There are two families involved. My mother was Kingsley Merrick's only surviving child. She married twice. Steven's cousin, Elizabeth Edgarton, was my mother's child by her first marriage, while I'm her daughter by the second, you see." Smoothly, smoothly did Alice Bradley lead them all away. "I won't bother you with the whys and wherefores, but the two families gave one another a very wide berth. It's not surprising that Steven wouldn't have thought of me. He's probably never even heard of me."

"But you already knew each other!" Claudia protested, then stopped when she saw at last that she was trespassing. "Old family spats are so intriguing," she babbled, trying to bridge the gap created by her gaffe.

Mom had never told him that Alice Bradley was a Merrick.

"See why I hoped you'd get back before the meeting was over today?" Mari enthused, returning from the door where she had bidden a guest good-bye. "I wanted to surprise you, Steve!"

"Well, you sure did," he said gamely.

Miss Alice's eyes were gentle as she watched him. "They tell me you're in the coasting trade now."

"It's called windjamming." His voice sounded strange.

"Quite an enterprise! Where do you sail?"

"Oh, just Nantucket Sound," he heard himself saying.

"Tell me where," Alice said chattily, and Mari pulled over a nearby folding chair.

"Here, Steve! Have a seat! I'll just leave you two for a nice little talk while I see everyone out. I'll be back when they're all gone."

Alice Bradley was the last person on earth he wanted to be left with, but he was still too stupid with shock to think his way around this impasse.

"Nantucket," said his voice. "And Vineyard Haven, Hyannis Port..."

"And Edgartown?" Alice asked casually, yet he was nearly certain that her words were not casually chosen. "Do you go to Edgartown?"

"Oh, yes, always," he said remotely.

"My niece Diana owns a cheese-and-wine shop there. You must look her up. It's called Vincent's. That was her husband's name. She divorced him recently—you do remember Diana, don't you?"

"Yes," he said, sweating, bound to the chair, to her, to her eyes, which held him with a purpose that frightened him. Yes, himself a man who rarely feared anything, was afraid now—he feared Alice Bradley as a man might fear the Lord, who held all the answers whether a man asked or not, who gave the answers whether a man wanted them or not.

"The girls are married and have families, living in the suburbs, and surviving it so far! Doug is with Digital, doing very well. Surely you remember him—of course! He was your CIT wasn't he? He's married and has two daughters. Unfortunately not all the news is good." Her eyes were veiled now, and unreadable. "Their parents are dead. They were in an automobile accident three years ago."

His ears were singing as he stared at her. Mari's voice was far away as she said, close by his ear, "Well! How are you two getting along?"

Tim Bradley was dead.

"Actually, all of you have been invited for cocktails and dinner," Claudia chimed in. "Let's adjourn the festivities for now. Steve and Mari haven't seen one another all week," she said to Alice Bradley. "So let's leave them alone for a bit. Why don't you come back with me, Miss Bradley, and I'll give you a guided tour of the Elijah Merrick house."

"I'd like that very much," Alice said. "I've only ever been there once. We'll talk later, Steven. I hope."

"We're in the middle of restoring the house," Claudia explained, leading Miss Alice away. "So it's in a bit of a mess. But it's coming along just fine. I really love the old Georgian places, don't you? Their lines are so pure."

It was as though all of him had caved in, leaving a void, empty like the huge parlor was empty now, its guests gone, echoing and without the spark that could warm it, himself cold, friendless. . . .

Mari followed him up the back stairs to the bedroom he'd made over the kitchen. "Isn't she grand? She knows so much! She has Kingsley Merrick's papers and everything, and lots of information about mills that have been on that stream since colonial days. Go ahead and shower, honey," she instructed. "I'll tell you all about it later. I'll go on over to the Marshall's now and you can meet me there."

There was no choice. "You'll have to go without me, Mar."

"What?" Mari frowned, dismayed. "I said we'd go!"

Pulling the holey, rancid T-shirt over his head, he mumbled, "I've had a full week. You shouldn't have committed me."

"Steve," she began as patiently as possible, "Claudia's counting on us."

"She's counting on you, honey. I'm bushed and I'm just not going over there." Wearily he watched the eagerness, the pleasure, the exuberance drain away from his wife's face. "I'm sorry," he said more gently, trying to placate her without upsetting the fragile balance within himself. "I'm just not going."

He peeled off his stinking jeans, stepped out of his sneakers, and pulled off his fetid socks.

"It was really embarrassing this spring when you went and spoke up at town meeting, but I understood you felt it was your duty. It's taken me a lot of time to smooth it over. Claudia has made a special point to include you..."

He headed for the bathroom to turn on the water for a tub.

"It's important to me, honey," Mari said, following him. But he was not listening; instead he was trying to contain everything, as though his guts were threatening to spill out and he had to hold them in, the least movement painful, perhaps fatal. He had to be alone, he needed time—yes, time to understand, to accept.

Tim Bradley was dead.

"A marriage takes two people trying and caring about the things that are important, and you aren't doing your share."

He shucked off his shorts and lowered himself into the soothing, steaming water, lay back, closed his eyes.

For eighteen years everything had been pushed down and out of sight. And now it had returned. All his memories of Tim Bradley, who had done so much for him in so short a time, eighteen years ago. All the pain of learning who he was. Of relinquishing the man he knew Tim Bradley to be.

"If you don't come, there'll really be trouble," Mari said coldly. "And I mean it, Steve."

Bradley was gone. Steven had hidden from him and all his family. He had not answered Diana's letters; when Doug had written, inviting him to visit, his response was cold and without a vestige of friendship. He had turned away and even if he'd wanted to, he could not repair the damage now.

Because now Tim Bradley was dead.

"I'm leaving for Claudia's," Mari said. "I'm taking the kids. You will please meet us over there when you've bathed and shaved."

"For Christ's sake, Mari! Will you please just go!"

She paused, shocked, and he lay numbly in the tub, waiting.

He heard her rounding up the children (Rick noticeably reluctant, since he did not like Junior Marshall). He heard the car motor and then the pebbles on the surface of the driveway, grinding and crunching against one another as the sound faded away. Carefully he soaped up, rinsed off, got out of the bath, shaved, put on new jeans and a shirt, took the pillow out of his pillowcase and filled it with fresh socks, shorts, and T-shirts, slipped out the kitchen door and into the rusted old truck which, fortunately, he'd parked back here where it couldn't be seen from Kaptainsholme, should anyone be looking.

He drove back the way he'd come, carefully absorbing himself with the details of the road, carefully closing his mind until he'd made it to the safety of the *Jenny Lawrence* where he believed he could cope with his wounds. And where he discovered the party: Bruno, and Bob, and Eric.

Damn! There was nowhere he could go to do what he had to do, to come to grips with something so deep that he hadn't realized it even existed! From the open window of the truck he listened, clutching himself against the growing grief and sorrow and the awareness of having lost something he had not known he possessed.

In the distance were the gulls and the bells of a church; within was a weeping from a lost, forgotten part of himself that had been covered by the rubble of past years, and he allowed it now to breathe as he had never done before, and the freedom and joy he'd experienced in Tim Bradley's presence came into focus, sharp and clear and fresh as the hour he'd first encountered it.

Tim Bradley would never suddenly reappear, his hand out-thrust. Now Steven saw: all this time he'd been waiting.

"Look who's here!" A very drunk Eric spoke very loudly, and an equally drunken Domenic Bruno from Jersey City said, "Who the hell is it?"

"It's Steve Sinclaire, by God."

"Has he got my truck?" asked Bob.

"No, you boob. He walked on the water."

"Who'n hell is Steve Sinclaire?" Bruno asked petulantly.

"Your partner, stupid."

"By God, you're right." Out of the darkness Bruno staggered up to the truck and inspected the driver. "It is Sinclaire."

"Are you okay, Steve?" Bob asked.

"Of course he's all right!" bellowed Eric. "The only trouble with this man is that he's sober. He needs a goddam drink! Come with us, Steve," he urged.

What else, really, made any better sense at this point? Privacy was not going to happen, and perhaps it was just as well. Steven allowed himself to be led, his preoccupation unnoticed, bridged by the hilarity of the others. They toasted one another, sang of Bruno's good-fellowness, which would no longer be available to them, because he must, at last, return to reality in New Jersey. They recalled their favorite events of the summer as the evening approached and then arrived, bringing darkness with it.

"I see headlights down the wharf," Eric announced.

Then the masts were lit up and shining as the lights closed in, then disappeared and the hum of a vehicle stopped.

"Steven?" Mari called.

"Is she by herself?" he asked.

Bob blearily looked over the rail. "Your neighbor's with her, I think."

"J. Barry?"

"Yes, indeedy."

"Steven?" Mari called again. It was tempting to stay low, out of sight, but of course he could not.

"Hi, honey!" he called back.

"Help me over the side, Barry, can you?" Mari asked.

"Sure," he heard J. Barry say, and the two of them scuffled their way to the after-cabin steps.

"What's going on?" Mari peered down at them.

"Party," Eric answered.

"I came to take Steven home," she said.

"And I came to help," J. Barry added.

"Well, I'm not going home," he told them.

"Steven!" Her voice was urgent. "What in God's name is wrong?"

"Nothing's wrong," he argued. "Not with me, anyway."

"And so there's something wrong with me?"

"Well, Mar, how would you like it if you came home from a hard week at the office and found your parlor filled with historically oriented finks?"

"What office?" asked Bruno.

"This one," Bob explained.

"That's a little too deep for me," Bruno pronounced. "Let's send Sinclaire topside."

"Not at bad idea," Eric agreed.

Of course he must go out and talk to her. Of course. He must tell her . . . tell her something. "Are they gone now?" he asked, when finally he was able to make himself obey his unspoken command to face her.

"Who?"

"The Historicals."

"Of course they are!" Mari cried. "They left when you were still home."

"They're in your head, Mar, all the pricks that voted against me in town meeting."

It was a natural. He was amazed, how one complaint just flowed into the other, completely obscuring the truth. "They voted against me. There I stood, laying it on the line, spilling my guts, pleading for my friends and their way of life, and they voted against me. Against the town. All of you would destroy the grail. Philistines, every one."

"Steven," Mari said, her voice low. "This isn't the time or the place to discuss the Historical Society or town meeting either."

"Well, sure as hell I can't discuss it at home," he complained. "Because the parlor's filled with the opposition. And because your head is filled by the opposition. Can you deny it, Mar?"

"You've never been this vehement about it before," she said wonderingly.

"True. But now I am, and I'd appreciate it if you went home."

"That sounds like you're walking out on me, Steven."

"Well, I'm not," he declared. "I'm only waiting here on *Jenny* until you tell me that the coast is clear of historical finks."

"Then you can stay aboard till she sinks." Mari had a temper, and it was in full cry now. Not that he blamed her. "I'm going home. Barry?" she called. "Can you take me back now?"

"Sure thing."

Marshall did not so much as glance at him, helping Mari over the side again and into the car. It pulled away....

It was a relief to know she'd be unable to disturb him until he'd settled down a bit. Wearily he rubbed his tight temples, looked up at the stars.

"I'm going to bed," he told the party in the after-cabin. "I'm pretty beat."

"Okay." They could understand that.

He went below to the little cubbyhole reserved for him. He did not sleep; he had not thought he would. He wanted only to lie in his bunk and let *Jenny* comfort him and listen to her night sounds and wait for dawn. It was all he could do in the face of knowing Tim Bradley was dead.

He slept at last, until a headache awoke him and he pried himself out of his berth, staggered to the after-cabin, where Eric sat alone.

"Where's Bruno?" he asked.

"On his way to New Jersey."

Steven poured himself some coffee.

"Where's Bob?"

"Do you see his truck?" Steven looked. No truck. "Casey finished up his chores and took Bruno to the airport. I expect he's on his way home by now."

"What time is it?"

"Eleven o'clock." *Jenny* was usually onloaded at noon. "Here's the strongbox and the reservation list, in case there are early arrivals," Eric said. "I'm my way over to the liquor store. Bruno's supply is gone."

Blearily Steven lined up the cashbox and the reservations, three pens, and a pot of coffee. He listened to the sounds of Hobbes Hole, of seabirds and the ripples of the tide.

Mary Harrington and Dolores Demars arrived with their suitcases and sneakers, straw hats and raincoats, prepared for any occasion, they told him. They were secretaries in New York City; they'd been planning this jaunt ever since they'd heard about *Jenny*. They surely hoped that he'd arranged good weather for them! Beneath their coquetry they sized him up: sufficiently handsome, unattached, well-mannered, no doubt well-educated. The voyage looked better than ever!

He explained the ship's routine to them in a performance he could deliver nearly by rote now; entered their money in the books; heard them trying to get down the steps of the companionway without exposing more than decent girls wearing skirts should.

He stared out the window, waited. A couple from western Massachusetts, who had never left their children with Mother before.

A man from Indiana whose grandfather had done some sailing. Ran in the blood, didn't you know?

A couple of kids from Dartmouth, handsome and well-groomed as the sons of the rich seemed always to be.

A lady professor, who dressed like one.

A Nubile Young Thing, whose parents should not have let her out alone after dark. Arlene would have competition.

A party of four middle-aged couples, who would be cliquey and loud, he predicted.

All of them eager to voyage out and beyond the periphery of their known worlds. Their excitement failed to move him today.

He deposited most of the money in their account at the Hobbes Hole Savings and Loan. *Jenny* cast off, accepting a tow out past the jetty because the yawl boat's engine sounded a little rough, even with the new carburetor, and Eric decided not to use it any harder than he had to. The ship wallowed until she could respond to the breeze, and then she picked up speed, lumbered out to sea.

Steven leaned on the forward rail, watching, the exultation of getting under way escaping him as he labored under his load. How strange it was, to be so overtaken, overcome by such passionate sorrow. Beneath the surface it had lain there as did all powerful emotions: grief, or jealousy, anxiety or elation, instantly ready to leap into life while the passionless person who harbored them suspected nothing until it was too late. Now, he supposed, his sublimated self had emerged because it was safe, with Tim Bradley gone. Safe to yearn. To hope. To need, to grieve.

The Nubile Young Thing was standing in the bow of the ship, her long hair streaming in the wind. She was wearing a jersey which the breeze plastered to her breasts, and like a figurehead, she pointed them seaward, clearly enjoying the sensation she was creating among the male passengers. In his isolation he laughed at her, at them all, at himself, all of them on vacation from their day-to-day lives that they could not escape but would strive perpetually to avoid.

It was Ferris's turn to stand watch when they reached Edgartown, Sinclaire's to run the yawl. Efficiently he ferried the passengers and crew, tied the yawl to Edgartown's pier when the last load was done. He would meet them at ten-thirty, and would ferry groups of them back until they were all accounted for.

"Where're you headed?" asked the Nubile Young Thing.

"Nowhere special."

"Buy me a drink?"

"Not tonight." She could have been his daughter. "Another time, thanks," he said diplomatically, and quickly lost her in the melee that was Edgartown at dusk. The business district was a scrambling mass of searchers for happiness and souvenirs, roaming the streets, crowding the taverns, trying hopelessly for seats at restaurants. He walked through it and out to the residential end of town, with its narrow streets and sidewalks running past white-painted fences. Everything was overhung by immense towering trees brought as seedlings to America two hundred years before by the captains who had built the town.

He cut over a block and walked back toward the harbor and into the throngs again, the same surging, excited, happy, hilarious crowd which he could bear now no better than before. He cut over and back to the quiet end again, his footsteps echoing behind him, and back to the waterfront, in and out of different worlds, back and over, up and back until he came across the object for which he had not been able to admit he was searching: Vincent's Cheese and Wine Shop.

There was a sign swinging over its front door, made of weathered wood with the name carved deeply. Painted beside "Vincent's" was a wedge of cheese and a goblet half-filled with red, indicating the business of the shop just as signs had done two and three hundred years ago—and more.

He went past it and back, past and back again before he could look, standing across the street, letting his memories of Diana Harrison as a girl wash over him, the girl whose eyes were the color of green and brown pebbles at the bottom of a clear stream, whose voice was rich and full, who, as he remembered her, was slim and supple, her hair alight in the sun, blowing gently around her alert, fresh face.

Through the distant window he saw the woman she'd become, a woman who was slim yet, he saw, laughing with a customer, turning to a shelf of wines, reaching for one.

They had shared first love, that quietly sequestered experience which could never be had again, and he'd dropped her just as he'd dropped Tim Bradley. Now she was here, in Edgartown. Now he knew where to find her. Did it matter?

He turned away before his loitering became obvious and she might discover him, stole past the churches and the graveyards and houses beneath their old imported trees, all woven into the placid fabric of their own identity, his footsteps echoing behind him, hollow as he was, empty as he was, lonely as he was.

He walked and listened to the summer night and its sounds and the downtown revelry rendered insignificant and small by distance, and then met the passengers at ten-thirty as he'd promised, going through the motions of life at sea.

CHAPTER

Diana

IF SHE SAW HIM enter the shop that evening, she gave no sign of it. Attentive to a customer, she continued to discuss the right sort of cheese to complement the right sort of wine. Perhaps she didn't recognize him. Twenty years was a long time, but it had done little to change her. She was still lovely, still slender and poised, and her voice was the same. He'd know it anywhere.

Perhaps, he thought, suddenly cold, she is ignoring you.

When she was finished with the customer he moved in quickly, afraid if he waited the chance would be lost.

"Hi, Diana."

Motionless, she stared. "Well, if it isn't Steven Sinclaire," she said, without noticeable pleasure.

"At least you recognized me," he said, forcing a smile. "I was afraid you wouldn't." It had taken all week to work himself up to this point, and now that he was here and saw her disinterest, his courage ebbed.

"Actually, I expected I'd run into you sometime, when I heard you owned the *Lawrence*."

"Oh? When did you hear that?" he asked, hoping he sounded pleased with himself.

"At the beginning of the summer, as I recall." Her eyes were steady, with neither warmth nor rebuff in them. Her voice held indifference.

The shop's bell rang, and she turned to talk to the customer who entered, and he was left to mull over the unpleasant understanding that she had known all season where to find him, and had not attempted to seek him out.

Why should she? he asked himself. What have you ever done that would make her want to see you?

She walked to the door with the customer, who had not bought anything, and stayed there, looking out at Edgartown's evening throng. Was she ignoring him? He waited, but she did not come back to the counter where he was standing.

"I met your aunt a few weeks ago," he said. "She told me about your place here."

Nothing. Panic began to grow.

"Hello, there," she greeted an approaching customer, and accompanied him to the wine section. Steven waited, looked over the polished pine paneling and shelves, gleaming pewter mugs and trays, wine richly colored in its bottles, cheeses wrapped in red wax and silver foil and cellophane.

The customer paid for a bottle of brandy; Diana gift-wrapped it, sent him on his way.

"Your Aunt told me about you and Doug and the girls," Steven struggled on. "And she told me about your parents. I was sorry to hear about it, Diana."

"Thanks. It was quite a shock."

"So this place is yours."

"Yes," she said, looking up from a note she was scribbling to herself. "My husband and I started it ten years ago."

"Your aunt tells me you're divorced."

"Aunt Alice loves to talk," Diana observed noncommittally, and was rescued by another customer.

Should he just give up? Certainly she was putting him off. Perhaps because she'd been hurt in her marriage and didn't want to encourage another man. Perhaps because another man, Steven Sinclaire, had stood her up twenty years ago. Perhaps because she just didn't want to be bothered.

Only one chance remained. Miserably he knew he must take it. "Have you ever been aboard the *Lawrence*?"

"No, I never have."

"How would you like a tour of *Jenny* in the morning, before we sail?" he asked. "Would you enjoy that?"

"No. I don't think I would." Stooping down, she busied herself with items on a shelf under the counter.

"Or a day sail, maybe. Over to Nantucket," he went on, hopelessly exposing his need. "You could take the ferry back. It's quite an experience, sailing on a schooner that large."

"I'm pretty much tied down here," she refused firmly, still rummaging around under the counter.

There was no way to avoid her hostility. "I guess you wish I'd just leave you alone," he said.

Standing up straight again, she looked him square in the eye. "Yes. I wish you would just leave."

Humiliated, defeated, he fled to the nearest tavern. It was not filled to capacity yet, the evening being young. Sawdust was strewn casually on the floor and fishnet hung nautically over exposed ceiling rafters. Buoys and lobster pots were stacked here and there in an attempt to create a fisherman's haven. Arleen Patterson was at the bar, as though she'd been there all along, waiting for him.

"You look awful," she said. "You need a drink."

"You're right!" Heroically he entered the spirit of the evening and ordered a shot of Scotch and a draft beer. "Do you need another?"

"Are you buying?"

"I am," he asserted. "You can have whatever you want. I'm the last of the big spenders."

"And maybe you'd like to hear the story of my life, too," she offered. "Now that you've asked."

"All right," he agreed.

"And then, when everybody's aboard the ship, we can row over to Chappaquiddick and you can tell me yours."

"My what?"

"The story of your life."

"Oh, that."

"We could make it like a beach party, for just you and me."

"Sounds swell," he said, and was aware that she'd moved closer to him, her breast softly nudging, her thigh slightly pressing. It was good to know that when everything else had failed you, the Arleen Pattersons of life were there, generous and full-bodied, kind and amiable. In that moment he was grateful, and he put Diana Harrison Bradley Vincent and her rebuff behind him, and Alice Bradley and his fear of her, Mari and the things she dubbed sacred—even Rick and Kathy and the *Jenny Lawrence*, and entered the refuge that was available just then.

The dinghy rocked gently. The Chappaquiddick ferry hustled back and forth with ducks following and gulls circling above, crying and jabbering. At Edgartown's dock, owners of boats went about their interminable antlike tasks. Steven remotely observed it all as *Jenny's* dinghy sank lower with the tide, gradually, gradually below wharf level. Then, because his visual range was now limited, and because the sun hurt his eyes if he looked out across the harbor, he concentrated on Jerry Ferris in the yawl boat, tied next to him and sinking with the tide at the same pace as the dingy. From beneath his seat, Steven brought up a bottle of gin still encased in its paper bag the way rummies carried theirs, and offered it across the intervening space.

Jerry helped himself, handed it back, went on patiently tinkering with the engine, tightening, cleaning, oiling.

Jenny was taking on quite a lot of water these days. Steven knew he ought to row out and pump her bilge while the clientele shopped and lunched and bought postcards to send home.

Yes. He ought.

Eric had assured him it was nothing to be immediately alarmed about, as long as they kept up with the pumping; the ship was old, unaccustomed to the currents and undertows of Nantucket Sound. She could take only so much before the old caulking worked loose. They'd have her seams redone this winter, even if they had to borrow to do it. But for now—if he didn't pump the bilge and *Jenny* sank, the summer would be definitely over. Yes, he must do it. But did not move.

"Hi!" called Arleen.

Turning slowly, so as not to jar his head any more than necessary, he looked up at the now elevated dock. Arleen looked down over the fullness of her very ripe figure and said, "Going my way?"

"If he's not, I am," Jerry volunteered, gazing up in admiration.

"Nice day for a swim off the ropes, don't you think?" she suggested.

"I sure do!" Jerry approved.

"I wasn't speaking to you," she said saucily. Apparently today was not Jerry's day. Blowing him a kiss, she climbed into the dinghy. Her nipples showed plainly beneath her jersey tank top; her tanned legs were endlessly and beautifully long. "How about it?" she asked. "Unless I miss my guess, no one's aboard."

"How about what?" Steven asked, refusing to play her game. In fact unable. He was definitely unwell.

"Swimming off the ropes."

"I had it in mind to pump the bilge," he said, giving her no encouragement.

"Okay. We'll pump it together." Expertly, she slipped the mooring, turned her face up to the sun. "Nice day."

"Ummm." It was awfully damn bright, but he decided not to say so.

"You work too hard, Steve," she observed as he rowed. "You're not having any fun."

"No harder than you."

"But I'm younger." She wrinkled her nose at him, to indicate that the years between them did not discourage her. However, he was not interested in whether she was discouraged or not, because just now he was interested in nothing at all.

"When's the last time you ate?" she asked, scrutinizing him carefully.

"I don't know."

"Would you like me to fix you some lunch?"

"No." He did not want her concern, because he knew where it would lead, and knew he didn't have what it took to satisfy her. Not today. God, his head!

The dingy coasted to *Jenny's* side. Arleen scrambled up the ladder and hung invitingly over the rail. Behind them, at the wharf, the bell rang, and squinting over his shoulder, he could see a group of passengers waiting.

"Sorry, Arleen," he called up. "I'm being summoned."

"Drat!" she grinned. "Another time, maybe."

The bell rang again, and he rowed back to the wharf where the yawl's ailing engine sputtered to life, then died. It had simply quit on the way out of Hobbes Hole yesterday, and they'd barely made it past the jetty. They'd been rowing passengers three at a time in the dingy ever since their arrival in Edgartown last night. It was tedious and unending, but it was exactly right for now. Between rowing and pumping the bilge and drinking there was just enough of a rhythm to halt the process of thought.

Jerry steadied the dinghy while three women from the waiting group climbed in, two seated in the stern and one in the bow. They settled themselves happily for the ride back to *Jenny*, telling him of a sale at one gift shop and some wonderful stuff (not on sale) at another.

Yes, rowing was better than lying alone in his berth, looking up at the bunk above, wondering what Rick was doing or how Mari had explained his father's absence, if his daughter was okay and if she hated him, like her mother did....

He'd lain in that bunk many hours, listening to the sloshing and groaning of the plumbing, the joy and laughter of the passengers, the occasional whack of an unprotected head on a supporting beam which, in their haste, passengers sooner or later forgot was there. Without interest he heard the distant arguments between Eric and Jerry, their patience wearing thin as the summer wore on, and tried to soak up the on-going solace of the ship itself. Was it true that alcohol made depression worse?

Perhaps tomorrow he'd better dry out a bit. It was already a little late today, but tomorrow would be a good time to start.

At *Jenny's* side he held the dinghy steady while the fat bottoms of the ladies disappeared up the ladder and over the edge of the ship's equally fat side, then set himself to the task of rowing back, facing *Jenny* as he went, *Jenny* whom he loved more than ever.

Rowing, rowing, he glanced landward over his shoulder to make sure of his alignment—and saw her, standing a little apart from the remaining passengers.

The oars had no lock and he lost one, grabbed for it, nearly capsized. Using the remaining oar as a paddle, he circled around the errant one and captured it, replaced it, continued on to the pier.

"Quite a performance for the holder of a Golden Arrow," Diana Harrison Bradley Vincent remarked, looping the painter around a piling.

Jerry was still laughing at the rescue of the oar as Steven climbed out and onto the wharf, all too aware that he looked awful and probably stank.

"I'd like a break," Jerry said. "Can I take a turn at the oars?"

Did Jerry know what being free just then meant? Waving acknowledgement and a thank you, he walked with Diana past the ferry slip and on up the road toward the inn. The silence between them was strained, but he knew of no way to relieve it.

Without warning she stopped and turned to him.

"I hardly know what to say, Steven. I'm really sorry if I've added to the hell you've been going through." Her eyes were kind and tender as they had not been two weeks ago. "I've spoken with my aunt. She told me—about you and Dad."

He swallowed past the obstruction in his throat while she looked at every detail of his face as though to confirm the truth of what she had learned. "There's a little sand spit down there where we can find some privacy," she suggested, indicating a steep, narrow path that ran between two houses and toward the waterfront.

"Sounds good," he managed to say, and followed her down toward the water and around to a dune where they sat.

There was a long, painful silence.

"My aunt told me you haven't been home since she saw you at the Historical Society meeting."

"No. I haven't." His guts quivered like jello. Waiting quietly, she clearly expected him to say more. "I needed time," he made himself tell her. "I still do."

"I just didn't understand . . . anything." She looked away. "My aunt didn't realize how it would affect you, either. Learning about Dad, I mean."

Her profile was nearly the same as when she was young. It was as though the barrier of years had been breached and the girl she had been spoke to the young man he had been. Tendrils of her long hair shimmered in the sunlight and flowed with the breeze.

"I came to tell you that Aunt Alice wants to see you. She says there are some things you should know."

"What kind of things?"

"She didn't say. She just asked me to find out when the *Lawrence* usually puts in to Edgartown—and see if you'll meet with her at my house."

There was nothing he wanted less to do. "Is it important?"

"I'm sure it's important to her. She wouldn't have asked, otherwise."

They watched the Chappaquiddick ferry leave its mooring and plow across the small channel.

"Steven," she said softly, "if you saw her and talked with her, you'd learn more about your father."

The moment hung heavily between them.

There were tears in her beautiful hazel eyes. "He's gone, Steven. He was a good man, and he belongs to you as much as to us. If you stopped running away and learned more about him, you might feel a lot better, about a lot of things."

Was it possible that Alice Bradley could help him close this part of his life, write the concluding paragraph to it while remaining within the bounds of manageable pain?

"All right. I'll talk to her."

"Will a meeting the next time the ship comes to Edgartown be OK?"

"Sure."

"I have to get back to the store. Business picks up right about now."

Following her back up the path, walking with her down the street to the town pier, was surreal. "I've really enjoyed talking with you again," he said tentatively. "Even if the subject is painful. Thanks for the chance."

"Maybe there'll be other chances," she smiled and turned in the direction of her shop. "Until next week, then."

Jerry had just arrived back at the pier with the dingy. *Jenny Lawrence's* customers, now a crowd, waited to carry their day's treasure aboard and begin happy hour.

"Three at a time, I'm sorry to say," Steven instructed. "All aboard."

Two dropped into the dory's stern seats, one in the bow as before. Steven exchanged places with Jerry and began rowing.

"What's for supper tonight, Skipper?" asked Richard Nelson from Wachusset, Rhode Island. "All this sight-seeing and gadget buying makes a man hungry."

"Have to ask the cook," he replied. "But my feeling is that we're going to broil steaks on the deck. In a charcoal grill, in case you were wondering."

Appreciatively, they laughed.

"Who's the pretty girl I saw you with, Skipper?" asked Mrs. Nelson, teasing.

"Old friend." He meant to say it briefly, without expression, but found that he could not stop his grin, observed by the woman in the bow.

"I think the cat just swallowed the canary," she said to Mrs. Nelson.

"Here we are." Sculling an oar, he eased up beside *Jenny's* ladder and helped them climb up. Quickly he rowed back, glad for an excuse that would whisk him away before any more comments could be passed. Jerry, who was putting the finishing touches on the yawl boat, regarded him speculatively, perhaps a little slyly, saying nothing as he helped three more passengers crawl into the dingy.

"When's that beast going to be ready to do this job?" Steven asked of the yawl.

"It's nearly ready now," Jerry assured him. "Stay aboard and pump the bilge. I haven't had a chance to do that today, and neither have you. I'll bring the rest of the passengers."

Bilge pumping would be a welcome respite, and a nice opportunity to let himself gradually, gradually, think his way back into the interaction on the dune. And his reaction to Diana. And hers to him.

His headache was gone.

The church bells were chiming 2:00 when he reached the town dock. Scrambling out of the dingy and securing it, he dodged tourists and Islanders as he hurried into town. It was improper to feel excitement at the prospect of seeing an attractive woman, he knew. He was a married man with a family, and his future lay with them. Yet the plain fact was that seeing Diana Bradley last week had been important. Without even trying to cut back, he'd been drinking less. He'd been sleeping better, his interest in *Jenny's* passengers reviving, his grief receding a bit, allowing a bit of room to live with it for now. Diana Harrison Bradley Vincent had shaken him loose, and if she did nothing more he'd be eternally grateful.

More? he asked himself, breathlessly approaching the shop. What do you mean, more!

You know perfectly well what you mean, he answered himself, and went in.

Looking him up and down, her eyes twinkled. "I must say you seem just a tad better than when I saw you last."

"I'm feeling a tad better too. I even shaved."

"I'm impressed, and very glad to see you. My aunt got here on the ten o'clock ferry. She's probably worn a rut in the rug with her pacing, so we'd better get to my house, pronto."

Signaling her departure to the young girl who was her assistant, she led him out the back door and into a small courtyard, around the side of the shop, and onto the street. "If I leave this way, no one will stop me for a discussion of wine," she explained. "Poor Aunt Alice would never survive more delay."

"Why is she so nervous?" he asked. "Should I be worried?"

"I don't think so. She's just keyed up—I'm not sure why. It seemed a little rude to ask!"

They hustled along without further conversation, leaving the business district behind.

"Here's my house." It was a traditional Cape, set well back from the street. A picket fence defined its boundaries; several old trees shaded it. "I lay claim to the downstairs, and the kids have the second floor."

"You haven't told me about them. Are they there now?" he asked. He could not talk to Miss Bradley if there were ears to hear.

"They're in Connecticut, working for my father-in-law. Earning money to go to college. They'll start in the fall."

Alice Bradley waited for him in the kitchen. Her face urgent, she rose as if to greet him, then wordlessly sank back in her chair, as though willing herself not to rush.

"Have to run," Diana told them. "I'll come back in time to take you to the four-o'clock ferry, Aunt Alice."

"Yes, dear, thanks."

They waited as Diana left, then turned to one another.

"Here I am, Miss Alice," he said, and took the chair opposite her at the kitchen table. "I think you wanted to see me?"

"Yes. I did. I do." She searched his face, then looked out the window and took a deep breath as though to settle herself. "There are two reasons I wanted to see you, Steven. The first is about your father. How long have you known about him?"

"Twenty years," he answered promptly. Facts, he could handle. "My mother told me after I came home from playing Canasta with you folks." Curiosity prodded. "When we met then, in East Waterford, did you know who I was?"

"Indeed I did, the minute I saw you. Charles Sinclaire couldn't beget a child like that. Besides, I knew Tim Bradley, my cousin, when we were both young. Your resemblance to him as he was then—well, it was unmistakable." Folding her hands, she leaned in a little. "It's important that you understand Tim would never have abandoned your mother if he'd known she was in trouble. But he didn't know, and I'm responsible for that, I'm afraid, and I want to ask your forgiveness."

"In what way were you responsible?" he asked.

"It all started way, way back, with my half-sister, your Cousin Elizabeth. You probably weren't ever told that she came to Waterford from Canada because our mother wanted to marry John Bradley."

"Your father."

"Yes. Elizabeth's father was quite a lot older than our mother, and his death wasn't unexpected. But Mama's marriage to my father was very much a surprise—and Elizabeth fought against living in his house. Eventually she came to live at Kingsland, with our grandmother, Julia Merrick, who was dead set against John Bradley, too. And it's really important that you know why."

"All right. I'm ready."

"There were four Bradley boys. My father, John, was the oldest. Then came my uncles, Abner and Robert. The youngest was Uncle David, Tim's father." Her gaze pinned him to his chair, and he made himself meet her eyes.

"David was Kingsley Merrick's bastard."

He commanded stillness, of his world, of his mind, of his heart.

"I think I'll make some tea." Abruptly Miss Alice pushed her chair back. "I'll make some for you, if you like."

"No, thanks."

He needed something a lot stronger than tea. "Do you know if there's any liquor in the house?"

"Parlor. Bottom cabinet beside the fireplace."

Searching, he found some bourbon, fetched a glass, seated himself while his world spun round and round.

From the stove, Alice Bradley said, "The only person in the whole world who knew the truth about Uncle David was my grandmother, Julia Merrick, who saw to it that neither my mother nor I were ever invited to a party or even a visit to Kingsland. A practice Elizabeth followed, once grandmother told her the reason. Of course, I knew nothing about any of that until Elizabeth and I had it out, just before the stock market crashed. Tim and I were engaged at the time, and she let me know that she'd reveal Uncle David's illegitimacy if we married. Illegitimacy was a terrible stigma in those days."

"It still is," Steven said. "Not all that terrible, perhaps, but a stigma none the less."

"But back then, it would have destroyed Tim's father. I can't even begin to speculate about what it would have done to mine. Elizabeth promised that everyone would know, if I married Tim. She'd raise objections on the basis that there was a mental problem in the Merrick line. Kingsley and Julia Merrick's oldest daughter, Caroline, was very slow. Perhaps even retarded. As double first cousins, it might show up again."

She brought her tea to the table. "She was using what she knew to keep me in line. I was making good progress in separating the young people of Kingsland's social set from the values of their parents, you see. My revenge for being excluded all those years. So what else could I do but tell Tim I'd changed my mind, and he'd be doing us both a favor by leaving town. That's what I wanted you to understand. He went to sea right away. He didn't know about your mother, Steven. If he had, he'd have married her in a heartbeat. Tim was as decent as they come."

More bourbon was definitely called for. Pouring it, he drank and looked out the window and watched a blue jay flapping around in the garden's bird bath. Uncounted, silent minutes passed.

Floating a little above the kitchen, thanks to the bourbon, he said, "OK. Let's hear the second reason you wanted to talk to me."

Miss Alice stirred her tea, which must have been cold by then. "When I was back in Waterford, when I met you at the Historical Society meeting, I visited afterward with a lot of the people I'd known when I was young. They told me about you—about what you'd tried to do on their behalf. This spring at town meeting."

"Can't win them all," he shrugged.

"I wanted you to know you were following a tradition and a legacy you probably don't even know about."

"Dare I ask?"

"Kingsley Merrick did everything he could to give an advantage to the working people of Waterford, and he succeeded."

The front door opened, closed quietly.

"The summer society was only spindrift. For years it provided cash, but was of little importance in town affairs. The Depression swept those rich people away, but Waterford itself remained the same. The local folks were content to stay here, living off the land. Gradually the next generation returned to the old places they'd known when they were children, fitting in with the locals as best they could. But the new people in Waterford now want to change everything, and they're destroying a whole way of life."

"I'm not sure they see it that way, Miss Alice."

"It's time they did. By going to bat for the townsmen, you started a process."

"Too little, too late. I lost. They lost."

"But you can seize the next opportunity, can't you? And the one after that, and the one after that? Why do you think I came here today? Why do you think I've told you all this? Yes, I wanted you to know where you came from. I owed you that. But after I talked with those people, I wanted to urge you to continue what you've begun. They haven't given up yet, Steven, but there's lots more local folks that don't realize what's at stake. They don't understand, but you do."

He met her eyes steadily and did not permit himself the relief of looking away nor the agreement that looking away would imply.

"Please, keep trying." Looking past him, her life's injuries and penalties were suddenly engraved on her old face.

Diana appeared in the doorway. "Do you still want to make the four-o'clock ferry, Aunt Alice?" She looked from one of them to the other. "Or do you need more time?"

Alice rose stiffly from her chair. "I'm supposed to meet a friend for dinner in Hobbes Hole at six o'clock." There was a minuscule pause. Did she hope he'd urge her to stay? He did not.

"Well, then, Steven, let's take her to the wharf," Diana said, counteracting the tension in the room.

The sidewalk would not accommodate three abreast, and he followed along behind. Like a eunuch, he thought, dodging pedestrians. I need a turban and a spear. He thought about that with determination, because he didn't want to think about anything else just then.

At the ferry slip throngs of people milled about, and most passengers were already aboard.

"Well, I'll thank you both and be on my way," Alice said. "It's meant a lot to me, to be able to meet you, Steven, and talk to you."

For himself there was nothing to say, nothing he could say. He shook the old woman's proffered hand and in silence stood with Diana, watching Alice Bradley disappear into the ferry's maw. Bells rang, horns hooted, people called, and the ship majestically backed out of its slip, turned, glided out of the harbor at the far side of which *Jenny Lawrence* rode at anchor.

"I've got to go back home now and grab supper," Diana said. "My helper leaves at 5:30."

Above them the gulls gabbled in the blueness of the late-afternoon sky and the voices of humankind on the streets of Edgartown blended into a kind of harmonious jumble. "Can I walk with you?" he asked. Being alone was a threat he could not face just then.

Warily, she nodded. "Sure."

They threaded their way through the crowd and, when it thinned, walked side by side. "Tell me about yourself," he said as they hurried along. "You know a hell of a lot about me, and I don't know anything about you."

"There isn't much to say." She waved a hand as though her past were insignificant, an irritant like a mosquito. "I was married young, and six months later my husband was drafted into the Korean War. We have two children—twins—born when he was overseas. A boy and a girl. The kids who live upstairs at my house."

"You were very young, to have married a man serving in Korea."

"I was eighteen. I'd just graduated from high school." That would have been a year after he'd met her. "My husband seemed pretty lost when he came back from the war, and after trying one thing and then another, we got a loan from his parents and bought the shop here in Edgartown and the house too. It was run-down, really derelict, and Paul spent most of his time fixing it up while I ran the store. Once it was in good shape, he had nothing more to do but drink. Eventually we divorced, and I bought my half of both the house and the business with one loan from his parents and another from Aunt Alice."

"Where is he now? Your husband."

"I don't know, thank God. Were you and Aunt Alice arguing? It sounded like a quarrel when I came in."

"Not really. I was trying to come to some conclusions of my own, and she was pushing hers, is all."

"Well, I'm sure meeting with you meant a lot to her, Steve. Thanks for going along with it."

Her neck was long and slender; he could enclose it in his hands and hold her life at his fingertips if he wanted to. Her skin was smooth and clean, like a child's.

"Do you plan to tell your wife about Dad?" she asked.

As if there were nothing more to think about, there was Mari!

"I don't know." They turned into Diana's front walk. The August-parched lawn looked cool now in the lengthening shadows of the afternoon. "Your neighbors will wonder about all the comings and goings at your house today," he remarked lightly as she dug into her purse for her key, turned to the door, her back to him.

"Oh, yes! They'll have a marvelous time, my neighbors, speculating on who that handsome man was they saw coming home with me." She glanced at him over her shoulder, teasing because, after all, he was a friend from long ago, wasn't he? With whom such a joke might be shared? And then her expression changed.

"Well, th-thanks for walking me back," she stammered, pushing open the door.

"Aren't you going to invite me in?"

"Certainly not! What would the neighbors say!" she retorted. "I have to go, Steve."

"I'd like to see you again," he said, fighting fear. Speculatively she looked up at him. "Will you let me?" It was not a polite, casual question: it was an important and critical one, and his intensity communicated itself to her. She backed a step into the entry, and he followed.

"Have you been home at all since you first saw my aunt?"

"No."

"Why not?"

"When Miss Alice told me about . . . Tim Bradley's death . . . I found myself in the middle of something I didn't understand and couldn't control. My wife wanted me to go with her to our neighbor's house, right then and there, but I was beyond her reach. I had to get away from her—from everything. And once I left, I found I couldn't go back. Is that what you wanted to know?"

She flushed but was not deterred. "You have children."

"Yes."

"Do you miss them?"

"Yes."

"And your wife? Now that you've been gone from her for a while, do you miss her?"

"No." He reached out to touch her hair. "Otherwise I wouldn't be here, would I?"

He looked deeply into himself and saw that Tim Bradley's death, whatever else it meant, whatever else it had done, played into his hands and hers. Once cleared of grieving, he would be able to put down the burden he had unknowingly carried, and would be free to return to love as he had first understood it.

"Meet me next week," he urged, "You don't need to be afraid of me," he said quietly, and heard a glad singing start somewhere, felt its rise. "I won't deceive you or run away again. I swear it." And then he carefully drew her to himself, kissed her lightly and then deeply, and more deeply, yet with great and terrible restraint, until she answered and her body became a part of his own, so well made for him that she was infinitely flesh of his flesh. He struggled desperately with himself as her own exquisite urgency betrayed her, gave her to him, and she became the girl he'd held twenty years ago. It required all his self-control to draw away.

"Good-bye," he said softly. "I'll be back."

"Yes. All right." Her voice shook.

"In a week."

"Yes." She leaned against the door as though she had no strength left and watched as he made himself walk away.

It was time to go to Waterford.

Summer had progressed. Now, in the harshness of late August, the lawns were brown and crisp and everything was covered with dust. The quaint old places, dressed up with shutters and wrought-iron railings and lampposts designed to look colonial, were drab, and the antique shops and art galleries unbeguiling. Leaves on the trees overhanging Main Street drooped; flowers were wilted in their gardens.

At Hall's Texaco, he pulled in for gas. "How's it going?" he asked Don Gray, who was manning the pump.

Don shrugged. "Can't complain."

"How's Roly?"

"Gone."

"Gone where?"

"Maine."

"When did he do that?"

"Couple weeks ago. The selectmen took his scanner. Said the new police chief would be getting a more modern, up-to-date one. They sold the old one and put the money in the town treasury. Fifty dollars."

"Rubbing it in a little, were they?"

"I don't know," Don said, his face impassive. "I don't take sides. I like to keep out of everyone's way."

Steven paid for the gas, drove on, pulled into the driveway at Kingsland. Listless though the maples were, they provided an oasis of shade. A no-vacancy sign hung from the porch railing, a collection of garbage cans roosted at the back of the house. The kitchen was empty; he walked into the parlor.

"Hello?" he called.

"Um, hello," replied a stranger, sitting in the reupholstered maroon velvet chair, reading the local newspaper.

"How do you do," Steven said quickly, and hastened to the billiard room, where Kathy was sprawled on the couch, watching TV.

"Daddy!" She jumped up, spilling her magazines and comic books, and flew into his arms. "Welcome home! I'm so glad to see you!"

"Hi, Sweetie. I'm glad to see you, too." He held her at arms length, wondering at the difference after six weeks of absence. Could she have grown up in that time? "How are things here?" he asked, hugging her again.

"Great!" she enthused. "We're making lots of money. Is *Jenny* repaired now? Is everything okay? We'd have come to visit you, but there was always something coming up on Sundays and Mom couldn't get away. And Saturdays, you know, are changeover," she said importantly, obviously very much part of Mari's enterprise. His absence appeared to have been explained to her satisfaction. Mari had kept his image bright, and he certainly did have to give her credit for that!

"*Jenny's* repaired for the moment," he told his daughter. "Where's everyone?"

"Mom's at the Marshalls'. Rick's at the Searses."

"So you're all alone?"

"Someone has to be here, in case the phone rings or someone comes to the door. It's my day to do that. Mom and I take turns."

It occurred to him that she was defenseless should the wrong person ring the bell. "No one's ever had trouble, Dad," she said, as though reading his mind. "And besides, we're wired to the new police station."

"Oh? I didn't know we had a new one."

"We do now. Right down the street at the store that used to be a church. The town bought it and moved the police into it until money for a real station can be approved at town meeting."

Everything was moving along. Fast. Too fast.

"All we have to do is touch a hidden switch and the alarm goes off," Kathy told him. "A cop comes right away."

Well, he could hardly fault that! You never did know, anymore, who was wandering around the Cape. Surely his family was protected better now than when Roly was Waterford's lone policeman. "When's your mother coming home?"

"Pretty soon, I think. Mrs. Marshall's having a meeting."

"Historical Society?"

"Not really. It's a just a bunch of people who're making up rules for the Old King's Highway Historic District."

"Don't tell me the District has been approved, too."

"No! Don't worry, it'll take years. They're just getting ready. Wait 'til you hear about their ideas." She laughed at him affectionately, knowing how he'd react. "They want it so that if you decide to change the color of your paint or build a garage or cut down a tree that's bigger than six inches around, you'd have to get District permission. Ricky wants to put up a flagpole while we still can."

The kitchen door banged, and several footsteps later Rick appeared.

"Dad! I saw the truck!" Breathless and boisterous, the boy manfully thrust out his hand, but the greeting turned into a bear hug despite his determination to be grown up.

"I see you've been keeping an eye on the place."

"I sure have. The grass has about stopped growing by now, though, so my troubles are over. Say, Dad, what do you think about putting a flagpole in the middle of the yard? I think it'd add a lot of class. If we do it now, we won't have to ask anyone's permission. And you don't need to tell Mom I said so, either," he said to his sister.

"I won't! I won't!"

"Like you say, it's got class." Steven agreed. "Great idea!"

Another banging announced the presence of Mari, and he felt himself tighten. Here it comes, he thought. Her footsteps crossed the kitchen floor and approached the billiard room.

"Why, hello, Steve." As though she'd been expecting him, she lightly kissed his cheek, and her voice was calm. "Welcome home."

"Thanks." It was hard to meet her eyes. "The kids have been filling me in. Seems as though everything's under control here."

"Oh, yes, they've been a great help! We're doing fine." She nodded their way in approval. "Full house!"

"I noticed the No Vacancy sign."

"It's been like that all summer. We're sure glad you're back, though. We can use your help, now that the *Lawrence* is taken care of. *Jenny* is fixed now, isn't she?" Mari's voice had an edge to it.

"Well, she's still afloat. We've had a full house each week, too, and the season's not over yet."

The front door opened and closed, but no one moved to find out why.

"There's no need to go out and see who's there," Kathy told him. "Unless the bell rings for the manager."

"Dad says he'll help put up a flagpole," Rick said to his mother.

"Oh? I didn't know you wanted one."

"I think we have to keep our image looking good. And I think a flag would look great out there where the driveway circles around, don't you?"

"We could hang a vacancy or no vacancy sign on the pole, too," Kathy added. "So people wouldn't have to drive up close to find out they can't stay here."

"Give Dad and me a chance to talk it over," Mari hedged. "Now that he's home."

The ball was in his court. "If Mom's in agreement," Steven said to Ricky, "we can get a big jump on it before I have to go back to the ship."

"Maybe you could give up the ship for a day or two," Mari suggested. The kids listened intently. "You could join her later, say, on Nantucket. You could take a ferry."

"Could you, Dad?" Kathy asked.

"I could," he said, "but I haven't arranged for it. There'd be no one..."

"Bob. There'd be Bob," Mari persisted, pushing, pushing, to see how far he would go to accommodate her.

"We could do most of the flagpole today, anyway," Rick was saying. "I could finish up during the week. I'm strong enough. Dad! Feel my muscle!"

The kitchen door rattled as he squeezed Rick's bicep and staggered away, as though overwhelmed. Kathy disappeared to see who was at the door, then reappeared.

"There's a man outside, Dad."

"Did you ask him in?" Mari asked.

"He didn't want to come in."

"Must be a native," Mari remarked dryly. "Must have seen the truck. They can't let you alone for even a minute, can they?"

It was indeed a native, old Mr. Shaunessy.

"Hello, Mr. Sinclaire," the old man said. "I hope you don't mind that I interrupted you."

"Not at all. Will you come in?"

"No, thanks. I won't take long. Mr. Sinclaire, they took my keys away and I wondered if you'd ask if I could have 'em back."

"What keys?"

"To the church." He gestured with a nod of his head toward the intersection of the Rockford Road and Main Street. "I'm the custodian. And the board took my keys, and said I'd have to meet whoever has them on a certain day. They'd let me in to do my weekly cleaning."

"Have they said anything before, about the keys?"

"Well, yes. They've been after me to clean at a certain time every week. But I never did that before, Mr. Sinclaire. I knew what needed tendin' and I always took care of it in between other jobs."

"Sounds like they just want to regulate things a little, John. I don't think you need to take it personally."

"Well, I do," Mr. Shaunessy said. "An' I was hopin' you'd speak up for me."

"I can't," Steven shrugged. "I'm not a member there."

"You ain't?" The old man was amazed. "The Merricks have always belonged to that church!"

"Not this Merrick."

"Oh!" John Shaunessy shook his gray head. "I ain't a member neither, so don't know who belongs and who don't. I'm real sorry to have bothered you, Mr. Sinclaire." He edged away, getting ready to leave.

"Are the board members old-time Waterford folks, or are they new comers?" Steven asked.

Shaunessy halted. "Flatlanders, most of them. That's why I thought you could speak to 'em, Mr. Sinclaire. They'd unnerstand you better'n me. But I don't guess you can, after all."

"No. Sorry." He patted the old man's shoulder; his body was thin and frail. "How are things going otherwise, Mr. Shaunessy? Around town?"

"Terrible. Did you hear they fired Greenleaf Stone?" Steven accompanied the old fellow back to his truck. "He let some young folks live in the house they was buildin' before all the permits was signed. They couldn't afford to complete everything, an' they'd hoped to finish up whilst they lived in the shell—but they was caught, and so Greenleaf was caught too. Used to be, folks who needed more time to build a house could get it. But not anymore." Shaunessy climbed into his old truck, started the motor, and sat a moment, listening critically.

"Sounds a little rough. Timing might be off," Steven offered.

"It might. It might." Shaunessy eased out the choke, pushed it back, and the motor resumed its normal pace. "Can't run the town the way it's always been done if more and more people are going to live here, I guess. Nothing's like it was, and maybe it just can't be." Shaunessy stared sadly ahead, through the windshield, seeing the days of his youth and strength fading to memory. "But it sure helps, Mr. Sinclaire, knowin' that you're here. Knowin' that when something goes really wrong, you can speak up for us."

"It sounds like it won't matter," he said. "I can't change anything."

"It'll matter to us."

The truck rattled and coughed clouds of exhaust as it left.

Mari was waiting at the door. "I got the kids to go to the beach and dig up some clams for supper," she said in her business woman's voice. "I'd like to talk to you unless you're too tired. There are a few things I want to tell you."

"It would probably be a good idea to have at it now," he agreed, his tone an even match for hers. "There's a few things I'd like to tell you, too."

They returned to the billiard room and prepared themselves for a showdown.

"I'd like, first of all, to tell you why I acted like I did," he began, "the last weekend I was home, when Alice Bradley was here."

"Yes, I'd like to know about that."

"Do you remember her telling me that her cousin, Tim Bradley, had died in a car accident?"

Mari thought. "Yes, I think I do."

"He was my father."

She stared. "Your... your father?"

"My father, though he didn't know it."

"Your mother..."

"Was already pregnant when she married Charles Sinclaire."

As though he were different from the man she'd known five seconds before, Mari only stared. "But your mother seems so nice," she protested, her traditional standards automatically in place.

"She *is* nice," he said calmly. "She made a mistake, is all. I knew about it a long time ago, but I'd never really dealt with it. I just put it away, because everyone would have reacted just as you did now, and I knew it."

"I . . . I didn't mean to . . ."

"I know you didn't. You can't help it. That's how we were all raised. Nice people are not born out of wedlock. So I buried it and moved on. But here's the most important thing—to me, at least. I knew Tim Bradley personally, when I was younger and involved with Camp Quivet. I didn't know who he was, then. I only knew he was everything my stepfather wasn't. I idolized him."

"And then Miss Alice told you he was dead." Even though he was accustomed to it, the word was heavy. Dead. "That's why you were so—so remote, then, after the Historical Society meeting, when she left with Claudia," Mari concluded.

"Yes. You insisted I go to the Marshalls, right away, but I couldn't. I needed time and space, Mari, and you weren't giving me any."

"And now?" she asked, without bothering to apologize. "How are things now?"

"Seem settled," he replied briefly, not at all sure how things were—or which things she meant, unwilling in any case to dissect them in her presence.

"Well, I can see how difficult it must have been for you. But I'm a little disappointed you didn't confide in me. I'm your wife, Steven. Don't you think I have a right to know about something like that?"

She couldn't help who she was, after all, any more than he could. She couldn't help automatically relegating him to a lower caste because of his circumstances. Younger people, maybe, could. The pendulum was swinging toward a more accepting position. But not their generation, or those that preceded it. "I didn't think you'd be able to deal with it, any more than I could. I'm still not sure you'll be able to deal with it. But now, at least, you know."

"Yes. I know."

"What did you want to talk to me about?" he asked, reminding her that she'd requested a confrontation even before he did.

"Well, I was going to take you to task for leaving like you did," she said. "But now that you've told me why, it makes what I've done seem mean."

"What have you done?"

"I wanted you to see that you couldn't just walk back in here as though there was nothing wrong," she explained. "And the more I thought about it, the more it seemed to me that you and I weren't seeing a lot of things eye to eye, anyway."

"I'm afraid that's true," he said agreeably, and she glanced at him quickly as though surprised by his complacency. The silence became protracted as he waited for her to say whatever she meant to say.

"I think we ought to get a legal separation." His dismay surprised him. "I've been to a lawyer. I had to do something when I knew you weren't coming home. I couldn't just stand around and wait. He's drawing up a legal document now. But you don't have to leave or anything."

"How generous. You'd like me to hang around the house for a while?"

"It's your house, too."

"I don't think I can share a bedroom with a woman who wants a legal separation," he said stiffly, "or one I can't touch." He sized her up. "And I take it that you'd prefer we didn't touch. Am I right?"

She hesitated. There was, after all, no reason to expect a man to stay around if such pleasantries weren't available to him—every woman knew that. Avoiding the obvious, she said, "I bought us twin beds."

She was serious, all right, and since it was about his running away, having nothing to do with her belated knowledge of his parentage, it was fairly easy to sort everything out. "All right. I'll sleep on the couch while I'm home," he said in what he hoped was a kindly voice. "Let's just let everything else slide for now, until the end of the season. It's only a few more weeks for *Jenny*. And the trade here will dry up after Labor Day."

"I don't know what the children will think when they see you sleeping on the couch."

"We're about to find out." His smile was a wry one. "You'll have to excuse me just now. I've got a flagpole to put up."

You are angry, he observed as he left the house, churning and hot. Well, no one likes to think they're dispensable, he told himself. Or that they don't measure up, even if they've already rejected the yardstick.

"Look, Dad!" Smudged and grimy, Rick held up a gold-leafed sign that said "KINGSLAND."

"Where'd you find that?"

"In the barn. I thought I remembered seeing it there a long time ago. I was thinking, Dad, that after we set up the flagpole, we can attach an arm to it and hang this sign from the arm and maybe plant a bunch of bushes and stuff underneath it."

"And hang a vacancy or no vacancy sign from it, too. Sounds fine."

"Mom agreed to the flagpole?"

In fact, he'd forgotten to mention it to Mari. "Yup. Let's rustle up a few shovels." Together they found what they were looking for, and together set out for the front lawn. "Why do you suppose such a swell sign was made in the first place?" the boy wondered, lugging it along. "I mean, it's perfect for advertising, but the house has never been used for tourists before, has it?"

"Heaven forbid," Steven laughed. "But the people who used to live here in Waterford did advertise—to each other. Everyone's house had a name—the more imposing, the better."

"Like Kaptainsholme?" Rick suggested.

"Quite," he smirked.

They settled on the most visible spot.

"Did you and Mom settle your fight?" Ricky jumped on the spade to sink it into a small clump of grass.

"What makes you think we were fighting?" Steven pried up a clod of his own.

"Kathy and I just didn't think you'd disappear like that unless you and Mom . . ." Rick glanced up, then back to the grass he'd pried loose.

They dug silently.

"We need a pole," Rick observed.

"Seems to me Bob Casey has a day-sailer with a hole in the bottom. Maybe he'll let us have the mast."

"Gee, Dad, do you think so?"

"I'll see him tomorrow, when I go back to the ship. I'll ask. Probably he'll be willing. I'll pick it up next weekend, along with some cement he's bound to have."

"That would have real class." Rick approved. "You'll come home next weekend, then?"

"Absolutely."

The boy glanced up, grateful that his father had returned to him. They smiled at one another, and set themselves to finishing the hole.

CHAPTER

Kingsland

"WE'RE RIGHT IN ITS PATH, from the sound of it." They'd been glued all day to the marine radio while the passengers poked around Vineyard Haven. Late August was the breeding season for hurricanes, and the weather dispatcher's expressionless voice delivered endless bulletins that could mean disaster for the *Jenny Lawrence*.

"How big is it?" Steven asked. "Should we go back to Hobbes Hole?"

"It'd be dark before we got there—assuming we could round up all the fuckin' passengers," Eric grumbled. "I won't sail into any God forsaken harbor in the dark. You know that."

"What do you want to do, then?"

"I want them back on the mainland." Eric's eyes were shadowed. "I don't want a bunch of assholes around asking stupid questions. We'll have our hands full."

"They aren't going to like being sent home," Steven hedged. "We'll have to refund their money."

"We'll put 'em on the first ferry out in the morning and worry about the money later. Good Christ, Sinclaire, do I have to spell it out?"

"OK. OK," he soothed. "I'll take care of it."

"Make sure that bitch Arleen leaves, too. She's more harm than help. You stay here and start working on the bilge. You can pump and explain the problem to the passengers at the same time. The emptier we are before the storm starts, the better. I'm going into the ticket office and arrange for the ferry. And I'll call Bob. He'll have to beef up our checking account."

The bell on the wharf rang; a group of passengers, their arms full of packages, looked expectantly toward *Jenny*. They'd shopped successfully and enjoyed themselves, and now hailed their taxi.

Jerry coaxed the yawl to life and took Eric with him. Steven dutifully pumped bilge and waited for the first load to arrive.

"Hi, Commodore," they hailed him, preparing to stow their packages. "How's it going?"

"Well, I'm afraid there's bad news," he told them, pausing momentarily. "There's a hurricane on the way. We'll have to ask you to get your stuff together so you can take the ferry back to Hobbes Hole."

"Now?"

"Early tomorrow morning."

"You're kidding!"

"I don't believe it!"

"We'll refund your money, of course. The captain's going to buy your ferry tickets too."

"Oh, nuts," growled a bald man with stubble on his chin, excused from shaving during his adventure at sea. "Here I am, all set to party it up for the week!"

"You're really serious, aren't you?" asked a pretty passenger.

"There must be a law," a man muttered. "There must be."

Pumping was a good way to avoid their anger and dismay, and he bent to it with a will.

"You folks are our responsibility," he reminded them as pleasantly as he could manage. "*Jenny's* an old ship, and we don't know how she'll hold up during a storm. If you'd rather stay here in Vineyard Haven and wait it out, that's your choice. But this week's cruise is cancelled."

"Is it dangerous?" asked someone stupid. "This storm?"

"It could be," he answered. "Please start packing now. When supper's over, we'll meet each one of you in the after cabin, with your reimbursement and a ticket for the ferry. Bring your bags and suitcases topside so we can take them ashore during the night. You can pick them up on the wharf in the morning."

It took forever. Pumping. Explaining. Pumping. Cajoling. Dispensing checks like confetti while balance in the checkbook dropped, dropped, and disappeared into the crater of negative numbers.

The crew—Jerry and Arleen, Eric and himself—began moving the luggage to the dock. The breeze was heavy, raising waves and blowing the tops off them. The bags were soaked by the time they were piled on the wharf, but at least the storm was taking its time, and the ferry would be able to run back to Hobbes Hole without interference.

Dawn attempted to lighten the sky as the passengers gulped down oatmeal and coffee, departing for the wharf and the steamship-authority slip, Arlene among them. Then it was time to move *Jenny* to safety. Eric had arranged to tie her at the oil docks, well out of the way of the inevitable drifting small craft that would break loose from their moorings. The water was turbulent, pushing the yawl away from *Jenny's* stern until its engine finally quit altogether—fortunately only three feet from their destination, a berth between two docks maintained by the local oil company. They snugged her up between them and rested momentarily.

"Here's the plan," said Eric. "Right now the wind is blowing us away from the dock—and that's what we want. The ship won't be pounding against it. But if the wind changes—and that depends on where the eye of the storm is—well, then we've got trouble. We'll have to try to tie her to the dock across from to us," he pointed, "so the wind, coming from the opposite direction, will keep her from banging into it." He pointed. "We'll row a couple of lines over and secure them now. When the time comes, we can attach them to the donkey engine and drag her over."

"Sounds hopeless," Jerry scoffed.

"Bull-shit!" Eric shouted. "Have you got any better ideas?" It seemed dubious at best, attempting to move a seventy-ton schooner with an antique donkey engine in the teeth of a storm, and Steven understood Jerry's lack of confidence. "I want you gone, Ferris," Eric commanded.

"What?"

"Gone. I don't want you here. You're a pain in the butt. You'll get paid, don't worry."

"Jesus, Eric!" Jerry looked ready for a fight.

"You go with him, Sinclaire," Eric shouted. "I don't need you here, either."

"Yes, you do. You forget you're talking to an owner. I'm staying."

Eric swore and turned away to the radio.

Steven walked down the dock and to the shore with Jerry. "Hang out in town somewhere," he urged. "We'll need you tomorrow morning."

Jerry looked toward town, a half mile distant. "I don't like it. If he fell overboard and drowned, you wouldn't know what to do. I could sail that tub single-handed, if I had to. You can't."

"We're not sailing anywhere."

"Still," Jerry scowled. "I don't like leaving you."

"Just go, friend. I'll be fine."

"OK, then. Good luck." Jerry shrugged, and departed for the nearest bar.

They rowed lines over to the neighboring dock, secured them, nailed down the ship's hatches and hammered boards across the windows of the after-cabin, put out the fire in the galley stove and stored the sails forward, then fortified themselves against the approaching calamity with beer and bourbon, procured at a bar where Eric had a running tab. The ferry blew its horn and left with the passengers; Vineyard Haven brought its lawn chairs inside, covered its windows and lowered its flags.

"Beer!" Eric cheered above the rising wind. "Just what we need. Sinclaire, let's toast the storm!"

"What about the bilge pump?" he asked, opening a beer for himself.

"No, let's not toast the bilge pump."

They settled themselves by the radio. "We'll take turns at it, in a bit. Half-hour each," Eric said.

"Spare me," Steven laughed. "*Jenny* might as well sink and be done with it."

"She'd better not," Eric said, opening the new bottle of bourbon and chasing his beer with a generous swallow. "I'm planning on living aboard this winter. If she sinks I'll be homeless."

Steven remembered that he might not have anywhere to live this winter, either.

"It's great, when you're in harbor during the cold season. It's warm and safe in the cabin while gales swarm around over-head. It's life reduced to its most simple terms, and clean, because *Jenny* is clean. You forget the rat race and how rotten people can be—how rotten they can make you be. You become worthy—if you know what I mean."

Such fluid and articulate expression also meant that Eric was rapidly returning to his former state of inebriation. Waving the bourbon bottle, he declaimed, "They bring it aboard with them, the passengers do. The meanness and rottenness. I hate them. Every one of those sons of bitches. Did you know that?"

"No. You hide it very well."

"Did you hate them?"

"The passengers?"

"The rats, dammit! You've worked in big business. There's plenty of them there and you know it."

"I don't love them. But they're not the problem, man. The problem is that if you want to hold your own, you have to become a rat yourself."

"There! Exactly what I mean! Were you ever afraid of turning into a rat, Steve?"

"Once upon a time, maybe. Not any more. Because I own *Jenny* now. Bob and me and Dominic Bruno and you."

"Bruno! What a hell of a guy! Let's drink to him."

They drank.

"What if she sinks, and you have to go back? Will you become a rat then?" Eric persisted.

"I'm in less danger of becoming a rat now than I've ever been." The alcohol, on top of fatigue, was doing its job, and Steven became eloquent too. "She's taught me the Tao of Sailing."

Eric groaned. "The Tao, for Christ's sake."

"The way of things."

"I know what the Tao is," Eric informed him.

"Well, here on *Jenny*, you're under the influence of the Tao of Sailing. You set out when the wind is right. Not before. Not after. And if it's not right, you wait, and live right where you are, the best you can."

"Sure, sure."

"I think I can move forward and remain true to myself, now that I'm under the authority of the Tao. I can be part of the race and not be a rat."

"But you won't get to the top."

"No. But maybe I don't need to."

"That's not good enough," Eric mourned. "If you—or I—go back to the rat race, it'll get us. But as long as *Jenny* floats, she'll protect us. So she can't sink," he said fiercely. "I won't let her. If I have to spend the rest of my life at that pump, she's not going to sink."

"It would help if you stayed sober, Captain O my Captain. We'll take turns pumping, and we'll repair her this fall. We'll borrow if we have to. We just have to weather this storm."

"Yes, the storm," Eric said absently. "Yes." His eyes closed, and he yawned.

"Can you grab a nap?" Steven asked.

"I don't want a fuckin' nap. If I doze off, I'll never wake up. I haven't had a decent night of sleep for a year." The eyes of haunted despair peered out from a deeply lined face. "After a while, sleep's all you can think about," Eric said. "So you do the things you want to do instead of just lying there, like reading a comic. Pumping the bilge. Screwing a broad. You want to sleep, but you can't. Something holds you back."

"Like what?"

"For me, it feels like there are dogs trying to catch up. It's like I can hear their baying, like geese in the sky, and if I rest for long, they'll catch up and find me."

"And?" Steven querried around another beer.

"Why, brother, you don't know what dogs do when they catch a rabbit?" Eric studied the bourbon bottle, picked at its label. "I need a good breeze to get *Jenny* going."

"Yes, I know."

"But a good breeze is too much for her. It's this goddamned sound, Steve. It's Nantucket Sound. Its waters are murder, and they're tearing her apart. I'm letting the dogs catch up, you see?" His face was contorted. "And she's so beautiful," he sobbed. "Now, will you get your goddamn ass out there and pump, for Christ's sake?"

Should he leave Eric in this state? "Maybe you should come with me."

"Maybe I'll stay here and relieve you in half an hour. Go, man."

Wisely or not, Steven struggled into a slicker. As soon as he was top-side, the full force of the gale struck him, shrill in his ears, the rain blinding. Pausing to get his bearings, he worked his way to the pump handle, commenced working with the Tao of the Bilge. Pull up, pause, push down, pull up, pause, push down.

He lost track of time, of himself; Vineyard Haven was no longer visible; only a few darker shadows in the sweeping rain suggested the oil tanks. Near at hand, small craft bucked and leaped on the waves; farther away he saw one racing for the beach, torn loose from its moorings. The water streamed from *Jenny's* bilge steadily. Were the cabins awash yet? There was no way to tell, and with everything nailed down, no way to find out.

She will not sink, he told himself, pumping to the rhythm of the words.

His whole body was beginning to burn with fatigue, yet he must keep pumping, and *Jenny* must not sink, because if he couldn't live with Mari this coming winter, if they couldn't bear to be housed together at Kingsland, then he'd live here, with Eric.

Another boat whisked by, and a dinghy crashed into the far side of the dock while the hurricane howled. Eric came up to relieve him; in another half hour he took his turn again.

Endlessly they pumped. By the time the wind eased off slightly, they were pumping together, too exhausted to do it alone any more.

"Think the eye's coming?" Steven called between gasping breaths.

"Don't know yet," Eric grunted.

They pumped a little longer. "It's definitely slackening," Steven said.

"You're right. When it gets really calm, we'll move. I'll keep pumping and you can get us more beer, if you don't think you'll get blown off the dock."

"You don't think we should move her now?"

"We can't, until it's calmer. Be a jolly good fellow, Sinclaire, and get me some more cigarettes, too."

It was better than standing around wondering what the storm was going to throw at them next. Steven jumped across the opening, closing, opening space between the ship and the dock. The wind, while less intense, was still considerable. He staggered ashore and looked back. The end of the dock and *Jenny* were barely visible in the yet plentifully falling rain. Now that he was on land again, his legs could barely support him, yet he must—and did—struggle on, to the center of Vineyard Haven, small and insignificant and without vitality beneath the wide, unkind sky.

Most of the bars were open and packed with the holiday crowd happily riding out the storm. At the Port-o-Call, where the appearance of a man from Beyond (himself) stirred everyone to thinking that they, too, should try their luck outside, he made his way to the bar. Reminiscent of college days and college taverns, the closer he got, the greater was the conviviality of those clustered permanently around the taps, by now caring little whether the storm ever ended.

Eric had long since made arrangements with the Port's owner, and the bar tender put a dozen bottles of beer into a large paper bag.

"Cigarettes," Steven shouted, and the fellow threw in a couple of packs.

"Sinclaire!" It was Jerry. "What the fuck are you doing? Why are you even here?"

"We're taking a break while there's a lull."

"Who's taking a break?"

"Well, I am, I guess. Eric's pumping the bilge."

"Has the ship been moved to the other pier?"

"Not yet. He's waiting for the eye."

"Jesus H. Christ!" Jerry swore. "This is it, man."

"But the sky's not clear yet."

"It's not going to pass directly overhead. The radio says the eye's over Provincetown. This is as good as it's going to get. We have to tell him." Jerry turned and Steven followed with his bundle, both of them churning through the crowd, then leaving the humid, fermented air behind in exchange for the pelting rain and wind that was stronger now, and coming from the opposite direction. Visibility was so poor that Steven could barely see Jerry as they raced to the oil tanks and the dock where *Jenny* was tied.

They hastened, leaning against the wind.

The sea disappeared in a gust of rain and the dock hung out into its nothingness, pointing its splintered finger at a horizon they could not see.

Jenny was gone.

Oh sweet Jesus, *Jenny* was gone.

"Eric!" Steven shouted to the uncaring sky. *"Eric!"* His voice tore at his throat.

Jerry stood, limp, arms at his sides. The ropes that had secured *Jenny* to the dock trailed in the water, cut cleanly. "He used the change in the wind's direction to get out of the harbor," Jerry shouted. "He's going to chance the open sea."

But there was no chance at all, and they both knew it. *Jenny* was unable to run before a storm—any storm.

"Notify the coast guard," Steven said.

"You're the owner. You notify them."

"If you don't move now, Ferris, I'll push you off this fuckin' dock."

Jerry saw that he meant it and lurched away while Steven, standing against the wind, tried to make sense of what he knew. Awareness stabbed at him, backing him savagely against the unrelenting wall of certainty.

Jenny was finished, and Eric had known it. There would be no living aboard her next winter, no way to avoid what he called "the ratrace" unless he simply wasn't present to join it. He wouldn't be plagued by sleepless nights any more, or whatever demons were chasing him. He would go down with his beloved ship.

Steven shifted his package, and the soggy bag fell apart, the bottles spilling out onto the dock. Putting one in each pocket of the slicker, he pushed the rest into the seething water and retreated to the beach. On a nearby rock, he knocked the top off one of the bottles and took shelter behind an oil tank.

The rain was harsh and cleansing, he decided, like a scrub brush. All other gods fell before it. The elemental nature of the moment was the proper setting in which to face the choice of his troubled friend, bid him farewell, mourn his desperate decision. And then to face the morass of his own life.

Eric, he thought, pouring the beer down his throat without touching the ragged edges of the broken bottle, you poor bastard, couldn't you have at least tried?

But depressed people, he knew, lacked perspective. There was only the ever-present moment of hopelessness. Recently he had been all too familiar with such moments. But he could not ever remember thinking that death was the only answer to them.

Finishing off the beer, he worked on the other bottle, crouching by the tank, and then decided it was time to leave. There was only one place to go.

The town was deserted, and he was a stranger in a desolated land inhabited only by himself. The hurricane had settled into a nor-easter now, the whole of the earth swallowed up in a vastness of rain and mist, without a living soul to see whether he fell to the ground, exhausted, or whether the damp drizzle on his cheeks was rain or tears. He didn't know, himself, as he started walking that unending, unwinding road to Edgartown on which he, a pilgrim, had been set for reasons he no longer understood.

There was plenty of time to think, as he walked. Should he decide his marriage was over, Kingsland, his refuge for so many years, would be compromised. Mari could claim half of its value, forcing him into some sort of well-paying work in order to support her and the children, such work as could be found in the corporate rat race, but there was no assurance there'd be a company that would take him on . . . .

Had he lost everything he'd hoped to gain, in one short summer?

You have a son, he reminded himself. You have a daughter. You haven't lost them. Yet. And, perhaps—just perhaps—you have Diana Bradley. If you can get to her.

A sheet of water rose up, arching like a plume, and fell on top of him. Ahead, the bloodshot eyes of brake lights glowed and a door slammed, a man ran toward him. "Oh, my God, I didn't even see you until the last moment! Are you okay, mister?"

"I think so. Wet is all . . . but I was wet to start with." He tried to laugh reassuringly, but no sound came out.

"No day to be walking the Edgartown road. Can I give you a lift?"

"Sure can," he told the fellow, whose homely, honest face peered out from beneath the bill of his dripping paint cap. Bundled up in hip boots and a slicker, a rather scruffy slicker that probably leaked, he was clearly a year-round resident of the island.

"Come on then. I got to hurry," the man urged as they climbed into the battered sedan and started on their way. "I'm on the emergency patrol," he explained, driving steadily, without hurrying. "Doesn't do anyone any good if I get into an accident."

The windshield wipers beat their poor best against the onslaught; there was little to mark their progress, other than the passing of the sandy verge. When they reached the edge of Edgartown, the road was littered with twigs and leaves; further on a telephone pole hung directly across their path, suspended from its sparking wires.

"End of the line," announced his driver. "Sorry. We'll have to walk the rest of the way."

"I've only got a block or two more. Thanks."

The Islander waved and headed on down the street, intent on his errand of mercy. Steven leaned into the storm again, walking along the boarded up business district with its rainshining brick sidewalks until he reached the outskirts. Only a little further on was Diana's house. There were no lights in its windows, and its darkness drew from the depths of himself a loneliness that he'd been able to avoid in his struggle to get here. The worst possible thing that could happen to him right now would be her absence.

Oh, God, he prayed even as he remembered his determination never to pray, never, ever to call upon that unresponsive, uncaring, nonexistent Deity. *She has to be there. She's got to be.*

He knocked on the door of his asylum, waited a long, cruel time before it opened to candlelight.

"Hi," she said. "Sorry it took me so long to answer. Can't see a thing."

"Can you give shelter to this benighted fool?" he asked, his tone as light as he could make it. "Seems I'm out in the cold, windy world with nowhere to go."

"Sure." Backing up, she let him into the entry, where he shed his slicker and boots. "What do you mean, you've nowhere to go? Come on, into the living room. I've got a fire going."

His fatigue and shock overtook him, and he had no strength with which to make light remarks about the storm and the absence of electricity. "*Jenny's* gone." Tears were near the surface, and he slumped onto the couch while she took a seat beside him. "Eric took her out to sea."

"What?" she asked incredulously.

"When the wind shifted. He sent me on an errand, and when I got back . . . he was gone."

"How could he do that, all by himself?"

"Cut the lines. Probably hoisted one of the jib sails. Those old schooners were often sailed by just one person. The ship was taking on a lot of water and he knew it. He went out so he could go down with her."

"You mean, he scuttled her?"

"He wouldn't have had to. She'd sink all by herself if no one was pumping the bilge."

Shocked, she was silent for a time, then let out her breath, as though she'd been holding it. "Why?" she asked softly. "Do you know why he would do such a thing?"

Steven rested his head against the back of the couch and stared up at the ceiling. "He was pretty depressed to begin with, and he wanted to live aboard, this winter. If she sank, he'd have to go back to living more conventionally, and he didn't want to."

"How did you get here?" she asked, impulsively reaching for his hand as every ounce of his energy drained away.

"Walked."

"All the way from Vineyard Haven, in this storm?"

"Got a ride, halfway."

"You must be awfully tired, Steve."

"Yes, I guess I am," he admitted, his eyes closing at the very thought.

"Stretch out, right where you are."

"Shoes," he mumbled, and felt them being removed and himself tipping over, stretching out. "So glad you were here." The room rocked. "I don't know what I'd have done if you hadn't been here."

"I'll get something to cover you," she said, tucking sofa pillows under his head.

The words to tell her not to bother were out of reach. The rasp of wool scratched his chin as blankets were tucked in around him. Gradually his body heat returned.

"You won't go away, will you?"

"No," she said. "I'll be right here. Have you been home since I saw you last?"

"I am home."

Silence and darkness entered the room as sleep, like an unexpected guest, suddenly arrived.

The house was quiet, with a stillness peculiar to electrical failures. The low, golden light of the distant candle coaxed him up from the pit of exhaustion into which he'd fallen, up, up into the present moment which he was unable, just then, to identify. Across from him was a fireplace, with flames licking lazily around a newly placed log. It was Diana Harrison's fireplace, he remembered, and this was Diana Harrison's living room. Then, in an awful opening up of cavernous consciousness, he remembered that *Jenny Lawrence* had sunk, like Atlantis, somewhere out in the sea, and that Eric Larsen had gone down with her.

From the kitchen came the sound of a page turning. Diana. Just the two of them here in her house, without lights or telephones. No one knew he was there, and no one would know until he chose to reveal himself.

Could he take up with her where he'd left her so many years ago? Would she let him? You're a married man, Sinclaire, he reminded himself, but knew it no longer mattered.

Every muscle was stiff and immobile. Cautiously he moved his shoulders up and then down, reached over the mound of blankets and stretched his arms, edged his way into a sitting position and waited for the pain of his sore and strained muscles to ease up. Somehow he got to his feet and staggered into the kitchen.

"Well!" The candle cast her face as in a portrait, highlighting her features.

How beautiful she was! Past the upwelling of desire, he smiled down at her. "Have I been asleep long?"

"Awhile." She glanced at a clock over her stove which wasn't going because the power had yet to be restored. "It's probably around midnight. You must be hungry!" Quickly she slid from her chair and opened the refrigerator door, busied herself with an examination of its contents by the light of her candle. "I have a six-pack of beer. And some ham. How about a ham sandwich?"

"Later, maybe," he said. "It takes awhile to wake up."

"All right. We'll see about it in a half an hour or so. Let's work on the beer first." She rummaged in a drawer and found a bottle opener while he seated himself at the table. "Tell me more about Eric. I didn't want to ask you too much before—you seemed so tired. Tell me why he would take *Jenny* out."

The beer was cool, smooth, wonderful. Hair of the dog.

"He wasn't the person he seemed to be. He surrounded himself with people, drank with them, partied with them, but I think beneath that, he was a loner, and depressed besides. I mean, really depressed, like unbalanced," Steven told her. "Just before the storm hit he told me he hadn't slept much for a long time. He said he was running from something—he didn't know what. His thinking was confused."

"Do you think *Jenny* would have sunk right where she was moored, if he had stayed?"

"Probably. She was taking on a lot of water. Her seams were surely working. We pumped all morning, but she was getting lower anyway. It would take a lot of repairing to float her again. I doubt the four of us could have afforded it."

"Maybe he went out so you wouldn't be facing that. So you'd have insurance money, instead of an old, decrepit boat that couldn't float."

Was that possible? His throat closed up and he could say no more.

"Are you sure you aren't hungry?" she asked, drawing him away from his sadness. "We could eat ham sandwiches by the fire. Stay warm. It's a little chilly out here."

"Not yet." He looked into the candle flame, the blue of its center, the golden nimbus around it; his sadness eased, desire returned. Steadily he watched the candle, waited, drank.

Into the silence she asked, "So. Have you been back? To Waterford? Since I saw you last."

"Yes."

"Did you tell your wife about Dad and you?"

"Yes."

"And?"

"She says I was unfair to have deceived her so long ago by saying nothing about it."

"Did you? Deliberately deceive her?"

"I suppose I did. I knew it would make a difference to her," he explained. "It makes a difference to a lot of people, even though they won't admit it. I don't ask for rejection, if I can help it."

She hesitated a moment. "Is that why you never came to Dad? When you found out who he was? Were you worried that he'd turn you down?"

It had never occurred to him, to seek out Tim Bradley. Quite the opposite. Past the candle he met her eyes steadily. "I had to get away. I'd spent my whole life, up until then, under the thumb of Charles Sinclaire—the man my mother married in order to give me a name. He's an awful man, Diana. He abused us both. I suppose we were an outlet for his anger. My mother had tricked him, you see, into believing he was the father of her baby."

"I didn't know that."

"No one knew that. No one knows it even now. But my mother and I screwed him good and proper, once we found a way to do it. After that, I was free of him, but I had to find a new way to be Steven Sinclaire. I worked as a carpenter, maintained the house for my cousin, Elizabeth, went to college, met Mari, climbed the corporate ladder, and deliberately put Tim Bradley out of my mind."

He reached for her hand.

"I couldn't see you again, Diana. If I did, I've have to see him. Knowing him showed me what I'd missed, and it was more than I could stand. That's why you never heard from me, after that summer. I couldn't answer your letters, though they meant a lot." The moment hung between them.

"Would you like another bottle of beer? I see you've finished yours. I'll have one, too." Freeing her hand, she pushed back her chair and dug two more bottles out of the refrigerator. This time the caps escaped her, bouncing along the counter and onto the floor. "Oh, damn!" she exclaimed, retrieving them. "I never even asked if you wanted a glass. Do you?"

"No," he answered softly, in an effort to put her at her ease—but she was not at ease, not at all, clutching the bottles and their caps. "Please, Diana, please sit down," he begged. "Let me tell you about my mother."

This distraction worked, and Diana resumed her place. "My mother is freed from Charles Sinclaire, as I am. Just now she's in Philadephia, with her old friend, Pris Warden."

Diana nodded her approval. "Good for her! And good for you, too, Steven, for getting free of him."

"The most free I've ever been has been aboard the *Jenny Lawrence*. My wife said it all: when I introduced her to *Jenny* for the first time, she complained that it was like meeting my mistress."

The word rose between them, unavoidably suggestive; the expression on Diana's face changed, and he suspected that on his own was the concentrated intensity of a man stalking his prey.

Her hand clutching the bottle caps tightened as she asked, "Have you ever had a mistress? A woman?"

"A woman, yes," he answered honestly, remembering Arleen Patterson. "A mistress, no." He continued to watch her, silently waiting for an answer to an unspoken question. "We were a strait and proper generation, after all. Have you? Had a lover?"

"I was faithful to Paul, if that's what you're asking."

"You haven't been married for a couple of years. Have you had a lover since?" he asked bluntly.

"No." They paid pointed attention to their respective bottles of beer and she let the bottle caps fall, one, then the other, onto the table, their tiny, tinny sound loud in the stillness.

"What will you do, now that your mistress is lost to you?" she asked finally.

"I was going to think that over while I walked here, figure out why *Jenny* was so important to me—what I'd found in her, whether it could be found anywhere else. Then that local guy came by and offered a ride and I took it."

"And never came to a conclusion?"

"Well . . . I may have come to a conclusion that didn't require thought." His eyes held hers, and he refused to release her.

"You must mean . . . you must believe it can be found—in another place," she faltered.

"Yes. I think it can."

In the silence, silence which no clock ticking measured, in which no motor hummed accompaniment, something hot and uncontrolled built up and reached out.

Quickly she jumped up, opened a cupboard. "Would you like some crackers with the beer? I have a fresh box up here somewhere." When she turned to get the answer he pushed his chair aside and came to her.

"I waited," she said and with difficulty looked up at him.

"I'm really sorry." He touched her hair, her cheek. "I couldn't come."

"Yes, I understand that now." At her temple a vein lifted and fell strongly. He touched it with his lips; he brought her gently to himself, found her mouth with his own, and felt her tension. She was afraid, and he must help free her. Drawing back a bit, he asked, "Was your husband unkind to you?"

"Sometimes. When he'd been drinking."

"You tighten up when I touch you. Do I remind you of him?"

"You're nothing like him."

"Do you want me to go away?"

"No," she whispered. "No."

"Very soon it'll be too late," he said, and from the deep of himself welled his need for her, his joy in her.

"Steve, I . . ."

She reached out, and they drew close again, and he found her breast, still youthful, firm, warm.

"I don't really know how to make love to a man," she said, covering his hand with hers. "Paul just took what he wanted."

"I'll show you. Is your bedroom on this floor?" In most cape-style houses, it would be on the other side of the stairway.

"Follow me." Picking up the candle, she led him into the living room to check the fire. "We'd better put the screen across it."

He did, and they travelled on, past the front door and into a small, snug room that took the candle's light and dispersed it. When their eyes became accustomed to the dimness, she pulled off the covers of her wide, wonderful bed, and removed what was left of her clothing while he stripped off his. They embraced in their nakedness, her lips seeking his more and more urgently, and gently he lowered her to the bed, lay with her in an exploration of their bodies, and because further discussion was not needed, parted her legs and covered her with himself and pushed, oh yes, into the hotness that willingly, urgently, awaited him.

"Steven." It was a gasp.

He had hurt her. Oh, Christ, he hurt her, and knew it was true, that she'd had no lover—perhaps had not even known her husband for a long time. She was like a virgin, but ready for him nonetheless, wet and warm. Waiting for her discomfort to ease and then to wane, he kissed her mouth and her eyes and her hair, the curve of her throat, and saw that her skin was softly pink, glowing. She was a woman in need, a woman craving, a woman who did not know how to tell him, nor take what he would give.

"You have to trust me," he murmured. "You have to let go, and let me catch you."

"I'll try," she whispered. "Oh, I will try."

He kissed her without hurrying, the pounding in his groin an agony that he willed himself to endure; he kissed her until he could fairly feel her aching need. Still, she held back and it was important, desperately important to break that control, demolish it so that there would be no restraint, no pride, no reservation. He must make her speak to him, he must make her admit that she needed him, he must make her beg, grovel if necessary...

He pinned her, every part of her, with every part of himself, immobilizing her, gambling on his certainty that the longer she would be unable to move, the harder it would be to resist the rise of her own need. Already she was starting to strain against him, her breathing shallow, starting to catch in her throat.

"Am I hurting you? Am I too heavy?" His lips still touched hers as he spoke, and he felt as well as heard her breathless reply.

"No. You aren't too heavy. You don't hurt... oh, God..."

He drew back slowly, as though to leave her.

"Don't!" Her eyes flew open, wounded.

"Don't what?" he asked softly.

"Don't—don't go away."

"Why not?"

She was silent, tears gathered, shining in her eyes.

"Why not?" He kissed her eyes closed. "Say it."

"I need you," she whispered. "I want you."

"Like this?" he asked, and slowly pushed in again.

"Yes!" Her voice was thin, drawn from a far place. "Oh, yes."

Beneath him her bones melted and became part of his, her breath was caught, and he had her—he had her . . . he knew it! He watched the torment, the tumult that he wrought. "Like that?" he asked, gently giving. "Like that?" he asked, cruelly taking away, slowly, slowly—oh, oh, the burning agony of it!

"Yes! Oh, yes!" she cried, over the edge now, past the self that feared him and what he could do to her, shuddering in the quivering agony of arousal, writhing and no longer in control because she was his, his own, part of himself, to do with as he willed for this moment, this hour, this lifetime, this eternity. All his awareness, all his being was centered in the beating, burning, aching of their coupling. Distantly he heard her call his name and felt the tensing of her flesh, and within himself there was a rending, a tearing, as a tree uprooted from the earth, as a cliff falling into the sea, and from a distant place he heard himself cry out as he never had, compelled to give voice to the depth of his experience.

The slam of orgasm rolled across his horizon like summer thunder, and he lost track of himself, somehow, and somehow came back, shaken and empty, lowered himself to her side, gathered her up. She twined her legs around his, clung to him, her face tight against the curve of his neck.

"I never knew I could fit with a man," she sighed shakily. "I can't get close enough."

Running a hand across her hip and waist, he felt her lips on his throat, felt the whispered texture of her skin, and knew that he could take her yet again, he who had believed the virility of youth was behind him.

"Even after I go back, Diana, we have to see one another," he said close to her ear.

"Yes." Somehow she moved closer yet, and he touched the curve of her spine and the rise of her hip, fullness of her thigh, pushed her away to kiss her breasts and roughly moved her beneath him. "Yes," she urged. "Yes," she cried, and he entered her again, found her ready, helplessly orgasmic, incredibly responsive, and he was sorry for the man she divorced who had not been able to unlock this part of her, glad for himself who had found her and her warmth and her openness as now she met him, aquiver in her eagerness, hot and deep.

Oh, Christ—the climax was drawn effortlessly from him, quiet, sustained, devastating. Shattered, he waited to be reassembled, and they were still for a long, long time. "I wish we could go on all night," he confessed gladly. "I wish I was twenty again, when I first knew you. I'd have been able to do it and do it and do it."

She laughed. "It would be grand, but I don't require more. I've just discovered I'm not frigid, and that's enough, all by itself."

"You've just been saving it up." He stroked her hair. "If only you understood how sorry I was, years ago—"

"Don't," she said, covering his mouth.

"I loved you then."

"It's okay, Steven."

"I loved you," he insisted.

"I loved you too," she said softly.

"And I love you still."

"I love you too. I love you!"

He held her as tightly as he could, grateful, joyful, humble, exaltant. "I have to start all over. You must know that."

"Yes, I'm afraid I do."

"Not only because of the *Lawrence*. I would never have come here if my marriage were still in one piece. It's not, and I can't go on pretending that everything's okay. A lot of things haven't been okay for a long time."

"I gathered that." Her lips whispered over his throat, his chest; he felt a little nip, saw she'd raised a welt on his shoulder. "I've branded you." She smiled. "Wherever you go, everyone will know you're mine."

"They'll know anyway, because you're coming with me."

"No."

His elation and joy drained away, and in his nakedness he was cold.

Pulling him to herself, she said, "I love you—you know I do—and that's why I'm not going with you."

"I don't blame you for not wanting to leave the Vineyard or this house, or the shop," he said. "But I wouldn't expect you to—not all the time. Just part of the time," he urged. "And I'll come here, part of the time. I'll build us fires to sit in front of, and read books to you, and bring you breakfast in bed."

She laughed shakily. "No. Let's just love one another now. Just now."

"And then?"

"And then you'll go back to do whatever you decide to do. But since you don't have any real idea of where you'd like to go or what you'd like to do or be, you have to go by yourself, and find out."

"I'd like any decision I make to include you."

"I know you would. But it's more important for you to find out what you think is right for yourself, whether I'm part of it or not. Don't you see?"

"No!" he said fiercely, clawing at the edges of the chasm of despair opening now beneath him. To have found her, after all this time! To have tracked her, pursued her, won her! "Why put us through it?"

"Because you have a chance to make a really free choice." Her voice was low, steady, strong. "You've lost all the ties you've had, except your children, perhaps, and soon they'll be gone, too. You're starting over, at the bottom. So much of your life has been conditioned by a secret you've been obliged to keep—by wounds you had no choice but to bear. Now that's not true. Now there's nothing."

"There's you."

"Yes. But that makes me an anchor. If I come with you now, all the decisions you have to make would take me into consideration. If I don't come along, every decision you make will come from the wellspring of yourself, and you'll see who you really are. It's the chance of a lifetime."

"I need you. You're the chance of a lifetime."

"Go find whatever it is you have to do," she begged. "Go find out what life requires of you. When you're done, we'll know whether there's room enough in your life for me. I'll wait, Steven."

He could only stare, defeated. "You really won't come with me."

"No."

"But you love me."

"I love you—and my not coming with you ought to prove it."

"You've got it all thought out."

"Yes," she admitted. "I had a lot of time to think tonight, while you slept. I've thought about a lot of things, ever since I saw you last."

"Like whether you'd let me make love to you?"

"Yes, that."

"Like whether you wanted to?"

"Yes." She touched his mouth. "And then, because we aren't the kind of people to take intimacy lightly, I had to think a lot about where it would lead, and where I wanted it to go—and where you'd need it to go. It's bound to lead us somewhere, and I'm willing that it should. But not now, Steve. Not yet. You've gone through so much, come so far..."

"And what if I can't find you when I'm done?"

But he knew the answer, saw it in her eyes.

"Trust me," she smiled.

CHAPTER

The Legacy

AS SOON AS the Hobbes Hole ferry docked, he called Bob, then Mari. "Casey's coming to pick me up," he told the stranger on the other end of the wire. "I'll be home in a couple of hours."

"How did you and Eric weather the storm?"

"Not so well."

"What's that supposed to mean?"

"*Jenny's* gone," he said. "I'll tell you about it when I see you."

"She was insured, wasn't she?"

There was a long pause. "Wasn't she?" Mari asked again.

"I think so," Steven said, and hung up. In fact, he didn't know. Bob had handled the details of the business, leaving everyone else free to sail.

The day was intensely and infinitely clear, as the day after a storm always was, and hands in his pockets, he wandered the Hobbes Hole waterfront, waiting for Bob. Flotsam and jetsam lay in tangled heaps on the beach. The storm had not struck here as harshly as it had on the islands, though, and the destruction had been pared to the proportion of a nuisance. A bench with fishnet and seaweed draped over one end looked out toward the jetty and he rested there, trying to make sense of things.

Home. It was time to go home to Waterford.

Home. To Mari. But how could he live with her, listen to plans for the Olde Kings Highway Historical District and watch the new comers pushing the local folks around?

Home. To Kingsland. To the house of Kingsley Merrick, his legacy, to do with as he chose while *Jenny Lawrence* and Eric lay somewhere deep down, in the arms of the bay or wherever the currents would take their remains.

Home. To his children, whom he would nurture and love and all the while hold Diana Bradley deep in his heart, living from the depths of the only truth he had left. From which he could move forward, whether *Jenny* was there or not. If that was what he chose.

An hour drifted by. Then a shadow moved up beside him. "Hi, pal," said Bob Casey. There wasn't room for him to sit; the net and seaweed took up the remainder of the space.

Steven levered himself to his feet. "Hi. Heard anything?"

They shook hands.

"I'm afraid so," Bob said. "I'm afraid there's wreckage washing up here and there that probably belongs to *Jenny*." Together they watched the sun dance in the harbor. "The insurance investigators are going to ask a lot of questions, I expect." It was Bob's way of seeking information without being direct about it.

So, Mari's question was answered. "I wasn't there," Steven said, still looking out to sea. "I left to get more beer. When I got back, the ship was gone, like I told you on the phone."

"Any evidence Eric untied her?"

"The lines were cut, actually."

Bob breathed a deep, despairing sigh.

"He told me he couldn't sleep and had nightmares when he did. He was determined to keep Jenny afloat so he could live on her this winter—"

"I remember we all agreed to that."

"He said he couldn't join the rat race. Wouldn't."

"The rat race being—"

"What people do to get to the top."

"And what is that?"

"Sell their souls."

"The insurance folks will want to know if he was suicidal."

"You mean, if Eric was using the ship to end his own life."

"Something like that. It'll seem pretty strange to them—going out in a storm."

"Eric died because Jenny went down." It was important that Bob should believe this. "Most likely he took her out to sea so she wouldn't be smashed against the dock, what with the change of wind direction." He watched a gull climb up and drop a clam on the rocks of the jetty, and did not tell Bob that he'd untied the cut lines and let them drift away. There was no need. The fragments were probably in Long Island Sound by now, and would provoke no questions.

The gull swooped down to pull the clam out of its crushed shell. "Did you put extra money in *Jenny's* account?" he asked. "Eric said he was going to ask you to beef it up."

"He didn't ask."

"He said he was going to telephone you."

"He didn't. But I transferred some funds anyway. We're not overdrawn."

"Why didn't Eric call, do you think?"

"Perhaps he was afraid I'd have time to get to Vineyard Haven. Then he wouldn't have been so free to make his own decisions." They turned and walked toward the Casey truck. "What are you going to do," Bob asked, "now that *Jenny's* gone?"

"Been wondering about that myself."

They climbed in and the truck labored up to the village.

"Have you thought about the building business? You're an experienced carpenter. I've been wondering if maybe you'd consider being my partner."

He did not look at Bob; he could not trust himself. "If I stay in Waterford, I'd be mighty pleased to be your partner."

"If? If you stay?"

"I may rejoin the rat race."

"Come on, Steve. You've got to be kidding. Why in hell?"

"I'd like to prove something, I guess. Besides," he said, switching to a topic they could both get their hands on, "I'm not sure I want to live in Waterford anymore."

"Hell, it won't always be like this. All these new people, they just want to make things better. Spiff the town up a little. But Waterford will get to them, in time, and they'll relax and go with the flow."

He thought of John Shaunessy, and Eben Gray. Of Greenleaf Stone and Don Slater. Of Roly Hall, who in his entire career had never issued a ticket, and had gone down east to Maine, the long-time refuge of Cape Codders.

"Staying around is like saying it doesn't matter to me, that the new folks are making the town into a suburb. And since I can't change it..."

"You'd rather your kids were brought up in the rat-race, I guess."

"That was below the belt, Casey."

"That's what it was intended to be. Maybe it'll help wake you up. You've taken quite a beating, Steve. I think it's a bad idea to make decisions now. Let's just put my offer on hold for a week or two. Or as long as you want. There's plenty of work, more all the time. I can always use you, either as my partner, or part of my crew, if you'd like that better."

"Thanks. I'll think it over." And he would. There was more than one way to help the townsfolk, and somehow Bob was the key. The mid-Cape highway passed by, its scrubby little trees coming out to meet them and then hurtling backward as the truck sped on, and he thought about Waterford and how it had accommodated the vision of the people who sought refuge there these three hundred years.

"Elijah Merrick lost his ship, too," he observed. "It totally ruined him."

"That so? What'd he do, after he lost his ship?"

"Came back to town. Got plain people to become Universalists. To spite the Congregationalists, I think."

"Huh." They rode silently. "My great-grandfather shoveled shit in Kingsley Merrick's stable," Bob said at length. "Only, his name was O'Shay."

"Must have gratified you, so many years ago, to see me shovel yours," Steven laughed.

Bob grinned, without taking his eyes off the road. "For about two seconds, it did. But you weren't like the Merricks. You were yourself. Anyone could see that. In fact, everyone did."

In fact, I'm a Bradley, Steven thought.

"Mr. Turner's resigned," Bob said.

"Who's Mr. Turner?"

"The fellow who was elected selectman this spring."

"Why'd he resign?"

"Too much work," Bob grinned slyly. "Seems he didn't plan on spending so much time doing town business. Says it's not good for his health. So the election has to be held again. In September."

"No, Bob. The answer's no."

"If you took his place...."

"It won't do any good. All it would accomplish is to buy time."

"Maybe time's all Waterford needs."

"Maybe I'll nominate you," Steven said. "And you can give it time."

They pulled off the highway and into Waterford. The leaves on the overhanging trees were beginning to suggest autumn, with a few yellow ones here and there as they drove past the square old houses of captains, and the more elegant ones belonging to the Greek Revival, and then toward the mansard-roofed monstrosity that was Kingsland. He thought of the Merrick who started a renegade church, and the one who amassed two fortunes and nearly made a third, who built the house they approached now, and of the descendant of the Merrick stableman, sitting beside him now, as much a part of the lore of Waterford as was Steven Sinclaire himself. The sequence was interesting, he thought. He'd have to consider it more carefully, sometime.

Kingsland's sign hung from the mast in the front yard, the flag drooped in the still of mid-day. "Looks like you and Rick have been busy," Steven observed. "Thanks a lot, Bob. The kid must have been jumping with joy."

"Well, in fact he settled right into the job and certainly did his share."

The clamshells scrunched in the driveway; on the front porch sat Rick, a rip in his shirt and mud on his blue jeans and a swelling lump beneath his eye. Steven left the truck without speaking, only holding his hand up in farewell.

"Gosh," he teased, sitting down beside his son. "How's the other guy?"

"You may find out soon." Rick grinned. "Since the other guy is Junior Marshall."

"What was it about?"

"Dan Sears's grandpa."

"Linc?"

"Yup. A bunch of us were over on the playground practicing basketball, and Junior was making some pretty raw remarks about Mr. Sears—he drinks quite a lot, you know?"

"Yes, I do know."

"Junior was saying things that Danny Sears could hear, trying to make him feel bad, so I told him to stop, and he began giving me a hard time. So I let him have it."

They looked at each other, man to man, there on the porch. "You're not here to stay, are you?" Rick asked, his voice soft.

"No."

"I'll sure miss you."

"No, you won't." Steven hugged the boy. "I'm only going as far as Boston. I'll be here a lot, helping your mother, and you can come up to Boston and stay with me during school vacations. You and Kathy both."

"What are you going to do there? In Boston?"

"Work at something. I don't know what, yet. Depends on what I can find."

"And you'll come down on weekends and help me with the garbage?"

"You bet."

Rick's grateful smile was a failure.

It would not be easy, Steven thought. But it would resolve itself graciously if he were patient enough, enduring enough, sufficiently faithful to his own search. It would resolve itself, and at the end of whatever he found was the occupant of the house in Edgartown, and perhaps, just perhaps, another chance here on the land of his heritage for the boy beside him. Another chance for another Merrick, in whatever way Waterford had to offer, in a time far distant from this one.

"Let's go find your mother, kid, and make some plans."

He extended his hand and they shook on it, man to man, and together walked into the cool shadows of Kingsland.

Epilogue

The children of the WWII veterans would become known as "baby boomers". Their parents made sure they had everything they wanted, and did not allow them to suffer the consequences of unpleasant behavior so they would not become unhappy.

When they grew into their teenage years, these children enjoyed the pleasure of recreational sex and drugs and set about protesting the inequalities they observed—the discrimination against black people and women in the workplace, the materialism that dominated American society, and especially the Vietnam War.

Then they grew up. Their children were given everything they wanted, too, and were left to watch constant television programming and entertainment while their parents pursued their own opportunities. Women entered the corporate world, politics, and into professions which had been the perview of men, while their husbands continued the climb to success their fathers had begun, inventing space travel and launching the Age of the Internet and personal computer.

Millions of people world-wide watched the wedding of Charles, Prince of Wales, and Diana Spencer. E.T. went home. The Berlin wall was taken down and the Cold War ended.

But peace was not to be had. Acts of terrorists began, and small wars no one wanted, and then larger ones. Drug use was endemic;

crack cocaine entered the market just as the grandchildren of the Baby Boomers entered their teens. The social fabric of the country began to unravel.

If they had ever been innocent before, Americans were innocent no longer.

THE BREEZE WAS JUST RIGHT, the tide perfect; gulls called and laughed and soared in the sun. Ahead, on the reconstructed wharf, Waterford's important people waited. On the beach, the cameras of the photographers winked and reporters scribbled on their note pads, describing the scene.

"Pretty amazing," Diana remarked. "A packet landing, after all these years."

Steven, preparing to change direction so that the little schooner would gracefully swing parallel to the wharf, was completely absorbed in not ramming it. There was no comment about the packet landing, but only, "Ready about."

"Ready," they called while Rick clambered forward to secure the jib as it fell and his twelve-year-old son, Tim, untangled the line and did his best to look nautical. He loved sailing, and was proud of Grandpa's boat.

Successfully turning, they coasted closer to the dock. Steven commanded, "Wave, everyone, so the committee knows you're glad to see them."

"How about you?" Diana asked as they obediently waved, and, like wind-up toys, everyone on the dock waved back.

"I'm busy," he explained, trying to hide his reticence. Today's observance and commemoration would put the finishing touch on the years of work he'd done with Bob Casey, but she knew he was uncomfortable being the focus of attention. Bad enough that he had to give a speech!

Jennifer was parallel to the small wharf now. The men caught her lines and secured her. At low tide, the little schooner would settle into the shallow trench hollowed out for vessels like her. Leaflets were distributed to the journalists, explaining that Mr. Sinclaire had agreed to use the new wharf today in Waterford's time-honored manner; his schooner would rest in the trench at low tide. The leaflet went on to describe the packet service in the days of sail.

This information was available on a plaque at the edge of the parking lot, too, along with others that described how the clams were protected and oysters raised and how beach grass helped to prevent erosion. Waterford was afloat with such plaques so that tourists, a crucial part of the town's economy, would understand the historical significance of everything they saw.

"Hello, there! You're just in time!" The chairman of the Board of Selectmen reached out a hand to assist and Diana took it gladly. Scrambling out of *Jennifer* was never easy!

"Thank you!"

Steven waited for Rick and Timmy to negotiate the wharf, then climbed over the edge to shake hands with the rest of the welcoming committee.

"Mr. Johnson."

"Mr. Martin."

"Miss Marshall."

"Mr. Snow."

Waiting at the foot of the wharf was eight year old Danny who, unable to contain himself any longer, broke away from his mother and raced out to take Steven's hand. "Grandpa! Come on!" he urged, tugging.

Cameras clicked, recording this heartfelt welcome.

"I guess it's time we were on our way," Steven told the group, whose members laughed indulgently. "Take Grandma Di's hand," he told the boy, "and I'll follow."

"Oh! OK!" Danny reached for her. "I'll take care of you, Gramma."

The boy was irrepressible, but his mother, Rick's wife Sherry, was not amused. "When we get back to the house, I'll take care of you, young man," she told him. "Take your eye off him for one moment, and he's gone," she mourned. "I'm sorry about that."

"We were about done with hand shaking," Diana assured her. "Don't be too hard on him."

"It rates a lecture," Sherry smiled. "Right, Danny?"

"Right, Mom," the boy agreed, undismayed. "Maybe tomorrow?"

"It's a deal." The girl was a wonderful wife to Ricky, great mom to their sons, fitting effortlessly into the family, in a sense becoming the daughter that Steven had lost.

Arnold Wheeler waited nearby, leaning against his old Ford truck. "About time you folks showed up," he remarked, shaking hands with Steven, nodding respectfully at Diana.

"Can't hurry the tide," Steven chafed. "You know that."

"Mr. Sinclaire! Can you say a few words about today's celebration?" The reporter had a microphone that he thrust in front of Steven's face.

"Later," he said, his tone firm. Turning, he helped Diana climb into Arnold's truck, hoisted himself in with a little grunt. "These things get higher off the ground every year," he complained.

"Ay-yuh," Arnold agreed.

Along with the truck were the cars belonging to the greeters on the wharf. Sherry would follow Arnold, driving Rick and the boys so they would be free to wave at whoever might be alongside the road. The others would follow her. The Commemoration Committee had not been pleased when Steven forbade a full-scale parade to escort him into town, but by now they were used to the low-profile way in which he operated. His modesty was just one of the traits Diana loved about him. There were many others that she never ceased to marvel at, even after so many years together.

The cars coughed to life, and slowly everyone left the parking lot, single file, and moved past the first house on the Rockford Road. Bob Casey had built it some forty years ago, using the insurance money he and Steven received from the *Jenny Lawrence*. It looked out over the bay, and had sold immediately with a substantial profit.

The next house, further up the road and without a Bay view, had been equally profitable because housing prices were rising fast by then, and just mere proximity to the shore was valuable. The third house, too, sold for a small fortune.

By then, Steven had become convinced that a man could be part of the rat race without becoming a rat. Having proven the point, he'd returned to Waterford and joined Bob in clearing the land for Kingsland Acres. Lying behind the three Casey-built houses on the Rockford Road, its entrance was just beyond the third, and a small mob had gathered there.

"Hi, Steven! Hi, Diana!"

Diana blew kisses while Steven waved.

"Bob's pleased as punch," Arnold reported. "I had a chance to visit him this morning."

"We'll drop by tomorrow and let him know how the day's festivities went," Diana said. She admired Steven's mentor wholeheartedly, incarcerated at a nursing home, his body was no longer able to sustain independence. But Casey was as sharp as ever. A wonderful old man.

They were passing the church at the corner now, gleaming in the midst of its surrounding lawn and benches and pergola. Across from it was its historic cemetery, chock-a-block full with more than one hundred and forty years of departed members. The town's cemetery was further south on the Rockford Road, and the Unitarians and Universalists joined the general population there now, since there was no more room in their own burial ground. That very fact made Steven happy, Diana knew. In death as in life, everyone in town faced the future together. His mother, who'd passed on twenty years ago, waited for them in the family plot he'd bought there.

Arnold turned onto Main Street, past the general store. It was housed in the ancient Inn of the Golden Ox, once the ancestral stomping ground of the Snow family. It was decorated with pails of flowers and swags of bunting. Across the way, an antique shop occupied the old

King house, and further along the road, a lawyer had set himself up in the Denning place, its many additions removed so as to present an authentically preserved remnant of the past. Most of the old captains' houses on Main Street were beautifully maintained by their owners, their signs unobtrusive, as required by the Historic District. All of them had their flags out.

The requirements of the District did not apply to the smaller homes and lots outside its jurisdiction. Nor did they apply to the older cottages of Waterford's native population, no matter where they were found, their shabby porches and cluttered out-buildings and sagging sheds safely sheltered by zoning's grandfather clause.

Arnold turned into Kingsland's driveway. The trees and flower beds and lawns that had graced the place in its hay-day did so still. Around the perimeter of the old mansion's footprint was a low wall topped by planks to sit on or climb over. In the center of the footprint was play space for toddlers, with ceramic horses mounted on heavy springs to ride on and an enormous sandbox. Swings with bucket-like seats dominated the far end, where the kitchen had once been. The house itself was gone.

The fence that once separated Kingsland from the Marshall estate had been replaced with one more ecologically appropriate, demarking the strip of meadow and bog between the two properties. Where the carriage barn had once been, a playground for larger children was installed, with see-saws and round-abouts and towers with fenced observation platforms on top, accessed by ladders. Connecting them, near to the ground, were swaying metal bridges.

The rest of the east lawn was reserved for parking. On the west a temporary platform had been erected with a refreshment table nearby. Benches were scattered here and there around the edges.

Arnold and the cavalcade stopped. Instantly Steven and Diana were surrounded by a crowd of townsmen and Kingsland Club members, while the Waterford band played incidental music, seated on folding chairs beneath a nearby tree. Children, some of them in Brownie and Cub Scout uniforms, cavorted on the lawns, waiting for their chance at the playground equipment which was, as yet, off-limits.

"I thought this was going to be small," Steven complained.

"It started out that way," Arnold explained. "But then everyone wanted to be part of it, not just club members."

"Well, that's got to be good," Steven conceded.

"Look, Honey," Diana put in, "they've even got refreshments."

"Thank the Waterford Ladies," Eben informed them. It didn't matter who you were or where you lived; any woman in town could belong to the Waterford Ladies Society, and it appeared that all of them had been busy baking.

"Well, then, let's get this over with," Steven sighed.

Along with the heads of Recreation and Conservation and History and the Board of Selectmen, they took their places on the platform. Everyone else claimed one of the folding chairs that had been set up by Scout Troop #2. The band played the national anthem, and then the crowd seated itself, the children cross-legged on the grass.

"We are pleased and excited to greet you all here today," the president of the Historical Society announced, too close to the microphone. Breathing heavily into it, she backed away a bit and started again.

Tim and Danny were eyeing the big kids' playground equipment, Diana could see. All the children, no doubt, were yearning for a chance to try it out, but waited patiently, no doubt well bribed by the Kingsland Acres Club. The Sinclaires did not belong to the club; it ran independently of Casey Construction, which had built and now leased the Acres' low-income houses, but Diana and Steven had offered a bribe of their own, even for Tim, too old for playgrounds, who waited as patiently as possible for the chance to toss a Frisbee or a football around with the older Waterford boys.

From her vantage point on the platform, Diana looked for Mari. Still living in town, she was married to someone else—a wonderful someone else who had persuaded her to grant Steven a divorce and exchange Kingsland for a handful of ancient Merrick woodlots, now very valuable. The new husband had built a magnificent modern house on the largest of them, all glass and fieldstone, far from the center of town where the District forbade such architecture.

But Mari wasn't there, thank goodness.

The Historic Society lady finished to polite applause, and introduced Steven.

He had not prepared a speech, though Diana had encouraged him to make a few notes so he wouldn't wander or reminisce. But he had thought reminiscence wouldn't hurt, if that's what came along in the natural course of things. "The Tao," he'd teased. "You're forgetting the Tao. I'll just go with the flow."

At this moment the flow took him up to the microphone. Reluctant or not, he faced up to the present challenge as though he enjoyed it.

"I think Kingsley Merrick, whose mansion was once here, would have been glad to see his land used for the benefit of Waterford," he began. "I'm not so sure he'd have been in favor of taking his house apart, though, one board at a time."

The group laughed gently; everyone knew that Kingsley Merrick's Victorian mansion was a monument to his financial success. Dismantling it would have hardly met with his approval.

"I'm quite sure he'd commend the Conservation Commission," Steven bowed to its chairman on the platform, "which has seen to the building of walking trails so that all of us can enjoy the gifts that nature has given us here on Cape Cod."

The enthusiastic audience came to its feet in applause for the chairman, who, modestly as possible, nodded and waved. Starting at the parking lot, the Conservation trail wound through the brush, all the way to the shore where a picnic table and grill awaited the visitor. The Kingsland Acres Club—a club that didn't even have a proper meeting place, that didn't keep minutes or make annual reports to anyone—had recruited every able-bodied male in town to lay the trail's walkways. The Club's women had rounded up Waterford's ladies to supply water and lemonade and cookies of all descriptions on those Saturday mornings of hard work.

As always, Diana was astonished by the Club's success. Comprised of the adults from Kingsland Acres, it took responsibility for the maintenance of its own land and the town's public beach access. And more. In the fall and spring, its members and their children were available for raking leaves, renewing flower beds, and washing windows. Its fees were modest and gratefully paid by for the Waterford's older people who comprised much of the present population. In this way, the low-income folks were an integral part of the town, and in fact, indispensable to it. Aunt Alice Bradley would be pleased, Diana was sure.

"We understand that dismantling the old mansion was distressing to those interested in history," Steven was saying now, with a nod to the chairlady of the Historical Society. "We are interested in history, too, but we believe each generation is responsible for bringing the past into the present. Kingsley Merrick's mansion—whatever were his motivations for building it—was a place where everyone in town met and mingled. Everyone. That was his goal—one that was lost sight of as time went by. We needn't pursue the why's and wherefore's of that, but we can pursue the renewal of his original goal now, in the twenty-first century. In that spirit, I am proud to convey, on his behalf, the new playgrounds—and the Conservation land—to the town. It belongs to us all now. Thank you."

The assembly rose as one, applauding and cheering. The band struck up a Sousa march as the children raced for the swings and towers or toddled toward the enormous sand-box. Friends and well-wishers crowded 'round. Hands were shaken, praise heaped up.

"And lo, good-will ran like honey from the comb," Steven murmured in her ear.

"And there was rejoicing among the people," Diana answered, as indeed was the case. They both enjoyed fitting old language into present occasions.

Tim had found a group intent on Frisbie. Danny had claimed an observation platform, along with as many little boys as could fit onto it. Everyone availed themselves of the refreshment table. Finally the

Sinclaire adults climbed into Rick's car and left, driving around to the Kingsland Acres access road. At its far end was home, standing on a lot carved out of the conservation land.

It would be held in perpetuity for the descendants of Kingsley Merrick. Joists and beams and flooring and trim from the old place had been used to construct a simple Cape house, its roof low to the ground, facing south to get the winter's sun. A deck overlooked the pond and the not-too-distant bay. Steven had worked long and hard with Waterford's various committees to achieve it. Since it was out of sight from Main Street, the Historic District glumly agreed to its presence. The Conservation Committee put a lot of pressure on them to do so, and to agree to the dismantling of the old house there in the middle of town with its tower high above everything else. "It doesn't belong here," Steven had argued. "It's at variance with all the other old buildings. The town's historical value will be greater without it."

His opinion had not impressed the Kings Highway folks, but the donation of all that land, forever protected from development and open to the public, carried the day.

The house itself was located in a wonderful spot, far enough from Main Street that traffic was only a murmur. An unobtrusive nature trail passed a quarter acre away, hidden in a depression created by the glacier countless centuries ago.

They paused for a moment to admire the house, then climbed gratefully onto the deck and took a deep collective breath. "Well, what's your opinion?" Steven asked. "We got through the day OK, don't you think?"

"Still have to take the boat back to Yarmouth Port," Rick reminded him.

"Not until tomorrow's tide." Steven stretched out on the chaise and folded his hands behind his head, looking up at the Cape Cod sky. "For now us old folks can just take it easy."

Sherry guffawed. Old folks, indeed!

"I think it's time these old folks had a gin and tonic," Rick said to her, "while others of us have a highball."

"A martini for me," Sherry said.

"OK. Let's go make the drinks and leave these old guys here, to rest in peace."

"What a wonderful idea," Diana sighed. And it was. Indeed, the accumulating years weighed heavily at the end of the day. It was a fine thing, to put their feet up and let the younger generation see to their comfort.

Afternoon was taking on a golden glow, its richness filling the marshes and meadows. Silence wrapped itself around them, and peace. Years of waiting had led to this moment. Waiting for Steven to come to her. Waiting for Kathy and Rick to grow up. Waiting for Mari to agree to a divorce. Years in which Steven saved carefully, worked with Bob to create Kingsland Acres. It complied with federal guidelines to provide housing for lower income working people like the Sears family, and the Halls, and the Stones. And their parents and grandparents. Provisions of the Affordable Housing Act gave preferential treatment to the local population and the income of Waterford's tradesmen, young and old, qualified them.

The boys, returning now from the playground, clambered onto the deck, bringing the hustle of the present with them. Peace receded.

"Those towers are great," Danny exclaimed. "Everybody likes 'em."

"Good." Steven didn't open his eyes. "Did you win at Frisbee, Tim?"

"No one wins at Frisbie," Tim told him. "We just throw it around."

"Were we good?" Danny asked. "Did we win the prize?"

"What prize is that?" Steven asked with a straight face.

"Oh, Grandpa!" the boy chided. "You promised a treat."

"If we were good enough," Tim reminded him.

"Were we, Grandpa?"

"You were great. Ice cream sundae of your choice, whenever you want it."

The boys looked pleased.

"Grandpa, can I live here when I get old?" Tim asked.

"What about me?" Danny demanded. "What if I want to live here?"

"It's not up to me." Steven sat up straighter, alert now. "It'll belong to your Dad. Maybe you'd better ask him."

"Oh! Ok!" The youngsters hurried off, looking for Rick.

The house could not be sold. It would be conveyed to the town if no Merrick wanted it, which seemed unlikely given the grand-kids' present enthusiasm. Kathy, far away in Chicago, had no interest in her father's present life or any property on Cape Cod. She had gone her own way as soon as she was old enough to do so, visiting Mari once a year and pointedly avoiding Steven. That hurt, Diana knew, but it was an unavoidable casualty of the failed marriage. Steven hoped it would change, if he waited long enough. Meanwhile, he'd deed the place to Rick.

The house, though it looked small, was commodious, and Diana's daughter would be down tomorrow morning with her family. Her twin, too young to have married, was buried in Edgartown, a casualty of the Viet Nam war. Sadness in remembrance filtered through the joy and pleasure of the present moment; Diana held it at arm's length, something she was good at by now.

Her son's death had brought Steven to her. He had come to Edgartown as soon as he learned of it. I'm so sorry, he'd whispered, holding her close. I'm so sorry.

He stayed, letting her grieve as she must, gradually making himself an indispensable part of her life. He'd quit his Boston job by then and was building Kingsland Acres with Bob. Unmarried couples were beginning to live openly with one another, and in its own time, they worked out a pattern; he lived with Diana on the weekend, at Bob Casey's house during the week.

That was when they lost Kathy, who was unable to accept such an arrangement.

By the time Kingsland Acres was well underway, Mari opted out. A housing development for poor people, virtually in the back yard? No, thank you!

Once she was no longer part of the equation, Diana and Steven were quietly married in a civil ceremony and together faced the zoning board and the Historical Society, the dismay of the town as Kingsland Acres rose up to shelter the dispossessed and the mansion was taken apart to build a new house here by the pond. They had kept some of the old Victorian artifacts—the Tiffany silver and the Limoges china and parts of the Aubusson carpet that could be restored and made into area rugs. To the Historical Society went the portraits and the papers, the land to Conservation.

A bird flashed by, the grasses rustled in an unfelt draft, and the voices of Rick and his family filtered out from the kitchen. Steven was asleep by now. His face in repose was gentle, its age-lines less apparent as the late afternoon light lay kindly upon it, and she watched him breathing slowly, his hands folded across his chest, his white hair—still abundant—stirring in a draft. He had taught her how to love, body and soul, and so at last she had learned to live fully, right up to the present moment.

Snacks and drinks would appear soon. The adults would chat languidly here on the deck, and the boys would probably play Monopoly at the picnic table, and everyone would witness the setting sun. Then they'd go in for supper, the house a welcoming one, somehow taking on the patina of age and tradition by its having been built from the elements of the old place, trimmed with its grooved window and door frames, foot-wide flooring and wainscot. It would welcome Diana's daughter and grandchildren tomorrow. Rick and his family would live here, in time, and if Kathy came back, it would welcome her, as well.

Kingsland, indeed, sheltered them all.

THE END

Merrick Genealogy

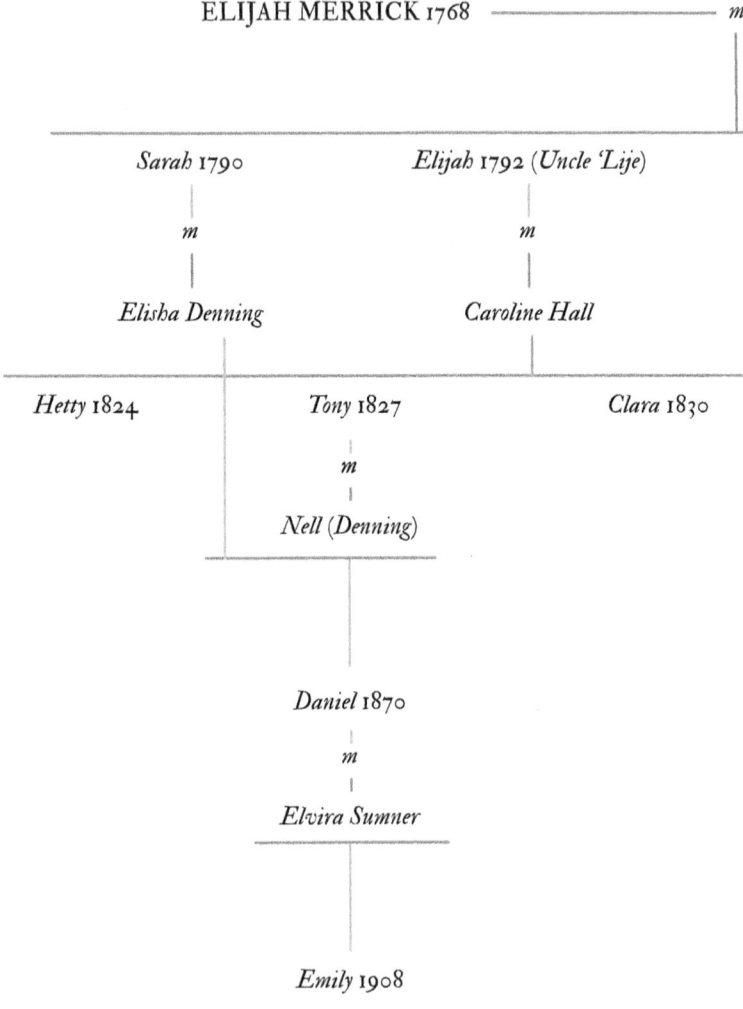

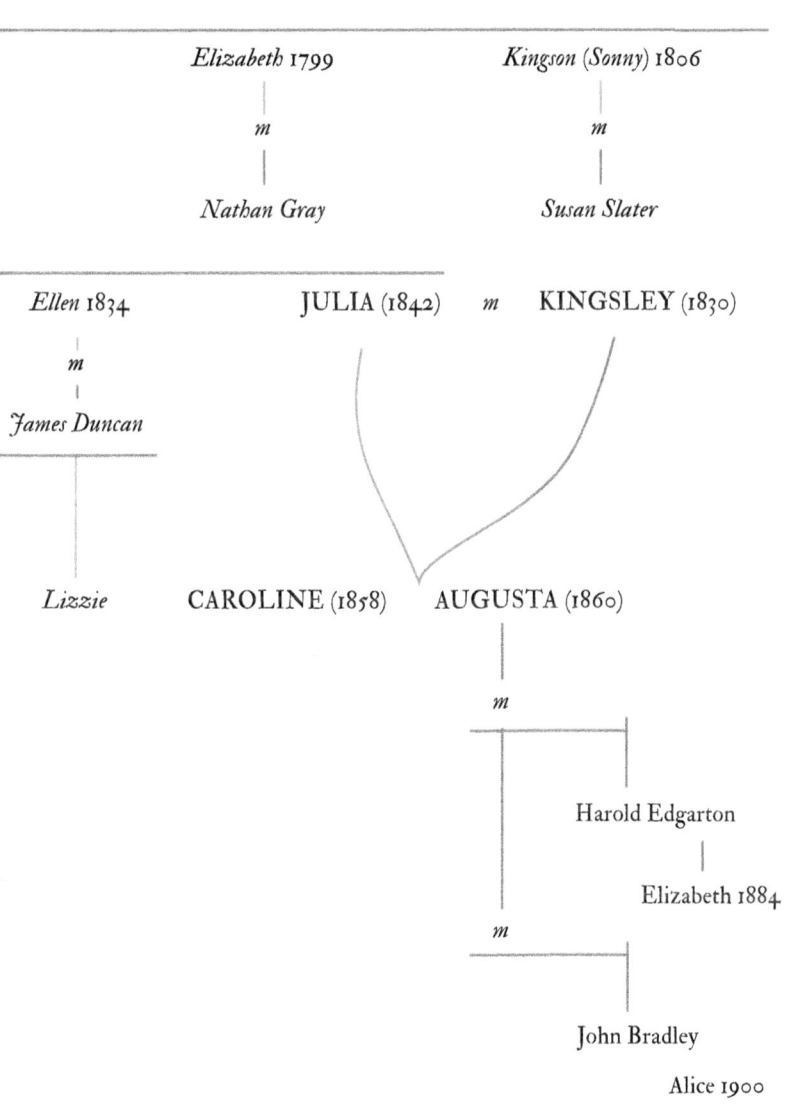

Did you enjoy
THE KINGSLAND SERIES?

If you did, follow Deborah Hill's blog at NorthRoadPublishing.com. Ask questions, share your opinions, explore the details of history that underlie each book of the series. Join the discussion about Elijah's monumental change of heart when he discovers that Molly has saved his house, about Augusta's excruciating choice of husband, about the devastation of Steven's loss—and whatever else interests you.

See you there!

CPSIA information can be obtained
at www.ICGtesting.com
Printed in the USA
BVOW11s2335061016
464416BV00006B/100/P